"STUNNING . . .

Smith skillfully takes readers into the dark world of the human psyche and spirit."

—*Romantic Times*

"The characters are so beguiling, the writing so evocative and detailed that one emerges from the book's pages—and the ancient catacombs of Arras—as from a dark movie theater, surprised by daylight and the real world."

—*The Orlando Sentinel*

"A compelling read—not merely an absorbing mystery tale that rises to heights of great suspense and terror but a profound study of human relations . . . Her understanding of people and their psychology never errs, and she communicates it in prose of beautiful simplicity and clarity. An unmissable treat for lovers of fine writing."

—Ramsey Campbell

"[A] stylish and literate historical drama . . . In addition to providing fascinating background on early filmmaking, the author adds French military secrets, murder, blackmail, and witchcraft. . . . Readers will care about the splendidly realized characters, whose fates are decided in an eminently satisfying conclusion."

—*Publishers Weekly*

By Sarah Smith

THE VANISHED CHILD
THE KNOWLEDGE OF WATER
A CITIZEN OF THE COUNTRY

A CITIZEN
OF THE
COUNTRY

SARAH SMITH

FAWCETT BOOKS • NEW YORK

A Fawcett Book
Published by The Ballantine Publishing Group
Copyright © 2000 by Sarah Smith

www.ballantinebooks.com

ISBN 0-345-43304-1

Manufactured in the United States of America

First Hardcover Edition: August 2000
First Trade Paperback Edition: March 2002
First Fawcett Books Edition: January 2003

OPM   10   9   8   7   6   5   4   3   2   1

We are born, so to speak, provisionally, it doesn't matter where. It is only gradually that we compose within ourselves our true place of origin, so that we may be born there retrospectively and each day more definitely.

—RAINER MARIA RILKE

To call [war] a crime against mankind is to miss at least half its significance: it is also the punishment of a crime.

—"Private 19022" [FREDERIC MANNING],
Her Privates We, 1930

It was as close as Reisden could come to talking about what was wrong with his family.

Financial security, at least, one can give.

General Lucien Pétiot looked like Father Christmas in a sky blue uniform; he had a cloud white beard and twinkling blue eyes and was in charge of procurement (Medical Section) for the French army. General Pétiot bought miles of bandages, barrels of mercurochrome, trainloads of cough pastilles—and tests for the French army. Intelligence tests, tests of mental competence; every man in France served three years in uniform, and the army needed to identify potential officers and potential problems.

Reisden's company, Jouvet Medical Analyses, did competency testing for the courts and specialized neurological testing for hospitals all over Europe. Jouvet could administer Berthet's intelligence test to large groups. In September 1910, just after Toby was born, Reisden first approached Pétiot. "We want to supply medical tests and neurological work to the army."

"You're an ambitious man."

"I have a son."

For six months Reisden and Pétiot ate dinners together, spent afternoons talking about the state of medicine in France, traded opinions, deplored the government, and tested each other. Pétiot toured Jouvet's half-completed building, under reconstruction after the Paris floods. "You want the money," Pétiot said, admiring the expensive new lab. "I want the job," Reisden said. "Let me talk to your staff," Pétiot said. Through the winter, Pétiot became as familiar at Jouvet as the concierge's cat, poking his nose into staff meetings, sniffing at a technician's bench, hovering outside the locked door of the famous Jouvet medical archives.

On a cold day at the beginning of April 1911, Pétiot came to Reisden's office at Jouvet and dropped his bomb.

"There's only one trouble with Jouvet's proposal, Reisden: it's you. Your background."

They were sitting on packed boxes of books in the middle of chaos, the wallpaper half up, the paneling still tacky with varnish, the air damp with the smell of wet plaster.

"This is a bad time politically," Pétiot said. "Germany threatens us, with Spain and Austria-Hungary behind her; the French army is small and underprepared; and at this very moment, the most intelligent of von Loewenstein's Orphans decides he wants to throw in his lot with us. One wonders what you mean by it. Isn't that what Leo von Loewenstein used to say?"

"The Orphans are a myth."

"A myth, oh dear, yes," said Pétiot. "But one of the mythical Orphans owns a French company that does medical analysis, of a kind that would give it access to embarrassing information about army men, government officials." Pétiot frowned. "Certain people are very distressed."

"I appreciate your difficulty," Reisden said.

"I knew you would."

Pétiot had been carrying a thin leather portfolio. He opened it on one of the cartons of books. "Alexander von Reisden," Pétiot read aloud, "born 1879, South Africa, only son of Baron Franz von Reisden, yes, yes, adopted 1889 by Count Leo von Loewenstein, a *diplomat*." Pétiot tapped the word *diplomat* and let his neat white eyebrows rise a quarter-inch. "Eighteen ninety-eight, you took as a mistress the sister of a radical Russian; Loewenstein wanted to know about the radicals. You married her 1900; she died that year, very sad. October 1906 you moved to Paris, bought Jouvet early 1907. January 1910, married Perdita Halley, heiress of the American millionaire Gilbert Knight."

"Tasy didn't know what Mikhail was doing and Perdita isn't Gilbert's heiress."

"Tell me about Gilbert Knight," Pétiot said.

"Better than that. I'll show you."

Reisden pressed a carved leaf on one of the bookcases and a section of paneling clicked open. Behind it a newly painted staircase led up to their apartment. The staircase was hung with photographs of Toby and Perdita and their friends: Roy Daugherty, Suzanne Mallais, Reisden's almost-nephew Tiggy and his dog. Reisden found the smallest and most blurred picture in the darkest corner between the windows. He handed it down the staircase to Pétiot. "Gilbert Knight," he said.

Pétiot looked at the picture and up at Reisden. "Remarkable resemblance. Really extraordinary."

"His lawyers were afraid I was an unofficial relative," Reisden said. "Perhaps his nephew Richard, who disappeared. I'm not." It had been unnecessary to say that, he thought.

"It wouldn't have hurt for you to be American. A better connection than Loewenstein."

"Who, precisely, is objecting to me?"

Pétiot pulled at his beard. Reisden raised his eyebrows inquiringly.

"Maurice Cyron," Pétiot said.

"*Cyron?*" Reisden put Gilbert's picture down on a carton of books.

"What does Cyron have against you?"

"I did something once he didn't like."

"Could you undo it?"

"I wouldn't want to." He thought of Toby, of protecting Toby. "What does he say about me?"

Pétiot shrugged. "I mentioned your name in his hearing, at a club. Explosion! He said you had ruined his stepson, you were a neurotic yourself and encouraged André's insanity; then he said you were a spy and so on and so forth."

Reisden stood up. "This is Cyron trying to control André. André asked me to be in one of his plays. He was still a cavalry officer then; you can't imagine how incompetent André was in the cavalry, he'd actually lost his horse once. It was the mediocrity of desperation. He couldn't bear not doing professional theatre. He'd found the building he could afford. He'd found Jules, who could play the roles he was writing.—André couldn't explain it to Cyron; he couldn't even face him; he couldn't talk about the kind of theatre he wanted to do. He asked me to go with him, to talk with Cyron, to explain to him why André, Count of Montfort, couldn't stick the life Cyron had chosen for him."

"Why you?"

"I wish I hadn't, of course, now." Gilbert's picture was still lying on the book carton. Reisden turned it upside down. "No, I don't. I knew a madman once who beat a child almost to death. I know madmen; it comes with Jouvet. I like to bring them back safe. You asked me why I want this job. Cyron was always a bully. He said André was insane to do the kind of theatre he does. André is odd and sad, but he isn't mad and he had to go into the theatre. Cyron was wrong."

"Have you seen André in the past year?" Pétiot asked.

Reisden shook his head. "I haven't seen anyone but my family and the builders."

"You know that he's married?"

"*André* is?"

"To a little girl from the country." Pétiot shook his head. "Maurice is very worried about them."

Chapter 2

Maurice Cyron peered through his automobile window. The line of cars and carriages stretched down the street; in front of Jouvet, the crowd had spread out into the rue de l'Université. Flashes were going off, illuminating men in top hats and women with diamonds. Cyron's lips tightened. "Take me to the side door," he told his chauffeur.

Even at the side entrance, cars and taxis were letting off people; there was a line waiting to be announced. "I'm not here, eh?" Cyron interrupted the man at the door. "Come to see my stepson's play, that's all."

"I'll tell Dr. Reisden, monsieur—"

"No." Everyone would think he was a patient, or approved of Jouvet.

A business is like a theatre: the fronts are all airy-fairy; it's the back of the house that tells you the tale. The party was at the front of the house; Cyron made his way downstairs first, into the newly rebuilt basement. Barred doors. Solid orderly shelves. Alcohol, disinfectant, pills. Straps, restraints, straitjackets. A cell mattressed on walls, ceiling, and floor. Bars and locks. A prison for secrets to be locked away. Reisden had built solid. He was supposed to be mortgaged to the hilt.

Upstairs, people jostled each other elbow-to-elbow. Along the corridors hung testimonials to Jouvet Medical Analyses. From the Keepers of Imperial Medical Asylums in Berlin and Potsdam and Vienna: the Germans. From the Salpetrière, the

9

Hôtel des Invalides, the School of Nancy, and a British veterans' group, for its work on mental patients: Cyron scowled. From hospitals and doctors all over Europe: *In cases of mental illness,* Cyron read, *when expert medical analysis needs to be done, Jouvet sets the standard.*

Cyron puffed up the circular stairs to the second floor, looking for things to hate. A big laboratory, new microscopes on the benches, everything white and clinical. Bars on the windows here too. Nothing was ever left entirely to darkness; small lights stood guard in the hall. Every drawer was locked against intrusion. On the third floor, he looked through a barred door to a large room filled with file cabinets, but the door was locked, and on each of the wood cabinets he could see the glint of locks as well. Beyond that room with its locks upon locks, a door of opaque glass blocked the way to still another room.

A place for secrets. Reisden had always wanted secrets, been searching for secrets, ever since he was a boy.

The director's office had Reisden's name on the door. Weirdly, all the doorknobs were red china, a bloody clear red. Gold titles and red spines glinted behind glass. *Clinical Pathology,* Cyron read. *Diseases of the Nerves.* The windows were open; from the courtyard below, Cyron could hear the buzz and mutter of voices.

Seventeen years old Reisden had been when André had first brought him to Montfort. Reisden had been one of those bony-pretty, nerve-ridden boys; black hair slicked down with pomade, the way the boys had done it then; skin almost paper white. He'd smoked incessantly and acted superior, and stared at him and André as if they were animals in a zoo.

You're good with your stepson, Reisden had said. *He must be difficult, a bit.* Reisden had been obsessed with nerves, madness. The very worst sort of friend for André.

And now Reisden owned Jouvet. Cyron sat down in the owner's chair. The desk was large, heavy, English-style, with drawers; the same style Cyron used himself. The drawers were locked.

How old would Reisden be now? Thirty-one. A bad man coming into power.

From down in the courtyard he heard applause and shrieks. Cyron rose and looked out the window.

Inside the porte cochere, an enormous black coach had appeared. The guests laughed and retreated. Two black horses reared showily, like clockwork, and a brass skeleton in the driver's seat raised its arm and flicked a whip over them. The coach door popped open, and out of it sprang a jumping-jack, skeletal, face painted like a skull:

André.

"I, Necrosar, King of Terrors of the Grand Necropolitan Theatre du Monde! Present Monsieur Jules Fauchard, the Most Assassinated Man in Paris! Together with the company of the Grand Necropolitan Theatre!" Behind the skull mask, "Necrosar's" voice was hollow and overprecise, every *t* distinct as a death-watch tick. He moved with the alert mincing delicacy of a skeleton or a spider, jerkily, warily, as if he were on strings. Cyron could see the muscles and build of the cavalry officer André had been once, should have been still. Should have been defending France against the Germans, not here playing the fool.

André climbed the steps leading to the clinic door and stood at the top of them. "Appearing tonight only! In a new—original—piece, in honor of the reopening of Jouvet Medical Analyses—*It's Enough; or, A Domestic Crisis Resolved*!"

Jules and a woman ran to the top of the steps, arranging themselves in front of the French doors. Two other women and two men placed themselves at the bottom of the steps. André and Jules smiled at each other. Cyron's heart squeezed painfully, unhappily.

"Mesdames! Messieurs! Madmen! The walls of Jouvet

have seen many sad stories . . . this is one of them." Necrosar extended his hand toward Jules at center stage and the play began.

"What a day at the theatre, my wife!" Jules complained, pitching his voice to the crowd. "Today, that hard taskmaster André du Monde has killed me five times!—crushed, impaled, guillotined . . . it's more than the mind can bear." Jules clutched his forehead.

"Ah, *mon pauvre ami!*" the "wife" said. "What will help you?" (Laughter, for some reason.)

"My dear—I regret—I've got to kill the parlor maid."

The wife rang the bell. "Sylvie? Monsieur Jules requires you." The actors moved out of Cyron's line of sight; there was a squawk and more laughter, as predictable as if it were being cranked out by a machine.

Silly stupid plays. Silly terrible stories. Tonight André's sweet little wife would be at home at Montfort, eating her heart out, waiting for her husband to notice her, and where was André? Making bad plays for people who didn't want him and wouldn't even pay him.

Theatre's a tool, my boy, Cyron thought; it's not a drug.

"I feel better," Jules Fauchard said from below, "*but not better enough*. It's a shame, but—the chauffeur too. He's got to die."

"How distressing, my husband! Who will drive the car?"

The woman was forcing her voice; she'd go hoarse in a couple of years. Jules Fauchard had no presence. He looked like a plumber, like a man who plays soccer on Sundays: ordinary, muscular, vulgar, a nothing with a moustache. From below, a property gun banged as Jules killed the chauffeur. The cook was called next and shrieked as she died. The audience laughed indulgently.

"Husband, are you finally feeling better?"

"Alas no. It's—"

"Not enough!" the audience shouted.

"But, my dear husband, we don't have any more servants! How annoying!"

"I agree! One can replace servants," Jules said, "but a loving wife like you—"

In Reisden's dark office, a piece of the paneling opened, a secret door, pouring out light. A slim, dark-haired young woman in evening dress stood balancing a sleepy child on her hip, her other hand outstretched.

She was young and very pretty, and obviously the baby's mother; no one else could have held the baby with such loving pride. All this solidity, all this security, she moved through it with the assurance that it had been made for her and her child. She gathered the bundle of baby up into her arms, resting his head on her shoulder. Light-struck, her eyes focused past Cyron. "Oh," she said, "is someone here?"

And behind her, Lucien Pétiot and Reisden came into the room. "I didn't know André was coming with the whole Necro," Reisden was protesting, and stopped. "Cyron," he said.

They change. The boys grow up. Cyron stared at him. "Cyron," Reisden said, "let me introduce my wife and son."

He had lost his accent. He was still too tall and thin, but solid now, muscled; there was wary pride in the grey eyes, which had been haunted once. A man. A father with a son.

Reisden was married. Reisden had a child. Reisden took his son in his arms; the baby made a determined grab for his father's white tie. "Not a toy, beloved," Reisden said, tickling the baby's nose gently. "Cyron, let me introduce to you Jean-Sebastien Louis Victor Reisden, known to all as Toby Belch." Reisden's son looked across his shoulder at Cyron and smiled, the beatific toothless smile of a baby who has always been completely loved. His black hair stood up in a dandelion-fluff. He looked like Reisden.

Why do you deserve a son? Do you know what you said to *my* son?

Jules was speaking from below. "It's a continual crisis. Again, faithful servants to replace! Again, an amiable wife slaughtered! And why? Why? I ask myself, why?"

It's all about families and death, Cyron thought; everything André writes is about death. And I can't change him. I thought Sabine'd do it if anyone could, but even she can't change him, he cares only about this cheap theatre, his fantasies of families and murder. And it's gone too far, I want him to die sometimes, I do; if André just left her with a kid . . .

But who gets a child—? Not André. Not my André.

"Look," Pétiot said from the window. "Cyron, Reisden, look, this is funny."

Cyron looked out the window. Jules was chasing André with a huge American rubber knife: "One man alone is the cause of my misery! When I go mad he's always there! Die, Necrosar, die!" Jules stage-stabbed André with the wobbling blade. "Finally!" he said, and the audience shouted with him: "It's enough!"

It's too much, Cyron thought.

"Look," said Pétiot, "he's got you in it too, Reisden; isn't that meant to be you?"

The supposedly dead Necrosar had produced a rubber ax and was jerkily creeping up on Jules. Crash! Jules staggered and fell against the balustrade. With the fatal dagger still quivering under his armpit, Necrosar rubbed his hands together and leered. Out of his line of sight, Jules raised himself on one elbow—holding on to the ax to keep it in place—and produced a gun; clumsy, that. Jules aimed—got ready to fire—

"Where?" asked Reisden.

"There you are."

A tall man in well-cut black made his way out of the audience. Cyron knew the actor; he had made a career out of playing gentlemen thieves. "Oh, my dear man, we really must talk about this. This one's dead— This one, too— Jules, how excessive."

"It's true," said Jules, flourishing the gun, looking at the bodies contritely. "Murder disturbs the harmony of family life."

"It's true," the dead bodies draped over the steps murmured.

"But what shall we do?" Necrosar hissed, producing a round object marked BOMB.

Cyron could see Reisden watching André's idea of himself. An amused face, dubious, human, the face of a father with a son. And there was Pétiot, laughing, and the girl laughing, and the baby smiling—

"Laugh, will you?" Cyron exploded. "Laugh at this? Have a party for Jouvet? André went to Jouvet once and it didn't do a d—n thing for him. I was the one who helped him, me; he wouldn't even speak when I adopted him; I helped him, me alone, no one helped me. And what happens when I've got him through college, I've bought him into a regiment, he's an officer the way his father was and his grandfather and every de Montfort before him? When I almost have him talked out of playing at actors?"

The baby shrank back at his tone and began to cry. "Stop that," Reisden said, "you're frightening my son." The girl took the baby and began to rock him in her arms. The baby stared over her shoulder, wide-eyed, plump-cheeked, dismayed, indignant.

"I'll tell *you* what he did; Pétiot, I'll tell *you*. This one makes André's acquaintance. They come down to Montfort together, André's all excited about him because 'he can act,' André says, which he can't, he's just a good amateur. It turns out that André's brought him to help persuade me to let André leave the cavalry. Him, this little seventeen-year-old—*dingus,* this *thing* with brilliantined hair—and he thinks he knows better than *me*. 'Go ahead,' he says to André, 'write plays. Go ahead, direct plays, you have a talent.' And to me he says—Do you know what he said to me? 'Why not let him,' he says. 'It's what he's good for.' It's *all* my son is good for. He told me that."

How dare he say it. Seventeen. How dare he think he knew André like that, at seventeen.

"Cyron—" Pétiot said, "after all—"

"You said, 'He'll be unhappy if he doesn't write plays,' " Cyron said to Reisden. "Do you remember that?"

Reisden nodded. "Perdita, love," he said, "take Toby upstairs."

"And now he's happy, eh? G-d save any family from being as happy as we are. It wasn't good for him, letting him write out all his fancies. All this death in families. He's married now, but his wife's frightened of him. And with good reason! The theatre has ruined him for marriage—ruined him."

Down in the courtyard, all the corpses had risen and were singing a song.

> *Whenever you start to get carried away,*
> *Instead of to murder, just turn to Jouvet—*

"Cure a sick man? You indulged him, Reisden," Cyron said. "And I mean to make you pay for our unhappiness."

Pétiot raised his hand; Cyron shook his head.

"I will ruin you," he said. "Jouvet has done nothing for André and I will say so. I'll talk about Jouvet. I'll talk about your guardian, von Loewenstein the spy. I have you in my hand," Cyron said, and raised his fist and closed it.

The girl had not moved; she was shocked and white, and the baby was sobbing in her arms. Pétiot had his mouth open, protesting, but he was saying nothing. When Maurice Cyron spoke, people listened.

"No," Reisden said.

"What?"

"The man you have in your fist is André. Jouvet consults on mental problems; we're supposed to be the best in Europe. You're concerned but you haven't brought him here."

"I haven't brought him here? I *did*," Cyron said.

"When you adopted him; that was thirty years ago, more, an eon in treatment of mental conditions. Do you want us to try with him, or will you attack us and lessen his chances?"

"You can't help him," Cyron said. Down in the courtyard, a three-piece band had appeared from out of the audience. And there was André, Necrosar, in his greenish black suit and his skull makeup, singing with his hand in Jules'. Was this André de Montfort, one of the oldest names in France?

> *Jou-Jou-Jou-vet,*
> *Go to see them today . . .*

Jou-Jou-Jou-vet. "You can't cure him," Cyron said. "I've worked on him for over thirty years. If I can't, you can't."

Not that *von* Reisden would even try. It was too convenient for *von* Loewenstein and *von* Reisden that the Count of Montfort was a clown. They laughed, they screamed, they encouraged him: oh, yes, Cyron knew what it was to be admired.

"Support us," Reisden said, "and I will try."

Sometimes the best exit line is silence: Cyron turned on his heel and left.

Chapter 3

The Reisdens' friend, the journalist Milly Xico, brought a bottle of vodka to get them all drunk, a string of amber beads for Perdita, and her pug, Nick-Nack, to adore her. "I can see Cyron, that old windbag. He gestured, and he strutted up and down like a rooster, like a big potato with a nose, and his hair flopped until it fell over onto one side and showed his bald spot. And he said, 'Trrraito-rrr! Trrrai-torrr!' " She made them laugh in spite of themselves. They were out in the courtyard, in the sun. She knelt down and called her pug. "Go, Nicky! Go right there!" she pointed. "Pee on his footsteps! Good boy!"

In the last year Milly Xico had begun writing and acting in moving pictures. The camera loved her but would never capture her: that foxy red hair; that distinctly Milly odor of perfume, cheap cigarettes, and dog; and those cynical blue eyes, which had seen everything in Paris.

"He has a point," Reisden said. "He's André's stepfather and something's wrong with André."

"Blaming yourself is boring; blame Cyron. Are you a spy?" Milly asked. "The old windbag's going round all the salons saying you are. Are you going broke?"

"No," Reisden said curtly, "neither."

"You should spy for the Russians, they pay best. Prrrropaganda," Milly rolled the word. "Bribes, I call it. Do you believe, this is what the Russians hand out to lady 'shapers of

18

opinion'!" Milly extended an arm, model-style, showing off her new jacket, sheepskin covered with colorful red embroideries that swore fashionably at her hair. "Men journalists get parties, vodka, caviar." Milly's sapphire eyes glittered mockingly. "Women . . . Us *ladies* get pretty toys. Amber—I have more earrings than I can count, I have necklaces, all courtesy of Ambassador Izvolsky. . . ." She twirled her long necklace of silver and Russian amber. "Isn't it pretty? As if we'd never heard of pogroms."

Perdita ran her fingertips over her own necklace thoughtfully.

"Just say 'thank you, Izvolsky,' and do what you like. *I* do," Milly said. "There's so much money going round no one will notice a few honest people. Put yourself on someone's side and hold out your hand."

"Don't joke, Milly," Reisden said. "What is going on with André?"

"Who is Maurice Cyron?" Perdita asked.

They looked at her oddly; everyone knew that. "An actor," Milly said.

"A hero," said Reisden. "Our French hero."

They had brought out bread and cheese; Milly scooped herself a piece of Brie and spread it on a round of *bâtard*. "A war hero once, who acts now. He has his own theatre and does military plays." She continued with her mouth full. "There's always a big fight scene, always a girl who weeps for him, the audience always cries if he dies and laughs if he wins. But now all his friends are out of the government, and he's old, and he isn't as influential as he was, not since Dreyfus. He wants to be immooortal," Milly said, drawing out the word mockingly. "So now he's making André—who isn't even his real son—have babies with that Wagny girl!"

"Is that the trouble with André?" Reisden asked.

"Dreyfus? Who is Dreyfus?" Perdita asked.

The two of them stared at her. She blushed.

"Don't you two ever do anything but have sex? Doesn't he ever talk to you?" Milly asked. "Men. Didn't you ever tell her about Dreyfus, darling Sacha? Nicky, he doesn't tell her a thing."

Nick-Nack, snuffling for scraps, looked up adoringly. Milly spread a round of bread with Brie and dropped it for him.

"Alfred Dreyfus," Milly said. "About fifteen years ago he was convicted of selling French military secrets, which is what Cyron said your darling Sacha is doing. But—" Milly paused dramatically "—*but* he hadn't done it. The man who did was another army officer, Esterhazy. Who had been born Austrian, just like your darling Sacha." Milly smiled sweetly at Reisden. "But Dreyfus was a Jew, even more foreign than an Austrian to the crowd that supports Cyron. So the other officers held a little trial, and what do you think they did? Did they convict Esterhazy and bring Dreyfus back from Devil's Island?"

Nick-Nack, who had swallowed all the bread at once, began to cough and retch. Reisden passed Toby to Perdita, picked the pug up, and thumped him; a horrible bolus shot out of his mouth and splatted on the cobblestones. Toby giggled delightedly. Nick-Nack blinked watery eyes, wriggled to be put down, and headed for it to swallow it again.

"No, they *acquitted* Esterhazy. With the letter in his own handwriting right in front of them. They loved their Esterhazy like a dog loves vomit," said Milly, seeing an illustration. "Don't you, Nicky? You love it because it's yours."

Toby was making blatting noises with his lips, trying to spit like Nicky. "Oh, don't learn, love," Reisden murmured. "Such a bright child, but please don't learn to throw up like a dog."

"You two are applying for citizenship, fine, *bien*. But are you really French? Do you wear Russian amber to honor our noble allies? Do you go to the Théâtre Cyron and stand up and shout 'Bravo!' and make him repeat all the big speeches? It isn't enough to be a citizen. You have to be someone's dog."

"Cyron's?" he said.

"Put your hands over your ears, Perdita," Milly said. "Have you seen the Wagny girl? Eighteen and mad for sex. And as far as getting satisfaction from André she might as well kiss her finger. That's what's wrong with André's marriage. She's young. She's rich. You could be her lover; she could give you money."

"Milly!" Perdita said.

"André doesn't sleep with her, you mean?" Reisden said.

"*And* she has Cyron turned round her little finger. Get in good with Sabine Wagny. Be Sabine's dog, and hold out your hand for the army contract."

Chapter 4

R eisden went searching for André's record at Jouvet.
There were two categories of records at Jouvet, third floor and fourth floor rear, the open and the closed. Open records could be used for research: generational studies, drug protocols. Closed records could be consulted only for the specific case. The system had started back in the 1850s when a Jouvet clerk had been caught blackmailing clients, but in the past year, since the flood, many more records had gone to the fourth floor rear.

For this the Loewensteins were responsible.

Just after the flood last year, Leo's son Sigi had come to

visit and offer help. The water was still waist-deep in the cellars and piles of rubble were being cleared out of the courtyard. Impeccable in a Savile Row suit, Sigi von Loewenstein had surveyed the walls held up by bracing beams, the smashed furniture and instruments, the boxes of rescued records in disarray, and the slick of pulped paper over everything, and he had offered Reisden a lot of money.

"Don't worry about money. Don't think about it; I can help; you do good business. Don't worry."

Be someone's dog. . . . Reisden had heard Leo make offers like that, offers it was hard to refuse. After Sigi's visit, he had begun to look at the Jouvet records with the skills he'd learned from Leo.

The army quartermaster with a Turkish young man on the side. The railroad scheduler with the kleptomaniac wife. The wholesale grocer whose son— Anyone with a family secret would be a weapon in the war between France and Germany.

Could they use André against Cyron?

The war had been going on for a century, and forty years ago, in 1870, the Germans thought they had won it. The Prussian armies had invaded and defeated France. Thirty thousand soldiers had marched through Paris (after which, street by street, the Parisians had scrubbed the paving stones with disinfectant). The Germans had taken the rich provinces of Alsace and Lorraine as war booty and imposed a crushing indemnity, which they thought would bankrupt France for thirty years.

But France had paid it off in three.

Since then France had made herself unexpectedly strong. She had made alliances with England, her traditional enemy, and with Russia, Germany's eastern neighbor. Germany was caught between two unexpectedly strong enemies. If France and Russia attacked Germany together, Germany would have to fight on both fronts, and it would lose.

Germany's only chance was to take the offensive.

Suppose Germany attacked France first, without warning. The Russian army, spread over thousands of miles, would take six weeks to reach the German border. If Germany could conquer France in those six weeks, Russia would back down from the war.

The key to Europe was France, and the key to France was those six weeks.

A day's delay was worth a regiment to the Germans. An army quartermaster could be blackmailed into forgetting boots or bullets. A railroad scheduler could be driven to a nervous breakdown. Hours here, a day there; too many hours and days and the Germans would reach Paris.

Reisden had sent the quartermasters and everyone like them to the fourth floor. André was a public figure and Cyron's stepson; that made him fourth-floor material. In a well-run company, André's file would now be between MONTFI and MONTJ.

It wasn't there.

It wasn't on the open third floor, or misfiled close by on either floor. It could be in the records still to be returned from storage. It could be anywhere. Or it could have been lost during the flood.

But it wasn't going to tell him what was wrong with André. André would have to do that.

Chapter 5

He and Perdita were spending as much time as they could with each other, awkwardly, unhappily on his part, because she was going to America.

Her New York agent, who had dropped her after she'd married, had sent her a letter. How was she, what was she doing, the agent had talked to someone who'd heard her play at a Women's Party concert in Paris, he had a couple of concerts, nothing big, the pay was nothing, it wouldn't be worth her while, but if she was interested and free right now—

Please, she'd said. I know we can't afford it, Alexander. *Please.*

So she was going to America; and Toby was still nursing, so she would take him; and so he and she went together, arm in arm, pushing Toby in his pram, to see André. But he made her stop in the park, down the street from the Necro. He had no intention of letting André frighten Perdita or Toby.

The Théâtre du Monde, to give the Necro its official name, was in the most sinister neighborhood André could afford, down the hill from the Place Blanche, the center of Parisian whoredom. At midday in windy early June, the street was deserted, incomplete without its shadows and sinister crowds. André was standing out front, supervising the repainting of the bat frieze.

Necrosar in the daylight: You noticed the stare first. He looked obliquely at you, as if searching out who you were, what hurt you could do: the stare of something caged. Off-stage, André was not skeletal but tall and solid. He was barefoot, his collar undone, his clothes ragged; he was wearing a boating sweater, which didn't fit him and was too hot for the day. André's pants bagged at the knees; he looked unfed and his hair needed cutting. It floated around his head like a corona.

"Come see my Egyptian mummy." André led the way toward the front of the house.

The Grand Necro was the smallest theatre in Paris; it followed that it wasn't profitable. But now the elegant green-and-gold lobby had been redecorated. André indicated the centerpiece, an enormous glass case. Reisden looked inside. A brown leather face stared out at him, grinning Necrosar's grin.

"Frightening?" André asked.

"No, André." Reisden had forgot how irritating André could be; he was a little boy who insisted on showing off his magic set.

"I'll frighten you."

André opened the door to the theatre itself. "You've redecorated," Reisden said. When André had been a young officer, he had directed his titled friends in comedies in château dining rooms. The new Necro looked like one of those private spaces: luxurious armchairs in Louis Seize style, moss green upholstery, green curtains. Precisely what a château theatre dreamed of being: apart, that is, from the little carved skulls grinning secretly from the arms of the chairs. André had spent money: the wife's, of course.

André turned down the house lights, leaving only the safeties on. Then the safety lights guttered and darkened, turning the house into wavering blue-green shadows, and went completely out. Reisden closed his eyes and took a deep breath.

"The dark," whispered Necrosar's overprecise voice, "the

dark . . . Everyone's afraid of it. Why? The dark ought to protect you, like a mother. It ought to keep you safe from all the dreadful things that want to find you. *But it doesn't.*"

There was a little sound, a series of bumps: something rolling down the shallow steps of the theatre. It came to rest near Reisden's feet. G-d, Reisden thought, what's he come up with now. Then the lights came on, shockingly bright.

The man's head was still oozing blood. It lay on the carpet, horribly hacked about the face, the neck toward them and the windpipe gaping like a mouth in meat. The rest of the body was sprawled over one of the chairs. Reisden took a step backward, stumbling down a step; he caught and steadied himself, let out the breath he had taken, and took another before he could speak.

"Very good, André."

"You're so rigid, Reisden," André said.

Reisden went over and poked the body experimentally. Wax hands; birdseed-filled cotton for the torso.

"To business," he said. "Your stepfather's accused me of spying, but the principal accusation is that I encouraged you to write Necro plays." André folded his arms defensively. "And this somehow is a problem between you and your wife."

Reisden's imagination suggested to him things André might have rigged up for the wedding night.

"Is something the matter? I'm not asking from sheer inquisitiveness; it wasn't my business until your stepfather made it my business. But I love my family, and I hope you are happy with yours."

For a moment the stare wavered, and André was not Necrosar, the King of Terrors, but André de Montfort, the beggared last of an old line, who had got married last spring. For a moment André was staring at his own troubles, and it humanized him.

"Family? My family? Oh, they're fine, they're dead."

"Your wife."

"My wife has gone to the country," André said, the whole sentence sounding rehearsed. "Yes. She likes the country." He laughed suddenly, stiffly. "She belongs there."

"Not with you?"

"Oh, *no* no no—" André said. "Are you afraid of your family?"

"Are you?"

"A family's an invitation to terror. Your wife is blind," André said; the stare of Necrosar slid over his eyes again. "Your wife is blind, and she's *looking after* your son. And you don't like to worry, Reisden! You don't like to be frightened!"

André had picked up instantly that Reisden hated the dark, and he used it every time. And he knew about Reisden's uneasiness with Perdita's sight. (How? From having seen Reisden lead her across the street?) André was odd but he wasn't stupid. "Is anything bothering you?" Reisden asked.

André smiled, the full, teeth-baring, menacing smile of Necrosar, King of Terrors, and the stare, the raggedness, the menace came together, the way André seldom came together except onstage. "What could bother *me*?" Necrosar breathed.

André might know what Reisden was after, but he didn't want to discuss his wife. Reisden talked for a bit about his family, hoping to get confidences from André, but André only wanted to meet Perdita because she frightened Reisden.

Perdita and Toby were standing outside, talking to a streetwalker. Toby was getting a cold; Reisden wiped his nose. Toby grabbed the handkerchief and tried to stuff it into his mouth.

André stood at Reisden's elbow, staring at the baby. André's pants legs flopped above his pale bare feet. André had always looked young, but in the sunlight his yellow hair showed white threads and his skin was ashy.

"Families," André said, reaching out one finger to touch Toby's cold-reddened cheek. Toby stared at him with the reserve of a baby who isn't sure this adult is friendly. "Nothing is happy. Nothing is secure. Oh, poor, poor child."

And André laughed, Necrosar's mocking, shrieking laugh, and Toby burst into tears again, as he had with Cyron.

"Don't do that to my son," Reisden said sharply, and André's face twisted, crumpled, childish suddenly, a boy adults don't like.

"André?" said Reisden more gently.

"I can't help it, Reisden," André said, and turned away from them.

Chapter 6

"**W**hy *do* you like him?" Perdita asked. "And what is it with him?" She was beginning to use her New Yorkisms.

"What is with him, I don't know. What can't he help?"

"He's scared of something."

Reisden's dressing room was the only room in their apartment not chaotic with packing, so that was where they were, he and his wife and their boy. From outside, they could smell the June night in Paris and hear a last carriage horse trotting toward the boulevard St.-Germain. In the next room, Aline, their ponderous invaluable maid, was packing, a rustle of concert satin being folded into tissue paper. There were more dresses than were explained by the number of concerts Perdita was supposedly giving. Very few, she had said. But her New York agent liked her, enough to give a married woman a second chance.

She didn't have a Paris agent. She'd tried.

Toby pulled himself up by the sofa leg and held on to Reisden's knee, swaying back and forth and yawning. On ordinary days they would have put him in his crib or let him fall asleep between them.

"Come, darling," Perdita said, "come to Mama and try to fall asleep." She unbuttoned her dress and the baby burrowed against her breast; her hand supported Toby's head, she rocked him, effortlessly close to her boy. One of Perdita's fans was lying on the floor; Reisden unfurled it and fanned her, a bit envious of that closeness.

The fan was feminine, white, scalloped, decorated with green letters. *Je désire voter,* he read. *I want to vote.*

"I was André's first Hamlet," he said, "before he turned professional and could afford actors. Cyron's right that I encouraged him to go into theatre. At least he's happy in that."

"What will you do while I'm gone?" she asked. "Can you help him?"

"I hope so."

"André's wife wouldn't know what hit her," Perdita murmured.

He laughed in his throat and caressed the edge of her breast.

"If Monsieur Cyron talks about you, could Jouvet go bankrupt?"

"I hope not. We'll be all right," he amended. She had not said, Gilbert would loan us money, but he wondered touchily if that was what she meant.

"I wish you would go with us," she said. "Gilbert would love to see you."

"We shouldn't tease Gilbert with what he can't have. Don't see him. At least don't bring Toby."

She sighed, letting her head droop back against his shoulder, affectionate, frustrated, as if she hadn't expected him to be quite so dense, but now that he was, she wasn't surprised. "I can't promise that. You know I can't."

You could, he thought. You should.

She leaned against him, nursing their son. He felt her almost imperceptible rocking, pressing against him, then moving away. Toby was nursing himself to sleep; his flushed little face nodded away from her breast, but his own falling asleep woke him again, and he nuzzled against her. She put him against her shoulder, patting his back, then moved him to the other breast. Looking down at him, Reisden felt a tenderness like an ache in his throat.

"Does André not like women?" Perdita asked. "I mean, the way Milly doesn't like men?" Milly lived with a French baroness.

"I don't know."

"You've known him since you were seventeen and you don't know?"

"Not everyone's as frank as Milly." Whatever André cared for beside the theatre, one only hoped it still breathed.

"Tell me about his theatre that you don't want me to go to."

"The performances of the Grand Necropolitan start"—he made his voice sepulchral—"at the stroke of midnight. André, as Necrosar, comes from behind the curtain in evening dress and begins to tell stories. The curtain opens and his troupe begins to act them out. Within five minutes the first character's been eviscerated at the zoo or chopped to bits in a butcher's shop, and André shows it all. He uses special effects, magic tricks, horribly convincing. You should have seen his *Hamlet*. . . . But it's a theatre for the eyes. You wouldn't be interested."

"Why does he want to frighten people?"

"No idea." Again. "It's a kind of closeness."

"His poor wife."

"I think André does theatre to protect himself from the world outside, which he doesn't find comfortable."

She reached out and laced fingers with his for a moment. For years and years he had done theatre, too, for just that reason. Toby was asleep; she lifted him gently to her shoulder and patted his back to burp him. Toby gave a great belch and opened his eyes in astonishment. "Oh, darling lamb, don't wake up," Perdita whispered to him, patting his back. "You're *so* nearly asleep."

"Give him to me. Come here, love," Reisden said, and put the towel over his own shoulder and took his son. Toby blinked awake, looking around the room, and smiled into Reisden's face. Oh love, he thought; oh my dear son. Later you'll be a good reasonable child and sleep; stay awake now and let Papa love you.

He put Toby down on the old American wedding-ring quilt by the fireplace, among his toys, and sat on the floor with him, overcome by the sorrow of leave-taking. Toby reached for his red ball, found it too far away, leaned forward toward it and began to crawl. "Ba-ba-ba," he said intently. "Ball?" said Reisden, holding it up, and was rewarded by a wonderful baby smile. *You understand me!* His son grinned, reaching out his hand and batting the ball away. Reisden retrieved it and rolled it back toward him. When Toby comes back, will he still be doing this? What first time will I have missed?

Reisden had gone on business trips two or three times since Toby was born; he had paced up and down Genoa or London, waiting to get on the train back to his son. At night he would watch by Toby's crib, just listening to his breath. Oh, my son.

Don't go, Perdita. Don't go. Don't take my son with you; don't let Gilbert so much as see our boy. How can you tease Gilbert with a family he can't have? He didn't say any of this, pressed his lips together, angry, full of the wrong emotions.

She was going to America because she still thought of

herself as American, and going to Massachusetts where she had grown up, where she spoke the language without thinking, going to visit Gilbert . . . going to what all Americans called *home*, when home should be Paris for her.

And could he entirely blame her? What did he have for her, what could he offer her, that was better than the Knights? Richard Knight would have had millions. Richard Knight would have lived in Gilbert's house on Commonwealth Avenue, where Perdita had been almost Gilbert's daughter. Richard Knight's wife would have had the vote when America gave it to women.

Richard Knight would have had no money troubles at all.

Reisden went with Perdita to Le Havre. It was cold that morning; when the luggage was stowed in the cabin, he went up with them on deck. He buttoned Toby inside his coat for warmth; the baby snuggled closer in his sleep, a warm, relaxed weight.

"Take care of our son," he said, "and I'll deal with André."

"Take care of *you*," she said, holding his hand.

"Everything will be all right; it'll have blown over by the time you're back." He hoped so.

"It's not just that your André doesn't like women," Perdita said. "He's afraid of family."

"He's afraid of his stepfather," Reisden said.

"He's afraid of something."

Perdita and he talked with each other until the last moment, quietly, so as not to wake their son. He had told her he was not going to stay on the dock while the boat left; she could not have seen him anyway; but he stayed, and he saw her, wearing her red jacket so that, if he was there, he would see her. Toby was in her arms. She waved uncertainly. He took off his hat and waved it in wide arcs, but he was not the sort of man to wave his hat, and he thought she would not see him and would not know him if she did, and of course his boy wouldn't.

He watched until the boat was a dot on the horizon.

Chapter 7

It was an American ship. Perdita stood at the rail when Aline took Toby down for his nap: a woman for once alone, going on a journey. Here people would speak English; here *she* would have to translate for *Aline*. She could ask about baseball scores; there would be real ice cream. She took deep breaths, then found the salon door with her white cane and ducked inside, smelling America. It is wonderful to be a child's mother, but wonderful too to rediscover who one is on one's own.

"Excuse me, miss, would you like me to lead you somewhere?"

Poor blind girl, a pity to all who know her. "Yes. Is there a piano in the salon?"

The room was deserted; she would disturb nobody. She told the man in charge that it had been arranged she would have rehearsal time. She took off her jacket and hat, put the piano lid up half-stick, and did her exercises. What would she play? The breeze came through the open door from the deck. That wind came from America.

In the spring before she had left New York, some friends had taken her uptown to hear a musician they'd found. The man's name was Blind Willie Williams. She let her left hand

slide into a walking bass, improvising with the right until a
tune found her:

> *The stars are a-shining, hear the turtle dove,*
> *I say the stars are a-shining,*
> *can't you hear the turtle dove,*
> *Don't you want somebody,*
> *Somebody to love . . .*

And then she had come to Paris and had found somebody
to love.

Sometimes you know so well what you want, you forget
what your limits are. All Alexander's friends had said he
should have married a Frenchwoman. A Frenchwoman with
the right connections could have given dinner parties for government officials and sailed right round this Maurice Cyron,
or charmed him. She would have cooked perfectly for
Alexander, dressed perfectly. Perdita had wanted to do all
that too, thought that somehow she would be able, just by
wanting to.

She had brought him worries. He didn't trust her to take
care of Toby. (She was very careful, she took no chances, but
in her heart she knew why he didn't.) He thought she didn't
know anything. In France, she didn't. She had to ask Aline the
words for things. At night sometimes, in bed, he would wake
up shuddering from dreams he didn't remember. She would
hold him in her arms and say, "It's all right." He would get up
rather than disturb her. Rather than believe her or trust her to
know he didn't.

She wasn't rich. She didn't have important friends.

Simple things she couldn't do for him. On the street once
he had bought them a cone of *frites. We don't get these at
home,* he had said, not meanly, but what she had heard was
that she would never be able to make French fries for her husband. She had burst into tears, stupidly, like a little girl. *It*

doesn't matter, he'd said. *We'll have a cook.* She didn't want a cook. She wanted his trust.

He didn't trust her not to leave him.

Perdita sat back on the piano bench for a moment, her hands still on the keyboard, thinking of that imaginary Frenchwoman in bed with Alexander. No; that was Perdita's place. But here she was, sailing away from him, leaving him on shore, and happy about it. *Going down to Third Street, put my mind at ease* . . . American music, American smells, her own language to speak, a new music under her fingers. She had a home in France, a husband, and she loved him, but her fingers struggled happily with the tricky rhythms, and she wondered whether Willie Williams was in New York and whether he'd let her sit in, and wondered whether Alexander was right not to trust her.

Who was she? Toby's mother. A pianist. Alexander's wife? Who was she?

Whom could she ask, who could help her and Alexander?

Chapter 8

No one needed Gilbert anymore. He lived in a tall cavernous house in Boston with his adopted son, Harry, and his son's wife. Harry and Efnie were seldom at home; Harry worked, Efnie had her charities, they both played golf. In the evening they were always at some party or giving a dinner to which Gilbert was not quite invited.

In the house there were also ghosts. One was everywhere,

unexpectedly, making a joke or a caustic comment, playing with his son in the garden. He was a voice, well remembered. *I am not Richard. You cannot say so.* This ghost needed Gilbert even less than Harry did.

The other lived mostly in the room downstairs that had been Father's office. Father was dead twenty-five years now, he was misty, hardly more than a voice too. *You will never amount to anything, Sir. When you are old no one will want you, only your money.*

There was only one person in his life who was alive and wanted him. *Dear Uncle Gilbert,* she wrote every week from Paris.

He filled his life with charities. He was the financial mainstay of the Children's Clinic. He sat on boards. He had discovered he had a certain cleverness with money, the restraint of a man who neither needs nor wants too much of it. He was a Harvard overseer and made donations of rare books to the libraries. Often he bound them himself. He liked to work with his hands; he would have been happy building shelves or cabinets.

One day, as he was walking down the street, he saw a dog in the gutter. The dog's leg had been crushed by a wagon and a man was about to kill it with a rock. "No," Gilbert Knight said and took the dog to a dog-doctor. He had not known before that dogs had doctors. He had never owned a dog. Father would not have approved.

The night the dog came back from the hospital, Gilbert made him comfortable in the kitchen. The two of them were alone in the house; it was the servants' night out. From the library upstairs, where he was rebinding a book, Gilbert heard a low mournful baying, and then a dragging and thumping like the chains of another ghost. Elphinstone had pushed open the kitchen door with his nose and was pulling his cast after him, stair by painful stair, to be with Gilbert.

Elphinstone's leg never completely recovered, but in spite

of his limp he turned into a trim, handsome little dog, resembling a beagle, who loved to go outside. Gilbert was himself a rather reserved man, but Elphinstone had no inhibitions. He would gallop three-legged down Commonwealth Mall, spreading chaos and happiness, yelping at pigeons, other dogs, statues, nursemaids, and children; *life, life, life.* And so, though Father's voice roared from the windows of the house, *You are idle, Sir,* Gilbert quite enjoyed walking his dog.

Then Perdita wrote that she was coming to New York, with Toby.

Chapter 9

Back at the office, there was no mail for Reisden. There was a part of him that was hoping for a letter from Perdita. She'd have had to mail it yesterday from Paris, in the rush of packing. (And why hadn't she? he snarled internally.—He demanded of her more than he should.) "Did Madame and the baby get off all right?" Madame Herschner asked him. Of course, he snapped, disappointed, and went upstairs into a silence that was already beginning to feel lonely.

The apartment had been one of their successes. When he had noticed she fumbled to find doorknobs, he had found someone to make them in red china. All the lower cabinets locked with patent latches, too difficult for exploring little hands. Perdita loved light, so they had put skylights in almost all the rooms and filled them with sunshine. Now, in hot June, the light was too much light, was heat.

He stood on the stairs and brooded at the photographs they had hung. Perdita, who couldn't see them, had wanted to display pictures of their friends and family. Louis Dalloz, Victor Wills, Tiggy and his dog Ponywolf. Five generations of Dr. Jouvets, miniatures and photographs.

He stared for a while at the picture of Gilbert Knight, then unhooked it from the wall.

He turned the picture upside down and, with his pocket-knife, cut the brown paper away from the back and removed the backing. Behind the backing was another photograph: a very young man, still a teenager, holding a baby. On the back was written, in Gilbert's hand, *My brother Thomas and Richard, his son, 1879.* The young man was grinning solemnly; the baby's head had moved during the exposure.

He looked at the young man: Thomas Robert Knight, nineteen.

Gilbert had sent the picture when Toby had been born; Reisden had held it above the fire more than once this winter. Thomas Robert was so very young, nineteen and gawky, with his struggling moustache and his regrettable striped vest, looking like a child playing papa. Exactly the sort of happy careless young puppy who would get a girl in trouble and marry her, and drown both of them four years later out of sheer carelessness.

What do you call a boy like that? Father? Reisden was almost a decade older than Thomas Robert would ever be. No. You take the boy by the shoulders and shake him. Be careful, you say to him. Don't take chances. Don't go out in the boat. You made a d—d will, Thomas Robert, but you didn't bother with naming Gilbert Richard's guardian, because you were going to live forever.

It was an embarrassment for Reisden even to want a father, like finding a French postcard one bought as a teenager; one thinks one's outgrown all that long ago, and still one reacts. Furious with him, furious, disappointed, wanting—oh G-d—

security, protection, all the things Thomas Robert had been too young and careless then to give and was far too dead to give now, and still too young, eternally too young, and Reisden was too old now to find them in anyone but himself, or need them for anyone but his son.

He looked hopelessly at Thomas Robert. Someone's grandfather now?

He laid the picture down, and the cardboard over it, and fitted the nails back into the frame; he cut a piece of paper from the roll of wrapping paper in the kitchen and glued it over the back of the frame. Covered up, not forgotten, not burned, not finished with; why did he torment himself this way? He turned over the picture and stared at Gilbert Knight's face, seeing Thomas Robert there, and Richard, and Toby, and himself.

Downstairs, the telephone buzzed. He hung the picture back on the wall and went to answer.

"Reisden? Are you there? This is Jules Fauchard." The Most Assassinated Man in Paris. "I wonder if I could come talk to you?"

"Of course." Put me out of my misery; my family's gone. Tell me about André.

"The thing is—I'm in a sort of trouble and it could make problems for André. And the man says, if I don't believe he'll do what he says, ask you. You know him."

"Trouble?"

"I'm being blackmailed. It involves André."

Chapter 10

Jules was meeting his blackmailer at the café at the corner of the Place St.-Germain. Reisden was across the street half an hour beforehand, inside the medical bookseller's shop opposite, which had a convenient plate-glass window. Jules came to the rendezvous the polite five minutes early. The blackmailer was five minutes late.

The Ferret was older and greyer, but still much the same: long-nosed, chinless, buttoned from ankles to neck in an old-fashioned narrow overcoat. He held up one hand close to his side, the little finger ridiculously raised as he ticked off points on the other fingers with his thumb. He was grinning, the predatory smile of a small carnivore.

When Reisden was seventeen, in the winter he spent in Leo's house in Paris, he had opened Leo's back door at night to the Ferret and people like him. The Ferret would waddle across the back hall toward Leo's office. And some time after, there would be the scandal, the suicide, the political crisis. But why was the Ferret blackmailing Jules?

Reisden watched until the Ferret shoved his chair back and waddled away. Jules waited perhaps three minutes. The Ferret had gone off without paying; Jules put money in the saucers. Then he stood up and came across the street as Reisden came out of the bookshop.

"Does he mean what he says he's going to do?" Jules asked.

"Yes. Tell me the whole thing."

Jules looked at him, shocked, as if he had only now realized that he had not only to meet the Ferret but to talk about it. He was a big brown ordinary cheerful man; he'd been a grocer before André had found him for the Necro. He was not an actor, he had always said about himself, just André's favorite victim. Now he looked ill with disgust and couldn't hide it.

"His name is Ferenc Gehazy," Reisden said. "Leo von Loewenstein bought political information from him. Gehazy used blackmail to get the information. What did he want?"

"I can't say."

"He has told you you can't," Reisden corrected. "We'll go to my office and talk this over."

Jules paced around Reisden's office, too nervous to sit, looking at the ominously titled medical books in the glassed-in shelves, the Vesalius etching of the flayed man, the crimson doorknobs. He sat down, took out his handkerchief, and wiped his palms. He balled the handkerchief between his big hands. He got up again, roamed around the room, looked out the window, checked the time on the clock on the mantelpiece, checked the clock against his watch. "I'll have to be at the Necro soon."

This was funk and not worth a reply.

Jules stared at the mantelpiece. On one side, the sandstone figure of a Renaissance courtier held up the mantelpiece. There had been two before the building had collapsed. Now, against the wall by the bracing, leaned a sandstone carving of a skeleton, smiling a deathly smile, holding a scythe bound with ribbons. The skeleton matched the courtier perfectly; André had an eye; but one does not necessarily want to be terrified in a medical office, a detail André would neglect. "That comes from André," Jules said. "It was at Montfort."

Reisden nodded. "He sent it as a present after the party."

"And you don't know how to send it back?" Jules said;

both men smiled. Jules let his breath out slowly, a small release of tension.

"André's not like anyone else in the world," Jules said. He looked again at the courtier and the skeleton. "People don't understand that.—If I told you—I mean, could I hire you or retain you or Jouvet so that no one, ever, would have to know about this?"

Reisden had seated himself behind his desk and Jules was in one of the clients' chairs. "Of course." Jules found in his pocket a louis d'or, the traditional medical retainer, and put it on Reisden's desk. Was that all right? his expression said. Reisden nodded.

"This man threatens to spread rumors about André." Jules took a deep breath. "André and Sabine went to Egypt for their honeymoon. He wrote four plays about mummies' curses, evil priestesses trapped in a tomb, all that, so from his point of view the honeymoon was all right."

André had sent the not-yet-born Toby a cat mummy as a present. What could one say about André that wasn't exceeded by what he actually did?

"But something happened in Egypt. Sabine—when they got back, André sent Sabine down to the country, and André—It's nothing like what this *blackmailer* says—" Jules took a long breath and let it out, slowly, slowly. He jammed his hands into his pockets, hunching his shoulders; red came up in his cheeks and suffused his face. "But he says that André and his wife don't get on because André and I have—an unsavory connection."

Jules was ordinary; it was his strength. Nothing unusual happens to people like him. A rival carpentry shop opens nearby, his soccer team loses. André turned Jules into a vampire, had him decapitated by a mad Russian countess, eviscerated him at the bloody hands of the inmates of Dr. Wardrell's Asylum every night and twice on Wednesdays, and the audience felt it all, because Jules was like them, only a little better, an ordinary handsome pleasant man.

Jules hadn't married. He lived with his sister in a flat near the theatre. He escorted women to play openings but never elsewhere; "I'm too busy to marry," he said with a smile whenever some mama hinted. "What woman wants her husband off being murdered every midnight?"

The Ferret specialized in rumors so awkward that their truth didn't matter.

"He can say whatever he pleases about me, but about André—*It is not true,*" Jules said, leaning forward. "Believe that. André's working on—" Jules hesitated "—a new project, he's been working on it all winter—something with Cyron. . . . Perhaps he's simply put her off to one side, to deal with later, you know how he is when he's working. But he ought to pay more attention to her. I—all of us at the theatre tell him to go home."

Reisden nodded.

"Sabine—she's pretty, she's rich, she wants attention—" Jules tilted his hand back and forth. "She's a little, you know; you know how those girls with money are, always on the defensive, they know it wasn't romance that got them married." Jules looked at him uneasily, as if hoping that he hadn't said anything unjust.

"That's awkward."

"Her father's dead, so it's *her* money." Jules left the rest unsaid. The new Countess of Montfort had brought with her, not a dowry, but an inheritance; she could take it if she left. "*She* went after *him,*" Jules said, and visibly felt this was unjust, and frowned, but couldn't prevent himself from saying the rest. "She likes him but she wants André, you know, to be—" Jules waved his hands "—more like Necrosar. You know, more—*there.* And she wanted children right away, on the marriage night, you know."

Reisden grimaced.

"Can I prove André and I don't—aren't—?" Jules moved his shoulders uneasily. "I work in the theatre, we spend hours together every day, of course we do, but it's not as though—" He blushed red beneath his olive skin. "We don't spend hours *alone*—André comes over to the flat sometimes, but Ruthie's there—at least she is sometimes— This is horrible. I'll have to give up the theatre."

"Don't. That would only make it look true."

Jules looked guiltily relieved. "Will this blackmailer do what he says, though?"

"I'm afraid he will. What does he want?"

"Something peculiar," Jules said, frowning. "He says there's a military secret at Montfort. He wanted to know about the new generator and he asked me for plans of the castle."

"Montfort has electricity?" The castle had always been lit spookily with flickering pitch-pine torches and candles.

"It's for André's film."

"He's making a film?"

"André and Cyron together." Jules' shoulders sagged. "Oh no. It's a military film, Reisden; what else would it be with Cyron in it? Cyron got his army friends to lend him soldiers for the big battle scene. You don't suppose that the black-mailer has heard about the soldiers—?"

It was possible. "André's been promised a battle scene with corpses and disembowelments," Reisden guessed. "And Ge-hazy's been sent to see why the armies are gathering."

"This film has been a disaster," Jules said. "I used to laugh about that superstition. Actors get sick, actors die, someone's eye gets knocked out in the middle of the fight scene, ha ha ha. But it's true. One thing after another. Pathé and Gaumont are trying to drive out the independent producers; they won't sell us film. We lost our first cameraman; we've had to hire an American who doesn't speak French. We had an American wrangler to handle the horses for the battle; he's completely disappeared with some girl."

"André's filming—" Jules held up his hands, stopping Reisden from saying the name. "André is filming *the Scottish play*?"

"Cyron's version, of course." *Citizen Mabet,* set in 1790s France. "Reisden, it's going to be a great film. We'll have a cast of thousands, the Revolution, the Terror, the guillotining in the actual Grand'Place in Arras—you should see the guillotine scene André worked out, better than *History of a Crime*, one shot, no dummies, no stopping the camera, no jumps, we'll leave the audience spattered with blood and screaming."

Cyron's adaptation of *Macbeth*. With André directing. The Revolution, the Terror, witches, battles, guillotines. Oh G-d, it would be wonderful.

"But why is Cyron letting André direct him?" Reisden asked. Cyron had never encouraged André.

"Because it'll get him down to Montfort," said Jules awkwardly. "Where his wife is. She's going to be in the film. I suppose, once he sees a lot of her, he'll get used to her." Jules didn't sound convinced.

"What's the problem between them?"

Jules shrugged, his cheeks reddening again. "André got sick on his honeymoon. In Egypt. He thinks—" Jules hesitated for much longer than he would have held a pause onstage. "He thinks she made him sick."

"How would she do that?"

Jules hesitated. "Poison.—He gets ideas," Jules said defensively. "He makes up stories."

"Not to that extent he doesn't. Why would André think his wife poisoned him?"

"I don't know," Jules said miserably.

"Are André and his wife ever together? I want to see them."

"André has to go to Montfort next weekend. He wants me

to go," Jules said. "I don't want to. Especially now. You can see what an awkward thing this Ferret has caused."

"I'll go," Reisden said. "And I'll think about your problem with the Ferret."

"What could he be looking for, though? What military secret could there possibly be at Montfort?"

Reisden thought. "We'll ask your sister to research it."

Chapter 11

Before Jules had become the Most Assassinated Man in Paris, he had been Josef Aborjaily, Lebanese refugee and carpenter's assistant; and when he had come to the Necro, he had brought along his sister, Ruthie, to make costumes and serve tea. Ruthie was warm and motherly with a streak of grey in her hair, a cheerful spinster who did André's research. Before he'd married she'd done his laundry too. The apartment the siblings shared clearly belonged to her: potpourri in a brass bowl scented the air, birds sang in a cage, and little roses bloomed in pots. In the front hall were framed their certificates of citizenship. Ruthie had spread papers and books over the dining room table. On either side of her rather pretty nose, red dints marked her skin. She got out her reading glasses and settled them firmly on her nose.

"The army might be testing something on the hill at Montfort, or in the fields," Ruthie said. "Traction vehicles with treads, which are supposed to work in the mud. Military uses of balloons, or radio, or planes. But Montfort castle? Juley, are you sure he asked about the castle?"

One could tell the politics of any Frenchman with perfect accuracy by his reaction to Montfort. When he had adopted André, Cyron had got permission to rebuild and add on to the castle. No doubt the authorities had had something tasteful in mind, a new roof, a bathroom or so. No indeed. Cyron had constructed a national monument or a national laughing-stock. But Montfort couldn't have sheltered soldiers against modern guns. Cyron had had no more money than any actor does, and he had spent it as actors do, on visibility. Montfort was made of chalk, locally quarried. The older towers were already losing their sharp edges.

No doubt Cyron thought it would be granite on the night.

"It's not on a railroad line," Reisden said. "It simply sits on a hill in a plain, surrounded by sheep and beet fields. It's close to the Arras road, which would be a military objective. But you can gouge the walls with a spoon."

"It has the well," Ruthie said.

"Useful in medieval times."

"No, no, no," Ruthie said, smiling. "*The* well. The *well*. The Holy Well of Montfort," Ruthie said. "It's in the deepest cellar of the castle. The witches think the water from it has powers. Perhaps the Germans want that."

"Witches, Ruthie?"

"They're a little old-fashioned," Jules said, "out there in the countryside. Herbs and stuff . . . chants at the full moon."

"Didn't Count André ever talk about witches when you visited?" asked Ruthie.

"If so, I discouraged him." The last thing one wanted was André telling scare-stories at night in Montfort, with the wind groaning in the towers and jerking the candle flames.

"Count André's country is full of witches. Girls use charms to see their lovers in mirrors. On St. John's Eve, everyone dances around bonfires all night, and on the next day the

women gather the ashes and the St. John's flowers, to protect
the ones they love."

Ruthie was handsome enough still, cheerful, with lovely
skin, olive blushed with rose, and only the glasses and the
grey hair to mar her. He had seen her in the background for
years at the Necro, dispensing her mint tea, knitting, doing
accounts, running errands, listening to actors' tales of woe
and André's latest schemes for murdering her brother onstage, smiling her shy, resigned smile, and the world had
gone on without her.

While his risky Perdita—*Je désire voter,* he thought.
Perdita would dance around a bonfire and make him worry
because she couldn't see the flames. Perdita would have flowers and ashes and the vote. There were times, even while he
distrusted her, that he remembered he loved her.

"You're thinking of your wife," Ruthie said.

"I am, I'm afraid."

She smiled at him. "You are lucky, Dr. Reisden.—I'll show
you a witch."

She went across the hallway to the library and stopped on
the way back to feed her caged birds. She stood there for a
moment, with her hand inside the cage, thinking, a pretty girl
once, left on the vine; and closed the door gently. "Here's his
picture," she said, taking a snapshot out of her pocket. "Isn't
he a darling?"

The witch was a man about sixty, posed by an ancient
building that seemed to be some kind of shop. He wore
glasses, unusual in illiterate Flanders, and an ordinary sheep-
man's ancient wool jacket and corduroy trousers; one could
almost smell the sheep dung. But his beard extended to his
watch chain, his hair tumbled to his waist, and they were tangled and felted in elflocks as if they had never been cut or
combed. "I know him," Jules said. "Omer Heurtemance. He
sells postcards in Arras. He's in the film."

"He's a white witch. He can cure toothache," Ruth Aborjaily said. "And infertility, infidelity, and diseases of cows. He can cast spells to get a woman a lover."

Jules laughed a little awkwardly. "We should try him on André and Sabine."

"Are there black witches?" Reisden asked.

Yes. White witches were curers; they guarded against tuberculosis, typhoid fever, cholera, or simple starvation. But if the disease were stubborn, if the cow gave no milk or the crop failed, the curer diagnosed *un mauvais sort*, an evil fate or spell, and sent the victim to a *sorcier*, to cast a *contre-sort*. *Sorciers* could be good or very evil.

"Most sorcerers are bachelors," Ruthie said. "Priests or shepherds; people who live alone."

"A family is a hostage to fate," Reisden said.

"That's a sad way to think."

"True, though."

"Sorcerers need time to wool-gather," Jules said, grinning.

"Jules," said his sister.

Sorcerers were supposedly to be found near all the old abbeys and monasteries, the Mont des Cats, Montfort, or near the old battlefields, Agincourt or Crécy. They used material from the Catholic Church and the battlefields: prayers, novenas, Masses, candles, dead men's bones. Holy water often formed a part of their rituals, as did the water in which the soul washed itself after death. (Reisden raised his eyebrows.) But those who did not use consecrated water set store by the Holy Well of Montfort.

This well had been struck out of the ground by St. Éloi in the sixth century. According to legend, the saint had exorcised demons from the water. During the medieval sieges of Montfort, not only had the well provided water but, the soldiers believed, all soldiers who drank it prevailed in battle. The use of the water in country medicine had persisted until forty years ago, when André's father, a freethinker, had forbidden the sorcerers to use it.

"I wonder André hasn't reopened it," Reisden said. "It seems very much his thing."

"His stepfather asked him not to," Jules said. "They use the water, of course. It's the water supply for the château."

"Can you imagine," Ruth Aborjaily said. "Drinking the water of a holy well, and bathing in it! Isn't there any romance in the world?"

"None," said Jules, who would be turned into a vampire on this evening's program at the Necro.

"Witches don't help us with the secret of Montfort," Reisden said. "Cyron might. Let's see him."

Chapter 12

That night Reisden and Jules went to see Cyron at his theatre, and arrived before the end of the play.

From beyond the auditorium doors Reisden and Jules heard his voice, thunderous and booming. "Courage, my soldiers! They're only an army—*we* are French—" The voice dropped to a murmur as Cyron exhorted his ragtag soldiers of France. They pushed open the door and stood at the back of the theatre, watching him, watching the audience, every one of whom was leaning forward, hanging on his words like the soldiers onstage, as if their lives depended on this sortie against impossible odds.

Cyron, their leader. He'd never been handsome; now, under his soldier's helmet, there were bags under his eyes and chin; he was an old potato with an enormous nose, tough as a chunk of wood. He came to the front of the stage—"There they are, boys, our enemies, there, and there, and there"— squatting with the remnants of grace, squinting out into the auditorium. *They're surrounded!* a bulky soldier's wife protested. *You'll see,* her bemedaled husband whispered. Someone else shushed them. "But here?" Cyron said. "In our hearts? No!"

Cyron's plays had always been about impossible odds, military miracles. He was every French drill sergeant who had ever trained a crew of left-footed conscripts; he was every soldier looking out over the fields, toward the enemy's overwhelming guns; he was every ordinary wordless man who had ever wiped a tear away over an old accordion song or a letter; every unexpected hero. He was Cyron; he was France. How does he do that? any actor wondered. How can I do it like him? Even Reisden wondered, who had not acted in years.

On a hill above the soldiers, the shadows of innumerable enemies moved on the red-lit gauze. Cyron, soldier of France, yelled defiance at them. "The Germans are a thousand strong, boys!" he shouted to his exalted soldiers. "Show them no mercy!" The soldiers charged the shadows; explosions shook the stage; the lights flickered, stage-smoke poured into the auditorium; enemy guns fired over the audience. From front row center to the heavens, everyone in the theatre ducked. Cries, shots, rumble of guns—the soldier's wife hid on her husband's shoulder—and Cyron, triumphant, appeared through the haze, waving the enemy banner.

While Cyron took his endless curtain calls, Reisden watched the audience. Soldiers, soldiers' wives and sons and daughters, officer candidates from St.-Cyr on an authorized outing, a Conservative minister out of power, two judges. Not many students—the French universities were leftist—but up in the cheap seats, rows and rows of the clerks, shop assistants, grocers, cooks, and waiters who would feed the cannons in the next war, all of them standing, applauding, shouting for Cyron.

The sort of men Jules played; the sort of heroes André eviscerated and blew up and fed to vampires in his theatre. André and Cyron were more alike than they thought.

Reisden and Jules were shown up to Cyron's office to wait. The office, upstairs in the theatre, was decorated with pictures of Cyron. Not the conventional publicity pictures, but Cyron and the Marquis de Morès, Cyron and Pétiot, Cyron receiving the Legion of Honor. The place of honor on the wall was given to an old photograph, a thin-faced, big-beaked, spiritual-looking Frenchman in army uniform, standing foursquare by a ruined wall. Reisden recognized the walls of Montfort, battered and unrestored, and with shock, in the face of a man younger than he was, Maurice Cyron. Sergeant Cyron, the hero; the real thing.

Forty years ago, when France had surrendered to the Prussians and given up Alsace and Lorraine, Cyron had been a wounded soldier recuperating at Arras. Cyron was Alsatian; his father had just been killed in the resistance. (There was a picture of him, too, Jean-Marie Cyron, standing on a Strasbourg street with two of his puppets.) On the raw January day when the French army had been ordered to lay down its weapons, Cyron had staggered out of the hospital, leading a ragtag group of farmers and soldiers thirteen kilometers to Montfort hill and Montfort castle, which the Germans had not bothered to conquer. On the hill below the central castle, Cyron had begun to pile the scattered stones of Montfort's walls one upon another and had declared war on Germany. "Alsace shall never be German property; France is and shall be free; I, Maurice Cyron, vow it; let it begin here!"

No army that defended Montfort had ever been conquered; Cyron's army never was. From Montfort to Arras, from January 1871 to 1874, Cyron's partisans carried on guerrilla war against the Germans. They raided and escaped like ghosts.

They dug tunnels below German storehouses, filled them with gunpowder, and set it off. The Germans took hostages; the partisans freed them. While the rest of France starved to pay off its billion-dollar indemnity to its conquerors, in Arras the war was still on and the Germans were losing.

From the window of Cyron's office, Reisden could look down and see the stage door. The actors were leaving one by one. The stage door was surrounded. Conscription-age clerks and old soldiers were elbowing each other to get a glimpse of Cyron.

"He'll be a few minutes yet, messieurs," Cyron's assistant told Reisden and Jules. Cyron would be holding court in his dressing room.

In 1874, when the Germans left France, Cyron had appeared in Paris, unshaven, ragged, and scarred, to a hero's welcome. A commissioned officer would have been invited to go into politics. But Cyron had been given only a theatre contract to re-enact his triumphs. No one had expected he would be more than a novelty. But the army had loved him, and in 1874 the army had owned France.

They still loved him.

In a showcase at one side of the office were some of Cyron's souvenirs. A pillow that an army widow had sent him, embroidered with one of his sayings: BECAUSE GOD LOVES JUSTICE, HE LOVES THE FRENCH SOLDIER. A scroll of appreciation from a group of officers. Medals that old soldiers had given him. His gavel as perpetual life president of the Friends of Montfort. A black-bordered photograph of him at a Mass mourning the loss of Alsace; he was in the second row, behind the generals, head bowed. Cigaret cards on which his picture appeared, together with the German decree banning the brand in Alsace.

"What do you lot want?"

The door banged open. Cyron stumped over to his desk and sat in his thronelike chair, his big hands resting on the arms. His assistant brought him supper on a tray: sausage, bread, cheese, beer, an apple.

While he ate, Reisden and Jules told him about the blackmail. "Someone wants 'the secret of Montfort,' " Reisden said. "Do you know what it is?"

"You know this blackmailer?" Cyron said.

"I knew of him," Reisden said.

"The secret of Montfort? The value of Montfort? Montfort is France. Montfort is soldiers. You wouldn't know." Cyron thumped his heart. Ridiculous gesture from anyone but Cyron.

"It has a propaganda value," Reisden said, "and that's all, is that what you're saying?"

In the myth that was Cyron, Montfort had come to have a central place. When Cyron had bought it (or, more accurately, adopted André), he had begun to rebuild it. Almost spontaneously, men and money had appeared in quantity. It had become a golden money-raising scheme. Raise a certain amount for Montfort and you could get your name on a stone. Raise more and you could have a tower. Old soldiers volunteered to work on the walls; young recruits mixed mortar under the eyes of a professional builder. Once a year there was a Montfort Night at the Théâtre Cyron. A general gave a speech, Rostand contributed a poem, a group of army wives and daughters dressed up as a Living Tapestry of France. As a climax, there was a moment of silence for occupied Alsace.

"Your support for the military is so well known," Reisden said, "that the Ferret's employer—whoever he is now—seems to believe you have some military goal in rebuilding the castle. Your goal is simple patriotic fervor"—propaganda, he thought—"but suppose that Jules were to tell the Ferret that Montfort does have a specific military value."

"What?" Cyron said.

Jules laid their offering on the altar. "Sir, we had thought of saying there is a wireless antenna on the tower. But only if there isn't, not that there could be. . . ."

In the unmagical twentieth century, the castle's only advantage was the height of its towers. With a Marconi aerial bouncing radio off the cloudy Flanders sky, the French army could send messages into Belgium, perhaps even into Germany.

"On the tower?" Cyron said.

"Powered by your new generating station," Reisden said.

Cyron slammed his hand against his desk. "You think about this, *von* Reisden, and you haven't found out anything about my son?"

"I have, actually. Jules, could you leave us for a moment?"

"For a thousand years the Montforts were soldiers," Cyron said. "I sent André to military school; I bought him a commission. I'm in the theatre, but I never encouraged him. It was *you who told him to do theatre.*"

In the cavalry, André had hid in a supplies closet, writing plays. No one had had to tell him anything. "The issue is not that he does theatre, Cyron, it really is not. The issue's that he thinks his wife poisoned him in Egypt."

Cyron sat back in his chair, staring at the desk. "That all started long before."

This puzzled Reisden. "Jules says after he came back from the honeymoon."

Cyron snorted. "Start with your records. The Jouvet records."

Reisden cursed silently. "I would much rather not tell you this," he said, "because we like to have a reputation for efficiency. But you know that some of the Jouvet records were destroyed last year. André's may have been among them."

Cyron looked up. "You can't find it?" He almost sounded relieved. There is only one force as strong as the family's desire to cure their madman, and that is the desire to have no one know about him.

"You brought him to Jouvet when he was young," Reisden prompted.

Over Cyron's rough face spread an unwilling, bitter sadness, and Reisden had seen that too before in the families of Jouvet's patients. He rubbed his face with his open palm, trying to rub the expression away. "I was going to buy the castle," Cyron said simply. "I was meeting with the notaries. Their men, mine, it was above my head; I was sitting in one corner of the room and this little boy was sitting in the other. I went over and began to tell him stories." Cyron said nothing for a moment, then, softly, "When the meeting was over the kid didn't want to go away; he wanted to stay with me. He took my hand and wouldn't let go."

"So you adopted André."

"Everybody says I just wanted the castle.—No.—I don't know what happened to him. His parents died. He was alone with the bodies for a while. One day. Two. He stopped speaking."

"You asked Dr. Jouvet to look at him," Reisden prompted.

"Just to make sure if"—he grimaced—"he had an infection, something like that. He had nightmares. And Jouvet said time would cure him," Cyron said.

"Time can do that."

"Unless," Cyron said bitterly, "unless some d—n Austrian told André he should give way to his fantasies, start writing them out, start putting them on stage?"

"But he always had fantasies?"

"Oh, yes," Cyron said.

"And they were—?" Reisden prompted when Cyron didn't say anything more.

"Murder in families!" Cyron burst out. "He said I was all right because I was only a stepfather. But *families* murdered each other," he added almost as an afterthought.

"Poisoned each other."

Cyron nodded silently.

"And he's said this for his whole life." Of course he had. He had said it onstage. "But you made him marry," Reisden said.

"It was his duty. It was my duty to make him."

Reisden said nothing.

"What, should I have let him neglect his duty?"

You shouldn't have neglected what he was saying. Neither should I. Reisden had been busy. . . . It's always easy to be busy. "What more did Jouvet say to you?" Reisden said. "Did he give details? Do you know what happened to André?"

"No."

"Then unless we find the records," Reisden said, "the only one who knows why he's saying it is André."

"Do your duty," Cyron said. "Fix him up. Binny's a wonderful girl."

Chapter 13

When she was ten, Sabine Wagny began to see death.

It started very suddenly on the street, one January day in Wagny-les-Mines. Though Papa had been rich even before the mines had opened, he was miserly; he always thought the Germans and the bad old days would come back. He kept no horse nor mule but always walked behind his dog-cart, he'd skin a mouse for the fur and the fat, and schools cost money since priests had given up teaching for free; so Sabine spent her days in the kitchen listening to the serving maids talk, and one day when Lalie the greying old cook-maid clopped off to the market, Sabine slipped on her sabots and went with her.

She already knew her destiny. Lalie had said, "Your mama saw a grand fate for you. 'This one will kill me,' that's what she said, your poor mama, 'but my child will live, she'll be the mistress of a great house.' " Sabine doubted. Who would be this master of a great house whom she'd marry, when she wore a grey flannel skirt and an orange blouse, Lalie's cut-downs? When would she go to school?

That day Lalie and Sabine had bought an old piece of steer-hock full of fat and gristle, which Papa would approve of because it had not cost much, and had bought rubbery whiskered carrots and sprouting potatoes, but with the coins they had left, they had gone to a patisserie for a *pain au chocolat*. They stood on the streetcorner to eat it. A man stopped in front of them. He was ragged, his plush trousers shone at the knees; his beard hung down in tangles. "Give me," he said to Lalie. He held out his hand palm up, and Lalie, wide-eyed and pale, broke off a piece of the chocolate-filled bread and gave it to him, then hesitated and thrust all of it at him. He smiled wickedly with black ruined teeth, taking it and turning away without thanking them.

"You gave him it all," Sabine accused her. "Mine, too."

"He would have cursed us," Lalie hissed. "Don't you know what he is? A man who never combs or cuts his hair?"

"I don't care," Sabine said, near tears. "It was chocolate, I don't care about being cursed." She followed the sorcerer into the street, curiously, resentfully, halfway admiring his selfishness. Lalie jerked her back.

"Shh! Do this." Lalie held up both her hands, fisted, the thumbs inside the fingers.

Sabine fisted both her hands, then unfisted them. "*I* curse *him* for stealing my chocolate," she said.

The streets of Wagny-les-Mines were steep and unpaved, but in the January cold, the frozen slush and mud were as slippery as cobblestones. A delivery wagon was coming down-hill from the butcher's. On the ice the horse slipped and fell; the delivery wagon fishtailed, struck the sorcerer, threw him against the curb, and crushed him.

Sabine opened her mouth, astonished.

Bystanders lifted the wagon off him. Its heavy iron axle had broken his head. Sabine ran into the street and crouched down beside him. She had never seen someone dying before. His brains were leaking into the mud and his right eye was bulging almost out of the socket. It was awful and fascinating. She took his hand and looked into his left eye, which could still see.

She had cursed him and it had worked.

The sorcerer smiled again, wickedly, recognizing her, baring bloody broken teeth. He held her hand tightly and murmured words at her. *Peur té seuc'*, she thought she heard. *For your sweets*. She felt some pulse flow from his hand to hers; then his hand went limp.

"Come away, come away," Lalie said, and drew her round the corner where she couldn't see the man. "Wash your hands quickly!" Lalie forced Sabine's hands under the cold splash from the street-pump.

"I was holding his hand while he died!" she said.

Lalie scrubbed at Sabine's hands with her skirt.

"He gave me something," Sabine said.

"*Qué des puces!* He gave you nothing," Lalie said. She made the fists against evil. "Do that," Lalie said to her.

Sabine thought about it and opened her dripping hands wide. If the sorcerer had given her anything, it was for her chocolate, and it was hers.

I am growing up, Sabine told her father. *It's time for me to go to school. She stared into his eyes until he blinked and sent her to the convent school at Arras.*

Arras was an old city, centered around two great plazas

with seventeenth-century arcades. Lime and chalk had been
mined here since Arras was Roman; now the old mines, tun-
neled and retunneled, formed a dark honeycomb under the
city. The shopkeepers showed the fascinated Sabine medieval
basements and crypts, ancient chalk rooms that stored wine
and cheeses and fresh flowers, an underground maze from the
shops to the city hall and the cathedral. The boves seemed to
her as strange, as fascinating, as the secret parts of her own
body.

From the postcard-seller in the Grand'Place, who never
combed or cut his hair, Sabine heard rumors that *des gens par-
ticuliers* met in the boves. She heard certain rumors about a
young dressmaker whose shop was in one of the seventeenth-
century houses in the Grand'Place, whose uncle was a hermit. She developed an intense interest in dresses and soon
was visiting Mademoiselle Françoise every week.

She studied the lore of her kind. When she saw anything in
the shape of a cross, she uncrossed it quickly and did the fist
or the horns to protect herself. She learned the uses of Saint-
John's-wort and wormwood, of pellitory and tobacco. She
knew about charms and love philtres and water from the Holy
Well of Montfort. "What a superstitious girl," her classmates
said.

Mademoiselle Françoise agreed to show her something
special in the boves. The dressmaker bound her eyes with a
piece of satin left over from a dress-measure. Sabine held the
dressmaker's skirt, stumbled down the stairs, followed eagerly through the darkness, and opened her eyes to find herself in a narrow cave. From a crevice in the rock, a carved
man's face smiled down on her, making her welcome.

At the age of fourteen, under the eyes of the Old Master,
she was initiated into the pleasures of her craft and learned
why a male sorcerer creates female ones and a female sorcerer males. She learned darkness and laughter, awe and wor-
ship and rejoicing. She learned that witchcraft was not spells

or curses, love philtres or charms, but flesh and the fate of flesh. A witch would not sit still with pale white folded hands and wait for Heaven but love the world and rejoice and tangle with flesh. A witch might burn. (Mobs had burned a witch alive in Germany only thirty years ago.) But until she died, a witch would live.

Every witch has special talents. Sabine had three.

First, of course, she would have money.

Second, she was pretty. She had thick brown hair and white teeth. Mademoiselle Françoise, who had studied in Paris, taught her to stand so as to make the best of her curves and to tilt her head to one side so she looked winsome. "Say *parler* and not *paller*," the dressmaker dinned into her. "Your voice must always be low, sweet, and demure. Sit up *straight*."

And most importantly, Sabine could see death. She saw the grey veil drop over Lalie's face; two days later her old nurse died of a stroke. Sabine often saw veiled people on the street. She knew that death was everywhere. So it made her happy to be young and alive while other people were going to be dead.

During the Easter vacation when she was sixteen she saw the veil drop over her father's face. She was extra nice to him, making sure that his meat was fatty and even a little rancid, so that he could be sure it had not cost too much. But when she got back to Arras, she rushed off to see her dressmaker.

"Make me black clothes," she said, "and make them pretty. I'm going to Paris."

It was Mademoiselle Françoise who had first told her about the great Count of Montfort. He lived in Paris, Sabine heard. He had never married. He suffered under a curse. He acted on the Paris stage under the name of Necrosar. Sometimes she had seen his black closed carriage waiting by the railroad station. In the illustrated papers she found a picture of him. She ripped all the other pictures off the inside lid of her trinket-box and pasted his there alone.

He was accursed; he was handsome.

It was hard to get to the Grand Necropolitan Theatre; at midnight one was supposed to be in bed long ago, a little schoolgirl! Sabine climbed out her window with her skirts hiked up and her shoes and stockings in her hand.

She fell in love the first time she saw him. *He, he, he,* tall and strong, white and strange, in black lipstick and eyes rimmed with black. The dark, Necrosar said. Everyone's afraid of the dark. It was true; no one knew better than Sabine how you could be afraid of what delighted you. The dark is power; the dark is death. In the dark everything happens. No one understood Necrosar like Sabine.

"I'm going to marry Necrosar," she told Françoise.

"André de Montfort has no money," her Paris friends said. Sabine knew that. She felt the threadbare chair-arms at the Necro; she saw the holes in the carpet. The lead actor helped to build sets; the lead actor's sister was the bookkeeper and swept the auditorium at night.

"I have money," Sabine said.

"He doesn't like women," her Paris friends said.

"I'll fix that," Sabine said. "He'll like me."

Chapter 14

The poison bottle arrived the day before Reisden went to Montfort.

Jules brought it. It was wrapped in black paper and sealed with Necrosar's skull-and-crossbones seal. Reisden unwrapped it and set it on his desk. The bottle itself was tinted an evil green and was corked and sealed; white powder smudged the inside. André had wrapped a note around the bottle: *This is what she used! She'll kill me!*

Reisden looked up. Jules was flushed red. "I told him I'd bring it," he said. "So here I am. I brought it."

Reisden pushed the bottle back and forth on his blotter with the end of a pencil. "Do you suppose it's rat poison? Or what is it?"

Jules flushed as if he had run a race and lost. "Why rat poison?" he asked miserably.

"The Necro has rats," Reisden said. "Well?"

Jules turned away, hands in his pockets, shoulders hunched, and looked out the window.

"My G-d, Jules."

"Do you think the Necro is bad for André, like Cyron says?"

"I don't know." But there André was, every night onstage, applauded for exactly the sort of *nécrotisme* that was sitting on Reisden's desk. Mysterious powders, sealed with mourning-wax and a skull. Perdita might not be in America, he thought, if no one praised her there.

Reisden showed the bottle that night to Philippe Katzmann, one of their specialists in patient assessment; then they went out to dinner. Katzmann was a Freudian, balding, with a wild fringe of black hair standing out on either side of his head. In imitation of Freud, he smoked cigars, and as he spoke he flourished one and scattered burning ashes over the tablecloth.

"The patient deals in secrets," Katzmann said. "He's an artist, a criminal, this time a dramatist. He's showing you a play through gauze. On the scrim, the patient paints the picture he wants you to see, big and colorful and dramatic, and shines a light on it so that the picture bounces back into your eyes. Poisoning! Bottles of rat poison! Mysteries! You must look hard, move the light, to see through the fabric to the real drama behind."

Reisden nodded. "What is his drama here?"

Katzmann pinched a burning fragment of tobacco off the tablecloth. "Two things. When a patient says his wife he usually means his mother. That's very powerful, he says his mother is poisoning him. What do we know about his mother?"

"Both parents died suddenly, of something fast and infectious. Possibly cholera. Cyron says André was alone with the bodies for days. He told Cyron that families murder each other.—I know a story, rather a legend, about his father."

"What?"

"After the war André's father is supposed to have doubled as the village doctor of Montfort commune. He took André to death-beds to cure André of the fear of death. Instead of being merely unafraid, André became fascinated.—Theatre gossip."

"Nothing about his mother.—Still, trauma." Katzmann knocked the ash off his cigar. "Cholera looks like arsenic poisoning, isn't that so?"

Reisden nodded. "André's remaking his parents' deaths as murder? Why?"

"Send him to me and I'll get him to talk about it. You know the talking cure, right?"

"Freud?"

"Freud says the patient can be cured," Katzmann said, "and his sickness can disappear, immediately and forever, 'when we succeed in bringing clearly to light the memory of the event by which it was first provoked.' The patient must *describe* the event, in all its details, just as it happened to him, with the emotions that it provoked then. If the patient was frightened then, he must be frightened again and describe it, he must banish the experience by putting it into words."

"André would rather think of murder than of their deaths?"

"Just that!" said Katzmann. "The patient *resists* going back to the traumatic episode, because it's so painful for him, and the resistance feeds his sickness.—Do you know the first thing they say after they say *it*, when you've spent months, years, trying to get them to describe what happened? The very next thing they say. Invariable. 'I could have told you that anytime.' "

I am Richard Knight, who murdered his grandfather. I could tell you that anytime. No. Imagine experiencing it twice.

"The other thing?" said Katzmann. "When a patient sends you a bottle of arsenic?" Katzmann did a decent imitation of a gibbering madman. "Be careful."

So there they were, he and André, ready for a weekend of persuasion toward psychiatry, but by the time they had been on the train three hours, Reisden had developed a respect for the myriad ways patients, and their confidants, can avoid speaking. André had brought work for the film, Reisden the same for Jouvet, mostly bills and budgets. They talked about sports. They deplored the French army's incursion into Fez. They talked theatre. By the time they had reached Wagny-les-Mines, they had said nothing.

From miles away they saw the pyramid of Wagny-les-Mines' mine tailings. The artificial mountain loomed over the town, over the whole plain. The one main street of the town was narrow and rotten with soot. Soot peppered the evening meals being cooked at the public ovens and the bread displayed in the baker's window; soot made a gritty crust on the street. Behind the main street was a grid of *corons*, rental houses for the miners. Coal tattooed the faces of the few men on the street; coal dust smeared the narrow windows of the *corons* and turned the bar-signs to shadows of gilt and black. André was photographed at the top of the shaft, in a group with miners, next to the ventilation fans. In the flashbulb explosions, the air danced with grit. André was at least six inches taller than anyone in Wagny-les-Mines, including the manager and the mayor. Counts, however poor they have been, are never as malnourished as miners.

André was reserved and sympathetic, exactly what *le patron* should be; it was a scene he knew how to play. But back in the train, in (fortunately) a private compartment, he relapsed to Necrosar. "I'll do a play in the coal region. 'Pollution oozes from the earth like pus from wounds. Around the mine shafts the earth falls away like decayed flesh from bone. . . .' "

"André," Reisden said, "you've no social conscience."

"It's evil there. Don't you feel it? Her country."

They sat in silence until Arras.

The yard of the Arras station was dominated by the Montfort coach. Not the rackety wagon drawn by farm horses that Reisden remembered; this was a sleek antique English mail coach, of the sort that rich men keep as pets, and the four bay horses were perfectly matched down to their white socks and pink noses. A footman was laying out English tea for them on the folding boot: sandwiches, cake, drinks.

"Poisoned, all of it," André muttered to Reisden.

"Shut up, André," Reisden murmured back, thinking of the miners.

A man and a woman descended from the train and greeted the driver like old guests; of all people to be here this weekend, the man and woman were cherubic General Pétiot and his wife.

André smiled at them skeletally, watching, waiting.

The coachman spoke to Pétiot and incidentally to André. "Madame la Comtesse is still with her dressmaker in the Grand'Place, messieurs, and we are waiting for one more guest on the next train."

"*She's* coming *with* us? In this coach?" André said sharply.

"Let's walk," Reisden said, taking him firmly by the arm

and steering him away from Pétiot. "Shall we see your Grand'Place, André, and collect your wife?"

"I'll show you the town."

Arras *centre-ville* is large for a county town, a couple of miles across, and they walked all of it—all but the Grand'-Place. They circled the enormous brick-walled Citadel, where André had been stationed as an officer, and André described dead men's bones rising from the military cemetery and walking the streets. In the stark grey Place Victor-Hugo, André conjured up vampires. In front of the eighteenth-century theatre, André spoke of Joseph Lebon, the Butcher of Arras. "It was like a slaughterhouse here, fifty or sixty guillotined in a day, blood on the pavement, the machine soaked with blood and stinking." Necrosar at his finest. But André's eyes darted past Reisden, examining the crowds for someone he was more afraid of than dead men, vampires, or madmen, and when from time to time they saw glimpses of a big central plaza at the end of a street, André quickly turned away.

Finally they reached the enormous town hall. "I haven't shown you the boves," André said. He was already ducking into the arched doorway. "Come on, come on." He flourished an enormous iron key. "You can't miss the boves of Arras."

"What are boves?"

"You'll be frightened." He led the way down an unlit side corridor to an iron-bound oak door and unlocked it. On the other side was a tiny dim vestibule, like a closet, and another locked door of iron bars. André worked the key into the lock, which was sandy with rust. On the other side of the bars lay utter darkness.

"It's dark." Necrosar made his voice high, eerie, like a bat's.

"We don't have time, André."

"Come on." André got the door open, reached up in the darkness, and found a cracked yellow end of candle. He lit it; a worn stone stair fell down into the dark. He plunged down.

The darkness was thick and resistant. Reisden felt he was inhaling it. He groped his way down the stairs, which were damp, slippery, and hollowed out by centuries.

"The oldest boves were Roman chalk mines," André said, playing guide. "Caesar had his winter camp near here." From their right came a breeze and the sounds of shouts, wagon wheels, and horses' hooves on cobblestones. "Can you hear the market? There's an opening like a well up into the plaza. The Romans used it to haul up blocks of chalk."

"How interesting. André, have we frightened ourselves sufficiently?" The dark was almost impenetrable; in the candle flame Reisden could see the rough-cut walls, part of André's arm, and that was all. "It's impolite to make the servants wait."

"*This* isn't frightening." André held up his candle, scanning the wall foot by foot for marks. Black flints glittered from the chalklike eyes.

"You said you knew where you were going," Reisden said.

"I do," André chuckled hollowly. "I *think* I do." André turned off into a still narrower side-passage.

"D—n you if you get us lost for effect." He forced himself to breathe deeply.

"You can't get lost so close to the plaza," André said. "Now *this* is frightening."

The tunnel widened into complete blind blackness. Even here, the faint reverberations of the market still came to them, thudding from rock to rock in the darkness. The floor was slick with something; Reisden slipped, caught himself, and swore under his breath. The footfall and his voice came back in deep murmurs.

"Saint Vaast," André said, and the reverberations hissed back his words like snakes. "He came to Arras five hundred years after Christ. The Roman Empire had fallen to ruins. The land was in darkness, the legend says, and ruled by a great bear. Saint Vaast tamed the bear. But he didn't kill it, just left it sleeping in its cave." And André raised the candle high.

Out of the darkness, man-high in stone, a white face thrust forward into the candle flame. The crude mouth lolled open, half-grinning, half-dead; mismatched eyes glared in the candle shadows, the thick lips writhed, the tongue moved. The candle guttered and the face struggled outward as if the chalk were trying to make itself a face.

"That's not the most frightening thing," André said. "This is."

André knelt down and held his candle close to the floor.

On the floor underneath the crude face were flowers, bunches of herbs, a pathetic bit of fur and bone that might have been a rabbit.

Offerings.

Chapter 15

The Grand'Place is one of those unexpected, enormous market squares that one finds in the Low Countries; after the pressing darkness of the boves, it seemed to stretch from horizon to horizon. A wool market was going on in one corner of it, the grain market in another; the tracks for the grain market's railroad spur curved across the cobblestones. A mackerel-seller was crossing the square, her red-and-yellow cart pulled by a dog, crying her wares: "Fresh mackerel, not dead yet!" On all four sides, seventeenth-century arcaded shops with top-heavy roofs displayed the local wares:

gin, beers, cheeses, tulips, chalk animals, and really dreadful chalk replicas of the Town Hall. There was a breeze, making the iron signs clack. Under the sign of a dressmaker's shop, a young woman in a violet dress was just taking leave of an older woman while her maid hovered with parcels in the background.

André shrank back. "*She's* here!"

Timidly, across the square, André's wife waved a white-gloved hand.

"We'll meet her," Reisden said. "Come, André."

Sabine, Countess of Montfort, Cyron's choice to be the mother of André's children, could not have been more than eighteen. She had thick, brown, curly hair, slightly freckled skin, and brown eyes ringed inexpertly with kohl. She was wearing a violet-and-white checked silk dress with rows of buttons, small clear glass buttons with pink roses. An old-fashioned cut (men with blind wives learn the anxieties of fashion) but so new that the cloth still smelled of dye. It had lost one of its buttons already, one of the vertical rows that outlined her high, large breasts.

And it was easy to see at least one of her attractions, for Cyron if not for André: Sabine was one of those women who would always have trouble with clothes. Buttons would undo for her, leaving bits of creamy freckled skin peeping out. Bodice lace would tear, needing intimate repairs. He thought—the first thing he thought was that Perdita had been gone too long; if she had been there he wouldn't have looked at Sabine in quite the same way. Bait, our Sabine. She was a woman one took to bed.

"This is Mademoiselle Françoise, my couturière." Sabine had a soft, slightly nasal voice, the accent of French Flanders. Mademoiselle Françoise sucked her teeth and giggled and ducked her bright blonde head, holding out a hot little hand like a chicken-claw.

"The coachman is waiting," André said finally, reluctantly.

Sabine held out her hand to him, but he only looked at it, smiling like Necrosar, and turned away. Sabine stared after him. Her mouth was lovely, the top lip slightly short, the bottom lip round and cushiony, quivering a little, from unhappiness or offended pride. A hurt, sulky, kissable mouth. Oh, Cyron.

"May I?" Reisden offered her his arm like a good guest. Sabine took it and trudged along beside him, shoulders rounded, face clenched like a fist.

The coach was crowded: not only General Pétiot and his lady, but an ancient sergeant with a stiff leg. There was luggage, the general's wife's knitting, Sabine's parcels. "I'll take the top," André said. Reisden offered to sit outside and was refused. Sabine leaned her head against the glass coach window, kicking her heels.

The men made stiff conversation; neither Pétiot nor Reisden wanted to talk about the situation with Jouvet. Pétiot and the sergeant had come at Cyron's invitation. The older men would mortar a few stones at Montfort, then amuse themselves wandering the countryside or watching younger men work at the building. "Yes, sir," said the sergeant, "they're a-sweat to get that new tower finished. And there's our boys from the Citadel—"

Sabine, sitting by the window, sighed explosively. She took out a magazine—a theatrical magazine, with a picture of an American moving-picture heroine on the cover.

Reisden had already been cast as the foreigner, so he asked the obvious question: "How does rebuilding Montfort build French defenses?"

"Rebuilding a sense of France," Pétiot said. "Not enough of that nowadays, is there?"

"It's," the sergeant said, and hesitated, "it's fine. You get up there, do your work, turn your face to the wind; there's a view, there's a vista, you see the land. . . ."

Neither of them could say why rebuilding a medieval castle was important to France in 1911, but they knew it was important to them. Pétiot had raised over a hundred thousand francs for the project. The sergeant had worked on it every year since the castle rebuilding had started. Montfort belonged to them.

" 'God loves the French soldier,' " the old sergeant said, quoting Cyron. "If I died there, with my hand on a stone . . ." Pétiot puffed on his pipe, agreeing. Sabine, sitting next him, gave Pétiot a look of loathing, pulled open the window, and fanned ostentatiously.

"Shall we change places?" Reisden suggested.

"Oh, that would be *wonderful*." Sabine made room for him with a wiggle. "Do you like films?" she said. "I *love* films." She gazed up at him from under the black tangle of her eyelashes; Reisden recognized the chaste-but-torrid gaze of a movie heroine. "This summer *I'm* going to be in a film. And then I'll have my picture in *L'Illustration* and in all the theatre magazines, just like this!"

And Reisden looked at André's wife: her disheveled clothes and hair, her ripe figure, her teenaged inexpert flirtatiousness; and he realized the other important thing about Sabine de Montfort. She would be good in films. If the camera caught anything at all of her, it would be that breathless warm aura. Perhaps she was able to act, but it didn't matter; when *Citizen Mabet* opened, Sabine de Montfort would be a sensation.

He wondered how long it would take her to know it.

Chapter 16

Montfort. He hadn't seen it for fourteen years, except in photographs, and the first sight of it took his breath away. Ridiculous, grandiose Montfort.

It dominated the sky. Montfort Abbey and the castle stood on top of Montfort hill, which is the biggest—the only—elevation between Arras and Vimy. One saw first, like scratches against the sky, the double black bell towers of the abbey, one whole, one partly fallen; and then, rising from the fields, the whole hill, spiky with towers—square ones, round ones, towers with pointed roofs, towers with battlements, all of them made from chunks of chalk mortared with cement. Round and round the hill, like a maze, ran a chalk white road with low chalk walls on either side. In the fields where the sheep grazed stood a profusion of little buildings, gazebos, garden sheds, simple memorials, all made of chalk as well, all in the shape of little pointed towers. At the back of the hill, visible as the carriage passed, was a vast white stone-dump, where blocks and chunks of chalk waited to be made part of Montfort.

"Did you ever see such a thing?" the sergeant enthused. "So many people! So many builders!" Pétiot puffed his pipe in agreement. On many of the little buildings, and even on individual stones in the wall, the late-afternoon sun picked out inscriptions. ILS NE PASSERONT PAS! They—the Germans—

won't pass this spot. VIVE LA FRANCE! VIVE LA RÉPUBLIQUE!
Many of the stones had names. DIED FOR FRANCE, 6 SEPT 1870.
It's easy to make inscriptions in chalk, but all this effort was
disconcerting, like art made by the insane. As the coach negotiated the hill, the sheep moved away from the road like bits
of the walls that had not yet settled in place.

Reisden had been given a room in the main building, André's actual old castle. Before Sabine, Montfort had been a
bad doss; one had pounded the mattress to scare the mice out.
Now the windows had been repaired, the cracked glass replaced, the corners had been swept clean of their accumula-
tions of dead leaves and dust-tigers. The old furniture had
been cleaned of its grime and polished until it glowed. The
bedstead in Reisden's room was eight feet high and carved
with medieval angels with slanted eyes, like a magnificent
tomb, very André. But what Sabine had added— Someone
had told her that Flemish medieval castles need Flemish medieval furnishings, so she had gone to, at a guess, the biggest
department store in Belgium and ordered a wagonload of
the Middle Ages. The walls were covered with bright wool
machine-made hangings featuring unicorns, armored heroes,
and droopy-haired maidens. The bedside clock looked like
the west end of Rouen Cathedral in brass and was an alarm
clock. Reisden, fresh from furnishing his family's house,
made shooing motions at it. He discovered the chamber pot
underneath the bed—finest medievalesque china, hand-
painted with André's coat of arms. He sat on the edge of the
bed and laughed. The house stationery featured a color print
of the castle. He wrote a note to Perdita, describing the clock
and chamber pot.

Downstairs, the Great Hall had tortuous new Gothic-style
dining chairs but was still lit by torches and candles; the
torches guttered and roared away in their holders and the candles melted away in a chill draft. André sat at one end of the
table, silent, refusing food, wine, even water, staring with a

fixed smile. From time to time, he took a notebook from his jacket pocket and scribbled a line of dialogue. Sabine cut her fish into scraps as though it were André's liver but only picked at her food.

She had changed to a yellow-green satin and was wearing a large, plain necklace of brown beads. Russian amber: she wore it with a stiff-necked consciousness that it was fashionable. It was—but not on her. She fidgeted in her dress, pulled at the weight of the necklace. Her clothes oppressed her.

After dinner the soldiers took over the billiard room (which now actually had a working billiard table) and André went into the library to write. Reisden stayed with the women in Sabine's new music room; if he couldn't have André, he would talk with Sabine.

He was reasonably good at small talk, and for a while they spun the wheels of polite conversation. Sabine said the weather had been so warm that the wheat and the hay were well along. Did he have land? No, he didn't; only in the Carpathians. She said she wanted to have more parkland around the house; it wasn't fitting to have only sheep-graze and beet fields. She asked if he would like her to play the piano, to which the only possible answer is *how extremely delightful*. With the flourishes of uncertainty, she began to make her way through a Chopin piece that Perdita would have made interesting. Montfort was a damp house, in spite of Sabine's new central heating, and the piano was correspondingly out of tune. Reisden listened with perfect outward attention; he was an experienced guest. Sabine threw her head back, smiling over her shoulder at him, imitating the swooning female musicians in Italian moving pictures. He smiled politely but not encouragingly.

From Pétiot's wife, who had had a long trip, came nothing but yawns.

The music came to its long-anticipated end. Reisden excused himself. It was moonlit out, a clear night. He let himself out the front door, breathing the night air with relief, and walked up the hill; he wanted to look at the towers.

Had she been flirting with him? Not personally. Most of the men she'd met had been suitors for her money. She wanted romance.

"Wait," he heard behind him in breathy nasal tones. With a rattle of pebbles, Sabine was making her way up the hill behind him.

"Where is Madame Pétiot?" he asked. "Is she coming too?"

Sabine, breathless, came up beside him. "I told her to go to bed," she said, self-satisfied.

My dear, has no one ever told you one doesn't tell the guests to go to bed? No. Clearly no one ever had, the way no one had ever told her that rich countesses don't buy machine-made tapestries. Perdita would say he was being a snob. It's not snobbism, he protested, it's a matter of class. He was being a snob. André would be too. Style wasn't the only barrier between André and Sabine, but it didn't help.

"I wanted to talk to you alone," she said. "Is my husband crazy?"

"Is he?" he temporized.

Over her childish face, in the moonlight, came a sudden darkness. "He locks himself in his dressing room at night," she said. "He makes me stay here."

"Do you know why?" he asked.

Sabine nodded. "He got sick to his stomach on our wedding night. He threw up all night. Now he says I poisoned him."

"Did he?" This was new. "I thought it happened in Egypt."

"That was later. Everybody got sick on our wedding day. It was the salmon."

"Tell me about that."

"Well." Sabine shrugged. "Everybody just got sick. But André made a big production of it, he threw up all night, every time I knocked at the door he said he was just about to be sick again. And then he kept saying he was still sick, and when we were going to Egypt he was trainsick or seasick, and then later . . . Are you going to put him in an asylum?"

"I want to cure him."

"Good luck!"

"Don't you?"

Sabine shrugged.

"How did you meet him?"

"I saw him at the theatre—" Her face glowed suddenly. "He was—Necrosar! When I realized he wasn't married and came from my region, when I knew I could marry him, I couldn't sleep, I stayed up all night every night thinking of him."

Reisden said, really dismayed, "Hadn't you met him outside the theatre?"

"He *is* like that," Sabine said simply. "It's not just the theatre, it's not just acting. I know he's like that. But he won't be like that to *me* and I don't know why."

No. Necrosar wasn't just acting. "Do you really want to be married to Necrosar?" he said. "Not André?"

"Better than what I've got! I'm not married to anyone!"

"Necrosar is a half-truth," he said.

She sighed impatiently and changed the subject. "Tell me about your wife," she said. "She's an actress or something, isn't she? She's off on tour? And you don't mind?" Sabine said, crossing her arms. "She goes off and gets all glamoured up for all those people out there, and she doesn't pay any attention to you?"

Of course I mind; I'm as frustrated as you are. And she took my boy with her. "She writes me," he said. "And I don't want the woman onstage, she's a construction; I want all of her, the one who gives concerts, the one who practices, my son's mother, my wife." Applause from the audience, he thought; what a hero our Reisden is.

"I don't get anything," said Sabine. "Backstage it's Jules fixing him eggs—eggs! Necrosar! Where am I? What does he want me for, but my money?" she said bitterly. "And when I spend it, he doesn't even like what I do; he laughs, hollow, *huh huh,* and then he ignores me."

They were standing by an unfinished low wall. She sat down on it, discouraged, tired; she leaned against a pile of chalk blocks brought up from the stone-dump, ready to be built into the wall. He watched her, a little concerned; she hadn't eaten much and she was pale. With both fists she grasped the tight waist of her dress and the corset beneath it and pulled both away from her body, as if her stomach hurt and she was unable to ease it. She sighed, then held her hands palm-flat over her stomach. The gesture was crude but extraordinarily sensual, as though Sabine were all flesh, as if her very flesh was sad, deserted, pained because André didn't care for it; still Sabine cared for it. She looked up and saw him looking at her; the look hung in the air between them for a minute, complete intimacy. Two deserted people. Two of the people backstage. She sat up straight and looked at him questioningly, challengingly: *You* might accept it, her look said, but not me.

"Let's look at the abbey, shall we?" he said, not wanting to share a moment like this with his friend's wife; not while his own wife was away.

He bored her to tears talking Perpendicular and High Gothic while he shone his torch up the towers. They were immensely old, shaggy with the grass and bushes that grew in the cracked stone. No wireless antenna snaked up among the gargoyles; at least Jules and he weren't giving away government secrets. Around the doorless door, the revolutionaries of a hundred years ago had decapitated every angel and saint; through the archway nothing was left of the abbey but rubble, blackened timbers too big to re-use or burn for fuel, bits of paving moth-eaten by the moon. Brambles snagged at their feet. The remnants of walls half-enclosed them. Where the crypt had been, a hole led into darkness. "Be careful," Reisden said.

"I was married here," Sabine said. "Last spring. My shoe heels sank right into the mud. I wanted to get married in Paris but I did it for him because Counts of Montfort have to marry at Montfort Abbey. He didn't look at me."

Reisden said nothing.

"He *did* it to me *once*," Sabine said, embarrassing him. "Papa Maurice talked to him about duty, and one night a couple of months ago he got drunk as a pig on old slops and came in and *did* it, and then he locked himself in his dressing room again. He acts as though it never happened."

The top of the hillside was hillocked with mounds and ditches. They had come back to the top of the path, and she needed to jump down to get back on it. He went first. She stood above him, holding out her arms, waiting to be helped down. She jumped clumsily, her foot slipped, she fell; he put his arms around her. Her mouth pressed against his, tentatively, saltily.

"No, Sabine," he said, moving back and depositing her at a safe distance.

She burst into tears. "I just don't know what to do."

He could feel her body in the palms of his hands. "Start by not doing that," he said.

"I'm sorry."

"I'm on your side," he said, "but not that way." He sighed. "Egypt," he said in a businesslike way. "What happened in Egypt?"

"Nothing."

"He was very ill."

"I didn't *poison* him," Sabine said.

He heard a half lie. "What did you do?"

"Everybody knew what was happening," she burst out. "What wasn't happening. Even my guide. So one day my guide *took* me to—a *place*—where they sold things. You know? The guide said they always worked and they were safe."

He stared at her, and tried not to.

"They were safe," Sabine said hotly. "I knew they were. Because—because why should anyone give somebody something like that when it wasn't safe? I didn't poison him, I *didn't*. It was a powder in a little paper packet and I put it on some sticky candy, thinking he'd eat a piece and . . . He was working all night, writing something, and he ate it all."

Reisden nodded. He'd seen André work; André grazed constantly and without thought, like a sheep.

"But," said Sabine, "there wasn't any poison bottle. If he showed you a poison bottle, it was *his*."

"I know that."

She clasped her arms around herself. The gesture was part pleasure in her body. But it troubled her, touching her own skin, half of it was almost a shiver, and her face went bleak again. "He has poison," she said. "And I have a feeling, I have feelings sometimes . . . just a sense about this summer, as if it's all bad somehow, something's going to go wrong.—Do you think he's crazy?"

She looked up at him through her black heroine's eyelashes, but this was genuine.

"Something *scares* me, Dr. Reisden," Sabine said. "I think—well, when he *did* it to me, I think—it worked. But don't you tell him. He doesn't want me, never mind—I don't want him to know."

Chapter 17

Montfort owned a new Rolls, courtesy again of Sabine's money. The next day, Reisden and André went out in it to scout locations in the Flanders countryside. They left the chauffeur behind and Reisden drove (André wasn't a driver). André sat in the front seat, his long hair blowing in the wind, the light making his cheekbones prominent and crude: Necrosar out in the daylight.

The hamper Sabine had packed for them sat on the back seat. When they had got beyond the next rise, André made Reisden stop and take a sample for analysis from each dish she had given them. Cold lamb with a confit of onions; a salad of early greens and palm hearts; fresh bread; cheese and apples; a bottle of wine. There could be ergot in the bread, André said; who knew what the palm hearts really were. . . . Reisden said that it was probably what it appeared to be, a rather nice lunch.

"Look at the apples. Did she inject them?"

"André, you know more ways of poisoning than I do." Of course André did.

"If you inject them next to the stem, the injection's invisible."

"Ass," Reisden said uneasily.

The day was glorious. Reisden drove with a controlled fury. André leaned out from behind the windscreen, letting the wind batter his face. His face looked thin, almost skeletal.

81

"She doesn't seem sinister," Reisden said. "She's un-happy."

They went round to a small, ancient, moated castle, Ol-hain, which André wanted for the house of Mabet's illegiti-mate son. André made sketches of battle scenes. From Olhain they motored to Arras and talked with the postcard-seller-cum-witch on the Grand'Place. The old man smelled like sheep; his postcards were fly-blown, and he had pictures of himself for sale, the same picture Ruthie had bought. In the back of his shop, Reisden noticed silver francs, pierced for a love charm, and small wax-corked bottles filled with liquids and drowned herbs. Witchcraft for tourists.

They ate a late lunch at a café on the square. The local cheese, Coeur d'Arras, smelt like something long dead. André liked it. They were washing the foul stuff down with beer when a stranger approached the café. He was about six and a half feet tall, with a long loping gait and a face like a monkey, and he was wearing, of all things to see in French Flanders, an American ten-gallon hat. He looked at them with a weary pessimism.

"Don't either of you boys speak English, I guess," he said.

Reisden had astonishing numbers of brothers-in-law in Arizona; one of them had visited Paris last winter. "Nope," he said.

"Well, tar me. Put 'er there, friend."

The cowboy folded himself down onto the café chair, ac-cepted beer, and declined cheese. André and he sniffed at each other like two dogs wondering whether the other was a dog at all. The cowboy's name was Zeno Puckett, he came originally from Lamapo Flats, Missouri, and he was looking for a friend he'd met riding in the Carver-Whitney "Wild America" show in Moscow. He reached into an enormous pocket and brought out a small, flat, badly printed grey book. "My pal wrote that. T. J. Blantire." The book had been published by a newspaper in Chicago, the title was *Through Russia on a Mustang*, and the frontispiece was T. J. himself in a Russian fur hat, sitting on a depressed-looking animal in front of a dacha.

"You seen T. J.?"

Between the hat and the enormous dark drooping moustache, there wasn't much to see of T. J. What there was looked like a badly stuffed walrus. But it was the only picture Puckett had of T. J., and, he said, T. J. was missing.

"T. J. writ to me from Paris and said he was signed on to a movin' pitcher here. Said he would be obliged if I'd come help, because there was more horses than he could rightly handle. Here I am in Ay-rass, though, and nary a sign of T. J. to be found."

Reisden passed the book to André. "André, is that your missing horse wrangler?"

André contemplated the moustache under the hat and shrugged.

"Would T. J. have gone off with a woman?" Reisden asked the cowboy. "Because I'm afraid that's what he's supposed to have done."

"Dang," Puckett said. "T. J. is a wild young thing. Don't know the gal, do you? Because I would sure like to get a hold of him."

André didn't. "Do you want T. J.'s job?"

They gave the cowboy an introduction to André's production manager and sent him off. Then, while the shadows lengthened across the square, André did geometry, figuring what time of day was best to film the guillotine scene in the Grand'Place if it were to be filmed in late July. They would be late for dinner; but André did not want to be at Montfort for dinner, or at all.

"André," Reisden said.

André was sketching in his notebook with a silver pencil. It was a new one, Reisden noticed. Sabine's money for a silver pencil, to fix the castle, to make the film . . . *I'm scared of him,* she'd said.

"Your wife," Reisden said with the slightest note of interrogation.

André looked up. "She'll be in this scene," he said.

"Not what I want to talk about. You neglect her."

André blinked. "But she's trying to poison me," he said.

"Did you always feel this way about her?"

André's shoulders hunched defensively. If he had felt something else, he wanted to deny it now.

"To a degree I understand she's not your style. She's young, she's from the country. But you have married her, it's her money keeping up your house," she may be with child, "and for her sake and yours, you should do your best to live with her."

"You won't have the lunch analyzed," André said.

"I will certainly have the lunch analyzed; that's not the point."

"I could write a play about her," André said. "A new bride. There's something she doesn't like about her husband. Something wrong. So she begins to poison him." He looked out blindly over the enormous cobbled square as though he could see the scene. "She tries to make him be close to her, but he can't be close to her, he's frightened"—he swayed back and forth in his seat—"and because he's frightened it all goes wrong, and she knows it's wrong, she feels it's wrong. She's afraid too." There was white all around the pale blue iris of his eyes. "And she doesn't know what to do, except poison him."

André didn't care about motivation, but once in a while he got it absolutely right. "Is he frightened, André? Why?"

"Why?" André made a gesture as if he were picking spiderwebs off his sleeve. "Do you want to know how she dies?"

Reisden nodded wordlessly.

"It's at sunset," André said, "here, in this square. As the sun sets, the shadows of the roofs rise out of the earth like giant men." He showed Reisden the sketches he had been making. Shadows of the Dutch-gabled houses crawled over the cobblestones, great men with shoulders and heads. André sketched busily; the shadows rose, eating the light.

In the midst of André's drawing a tiny guillotine glittered, ferocious as a knife.

"She comes out with Mabet," André said. "She goes to the guillotine first. She leans down. Her feet are bare. She puts her body on the plank, extends her head out beyond the end of the plank. The executioner ties her down. She's writhing, she's screaming. No cut, no dummy, then, *whack*! The knife comes down and her head falls off, blood sprays from her neck, her head comes falling off into the basket," André said exultantly.

He was making no attempt to keep his voice down. He was Necrosar, King of Terrors. From other tables in the café, heads turned toward them.

"André," Reisden said.

For a moment they were the center of a ring of eyes; the other people having lunch at the café knew what they were hearing.

They were listening to a man thinking of killing his wife.

Chapter 18

Cyron had come down late on the Saturday night, bringing his private chaplain. After Mass they had breakfasted to the sounds of motor buses and horses arriving; the League for French Freedom, the Church Restoration Society, miners from Wagny-les-Mines, tenant farmers from André's lands, old Uncle Tom Cobley and all, coming to build Montfort. It was a production. Tables of wine, cheese, coffee, bread, all donated; Cyron's master builder and his assistants, sorting the men into work groups; fragments and small fresh-cut blocks of the local chalk on sleds by the work areas; men ready to lift them into place. Cyron set the first stone. Helped by stronger arms, General Pétiot and the old sergeant each cemented their chalk into place; the crowd cheered them. Then the work began; soldiers, ultra-patriots, and pious architecture students labored under the strong spring sun, trundling wheelbarrows and cranking the rope-driven cranes. André had been persuaded to set a stone. Reisden did what Pétiot did.

Sabine sat on the ramparts, holding her hat down in two flaps against the wind, squinting. Reisden sat on his heels on the stones beside her, looking out over the country. It had rained a little overnight; a reddened rainbow stood over the fields. The sky was enormous, tinged with grey and opal. The fields stretched flat in every direction; from the top of Montfort hill they were checkered blocks, mortared by hedgerows and ribbons of streams.

André came to stand beside Reisden, but on the other side of Sabine. Reisden had to turn his head one way to speak with André, to the other for Sabine, who was looking half-apprehensively at her husband. André looked at Reisden looking at Sabine and took him aside. "Have you seen enough? Have you seen her? Do you believe she's poisoning me?"

But Reisden was looking at a shabby carriage winding its way up the hill.

What is it about police wagons? One can always spot them. They have the air of belonging to no one in particular, of conforming to a standard; they're orphans who have become soldiers. Two men got out. Only one was in a policeman's uniform, but from his posture and gait, the other might as well have been.

Behind every superstition there is a reality: two gendarmes together deliver news that one gendarme would not want to give alone.

They called André aside. "Dead?" he said in Necrosar's hollow tones, and smiled with a baring of teeth. "My wife's friend, poisoned. Hah." Sabine went aside with them—listened—and put her fist to her mouth. "Suicide? No! I saw her yesterday!"

"Françoise Auclart?" Cyron exclaimed. "She was the niece of one of my men."

André called Reisden to them. "This is Dr. the Baron von Reisden of Jouvet; he knows all about poisons. Mademoiselle Françoise," André explained. "She's dead."

"It was an accident! It must have been," Sabine said.

"She was our costumer," André said. Another disaster to the film.

The dressmaker's house was on the Montfort road, between two villages, at the edge of a copse of woods. French farmers usually live in villages; Mademoiselle Françoise had lived a hermit's life. A woman's bicycle leaned against the wall that enclosed the kitchen garden.

Inside the house, a clock ticked in the ancient smoky-smelling shadows; the sunlight shone on a cherrywood table. One of the downstairs rooms was a workroom, with two sewing machines catching the light from the windows. On a rack were hung uniforms and peasant costumes from the last century, and on the table was a half-finished jacket. Cheap cloth, exaggerated detail, for the film.

The other room was the kitchen, dark and hung with bunches of dried herbs. By the door to the garden stood a middle-aged pop-eyed woman, wiping away tears with the heel of her hand.

"No, monsieur, she had no troubles at all! She was so happy," Mademoiselle Huguette quavered. "She was going to treat herself to a week at the beach this summer, she'd made so much money from the costumes. And she was so proud of working for Monsieur Cyron's film. Why should she poison herself, or poor little Merlin?" She glared at the policeman. "Suicide? You should be ashamed!"

The police had taken away Mademoiselle Françoise's body, but the cat, a black tom, still lay stretched on the flagstones under the stove, a little foam dried on its nose and mouth. Sabine knelt down, hugging her knees, stretching out her neck to look at the cat. André stood behind her, staring intently. For a moment they seemed like a couple, until Sabine wiped tears away. André was breathing through his nose, deep breaths, as though he could smell the death in the house.

"She was my friend," Sabine said. "Now I'm alone."

"But how did it happen?" asked the policeman, and turned to Reisden. "Your company has experience with poisons, Baron de Reisden?"

"Don't touch anything," Reisden said. "Leave it for the Sûreté." The policeman wiped his face, relieved.

They went out in the garden and stood by the rabbit hutch,

out of the way, among the pungent-scented herbs. The back wall of the garden was a long sandstone garden shed, almost a barn; on its south side, vines twirled up a set of newly replaced strings. Suicide? The rabbits blinked and twitched their noses in the sunlight.

Mademoiselle Huguette wiped her eyes. She sewed for Mademoiselle Françoise, she said. She had arrived by bicycle from Arras on the previous Wednesday to finish the costumes for *Citizen Mabet*. "Mademoiselle Françoise went to town during the day, to take care of her business, so at night we were both sewing, in the daytime just me."

Yesterday, market day, Mademoiselle Françoise had gone early to the city by the Arras coach. (Cyron's coach served as unofficial common transportation up and down the Arras road.) She had got a ride home with a farmer, who had stopped at the house; they had all eaten cheese and drunk cider. After the farmer had left, the two women had eaten supper: fresh bread from Arras, a salad of greens, half a bottle of wine, and cold rabbit.

"But me, I ate an egg," Mademoiselle Huguette quavered, "because I'm vegetarian."

The commune policeman looked at her suspiciously.

The remains of the cooked rabbit, stringy and dry, were still in the cat's dish. Reisden collected samples while Mademoiselle Huguette told the rest of her story. Both women had sewed until about nine at night, when Mademoiselle Françoise had complained that it was too dark to see. She had gone upstairs to bed. Mademoiselle Huguette had sewed for perhaps an hour more. Then she had looked in on her friend, whom she found irritable and feverish. "She was afraid that she was getting a cold; she said she felt quivery and her eyes were blurrish," said Mademoiselle Huguette, putting her hand on her chest. "I offered to make her my special tea for colds, but she didn't want it. And so I went to bed." Mademoiselle Huguette broke down into frank tears.

"And the next morning?"

"There she was, fallen down in the hall, barely breathing. And poor little Merlin in the kitchen." Mademoiselle Huguette had huddled on some clothes—she was dressed in a skirt over her nightgown—and had gone for the priest. She had had to bicycle to Ste.-Catherine; since the separation of church and state, the priests came to the smallest towns only once every several weeks.

"You didn't go for the doctor?" Reisden asked.

"Ah, no, monsieur; she was past that, *barely breathing* I tell you; it was time for the priest."

The policeman plucked Reisden's sleeve and explained in a whisper. "Barely breathing, you understand, monsieur, these country ladies are superstitious. If you die before the priest comes, then that's it, God won't take you into Heaven!"

Reisden nodded. In the Jouvet files was a case of a man found "barely breathing" but decomposed by about a week.

"What salad greens did you eat?" the policeman asked.

Mademoiselle Huguette wrung her hands and protested vaguely: this, perhaps a little of that, but perhaps the other; she had been looking for eggs under the leaves. "And we had the same salad, after all, but poor Merlin had the end of the rabbit, poor *minou*—!"

Yes, the policeman agreed, it must have been the rabbit. He hadn't meant to say suicide, he apologized; it had just come out of his mouth.

Reisden left the commune policeman and Mademoiselle Huguette talking about vegetarianism. ("But what do you *eat*?") The women had slept upstairs, Mademoiselle Huguette on a cot in the storeroom, Mademoiselle Françoise in the only bedroom, which was cluttered with a double bed, a dresser, a painted wardrobe, and many pictures. On the whitewashed walls were pinned colorchrome prints of the Sacred Heart, Sts. Barbara and Isidor, and the Virgin Mary, surrounded by herbs dried in bunches; there was also a panorama postcard of Malo-les-Bains. In the center was a photograph of the bachelor uncle who had owned the house previously. He wore his army uniform. Reisden wondered if he had ever helped to build Montfort.

Reisden looked inside the wardrobe. Smells of perfume, perspiration, and garlic. A Sunday dress, plaid, with dusty frills and old-fashioned mutton sleeves. Two plain black dresses of the sort worn by shopkeepers; two skirts; several blouses with necklines surprisingly low. Two pairs of pointed shoes. On the dresser, assorted perfumes, face washes, creams, ointments, skin bleaches, and hair pomades. In the dresser, women's lisle underwear and stockings.

In the bottom drawer, wrapped in tissue paper, was the ritually elaborate white nightgown every country Frenchwoman owns. She wears it on her wedding night, then folds it away for her burial. Françoise's was as embroidered, as heavy with lace, as a wedding gown, and it had been used; it was crumpled, folded away hurriedly, with the smell of sex in it. Below it, hidden between the lace and the tissue paper, was a grey book he recognized.

Through Russia on a Mustang. It was inscribed, in T. J. Blantire's handwriting and in ungrammatical French, *A ma chère petite Sorcière d'une Fille.* To my dear little Witch of a Girl.

Mademoiselle Françoise, Blantire's woman? Reisden tried to remember her. In the Grand'Place, when they had been introduced, he had been looking at Sabine. She had been older. Thirty? He remembered only the heat of her thin narrow hand.

T. J. was a wild boy; Françoise Auclart had sewed herself blouses with low necklines and lived at her uncle's solitary house. He pictured them meeting in Arras. "I'm working in the movies." "So am I." Theatre company love.

But now Mademoiselle Françoise was dead.

Where was Blantire?

* * *

There was one more odd moment in that odd weekend. Late in the same afternoon, the guests were about to leave. Reisden, who packed light, came into the Great Hall to wait for the rest. André was already there. The Great Hall had almost escaped Sabine's improving touch; the new chairs were Selfridge-medieval but the great walnut central table shone with five hundred years of elbows and meat grease, and if there were a few too many banners on the ancient walls, at least they were real ones.

On one side of the hall was a minstrels' gallery. André was looking at the other side, the side with such a profusion of faded banners. He was staring at it, as though he were seeing something. Reisden looked, too, and saw underneath the banners a set of scars in the ancient plastering, marks of a staircase that had been there not so long ago: a staircase, gone now, and a railing that had disappeared, and the outline of a door, bricked up and plastered over.

Something had been there, some room or balcony or wall. André was staring at it. "What was it?" Reisden asked. But André didn't answer, and Cyron, coming through, gestured them both impatiently toward the coach. "Come on, come on, eh! Don't stare!" He hurried out, taking André with him, leaving Reisden to wonder why Cyron, the builder, had torn something down.

Chapter 19

Reisden went to the Bibliothèque nationale and looked up the newspaper stories around André's parents' deaths and Cyron's adoption of André. The Paris papers had nothing; the Count and Countess had both died of cholera within a day of each other. The single odd detail was that only the time of the Count's funeral had been given. Wouldn't they have been buried together, and if so, why not list both names? He ordered up the files of the local papers. The *Echo d'Arras* added the detail that their only son had also been ill but was recovering. The *Lion d'Arras* gave a slightly different story. The Count had died of cholera, but the Countess of grief.

Grief was a polite fiction, like *barely breathing*, and no paper had given a time and place for the Countess's burial.

He went to see Jules and found him at the theatre with André.

André wanted to know whether there had been poison in the lunch. Reisden had sent the samples off to Callard, the poison specialists, but had had a Marsh test done first at Jouvet.

"No arsenic," he said.

"There'll be poison," André said. "It will be the same thing that killed her friend. She's practicing for me," he added in the tone that made audiences giggle and scream at the Grand Necro. "She sends pears in wine every week from Montfort. But I don't eat them."

93

Most families with country estates sent hampers of fresh food up to the city. Reisden and Jules exchanged glances; André's wife was simply doing her duty.

Jules held up an egg. "Bought it myself just now in the market; do you want one?" On a shelf in the corner of the office, someone had installed a gas ring. Jules reached underneath the shelf and brought out an omelette pan, butter, a not-too-clean spatula, and some spices.

André snatched the egg out of the pan as soon as it was done, scraping the fat with stale bread, shaking his hair away from his face so as not to get it in the food. He was starving.

"Come see the set models," Jules said to Reisden.

They went down into the basement of the theatre, into the room that was usually the set designer's and that now housed the models for the film. They had already made the model for the Grand'Place, a cobblestoned square surrounded by tiny cardboard cutouts of Dutch-roofed houses. Jules held a student lamp in his hand and made the sun set; shadows reached across the square like hands. In the middle of the square, the tiny guillotine glittered.

"He didn't eat at Montfort," Reisden said.

"I make him eat," Jules said.

"He'll be at Montfort for—how long is your shooting schedule, three weeks?"

"I'll cook for him," Jules said. "Lots of eggs."

"He's afraid of eggs at Montfort."

Jules set down the lamp and slumped into a chair, staring at the model. The shadows raked across the square, light from a sun that had gone down.

"He'll eat in Arras," Reisden said.

"I'll drive him to Arras, then."

"Do you know," Reisden asked, "did his mother commit suicide?"

Jules blinked: kindly, innocent Jules. "No." It was the flat *no* of a practicing Catholic.

"She didn't have a funeral." Which meant, unless she was not a believer, that her priest had refused to bury her with the rites: an almost impossible thing for a countess. "She wasn't a freethinker, was she?"

Jules shook his head.

He thought over it that night, while failing to write a cheerful letter to Perdita. André was obsessively acting out an endless drama in which members of a family kill one another. *My wife is poisoning me. A mother is poisoning her son, a son his mother.*

One wonders what he means by it.

Leo's phrase.

Leo had been a good man, in his way, a good guardian, and there really had never been Orphans as such, only Leo's wishes, which one wanted to fulfill. "I wish I knew more about the Such-and-so family; Mr. Such-and-so has some very inconvenient opinions, I wonder what he means." One was expected to find out. "Mrs. Such-and-so, a pretty woman, and so bored; pay her a little attention, you dog you." When one was at a friend's house, one should notice what newspapers were on the table, open to what stories; one should talk with one's friends, and the friends of the friends, the uncles, the mothers, the wives, the servants. (Never take your own servants to a weekend unless they are your accomplices; use the ones the host offers you. You are young, so they will be the least experienced and the most likely to talk.) For a while, one had been asked to wonder what Cyron meant by all that obsessive building. . . . It had seemed not too much different from amateur theatre, an amusing game that everyone was playing; at least Reisden had thought everyone was playing it, as a new whist-player thinks everyone is playing whist.

In Leo's world, of course, everyone *had* been playing; and no one could imagine not playing, or ever ceasing to play, leaving the cards on the table and the Great Game not won. Leo had been a good man, almost a good father; they had

shared tastes from Sherlock Holmes to good coffee and
chess. Perhaps an uncle, the cynical disreputable uncle who
introduces one to women and teaches one good taste, and has
a dark side. They had certainly liked each other. But when
Reisden had wanted to lay down the cards, Leo had not let
him go, or ever stopped wondering what Reisden meant by it.

He tapped his pen against the inkwell, looking at his unfinished letter to Perdita.

There was no military secret of Montfort; at least he'd
never found one. It didn't matter. Family secrets are explosive
enough. And it suddenly occurred to him, with a little stab of
surprised panic, that for all Perdita knew about him, he had
never told her what he had done for Leo.

He would have to, he thought. Eventually. But she was
American, she was young. In the end he'd been disgusted
with the life, appalled at the things he was getting into; how
would she feel? He didn't trust her with this any more than
with Toby's safety. And he was saddened, and frightened, because he couldn't trust her whom he missed so deeply.

"Tell me about your mother."

Reisden cornered André in the effects room at the Necro,
where André was inspecting a severed head. André didn't
want to talk, tried to tell him about the film, tried to show him
the head. Reisden persisted. "Your mother and poison."

Finally André folded up into a chair, his shoulders
hunched, the severed head at his feet. He clasped his hands
between his knees as if he were cold. "Jouvet didn't believe
me," he said.

"I might."

"My mother poisoned my father and me," André said in a
single rush of words.

This could be anything, metaphor or more of André's perpetual testing. Still it hung in the air between them, a little
shock. Reisden nodded.

"She poisoned us all. Papa first," André said. "Then herself and me. The poison was in a green bottle. I saw her mixing it. I pretended to take it but I spit most of it out."

Reisden waited. André didn't go on. "And then?"

"Well, she died," André said. "And Papa died."

And nobody discovered you for a couple of days, and you were five years old. "What was that like?"

"What was it like?" André said. "I don't know. They died of cholera. You shouldn't believe me."

"Shouldn't I?"

"I'm mad. Papa Cyron says. Don't believe me."

Reisden didn't know whether to believe him. There was no center to the story. *I saw her mixing the poison, I spit it out, they were both dead.* Either André was still shocked or he was lying. The two are so much the same. Reisden raised his eyes and saw André looking at him, blue eyes flat as marbles, angry, defensive, unsure.

"You don't believe me," André said. "Don't believe me. It's all Necro."

I do believe you, he almost said. Then he remembered what Katzmann had told him. *They always say "I could have told you that anytime."* André hadn't. He'd said, *Don't believe me.*

Is he telling me he's lying?

"I can see marriage would be difficult whether you made the story up or not." It was all he could think of. "What did she use? Arsenic? Have you ever found out?"

André blinked as if he had suddenly heard a loud sound or put two ideas together. "What sort of son would tell a story like that about his mother?" he said, speaking beside the point too, or maybe not. "No. It's wrong of me."

"It could be checked, if it's arsenic. It might be in the body. Would you like to know?"

Reisden didn't feel he was handling André well. André was barefoot, the way he usually worked; he drew a leg up, holding one bare foot between his hands, massaging it as if he were comforting it. He wanted comfort; all Reisden was offering him was facts. "They died of cholera. Dr. Jouvet said." He doesn't want to know, Reisden thought, just as André raised pleading blue eyes to him.

"When *she's* not at Montfort, go there with me. Help me dig up my parents," André said. "Run the arsenic test on them."

Chapter 20

Perdita had written to Gilbert first from Paris, and got a delighted reply and an invitation to stay at the house on Commonwealth Avenue. She had written again as soon as her plans were clear—and heard nothing, no reply at all. This she did not tell Alexander; he would have told her she shouldn't go to Boston. She wrote to Gilbert from New York, three times, and three times she got no reply.

So, with the air of a woman who had much more to spend than Perdita did, she reserved rooms at the Parker House; and there, on the morning after she arrived, Harry came to see her.

"He won't see you. None of us want to see you. So you might as well go home."

"I don't believe so yet, Harry; I want to introduce Toby to baseball, and I have a concert to give for the Massachusetts Women's Suffrage League."

"None of my friends will come to your concert."

None of his friends would have come anyway, she thought

a little sadly. She knew his friends; she had been queen of them when she had been going to marry him. "How are you and Efnie, Harry?"

"We're none of your business, Perdita."

She expected that Harry was fighting with Uncle Gilbert over seeing her, but Gilbert would come to see her anyway however he had to do it. She must simply bide her time. So she introduced Toby to the swan boats in the Public Garden, which he loved. They saw a baseball game at Nickerson Field and strolled Toby in his perambulator past the enormous new ballpark that was being built on the Fens. Every morning she practiced piano on one of the rentals at Steinert Hall. In the afternoon, before Toby's naptime, she rehearsed or went to the offices of the League in a tiny third-floor walkup office on Stuart Street; Toby napped on the floor while she talked with the other women.

Uncle Gilbert didn't come to see her.

The concert was being given in a Unitarian church hall just off Commonwealth Avenue. Perdita and two women students from the Conservatory, Betsy and Joanna, violin and violin-cello, doing Brahms' Piano Trio #1. Three days before the concert, when all the posters had been put up (and most of them torn down), the League was called by the police. "Ladies, you can't have your concert. Too rowdy. The neigh-bors complained." What was rowdy about a piano trio, they asked? "D'you mean to say there won't be pickets out on the street? I can guarantee there will. You bring it on yourselves, acting unwomanly as you do."

"I know some of those neighbors," Perdita said. "May I call round?"

"You'll find—" said Miss Grey, the secretary of the League.

"Let her try," said Miss Rutherford, who was treasurer.

They had been *her* neighbors. The boys from the Iroquois Club and their girlfriends; Lothrop Ames and his cousin; the

Blackstone sisters. They had all come to Harry's coming-of-age party. They had all applauded when Perdita gave concerts as a girl. Now she was back, a better pianist with something to say; and they wouldn't listen.

"It would be *so* disruptive," Amelia Ames said. "I'm *so* sorry I won't get a chance to see you; I am *so* busy with the baby now." The old girlfriends were now the wives. "We're at the farm most weekends." "I just don't take an interest in such things." "You know George wouldn't like my being *political*; you know how he is!"

And, awfully, "Your Harry called my husband, dear."

"I'm the cause the concert was canceled," Perdita said to Miss Grey.

"Oh no, my dear," Miss Rutherford said mildly.

"This time," Miss Grey said. "Last time someone else. Next time some other reason."

"My dear," Miss Rutherford said, "if we had a tenth the money and the power that people like Harry Boulding do, they would feel they had to listen to us. And so they try to keep us from getting money and power. They prevent us from marching, from raising funds, from acting as lawyers and doctors and owners of business, everything that would make us serious people."

"But the women—" Perdita said.

"The women take their cues from their husbands. What their husbands believe, they must believe, or, they think, their husbands will come home late, because other women are more pliable. And other women *are*," Miss Rutherford said. "I had a father, and I have a stepmother; I know what women will do."

"We are difficult," Miss Grey said. "We are troublesome."

"Women are not to blame for everything," Perdita said. "Everyone wants to do the easy thing, don't they? Men too."

Uncle Gilbert had not telephoned her, not written, not anything, not once. It would have been difficult for him—Harry was probably giving him troubles about her—but she and Uncle Gilbert had been true friends.

Didn't he want to see Toby? Was he thinking like Alexander now, that they should never meet? Alexander wouldn't have written to him urging it—Alexander wouldn't do that—but Gilbert and Alexander were so close in all that they thought, all they believed. . . . That was exactly why they should talk to each other.

She thought of how Alexander would feel if she forced herself on Gilbert.

The last day she was in Boston was what would have been the day of the concert. Aline had packed everything; they were ready to go; there was nothing left to do but to be truly miserable and homesick before she had even gone. "And we won't do that," she told Toby, "will we? No, we'll go out and take one last walk and go to the swan boats again, and then we'll go back to Paris and you will be your papa's boy."

And I will cry, she thought, but when no one is looking.

"Mrs. Reisden, Mrs. Reisden!" Betsy and Joanna from the Conservatory, the ones she would have played the concert with, piled into the room. "Would you still play?" The two girls had brought their instruments; she could hear the strings sounding from inside the cases. "Right now? We have a piano in a wagon, and our friend Fred to drive it," Joanna said.

"Do you want to make some mischief?" Betsy said.

They had actually stolen the piano from the Longy School—"just borrowed!" Betsy corrected. Perdita felt so much older than they were. You will get in trouble, she thought; you'll get expelled. I was at the Paris Conservatory; I know. They are only looking for excuses to get rid of us. And then she thought, Women ought to be pliable. Other women are more pliable.

"Any kind of mischief will do," Perdita said. "Just lead on." She wouldn't spit in Uncle Gilbert's eye or Alexander's, but she would be delighted to spit in someone's.

On Commonwealth Avenue they arranged for the wagon to have its "breakdown." Fred cut the harness. It was the middle of the day; mothers and children with their nursemaids were walking up and down the strip of park in the center of the avenue. Joanna and Betsy emerged, disheveled, carrying their instruments and wearing their Votes for Women sashes. Fred hauled the canvas back and revealed VOTES FOR WOMEN hurriedly painted on the inner side.

And they played.

They got through the first movement of the Brahms First before the police arrived. Traffic was snarled almost down to Copley Square. "Oh, *look* what we've done," said Betsy unrepentantly. "Isn't it *awful*," Joanna agreed. Fred was arguing with the policeman. "And all we've done is play music," Perdita said.

All we've done is play music. She knew every tree on this block by the sound of its leaves; she had played in this park as a child. I've cut myself off, she thought, I don't belong here anymore; she felt desolated, surprised; relieved, but sadly relieved. Now she could go back to Paris homeless, ready to find a home. It was like the morning after a funeral. I could have stayed here, she thought. I could have been like those women, telephoning the authorities to get rid of those dreadful suffragettes because my husband's club friends didn't approve of them.

For funerals there is only one kind of music: jazz. She had seen Willie Williams in New York and got new tunes to play. While the policeman argued with Betsy and Fred, she let the blues stomp all over Commonwealth Avenue. *Homeless girl, put your red dress on.* The police arrested Fred but not the rest of them; police never took women seriously. She got up from the piano only as it was being towed away.

Aline was waiting with Toby. Perdita gave Toby a big hug, glad it was over after all. *"Mais c'était magnifique, madame!"* Aline giggled. "That was grand!"

"Oh, it wasn't, Aline. Let's go get tea."

"You should have seen all those faces, like a row of gherkins— Scram, you!" A wet nose was snuffling at Perdita's skirt. "Never mind, madame. It's only a dog. But oh, isn't that strange—"

"What?" she asked casually.

"That man over there looks like Monsieur Alexandre."

Chapter 21

"Oh my dear," she said.

"My dear," said Uncle Gilbert.

"You didn't *know* I was here?"

"I had no letters," Uncle Gilbert said. "Only the one from Paris. Why did you not write?"

He took her to a coffee shop near the Museum of Fine Arts. Uncle Gilbert urged her not to drink the coffee; tea at the museum would probably not be bad for her, he conceded, but coffee of any sort! Perhaps they had not washed the pot recently! Perhaps not in a long time!

"Oh, Uncle Gilbert," she said, taking his hands. "Don't fuss about that."

Fuss about what we've come to, she thought. He had not taken them to tea at the Athenaeum, where his friends would have seen them, but here. How *could* Harry have done that to him, she thought. How *could* he. She was ashamed of her own reluctance to call. She had been willing to make a scandal for music or the vote, but not for him.

They sat for a while, simply holding hands. And then they talked. Toby was asleep in his pram by the table. "He looks like Tom," Uncle Gilbert said.

Alexander had said he wished Toby looked like no one but himself. She didn't say that. "He's a wonderful baby," she said. "He even liked going on tour; he likes a good audience, just like his mama, don't you, sweet? He loves to get attention."

"Are you happy?" Uncle Gilbert said. "I hope so."

"I miss America," she said, but no more than that, not talking about how she needed the smells and the music. "I don't miss Boston! I miss you."

"I miss you, my dear." There were things he might have said too, she thought, and he didn't. She didn't ask him whether he was happy. She didn't want to talk about why the letters hadn't come.

"Is—Alexander—is he happy?"

She had never quite thought about this; she had been too focused on whether Alexander loved her, what he thought of her. Uncle Gilbert, she thought, I needed to talk with you. "He isn't," she confessed. I don't think he loves me. "I don't think I can do enough for him." I don't think I'm right for him. "He needs someone to take care of things for him." I can't even make French fries. And I won't complain to Uncle Gilbert.

"Alexander was doing research with the department head of Physio. Psych., a combination of biochemistry and psychology. When the building collapsed, he took leave from the Sorbonne. While he was gone his research partner died and the group fell apart. That hurt him.—So now he spends all his time at Jouvet. He loves Jouvet and he says now he doesn't want to do anything else, but it's a huge responsibility. Not that it won't go very well in the end.—He's never had a family before," she said, "not one he likes. He's never rebuilt a building or been a father. And he has to do everything; he has meetings and more meetings and, with all that, he has to check little things like whether the plasterer did the walls right because—" She put out her hand and gestured as if she were patting wet plaster. "There's so much I can't *do*. He needs to come home and have someone take all his cares away, *do* things for him, make things *right* for him," she said, and then she added something she hadn't even known about her husband. "He's lonely," she said.

"Yes," said Uncle Gilbert.

You know, she thought. You're lonely too. I suppose we're all lonely.

"How long will you be here?" he asked.

"This is my last day," she said.

"Oh," he said, a long drawn-out *ohhh*.

She should have said that she would change her ticket and stay. She didn't have the money for it. She could have got it somehow. Not from him. "Why are things going so badly?"

"It is my fault, it is *I*, I should try harder with Harry. I really believe I say more to Elphinstone than to him."

"I don't mean Harry. Harry can jump in a box, I have no patience with him.—I feel as if it's my fault Alexander has to take everything on by himself. Alexander doesn't trust me to be what he needs. I don't trust myself. He misses you and he won't write to you. And if I go back to Paris now, with things—as they are here, what shall I do, Uncle Gilbert? I shall be thinking of you."

"You must not think of me. It isn't your fault, my dear."

"I 'must not'; but I will; how shall I help it?"

"My dear," Uncle Gilbert said, "I know what Alexander feels. He wants to save your boy from what happened to him."

"From you?" Perdita said. "Not from you. It isn't your fault either."

He took her hands. "You will save him. You have grown to be such a good and kind and loving woman, my dear. You will be his family."

No, I won't, she thought. I'm the one who loves America and leaves Alexander deserted in Paris because I want to play the piano. I'm not good enough. I don't always want to be good enough. "I can't be all his family by myself! I need you. Why can't you at least write to him?"

Do it for me, she thought. Write us. Come to see us. Visit us in Paris. You would like it. It would scare Harry half to death and perhaps he'd start being nice to you. She took a breath, about to say *Don't just write.*

"I am his bugaboo," Uncle Gilbert said. "Do you remember how everyone said he and I look alike? When he was here in America, he used to wince at it. He said, 'At least no one can see you in Europe where I live.' "

"He was being cruel."

"No," Uncle Gilbert said. "I feel—sometimes, still—haunted by Father." So does Alexander.

Gilbert is doing what Alexander wants, Perdita thought, feeling disloyal. And I am supposed to do the proper thing too, to support Alexander who won't take support from me. We all have to be nice to Harry, who is *not* being nice back— Oh, we're so proper, so dreadfully polite, all of us; how can we ever depend on each other when we don't dare to talk about what we feel or ask for what we need? We silence each other. It is like not having the vote.

"Here, my dear." He pressed something into her hand. A little box. "I wish that it were more; but when I heard that you were coming, I felt it was to say goodbye . . . and that should be," he hesitated, "celebrated, I hardly like to say celebrated, but I believe that you are going to where you will live happily. And I have seen your boy," he added softly. "Thank you for that. Thank you."

There is a difference in the hand between cheap jewelry boxes and good ones. This was thin cardboard, covered in paper that was peeling away on one corner. She held it in her hands, puzzled. "Alexander told me a story once," Uncle

Gilbert said quickly, nervously, apologizing with his tone of voice. "When he was about to run away from Vienna with his first wife—his family disapproved of her, you know—he bought her a pin because they were going to get away. It was not an expensive pin, but it had value for them; they were going to escape. You have escaped. You and your boy and Alexander. I am glad for you. This is for you. There is a letter with it for Alexander."

No, she said to herself as if she were going to say it out loud. That's not the point. There are situations that it is worthwhile not escaping from.

She opened it, at his urging, and felt it and held it close to her eyes. It was a silver-colored pendant, thin base metal, lumpy on the back, decorated with three big staring rhinestones and some smaller ones. She felt the edge flaking away, the silver color or a bit of glue. It was shaped like an oval with a point on the bottom: a heart, but a disguised heart.

"Wear it for my sake," Uncle Gilbert said. "Show it to Alexander with the letter. Tell him that I shall never bother him and that I remembered the story of how he escaped. I shall not disturb him. I only wish him very well with Jouvet. Here, here, put it on."

She clasped the chain around her neck because he had asked her to wear it. Women are so pliable, she thought. I am to be your last letter to Alexander. You are to stay here; you are not to escape; and I am not to think of it. She was having trouble with the clasp; her fingers were shaking. A little part of her simply hurt because he had given her something ugly. It was not the money, though anything having to do with Uncle Gilbert took on an air of money. She wondered whether he thought she would not notice, but that was so unlike him, and then whether he had thought giving her something would make Harry jealous. That worried her. All the time, she thought, all the time in Paris I shall be thinking of

you and those letters you never got. What good will that do
Alexander and me?

She put the necklace down on the table between them.
"No," she said. "I will not. I cannot do it. You must write to
him—No. You must come to Paris and tell him yourself."

After Perdita had gone, Gilbert Knight walked slowly and
tiredly back to his house with Elphinstone and went upstairs
to the library, where Harry and Efnie never came. His eyes
were tired and blurred. There were two chairs by the window;
he sat in one of them.

In the chair across from him he saw a ghost of Alexander, a
ghost with haunted eyes saying *I am not Richard. We simply
look alike.*

I will not haunt you, Gilbert thought. Though she asked
me—

Father's ghost-voice echoed through Gilbert's heart. *You
have wasted your life, Sir. You have failed all who love you. At
least show a little spirit now. Do your duty! Stay at your post.
Here.*

Alexander looked at Father in tired exasperation, snapped
his fingers like a scornful magician, and melted away, in
charge of his own disappearance.

Elphinstone came into the room, holding his leash in his
mouth. "Yes, let's," Gilbert said. The house was full of
ghosts.

They walked down Commonwealth Mall. Elphinstone
kept close to Gilbert. But when it came time to turn around,
Elphinstone tugged to go farther.

"We must go back." It was almost dinnertime. Harry and
Efnie might be there for dinner. He must try with Harry. He
had been trying for years. "Come now, Elphinstone, come."

But Elphinstone wanted to go on. They crossed the street
to the Public Garden, past the Frog Pond and the swan boats.

Elphinstone tugged at the leash; even farther, across Charles Street, into the Common.

How can Perdita ask me for help?

And then suddenly Gilbert stooped and picked up his dog, and, holding Elphinstone over his shoulder like a baby, he began walking, striding in a way he had never really done before, across the Common and down past Washington Street. At his bank he took out quite a lot of money. He felt guilty, sick, exalted, as if he were robbing someone.

South Station has public telephones. Gilbert dusted off the earpiece and mouthpiece and called his housekeeper. "Tell Cook I shall not be home for dinner." Across from him, the New York train was chuffing on the metal rails, which stretched out beyond the station, dizzyingly far, forever.

"I do not know when I shall be back."

Chapter 22

Jules invited Reisden to the Necro for André's birthday. "There'll be a party after the show," Jules said. "Sabine will be there."

"André invited her?" That would be an interesting change.

"I invited her," Jules said, sounding uncertain. "Bring a guest. A woman, you know, someone Sabine can talk with."

Reisden brought two.

No two women in Paris were less alike than Milly Xico and Reisden's cousin Dorothea, the widowed Viscountess de

Gresnière. But they shared a single precious trait: they disapproved of everything and everyone else in life at least as much as of each other. It followed that they never lacked conversation. Dotty had never been to the Necro before; she gazed at the mummy and the carved skulls with a distant, horrified fascination. "My G-d," she murmured. "But, darling, my *G-d*." Milly arrived just at midnight, vivid in newly hennaed hair, wearing her Russian peasant jacket, a red skirt slit up the side, and strings of amber. Nick-Nack trailed resignedly behind her.

Dotty and Milly exchanged air-kisses. Milly sat down and looked admiringly at the ceiling, where winged baby skeletons held festoons of withered leaves.

"Chou-*ette*, look at all the money he's spent!"

"So *utterly* vulgar." Dotty raised her mother-of-pearl opera glasses to examine Cyron and Sabine, who were sitting together front and center. "Where *did* she get that dress?" Dotty whispered. "Dear heavens. It has fringe."

"That's what that old—Cyron wanted to play Madame Mabet," Milly said. "What idiots men are. Do you suppose he's sleeping with her?"

"Darling, she has to sleep with someone, doesn't she?"

Reisden held out his hand for the opera glasses.

With Cyron, in the intimate ring of the opera glasses, Sabine was a different person. Cyron was exerting his grumpy charm on her and she was almost blushing with happiness. *Something scares me*—Not with Cyron. Beaming too, Cyron patted Sabine's hand.

"No," Dotty said decidedly. "Father-in-law. He likes her too much to love her."

In the interval, he took the women up to meet Sabine and Cyron. Dotty took Sabine aside for women-talk; Sabine gazed at Dotty's exquisitely plain dress and opened her eyes even wider when she learned that Milly wrote for the movies. Cyron glared at Reisden. Reisden smiled politely, thinking,

Wait until you hear that André wants to exhume both his parents.

The play after the interval was *Obsession*, which André had written a few years ago. Jules was Henri, a young engineer, the father of a small boy. Henri is haunted by the idea that he will kill his son. Henri is a decent and responsible man. He talks openly, desperately, to his doctor, and then to a specialist in mental diseases. "But I *feel* this, as if I *must* do it," Henri says, bewildered, spreading his hands helplessly. "Should I have myself committed?" *Yes,* people actually shouted from the auditorium. *No,* all the onstage authorities reassured him cheerfully. "But I know what I must do," Henri said despairingly when he was alone. Reisden foresaw how the play would end. He went out into the bar; he wasn't going to watch this.

Dotty joined him and accepted a glass of white wine. They sat at the near-corner table. The corner table was occupied by one of André's decorations, a pair of cobwebbed skeletons holding hands over drinks. Dotty ostentatiously turned her back. "I don't know why I come to these things," she said.

"For my sake."

"Is André a case, darling?"

He shrugged, meaning *You know I couldn't tell you if he were*; *He always has been*—something like that. "I hope we'll be able to do something for him."

"Sacha. Dear. One hates to be discouraging, *but*— Look at the poor girl, depending on her father-in-law to make her welcome in her husband's theatre."

"Something happened to André that put him off family life; but now he's got a family, like it or not, and I mean to teach him to like it."

Dotty shook her head. "You are pursuing the difficult for its own sake, darling."

"Actually," he said, "for their child's sake."

"No!" Dotty said, surprised. "Is it André's?"

"*Don't* make mischief, Dot," he said, startled.

"Sacha. Dear. And how are *your* wife and baby?"

The transition was pure Dotty. "No, I am not," he said.

"Darling?" Innocently.

"Recommending marriage and children to everyone because I love mine.—To answer your actual question, Perdita is enjoying herself in New York and has given a concert for the benefit of the Women's Suffrage League. I am very proud of her." He sighed. He took a photograph from his wallet. "Toby in Central Park," he said. "Perdita sent it. Look at him smile."

Dotty's face softened as she looked at it. "How can you bear to be apart from him?" she said. "They go away to school so quickly."

"I count the days until he's back."

She contemplated the little stiff square for a moment. "The trouble with love," she said, "it hypnotizes one. The love of children. One wants them, one wants more. . . . Sometimes I actually think of marrying again. I do. But, darling, all the things that are wrong with marriage, all the reasons one shouldn't dream of marriage . . . André is not meant to be a father."

"One never knows what children are like until one has them," Reisden said. "Or who one is oneself."

"You will simply make two people unhappy; three if they have a child."

This was what she'd said about him and Perdita.

"Four," Dotty amended.

"The fourth?"

"Jules Fauchard, of course."

Reisden shook his head dismissively.

"They're very close," Dotty said.

"Of course they are. André needs to know that he's a decent, sane man. When he writes *Obsession*, he's acting out both his feelings and his revulsion at them—oh, G-d, I sound like Katzmann. So he picks the sanest, most ordinary man in Paris to act his madman.—That's why I don't let go of André," Reisden said. "He does keep asking to be sane."

"Darling, how often one wants to be what one isn't."

"You *will* help?"

Dotty sighed in irritation. "Sacha, I do hate it when you push your reclamation projects on me."

"Take her round. Polish her a bit. Her ideal of good taste is the Samaritaine department store, and André knows better. Make her appeal to him."

"*Very* pale powder?" Dotty murmured. "Blue lip-tint?"

"Be nice, dear."

The play ended; they went back into the theatre. Waiters moved chairs to the side of the room and brought out a buffet, which the theatre company rushed at. Milly's Nick-Nack wriggled out of his collar and stationed himself in the middle of the crowd, yiking hopefully. Reisden saw Ruthie, hanging back shyly at the side of things. Jules toasted André's health in champagne. "It's not possible," Dotty whispered pointedly. "André is forty years old! *Do* people change at that age?" Cyron sat next to Sabine; Reisden went across the room, sat next to André, and tried to draw his attention to his wife. André sat next to Jules, keeping his business partner between himself and the room that contained Sabine. Sabine glared at Jules when she thought no one was looking. Cyron smiled at her again, drawing her out, making her eyes sparkle, making her the happy girl André had never met.

The theatre orchestra began playing. Cyron asked Sabine to dance. They moved around the stage, Sabine a little heavy-footed, Cyron hopping about with her until her skirts pranced like horses and she laughed.

Nick-Nack began barking at them. Milly collected him and brought him back to Reisden and Dotty. "Bad Nicky" cooed at him. "How could Cyron give Madame someone who dances like a chair, when he had *me*? Have some more ham, Nicky, and throw up on her shoes."

Nick-Nack gazed up at her adoringly and drooled on her sleeve. Milly kissed his ear; Milly liked male dogs.

"Jules invited her," Dotty said in an undertone, "which means that Jules knows that she and André are not on good terms; and she knows that Jules knows; and now Jules has made it obvious to everyone, though he is such a dear that he could not possibly have meant it, could he? But of course she could not afford not to come, since she was invited. . . . I am translating, darling, from the Feminine."

"And there's Jules' sister," Milly said, "who'd throw herself into a mud puddle to keep André's feet dry. When I finish *A Woman by Herself*, women like that won't exist anymore."

"Darling, there will always be women like that."

André left and reappeared; he was dragging a film camera and lights. They all crowded up onto the roof, where it was just dawn. André set up the lights and filmed them as the sun rose: his whole company, then the principals. Cyron, as Mabet, fought an imaginary sword duel with Jules. Cyron described Mabet's vision of France; Sabine applauded, an appreciative audience. Finally Cyron, Jules, and Sabine stood by the cupola, holding hands and smiling at the camera: Cyron on one side, Jules on the other; in the middle Sabine; and André, not Necrosar at all, bent his back behind the camera.

"At least," Dotty murmured, "André looks at her from *there*."

Milly gave a little crowing sound. "That's it! That's why Cyron wanted her, not me. Isn't it, Nicky? He's going to make her an *actress*," Milly said. "She'll be pretty on film, I grant that. André's filming her, André edits the film— Poof!" Milly said. "André has to look at her. André pays attention to actresses."

"Jules thinks so," Reisden said.

Milly snorted. "But André hates her, so he'll light and edit her badly—"

"Unless André has a change of heart," Reisden said, "and wants to like her."

"But," Dotty asked, "what *does* André want?"

Milly fixed him, sapphire eyes beaming under her hennaed hair. "What does darling Sacha want, that's the question! Do you want me to *teach her to act*?"

"My dear," Dotty said, "he's asking me to teach her to dress!"

"What a horrible man."

Reisden spread his hands in masculine helplessness.

"I suppose I must talk couture with her." Dotty wrinkled her perfect nose. "I am the century's most put-upon woman."

"It's why I love you," Reisden said.

Milly groaned.

"But you are forcing it, darling," Dotty said, "you know you are. They'll never make a happy family. They're hopeless. Doomed."

Chapter 23

Sabine had always wanted children. If one is a sorceress, one's children will be too, and the children of a sorceress and Necrosar—! The enormous black cloak, the face made up like a skull; she wanted to lie naked on that cloak, shivering in the chill of underground, while he took h̶ masked and anonymous in the fur of a beast. Their f

would be Count of Montfort, keeper of the Holy Well. He
would drink the water of the Holy Well, bathe in it. In his sev-
enth year, on Christmas Eve at midnight, when powers can be
multiplied, Sabine would give him her talent for seeing death.
Sabine's son would be a great sorcerer, a force in the world.

And so Madame des Poirées was sent, grumbling and tot-
tering on her high heels, to make discreet inquiries; and in the
course of time, in a room crowded with lawyers and interme-
diaries, Sabine and André met and shook hands, and he gave
her the big old diamond that had been his mother's, and he
smiled cynically, as if there were a secret between them. That
smile tore her heart as a hook tears a fish; she was ecstatic,
pulled out of her element into a new atmosphere, breathless,
airless with delight; she was afraid with love. On a windy day
in May, in another room filled with lawyers and witnesses,
they signed papers, and then, in the ruins of the old abbey
church at Montfort, with her veil blowing in her face and the
witnesses standing silent in black, Sabine took André's chill
hand and swore to be his wife.

But Necrosar was cursed, and sorceress though she was,
she could do nothing about it.

They went to Egypt. Sabine shopped in the bazaars and
came back with silk bustiers and colored veils. Necrosar
bought a mummy, visited the pyramids, and stayed up all
night writing *The Pharaoh's Revenge*. He no longer said he
was sick, but he seemed to have assumed that their life had
fallen into a pattern, while she was still waiting for it to begin.

Who could have done this? Sabine looked through her husband's baggage for strange knots, bits of soil. She threw out
his favorite English tea "by accident"; you know the English.
One day she walked moonwise in his dressing room and
counterspelled every object in it. His mirror? From her
pocket Sabine took a little box of black wafers, which were
always with her, and stuck one to the back of the mirror so
that his thoughts of passion would not be reversed. His

daybed? Sabine ran her hand under the mattress, looking for knots tied in the sheets. She changed the sheets for ones of her own; it was not unknown for a malicious person to weave sheets with crossed threads.

Each photograph over the desk she marked with a wafer. In André's closet, she counterspelled each piece of clothing. She marked the knob of the door, the key, the lintel, and the door frame. She opened the dresser drawers to say words over each of his underclothes and to mark them, and one pair she carefully unfolded. Taking off her own lacy underclothes, she put on a pair of André's inside out.

As you walk, think of me; as you put on your clothes, think of my skin; may this mark protect you from all harm, and this lend strength to nature. As this is close to me, may I be close to you. As this key opens your door, may you open to me.

She wore the underclothes for three days, with no success at all.

"Everyone *dies*," André said. They were watching a funeral on an Egyptian street, a little white coffin being carried toward the river. "Everyone always *dies*."

"But that's the fun of it," Sabine said. "*We* don't, we live." She wanted to live. She looked around the crowd. One or two people were veiled with grey: a blind old man being led by a boy, a fat auntie in the funeral procession. But she was alive, alive, and it was a hot sunny day. It would be cool behind the shutters, on soft Egyptian cotton, their bodies striped with sunlight. She had not even seen her husband naked. Not once.

She could divorce him if he refused to sleep with her. He would be poor again if she divorced him. But she wanted Necrosar.

One day, in the souk with a new guide, she came across a tray of love potions, and among them was a powder that she didn't know. "Lady no try that," her guide said. "Powder ve~ strong, very strong, no good." But the spell on Necro~

strong, too, and she was sure, of course, that it wouldn't harm him.

André couldn't stop vomiting. He threw up blood. In the hospital, his eyes followed her, then slid away. "Go away," he whispered. "I don't want you."

They came home from Egypt—home? He sent her to Montfort and stayed in Paris.

On Epiphany night, girls use a spell to see their future husbands. From dusk on, Sabine sat motionless in her room, eyes turned away from her big mirror, reciting the verses. As the bells rang for midnight from Ste.-Catherine, she stood and walked backward toward the mirror; as the last bell struck, she looked over her shoulder.

In the mirror, she saw a coffin, the spinster's sign. As if she had never been married at all. As if she would die and be carried in her coffin, never knowing her husband's love.

She made the fists and the horns at the mirror.

There is a spell against unknown enemies, a spell that will eat the strength of a curse and spit it back at the giver. Sabine used five mirrors, holy water, and the bone of a dead man, and with all her heart she cursed the unknown who had set this spell between herself and Necrosar.

No one had unusually bad luck, that early spring, but her husband and her father-in-law.

They were making a film and everything went wrong. Sabine's father-in-law told her about his problems every Sunday morning at breakfast, before the Friends of Montfort came to help build the castle. At first, of course, she suspected Cyron. Why had he had this bad luck, if she had not cursed him?

And then he explained to her that André was directing the film.

She had turned the curse back, and it had fallen on her own

husband. The film was Necrosar's. Necrosar himself was the source of everything that had gone wrong with them.

Love embittered is perfect hate. "I despise him!" she burst out (surprising Cyron, who had only told her that André was directing). "I love him and I married him but he didn't mean it. I want a child!" she wailed. "I want *him*!"

"Oh, Sabine girl, my poor Binette." Papa Cyron patted her hand.

Her hate wanted to turn back to love, as vinegar wants to turn again to wine.

At past midnight on a shivering March evening she rang her friend Mademoiselle Françoise's bell. Mademoiselle Françoise answered the door in her nightgown, her hair up in its leather tails to curl it.

"Françoise, get up and get your books. I will have a child from my husband, whether he wants or no."

Chapter 24

" 'It has been the experience of all times and all nations, that witches practice coition with demons,' " Sabine read aloud. " 'I add that a child can be born of such copulations with an Incubus devil.' " Sabine put her finger on her notes and looked up triumphantly.

"Well, I don't know," said Mademoiselle Françoise.

" 'Devils cannot, as animals do, procreate children by virtue of their own strength and substance; but the devil can collect semen from another place, as from a man's vain dreams, and by his speed and experience of physical laws can preserve the semen in its fertilising warmth. . . .' It'll show the bishop up if we do it," Sabine said cunningly.

When Mademoiselle Françoise's uncle had died, a blacksmith from Ste.-Catherine had been named bishop. Mademoiselle Françoise had done all the gardening for her uncle, supplying fresh herbs to the coven, but now that business was going to the blacksmith's aunt, who lived two villages away. Instead of sitting by the altar, Mademoiselle Françoise was now just one more member of the congregation. The herbs always arrived wilted, Mademoiselle Françoise complained, and as for the aunt's flying ointment, one might as well hop on one foot and flap one's thumbs.

"You're right. I'll do it."

For nine days before the ceremony Sabine drank only water and ate only bread; she avoided human society and abstained from labor and from luxury. She prayed five times during the night and four during the day, *that those things which I conceive in my mind may happen in the flesh*.

"You must bathe in water from the Holy Well, exorcised water," Mademoiselle Françoise said. "Not from the tap, but from the well itself."

The Holy Well was in the deepest of Montfort's three basements, which was supposed to be dangerous because of rock falls and bad air. Sabine stole the key from Papa Cyron's desk and went down into the cellars. Down, down she went, through the first cellar with its wine bins, through the cobwebbed second cellar, and down the deepest narrowest stairs to where twisting tunnels drove through the hill like Montfort's roots. And so she found the Holy Well.

She found the Holy Well by the galvanized pipe that led from it. The Well had been covered over, boxed in with wood. A gas-powered pump crouched by it. Everything was huddled behind thick modern iron bars. She stared at it in horror. I'll fix this, she promised the Old One.

She brought a bucket of water back to Mademoiselle Françoise, and from the crown of her head to the soles of her feet she purified herself with exorcised water, then clothed herself only in linen.

Meanwhile Mademoiselle Françoise made the ointments. This you can't do in your own kitchen, not if you value your life; Mademoiselle Françoise had a workroom deep in the chalk under her farm, a room that had been an old animal byre. Tunnels led away into the earth. Shivering in her linen dress, Sabine sat on the stone bench carved into the chalk walls, nodding from the heavy green scents of belladonna and nightshade, drinking tea Mademoiselle Françoise had given her. She was light-headed from lack of food and sleep, from cold and drugs, and hate and love churned in her like a heavy sluggish fire.

She would be Necrosar's at last; he would be hers.

On the thirty-first of March, which was a Friday night, the two women scrubbed the stained, hoof-scarred floor of the old byre. Sabine took off her stiff linen dress and cast it aside. She stood naked in the low cellar. It was so low that her hair brushed the ceiling. Mademoiselle Françoise drew around her the symbols that would wall her in with the demon, then chalked signs of protection, pressing the soft chalk hard against the irregular flinty floor, muttering, holding up her skirt to make sure she didn't smudge a line. Sabine watched the candle flame, Mademoiselle Françoise's swinging gold ear-drops with the little pearls, her scuffed suede slippers piled in a corner. Who would come? Lucifer, who appears in the shape of a handsome boy? Ashtaret, a fiery cloud? Vapula, a lion with griffin's wings?

"I conjure you . . ." Mademoiselle Françoise prompted her from the book.

"I conjure you, I abjure and call you," Sabine said, then more loudly, "I constrain and command you: come, and obey. . . ."

Nothing. No naked man, horned or tailed; no fire; no black goat or long-tailed donkey or lion. No Necrosar; no husband; no child. Nothing. Sabine was shaking from the cold.

"Louder!" hissed Mademoiselle Françoise.

The lights were surrounded by rainbows. The cave was thick with smoke from burning sage branches. "I call upon you," Sabine shouted, "with my flesh I call you, with my body I call you; come, obey—"

And he was there, in the shadows beyond the fire. He had come from the tunnels. His face was dark but his body was white. For a moment Sabine doubted; that is how men look who work in the fields.

"Françoise, he's just a shepherd!" she hissed.

"Look, though: have you ever seen him before? It's no one from around here! Because it's not a man!"

"He isn't Necrosar!" she said.

"Why would it look like Necrosar? It's a man of air—"

The man beckoned to her. He had a round flat face, thick lips, and strange slanting eyes, almost Chinese. She had been expecting something that looked like her husband. He beckoned her to him. She hesitated. He said something in a thick-tongued language, nasal and throaty at once, and beckoned for the third time, then put his hands on his hips and simply looked at her.

He was not a man of air; he was a man. The incubus had brought him, slipped into him like a hand into a glove, made him its own, but he was not Necrosar; something stranger was going to happen than what she had prayed for. She moved around the sage fire and took his hand (it was callused, a living man's hand). She looked up into the face, the hot fire-lit eyes.

And the incubus took them both. They moved back away from the smoky firelight, into the cracks and crevices of the tunnels. His hands moved over her, rough like the pads of a big cat. His body was hot. She shuddered and wrapped her leg around his. He knelt and laid her down on the live rock. All this time he was talking in the guttural language of demons. He took her breast in his hand. He lay on top of her. She was swaying inside, liquid as fruit; she felt a pain, light, a heat gathering around pressure, and then something she had never felt before burst out from them together, so that she shrieked from the deadly pleasure of it. Necrosar! Necrosar! She died, she fell, she burned, she cried, she hated; she loved her husband and no one but her husband; she despised him and had taken a lover; it was not a lover or good or evil or anything, it was herself she was finding.

As Sabine stumbled up the stairs and out the door of the garden shed, she looked up and saw trails of fire in the sky.

She thought the man of air would come once and no more, but he came to her next at Montfort.

He came to Montfort on the day of the early spring washing. In the kitchen, every pot was being scoured. Every featherbed and pillow had been pulled down out of the bedrooms and the maids were shaking them on the lawn; they scattered feathers like little flowers among the grass.

This time he was dressed, but he wore a huge hat (to cover the horns, Sabine thought, smiling) and he wore boots, preternaturally long and thin and pointed. He said he was to be part of her husband's film. He was here to look at everything. No one else had time for him that day; he had been clever.

She took him by the hand and led him down into the cellars, to one of the cobwebbed tunnels of the second level. She motioned to him to take off his leather coat. His skin was leathery, too, dark in the candlelight and cracked. She unbuttoned her dress. His eyes went wide; he laughed and said something in the guttural language of demons. She lay on the leather coat, which smelled of smoke, of animals, of kingdoms on the other side of death, and opened her arms to him.

He needed to know everything about the land around Montfort. Together they explored Montfort in the spring. In those warm days the castle seemed to be infinite, white room after white room open to the sun, shadowed places under stairs, tunnels leading nowhere from the dark basements, not meant to be lived in, only to be built and built and forever to be built. She stole Papa Cyron's keys and together they explored the locked Bluebeard-rooms of Montfort, which had in them nothing terrible but only supplies for the builders, mortar for cement, rooms piled with boxes of nails and hardware.

Above them, a gull hovered in the clouds, an eye watching over them where the trails of light had been.

On horseback, they explored the woods near the castle. Instead of using a whip, he slapped the horse with his hat. He had no horns. He took pictures of her with a Kodak camera, which made her laugh; what did demons want with pictures?

If he was human, it didn't bother her; he was not her lover, he was simply part of what she had wanted. She accepted it all. His thumb on her nipple, his tongue on her breast. Her legs around him as they lay under the trees. He gave her a present, a set of amber beads, blood red, a present for a witch. She wore them everywhere; they were from Necrosar.

Her breasts swelled and grew tender. She yearned constantly for fruit. When she walked on the castle wall, the pigeons flew down and strutted around her, spreading their tailfeathers and cooing; this is an infallible sign of being with child. The gulls haloed the sky above her.

She wrote to Papa Cyron and went secretly to Paris. Papa Cyron got André drunk and Sabine added a preparation to the wine. It took two servants to carry him upstairs. She went in to him. Mademoiselle Françoise had prepared a salve; she rubbed it onto his parts and said words over them until they unfolded and grew. It was fascinating, beautiful, like butterfly wings unfolding. She crouched over him carefully, softly, she sank down upon him. It was nothing like with the incubus; it was something so tender. She felt so connected to him, so alive, it was almost as if he were going to die.

"There it is," she whispered to her husband's sleeping ear. "You have given me my son."

Chapter 25

By the end of that week no one would think the film was going well, but on Monday it seemed to be. The new cameraman and the first technicians had already gone down to Montfort, preparing the way for the arrival of the cast on the weekend. Jules visited Reisden on Monday, jubilant because he was looking forward to a role he liked, and because he was about to pass his false information to the Ferret.

It takes a great deal of effort to make a false secret. Cyron's friends at the Ministry had provided Jules with an elaborate packet: photographs and specifications of wireless equipment, details of the Montfort electrical plant. The taller of the abbey towers had been given a "concealed" antenna, complete with rather conspicuous Marconi reflectors. Jules had spent two days at Montfort with a camera, supposedly spying, taking pictures that were not any better than Jules would take, and had written out in his own hand the secret of Montfort, the generator and the Marconi station.

"Look at that," he said, spreading out the packet on Reisden's desk. "It goes today to the Louvre post office. I think the police are watching to see him pick it up. It's pretty exciting, isn't it?"

"Just like a film," Reisden agreed wryly.

Jules grinned. "Friday is the last day of the Necro season. Saturday morning we're off! And on Monday morning Mabet and Méduc meet the witches and they tell both of us we'll be important to history. And we will, this'll be the film of the year.—Reisden, you ought to come. It's going to be just tremendous fun; they're casting some of the little roles down there now, with locals. Why not you? Come for a couple of days and get in on it."

"I may come down to watch you."

"You're too sober," Jules said. He had brought the costume sketches for his role and had shaved his moustache for the part. He was an actor in love with his role.

"Jules," Reisden said, "I want to talk with you about what'll happen when you're at Montfort. André will have at least one shock during the filming, and I don't know how it'll affect him. His wife thinks she's with child."

It took Jules a moment to understand. Then the light went out of his olive face, leaving it muddy. "That's wonderful," he said, flushing.

"André doesn't know. He will find out soon. He'll be disturbed. When he's disturbed, he turns to Necrosar or depends on you. This time he can't do either; he needs to talk with his wife, if he can."

Jules thought this over, his eyes on the floor.

"But he needs you to watch him," Reisden said, "because he might become—very disturbed indeed. Can you do that? Will you call for help if you need it? Cyron won't."

"Ruthie and I will," Jules said. "Count on us."

And Jules went off to deliver his packet of lies to the post office, his face more somber, a little older; thinking of his expression later, Reisden would decide that he had looked as if he had been told he would be the father, not André; it had been that look of responsibility. One would trust Jules to be responsible. But after he had gone, Reisden found the costume sketches; Jules had been shaken enough to forget them.

As far as the police could reconstruct Jules' movements afterward, he went to the post office and then to the Necro, where André sent him off to do some errands. Jules did not seem unlike himself, André said; but André wouldn't notice. Ruthie had expected Jules back at the apartment for early dinner. When Jules didn't show up, Ruthie left a message at the theatre, presuming he'd forgot. André had been meeting with the set dresser and barely got back in time to do the show. Jules wasn't in the first half of the program, so it was well past midnight before anyone noticed he wasn't there at all.

As the police told the story, Jules finished his errands, left off packages at the Necro, then walked to the Minaret, a neighborhood Turkish bath frequented by homosexuals. There, again according to the police, he rented the services of a Marcel D., twenty years old. Marcel D. was flattered; he recognized Jules. After the encounter, Jules asked Marcel to buy them a bottle of eau-de-vie. Marcel got the bottle, hoping to talk with his client about the acting business, but when he returned, Jules had left without paying.

And what did you do then? the police asked Marcel.

I gave Big Fiboul thirty francs and told him to beat the bastard up.

Chapter 26

Jules was released from hospital four days before he would have gone to Montfort to act Méduc. Reisden took him back to the apartment. Jules had to be helped to lie down on the chaise longue in the library. He gestured for the blinds to be drawn, for the papers that littered the library to be taken away. Jules could not speak; his broken jaw had been wired shut.

André awkwardly, carefully gathered up the papers that littered the floor. André, whom Jules usually waited on like a slave, was trying to reciprocate. Reisden, passing him papers, saw they were part of the script for the film.

Flung across the back of a chair was a wine red coat in the eighteenth-century style. The sketch for it was still back in Reisden's office. Reisden remembered Jules laughing, excited about the film.

Jules looked half medical machine, half vulnerable human. His neck brace immobilized his head so he could not look at any of them without turning his whole body; he could not look up or down, only stare straight in front of himself. The lower half of his face was in an iron-mesh protective mask attached to the brace; his mouth was swollen and wet; he couldn't swallow easily because his attacker had hit him in the throat. Both eyes were blackened, yellow-purple. Between the swollen lids Jules' eyes glared with an angry defensive pain. Go away, Jules gestured, not looking at André; go away.

The police had let Jules' attacker go, because Jules had refused to testify against him. André had told him he should; Jules had scribbled *NO*, time after time. The story would have come out and André was part of the story. It was a declaration of loyalty; but loyalty that is a weight, a mistake.

Reisden took André into the dining room. "Leave him alone for a while."

André sat down in one of the dining room chairs. He wrapped his arms around himself, as if needing to be enfolded by care. He was moving like an old man, as if the shock had brittled his bones. He hadn't done Necrosar, onstage or off, since the first telephone call had reached him at the theatre. Necrosar would have said things that André couldn't bear hearing. Ruthie patted his shoulder awkwardly, tenderly, like a sister. "Would you like some mint tea?" she asked both of them. Reisden accepted, to give them all time to settle themselves. She made tea; she began to pour it into small cups painted with flowers. Suddenly, with his arms still around himself, André moaned and laid his head on the table. Ruthie stood rigid, like a pillar, a woman of wood, not moving anything but her arms, finishing pouring the tea, closing her eyes behind the glasses, and bowed her head and opened her mouth and made a sound, not loud, but as if someone had stabbed her, pain so unexpected it surprised her; she took off her glasses and jammed them into the pocket of her sensible skirt. She sat down at the table herself, one hand over her eyes, one hand outstretched, as if she were comforting André by touch, or asking for comfort. He put out his hand, close to hers. He touched the ends of his fingers to hers, patted her hand.

It was probably the first time in André's life that anyone had asked for comfort from him. Reisden left them in the dining room with the roses and the singing birds; he closed the door gently behind him.

Squaring his shoulders, he went back into the library, where Jules was lying in the dimness, and closed that door, too.

"First," Reisden said. "Whether the story's true. Once I remember you'd raided the Necro's petty cash to buy makeup for the company. You came back with a box of greasepaints and four francs seventeen centimes in change. I remember you counting the centimes out, fifteen, sixteen, seventeen. We all laughed at you. If you'd hired a Marcel, you'd have paid him. And drunk with the d—n man and probably listened to him recite, bad as he was. You don't cheat anyone. I know you."

For a moment, in the dimness, Reisden thought Jules was choking—his breath rasped through his broken nose and bruised throat. But it was laughter, or something that might just as well be taken for laughter. Jules' bruised hands counted out imaginary centimes in the air, explaining. He began to cough from his own spit; Reisden gave him a handkerchief, and Jules wiped his mouth and eyes. It left a bloody streak on the handkerchief; Jules looked at it apologetically. Only Jules, Reisden thought, would apologize for bleeding.

"Tell me what happened, if you can. Then I'll tell you what I've found."

Jules reached painfully, with bruised muscles, for paper and pencil. *Don't know,* he scrawled, holding the paper against the wall so he could see to write.

He didn't remember the attack. The last thing in his head was the middle of rehearsal. He must have done the errands; he thought he had been walking back toward the apartment. He thought he remembered a van with two men, maybe three.

"You broke the biggest one's nose," Reisden said.

Jules turned his thumb up wryly.

"To a degree I misled you. I know the story's wrong because I've talked with one of them. Gehazy hired them."

Reisden had found Big Fiboul at the workmen's club where he hung out. Fiboul was the size and shape of Wagny-les-Mines' mine tailings, three hundred pounds. *Moi, c'est mon métier dans le monde,* he had explained in a gravelly voice. *I beat guys up.*

Marcel hadn't hired Fiboul. "The guy who hires me, he's wearing an overcoat, in this heat, and he has a little smile like this," Fiboul had said, sliding his lips away from brown uneven teeth. "He said take some friends." The only instruction was that the beating was to be severe, visible, and long-lasting.

"Gehazy knew what he wanted you to tell him," Reisden said. "He thinks you know this secret."

Jules looked up at him sharply from his blackened swollen eyes, as if hoping what Reisden said next could define his experience.

"You left the package for Gehazy at about ten in the morning. Gehazy picked it up before noon. According to Fiboul, Gehazy hired him at around three in the afternoon. He had barely enough time to read your packet. He was looking for something specific."

Jules thought and tried to nod with his immobile head.

"Something either so blazingly obvious that you must have noticed it, so that he knew you were lying when you didn't mention it—"

Jules moved his hand, denying it.

"Or something you were supposed to know and deliberately didn't tell him. Did they ask you for information?"

Go after lost memory quickly and hard and sometimes you'll get it back. They worked out a system for Jules to answer without writing: left hand raised for no, right for yes. Reisden asked the same questions repeatedly, with all the variations he could think of. Did they say anything to you?

Did they ask you questions? Jules raised both hands help-lessly. Yes, no, maybe.

Reisden got up, paced the room, fiddled with the closed blinds. "Do you mind if I open these?" Light was not kind to Jules' purple-and-yellow face. Reisden tilted the shutters and looked down into the street. No one was watching Jules' building, though the police had promised protection.

"What would Gehazy presume you know? You've been to Montfort; you've known André for years. What's the secret of Montfort?"

Jules raised both hands, shrugged, and winced in pain.

"Anything!" Reisden said. "The most obvious thing. It's in plain sight. Anyone who knows the household knows it. What is it?"

Jules raised both hands, then pointed his finger at Reisden. He reached for the paper and scribbled.

You would know it too.

Chapter 27

"Jules is out of the film," Cyron said. "Out of the Necro. Out of my son's life. The whole world knows that my son's business partner was caught in a male brothel."

"That story is a lie," Reisden said. "As you like to remind me, I was Count Leo's ward. I knew Gehazy. He never cared whether the story was true; he simply made it scandalous. I saw the manager of this Minaret, which is a respectable place as these things go—" As these things go, Cyron thought. "No visit from Jules. Fiboul was hired by the blackmailer. So was Marcel, who's been fired."

Cyron felt a moment of unease. "The story's true," he said.

"No. You don't like the Necro, you don't like Jules, but the story is not true and you cannot use it as an excuse."

"It doesn't matter if the story isn't true, I won't have it get round—"

"Cancel the film," Reisden said.

"What?"

"André's mental state was precarious before Jules was hurt. He depends on Jules, not only as his business partner but to run errands for him, cook for him, everything; what Jules didn't do, his sister did. Jules and Ruthie were going to watch him. Now André doesn't have any support."

"If I'd say he has me," Cyron said, "you'd say that wasn't good enough, wouldn't you, boy? According to you I don't know him. Never have. Not the way you and his friends do." He nodded his head bitterly. "So. All right. You watch him. Didn't you say your *friend* Gehazy was looking for the secret of Montfort, which doesn't exist? He didn't get it from Jules, did he? So he'll try again, won't he? There'll be a lot of people at Montfort these next three weeks. I don't want to watch all of them to look for German spies. The next man Gehazy wants to blackmail, I want it to be you."

It took Reisden back; Cyron could see.

"Here's your chance to be loyal, eh? Prove yourself? Find out what this man wants, who he's working for. Find out what he's looking for, with this 'secret of Montfort.' You do that, I'll talk to Pétiot. You'll have your contract."

Reisden sat back, looking at him, trying to figure out Cyron's angle.

"I'll put you in a role." Cyron had got back Jules' annotated copy of the scenario. He slid it over the desk to Reisden. "Jules' role."

"You're mad, Cyron. I'm an ex–amateur actor."

"André wants you. He's worked with you before."

"I couldn't do it."

"I'm reconsidering my opinion. During the filming I'll be talking with you." Cyron's lips went wry over the words. "I'll look like I'm beginning to trust you. As for the acting, I'll take care of it."

"I—"

"Nobody's coming to see you, boy. Just stand still and let me act around you. You want to help André, or not? I want him helped. You say you can."

Got you, boy, Cyron thought.

"Come rehearse with me tomorrow, ten-thirty. Know the scenario cold by then."

Chapter 28

Dotty telephoned him. She was at one of the end-of-season parties; in the faint background he could hear the sounds of an orchestra. He imagined Dotty in a Poiret lampshade ballgown crushed into a telephone cabinet.

"Darling, I've heard André du Monde is trying to get *you* into his film."

Paris was a very small town. Gehazy would have heard too.

"Darling," she said, *"don't."* Her voice was high and nervous. She had never liked him acting, but this was more than that. *"Don't,"* Dotty repeated. "Say no to everything. Lose Jouvet if you have to, darling, but—"

"You know I won't do that."

"Darling," Dotty said, at her most brittle, her most high-society, "I absolutely *must* have an escort to the Spanish Embassy party tomorrow night. There is someone who wants to meet you. Can you possibly, possibly do it? You simply can't say no."

France was continuing to quarrel with Spain over Morocco, which meant that there would be a large German and Austrian contingent at the Spanish Embassy, supporting Spain, and a French demonstration outside condemning Spain as a bloody-handed imperialist invader. Not a place to be seen, most particularly if one were spending the next three weeks with Maurice Cyron. "Can't, darling."

"My house then. Seven, tomorrow." Her voice took on an edge like crystal being rubbed.

Dotty lived on the Île de la Cité, in an ancient house on the Place Dauphine. When the butler opened the door to the yellow salon, Reisden saw her first, dressed for the Spaniards in pastel silk and pearl ropes. She was not so much standing as backed up against the mantelpiece, with her painted ivory evening fan held in front of her like a broken sword. Makeup stood out on her face. A man was seated facing her; Reisden could see only the top of a grey head over the gilded back of the chair.

"Leave us, Dumézy," Dotty said. The butler bowed, retreated, and closed the mirrored doors behind him.

"Good evening, Baron von Reisden," Ferenc Gehazy said, standing and holding out his hand.

Reisden looked at it without comment, thinking of Jules. "Dotty, love, leave us."

"I want to stay," she said.

"You really don't."

The Ferret sat down again in Dotty's Louis XV armchair, wriggling his bottom against the seat. Reisden stayed standing. The Ferret looked up at him, bowing in the chair and rubbing his hands. "Your beautiful cousin has been so kind to invite me to her lovely home, to introduce me to you. I was a great friend of your guardian, her noble uncle. With respect, kind honored sir, I have a little favor to ask of you, a little favor you can do, in the name of your esteemed uncle Count von Loewenstein."

The blackmailer was speaking to them in German, a language well-suited for groveling, but he smiled slyly and appraisingly up at them as if he were considering how they would taste.

"I've come to warn you, first of all, honorable Viscountess, honorable Baron, that I have heard a terrible story about you, terrible. I hear that—but no, it is too indecent to assault the ears of the wellborn Viscountess."

Dotty closed her eyes.

"This terrible story is about the family"—the Ferret bowed sympathetically toward Dotty—"and the wards"—with a nod toward Reisden—"of the late noble Count von Loewenstein. It is said by people of no conscience that in former days the late noble great Count was involved with the Secret Service of our Empire. His family and wards were trained as spies, to do favors for influential people and to gather information—"

"It isn't so," Reisden said, trying not to overplay.

"Among this Secret Service," the Ferret continued, "people of no conscience said that one was worse than the others. He was very young and he was nobody, a boy that the late noble Count found abroad—who would tell these stories about such honorable people! This boy did—certain favors. For this he was given the name of honorable dead people," the Ferret said. "At one time he tried to infiltrate the Russian underground by marrying a Russian socialist; he distanced himself from the noble Count, but this was all a trick. Now he has moved to Paris to gather information among the French. He has married an American heiress for money, but he is a colonel in the Imperial and Royal Secret Service.—Such a dreadful story," the Ferret said, crossing himself piously, "*G-tt sei dank* it's not true."

"All that is nonsense, and old nonsense." His face felt numb. He risked a look at himself in the mirror above Dotty's mantel. He looked all right, pale, but he was always pale, and his voice sounded all right as far as he could tell; but his ears were ringing. *He was nobody, a boy Count Leo found and gave an honorable name.*

"It's unfortunate," the Ferret said, "in such political times, foolish people believe stories about spies."

"When they're spread by one of them?" Reisden said. "Who sent you?"

"Don't, darling," Dotty said.

"I will not be blackmailed." Don't sound like a melodrama, he told himself.

"Darling"—Dotty took hold of his hand—"talk privately with me for a moment. Herr Gehazy, you'll excuse us."

Dotty's house had two salons, with a door between them. Dotty drew him into the other salon and closed the door. It, like the other, was strict eighteenth-century but for the piano, which was closed and covered with a Chinese shawl. The shutters were closed; dim gold spears of light fell onto the carpet, on a leg of the piano and the fringes of the shawl. The glass windows were open onto the Quai des Orfèvres, letting in the sounds of the twentieth century, a water bus chugging down the Seine and a horse-drawn sprinkler hissing against the dusty hot pavement. He could smell heat, wet dirt. They stood by the window to mask their voices from Gehazy.

"Please, darling." Her thin cheekbones reddened.

"He's threatened to spread rumors about you too?"

"About both of us, darling. That we're—still doing it." She looked up at him as if there were something he should say.

"You aren't still doing it?" she said after a moment.

"No! After everything that happened? You?"

"No."

They regarded each other as if they hoped to believe each other. Her face was reddened still; she looked down at her fan, opening and closing it. "No?" he said.

"No! No." She looked up defensively. "I'm ashamed," she said, "that's all."

"That settles one issue at least," he said, "whether anyone else will believe the Ferret. Does he want you to do anything?"

She shook her head, still looking at the floor. "Only you."

"What does he want?"

"I *told* you," Dotty said in a low voice, "you shouldn't be involved in André's film.—He wants the secret of Montfort."

Of course he did. "Let's go back."

He opened the doors. Gehazy was looking at Dotty's display case of eighteenth-century snuffboxes; he had the air of a man who has just tried the lock.

"There is a military secret at Montfort," the Ferret said, straightening up. "I want you to tell me what it is."

"No, there isn't," Reisden said. "I've been at Montfort; there isn't anything. Leo was interested, long ago, but he didn't find anything. You asked Jules Fauchard to find it before me. He didn't find anything. Nothing is there."

The Ferret grinned, but uncertainly. "You will know it when you find it," he said finally, with the air of a penny oracle at a seaside arcade.

"Talk with the person who hired you," Reisden said. "Tell him I need more information."

"Did you tell Jules Fauchard to lie to me?" the Ferret said. "You see what happened to him."

The Ferret left several minutes later. Dumézy showed him out; Dotty collapsed into a chair; Reisden went back into the second salon and folded back the right half of the shutters. He leaned out. Gehazy was visible through the trees, slinking away from the Pont-Neuf toward the Palais de Justice. Reisden had taken precautions; Roy Daugherty, their detective friend, was strolling after him, his hands in his pockets, discreetly shadowing him.

"Who is he working for? Our esteemed cousin Sigi?" Reisden asked. His voice sounded tinny and distant, like a phonograph record. "I wouldn't put it entirely past Sigi.—I hope Roy doesn't lose him."

"Darling." Dotty laughed rather hysterically. "Sigi would love to know. Sigi came to see me this afternoon. He's being blackmailed too. You see," Dotty said, "how much someone wants the secret of Montfort."

Chapter 29

On Friday, Reisden did a rehearsal with Maurice Cyron. Cyron took him into the rehearsal studio—Cyron had a studio in his town house, with full-length mirrors—and showed Reisden what he wanted and how it looked, making him practice it until he got the face and gestures right. Cyron wrote it down in Aubert's pantomime annotation: stick figures to show the attitude of the body, sketch of the face to show expression, sketch of the hand to show gestures. Reisden grimaced in the mirrors, widening his eyes for "Uneasy Listening" and squinting for "I Have My Doubts."

Citizen Mabet is yet another of Cyron's homages to militarism. It takes place during the French Revolution. The hero is Edmond Mabet, an old army man and a minor noble. The country and the countryside are starving while King Louis carouses at Versailles. Despairing of the King, Mabet renounces him and throws in his lot with the revolutionaries. He becomes a judge, sentencing the royal tax collector to death.

Mabet has a wife and a son. His young wife is a woman of the people, idealistic and proud, representing the countryside at its best. *Her* people, she says, will be able to govern France! The suffering of the peasants will be their teacher; they, who have needed compassion so long, will govern with compassion.

His illegitimate son is named Méduc. Méduc is fully recognized by his father and has a respectable place in society, but he is gloomy, a conservative, a doubter. The people cannot govern themselves, he says; the Revolution will fail. Méduc would be Reisden's role.

Mabet and Méduc clash. In a dramatic scene, Méduc confronts his father; the Revolution has gone too far, it is drowning in blood. Mabet condemns his son. The mob marches on Méduc's estate and, finding him gone, kills his wife and young son, Mabet's only grandchild.

Cyron broke the scene and came across the room to Reisden, held his shoulders, and looked up into his eyes. "And now, next, this is your scene," he said. "This is your only reason to be in the play. You have held back. You haven't supported the Revolution but you haven't emigrated. You have been on no one's side, you've thought you could stay out of it. And now your family is dead. So who do you curse? You curse me! 'He has no children.' Show me that." Cyron stepped back. "Hate me. Hate me."

Reisden tried. He worked on an expression that would stand in for that line. He tried everything, from a horrified Garrick-style forehead-clutching to bared teeth and a dazed grimace. He didn't need Cyron's expression to tell him how badly he was doing.

"It isn't that hard, eh," Cyron said finally. "You have a son. What would you do if someone killed him?"

"Kill them."

"Even if he's your father."

Especially, Reisden thought.

"How would you kill him?"

"I would beat him to death," Reisden said without thinking, and saw how oddly Cyron looked at him.

"No. That's simply brutal. Not Méduc. He's a man of the law. He wants to defeat his father and shame him, by killing him in the public square, on the guillotine."

Mabet's wife goes insane, haunted by the dead innocents her husband has killed. Mabet leads the Reign of Terror in Arras. Méduc raises an army and defeats him. Mabet and his wife are condemned to death.

The curtain rises on the final scene. Madame Mabet is led first to the scaffold, confused, singing the little folk song from the first act, not taking up too much stage time. Mabet watches her die. Mabet is then led forward for his great scene. He begins by execrating the people. "You have killed the best among you!" He curses them: "You will die like me." And then—Reisden wondered how André would ever do it on the Grand'Place—the stage lights dim, and baby spots pick out two persons: Mabet and his son. Mabet gives his great speech. "I have loved France," Mabet's voice rises to a climax; "for France I have lost everything, my family, my son—"

"No, no, Father, not your son!" Méduc says, repentant, casting himself at Mabet's feet—

"Ah, my son!"

"My father! I will die with you!"

"No, my son, live! Live for France! If you die, die for France! Sacrifice for France!" By now, in the theatre, the whole audience would be on its feet, hoary old sergeants shouting "For France!" and weeping into their handkerchiefs—

Cyron sighed. "We won't take the last scene today. I'm defeated. You have no face. Even that—that Fauchard would have been better."

Reisden massaged his nonexistent face with the ends of his fingers. "I don't understand why you wrote the relationship that way. Why is Méduc Mabet's son?" In Shakespeare's original the character had been Macbeth's friend.

"Ah, fathers and sons—" There was something in Cyron's voice. "Did I ever tell you about my father?"

Reisden shook his head.

"My father." The rough old rooster-face momentarily softened. "He was a woodcarver in Alsace, carved puppets, heads and hands; my mother sewed the costumes. He sold puppets and dolls and clocks and he had a puppet theatre. I was doing my time in the army. He was in the Territorials, what they call the Territorials now. He died defending Alsace." Cyron made a face. "Still sometimes I think he's in the audience at the theatre. I act for him.—So you see about Méduc?"

"No," Reisden said.

"The thing Shakespeare did wrong—it's not his best play, eh?—is that no one cares about Macbeth. In my play, his son mourns for him. 'What a terrible thing I did to you,' the son says. 'It's our tragedy, I didn't understand your nobility.' You wouldn't understand, you never had a father. A man's not complete unless he has a father. Do your best with that line," Cyron said, "but you won't get it."

"May I ask you a question?" Reisden said. "Your father was in the theatre. You're in the theatre. You never wanted André in the theatre; why not?"

Cyron thrust his chin forward, insulted. "Is he my son? I know better. I brought him up to be his father's son. A soldier was what I wanted for him."

Chapter 30

"Did you bring Dotty into this?" Reisden said to Sigi. "What? Why do I bring Dotty in, when it's me, I'm being also blackmailed?"

Sigi von Loewenstein was a big, blond, muscular man, strikingly like Leo, and from the moment he had come to Paris, three years ago, he had made a joke of who his father was. He would introduce himself, "Hello, I am Count Sigi Loewenstein, son of the late chief spy of Austria-Hungary in Paris," and then, with his broken French and his obvious questions, tried to make everyone take it as a joke. "I'm just a *military attaché*, you know," he would say solemnly. He had suggested to Reisden that they meet at Ste.-Clotilde, a church so notorious that it had been nicknamed St.-Spy. Reisden chose instead the chamber of horrors of the École de Médicine, where no one ever visits. In the churchlike dim room, among the row of monstrosities and wax statues, Sigi in his white suit, with his soldier's straight back and his decoration in his buttonhole, stood out indiscreetly, but no one was watching.

Sigi had the French *Racing Form* under his arm. How he brought back Leo, who had loved the races.

"This is funny," said Sigi. "What is this Montfort? Do you think I would send someone like Gehazy on you? That's *Quatsch*; I don't use him. I come myself," he said, spreading his hands. "And the secret of Montfort? I want Jouvet, Sacha.

There you've got secrets I want. You want money? I can give you money, everything what you need; I could give it even from French bankers or English. You give me nothing, you don't help me with nothing, but you know it's not me what's trying to get you out from Jouvet, right? Do I get rid of my cousin to deal with a stranger?" Sigi thumped his chest with his flat hand. "What is it, I'm stupid?"

"What did Gehazy want from you?"

"The plans of d—n Montfort," Sigi said.

"What *is* it about?"

"You said it was nothing."

"I'm beginning to doubt. Sigi, who wants it?"

"The Germans maybe," Sigi said. "Maybe the Russians. The Russians want to know if it delays the Germans. Maybe black men from the Fiji Islands want to know."

Sigi was examining a row of pickled things in glass jars; he picked one up. Bleached morbidities swirled. "Watch that," Reisden said, "it's probably interesting."

"I don't know who," Sigi said, "but I know why.—Someday, someday pretty d—n soon, the Germans are invading."

"Is that what they tell you?"

"I read the papers.—It's true what Dotty says, you are becoming a French citizen?" Reisden nodded. "It's a picnic in front of the guns, Sacha. With your wife and your baby. It's not so smart."

"I live here."

"You should protect them. I can help."

"Your story of being blackmailed is faked," Reisden said, "isn't it?"

"What did your man say, your detective who followed Gehazy? Did Gehazy meet someone?"

"How did you know I had someone follow him?"

"Because you're smart, Sacha. But he didn't find who it is Gehazy works for, no?"

Reisden shook his head, no. "Does that relieve you, Sigi?" Gehazy had spotted Daugherty—too easy in the crowds of short Frenchmen—and had lost him at the Gare St.-Lazare.

"You find out what is the Montfort secret," Sigi said. "You can tell me. But what I want from you? It's the fourth-floor back room at Jouvet."

Chapter 31

Four o'clock in the morning, Saturday, just dawn. He would leave by the ten o'clock train for Arras. It had been too hot to sleep, and he too nerve-ridden. He had packed, unconsciously allowing the time required for one of their family expeditions. Without piles of diapers, toys, baby blankets and baby clothes and bottles and the baby-food grinder, his luggage seemed very small. The only equipment he had was the Braille typewriter on which he wrote letters to Perdita. He felt he was leaving vital things behind.

He haunted his office, pretending to do paperwork, pretending to study Méduc's part, and staring instead at the pictures on the walls. Gilbert Knight, and, as visible through Gilbert as if he'd been transparent, nineteen-year-old Thomas Robert Knight.

There is a panic in going off to the country, where it's hard to reach you; things will go wrong as soon as you leave. He had not heard from Perdita in two weeks. He looked over everything he had left for Madame Herschner: the telephone number and telegraph address for the château, what she was to do in case any number of things happened. . . . Something would go wrong with Jouvet as soon as he left.

Perhaps not, he thought tiredly. Jouvet was all right fundamentally; Jouvet was fine. Perhaps all Jouvet needed to bob up again was for him to leave.

He picked up his boy's picture and stared at it. Toby, laughing, utterly secure. But, my dear love, you aren't.

The phone rang. "Darling, you spoke with Sigi?" Dotty, back from whatever party Society had most favored tonight.

"He says he isn't behind it," Reisden said.

They had both seen blackmailers pretending to be victims; it was one of the easiest ways to get information. "What will you do, darling?"

"Something clever. I don't know."

When she rang off, he sat in his office and thought of the conversation with Sigi. *You know it's not me trying to get you out of Jouvet.* Sigi had been the one to mention that: Not bankrupting Jouvet, but getting him out of it. . . . In favor of whom? Someone more malleable, with more dependable ties to Austria-Hungary.

He looked around his office. The rows of gently outdated books, from the last Dr. Jouvet's time. Descriptions of mental diseases, most of which he would never have the patience to read; some of which he shouldn't read because they were out of date and wrong. Occasionally he didn't know which were which. He was making Jouvet up as he went along, making up as much as he knew.

Jouvet would do better with a Frenchman, a doctor, preferably a specialist in mental diseases.

But he didn't want to lose Jouvet. He was tired of always having to be careful that no one looked too closely into Alexander von Reisden's background, tired of making himself up as he went along; he was tired of Alexander von Reisden never really existing in the inexorable way Richard

Knight had existed, tired of being a thirtyish ex-lunatic with the wrong background; but he wasn't tired of Jouvet.

He went down into the cool damp just before dawn, to turn on the lights and look at the lab. He went up to the third floor and unlocked the glass door to look at row after row of file cabinets. Five generations of mad patients; five generations of knowledge. He had reached that vicious stage of insomnia where one can't think, only feel, and what he felt was how powerless he was for them: for André and Sabine; for all of them; how powerless he was against whatever was brewing politically, against Gehazy. He looked at the waiting room, the testimonials on the walls; he went into an interview room and touched the desk, the chairs, the bars on the windows.

Someone was using the elevator. He went out into the hall curiously; it was Roy Daugherty.

"What are you doing here?" he asked; four in the morning, after all.

"Goin' home. Ain't found your guy's file yet." Roy had been hired on to help the librarians hunt.

"You've been here all night?"

"I got a feelin' it's there."

"Go home." Roy Daugherty's first marriage had broken up over his work. Now Roy was living with Suzanne Mallais— *lodging* with her, he put it; she was older, he wasn't French, for the first time in twenty years Daugherty didn't have an important and endless job. What do we do without our jobs. . . . Perdita and Reisden had ceded the Courbevoie house to them, with the right to come out on weekends, but when they did come to visit, they felt as though they were walking on souls. "Get Suzanne to make you breakfast. Enjoy her."

Daugherty smiled: dawn breaking in winter. "I know it's there, though," he said, shaking his head.

"Then you'll find it later; go home." He went outside with Daugherty, locking the door. He stood in the courtyard a moment, looking back at the building. Barely visible repair-lines marked the frontage, making the building look, oddly, not damaged but cared for. One more bit of Jouvet's history. It was a beautiful building. Jouvet was his. Inadequate as he was to it, Jouvet was his own.

"Admirin' it, are you?"

"This is what I want," he said. "So. We keep looking. You do. And I go off and pretend to be someone's son, again . . . and watch André."

"You take care, now."

They said goodbyes. He wouldn't be long; the film was supposed to take only two and a half weeks. Perdita would be back just after he was. They'd go out to Courbevoie and see Roy and Suzanne. He watched Daugherty trudge off toward the Métro station.

He walked up as far as Les Halles and had a bowl of onion soup at one of the cafés. The flower market was quiet under its glass eaves; *le monde* was beginning to desert Paris for its yachts and country estates. When Perdita was here and he was restive at night, he would sometimes come here at night for the walk and buy her flowers for the pleasure of looking at her as she smelled them; she would close her eyes, fanning scent off the flowers as if she were splashing water onto her face. Oh, love, love, he thought. He bought a bare-root rosebush for her, a well-scented variety, and added to it a bunch of the flowers as a bribe for Madame Herschner to pot it. Roots in a pot now. Someday, roots; someday a past on which to build a future, and a self, and security for them all.

When he got home, at about six in the morning, Perdita was there.

Chapter 32

It was Toby he saw first, crawling intently across the front-hall carpet into a patch of sun. Reisden stood still, lightning-struck, then dropped the rosebush and the roses and scooped up his boy. Toby stared at him, startled, and burst into tears, and took hold of the buttons of his coat and wouldn't let go. He hugged his baby, they hugged each other—"Oh, Toby, Toby my love, I've missed you." Toby sobbed as though his heart would break. Reisden wanted to cry, too; he took deep breaths instead, smelling Toby, who needed changing, but never mind. "Why did you come home so early, dear little one? Where's your mama?" And there she was at the hall door. For a second he saw her as one sees people who have been away, a little strange, such a grown-up beautiful woman, and then he crossed the hall in two steps and held them both.

Man and wife is one flesh. True. Man and wife and child. He felt as if home had come home to him.

He gave her the roses; she held them, fanning them, as he'd pictured her doing. "Think of your bringing roses," she said. "As if you knew I was coming." They went into the kitchen where Aline was cutting bread. He wadded a kitchen towel under Toby's wet diaper and held him, surrounded by stink and wordlessly in love. "You'll get all red and chapped. You'll have to let Aline change you," he murmured into his boy's little pink milk-smelling ear, but Toby just gave a hiccupy sob and held tight. "All right. Soon, but not now."

"But you're going someplace," Perdita said, bewildered. "I found your luggage in the bedroom. Where? How long? I thought you would be here; you didn't say you were going anywhere."

"Come with me to Montfort." He told her the story briefly.

"But I thought you would be here," she said.

You came back early, he was about to point out. He had missed her desperately enough, this last six weeks, to know that she was missing him.

"We need breakfast," she said. He sat with the baby at the kitchen table and relaxed back into his too-long-missing center: unreasonable demanding baby, smelly and inconsolable and too young to be talked to; equally unreasonable Perdita, making coffee, lighting the gas-burner while he held his breath, wondering whether this time she would go up in flames; family life, half-irritating, wholly what he wanted. Perdita sent Aline off for eggs. He looked at her critically; you don't need coffee, he thought, you need sleep. Preferably with me. Perdita, who didn't usually have nerves, was pale and tight-wound, fussing about the kitchen, moving things an inch to the right, an inch to the left, tidying her way back into being at home.

"How did the concerts go?" he asked.

"Oh, fine." Not fine. Something to talk about later.

"Come, sit down."

She stood at the kitchen sink. "Why you?" she said. "Why do *you* have to do this, Alexander?"

He told her again in a little more detail. She brushed her hand over his face. "You haven't been eating," she said. "You're thin."

"Everything will be all right," he said. "André wants to talk about whatever's bothering him, I hope."

"André," she said, and made a face.

Aline came back with food. They changed Toby in the kitchen, because he howled when they tried to put him down for a nap. Aline brought the bassinet in, fixed them omelettes, and disappeared discreetly. They brought their chairs around to the same side of the table, so they could touch as they ate, and fell on the food.

"André's wife is pregnant," Reisden said, finishing his toast. "He's not talking to her, she hasn't told him. She did give him something—once, in Egypt. She didn't mean to. She's a little frightened of him."

"*I* don't wonder."

"I'm going to listen to him," Reisden said, "while he talks."

"That'll take you a long time," Perdita said. "He can talk for hours and not say a thing."

"Come and talk to her. If you would. She's lonely."

She leaned against his shoulder and sighed explosively. Something was making her nervy, he thought. Not André's troubles. He laid the backs of his fingers against her cheek. She took his hand as if it were a lifeline, holding hard with both of her hands.

"Oh, dear. Oh, Alexander."

"What?"

"Not yet," she said. She undid his cuff link and ran her fingers up the underside of his wrist, bent to kiss his wrist.

Men are used to being sexually frustrated; happily married young women are not. Good, he thought, finding the little buttons at the back of her collar.

They lay beside each other in bed, in a tangle of sheets. Toby's bassinet was beside the bed, with a baby blanket over it to keep the sunlight from him. They had tried to put him in his own room, to spare his blushes; he had only started wailing again. In their room he had fallen asleep, lulled by his parents whispering to each other.

"Are you sure you have to go?" Perdita said. "We *need* to talk."

"I don't want to go, but yes, I'm sure. What happened in Boston?"

He was sure it was Boston that was worrying her. Her eyes widened and she sighed, confirming it for him.

"It was as awful as you said it would be," she said.

Good, he thought. "I'm sorry," he said.

She was wearing a silver necklace, which she hadn't taken off. It nestled in the hollow between her breasts. He admired it there, but it was Woolworth's finest: a lavalliere studded with gaudy rhinestones on a nickel chain. She tugged at it as if it were part of the story. "Uncle Gilbert gave me this," she said.

Gilbert's style was not Woolworth's. Especially not for Perdita, precisely because she couldn't see it. He unfastened it from her neck and turned it round curiously in his fingers.

"I went to Boston," she said. "I didn't hear from him. I wrote several times and got no reply. Harry told me no one wanted to see me. I stayed in a hotel." Perdita said the word *hotel* as if she were holding it with tongs.

"But you saw Gilbert," he prompted.

"The last day. Alexander, *they hadn't told him I was there*. I had written letters to him. He didn't get them."

Reisden swore to himself and said nothing.

"Was that what you thought would happen?"

"No," he said, surprised. "I thought Gilbert—" He broke off.

"Would love Toby. Of course he does, Alexander."

"I'm sorry Harry feels it threatening—"

"Alexander," she said. "Don't act so tough."

"All of that isn't our business," he said.

"It's my business," she said. "He wasn't being treated well. It is *our* business because you're my husband."

"But you are *my* wife," he said. "Not Richard's."

She looked aside for a minute. "I thought you would be sorry that he isn't being treated well."

"Harry and Gilbert should get on better. They don't; Gilbert's sorry; I'm sorry; Harry's guilty about it, from the sound of it; but it's not our business."

"There's more to it than that," she said.

"I don't want anything to do with it," he said.

"When I talked to Gilbert," she said, "he asked me what you were doing. I told him that you were working hard to build up Jouvet, and that you had spent all this year working on business, not doing much science; that it looked as though Jouvet would be very successful; that it was a change for you, and I wondered whether you were doing what you really wanted, but I knew you wanted Jouvet. We talked a lot about Jouvet, later. Do you know what he said? I wanted to talk about it," she said, "because it startled me."

"What?"

"He said you reminded him of William."

He stood up from the bed as if it had been burning. He stood beside it, naked, and looked down at her. She looked up at him, not quite up at him, half-focused beyond him, seeing something other than him. Family. Violence in a family lives in the very blood. He turned away from her and hit the wall beside the door, flat-handed, so hard it stung. It woke Toby; Perdita felt for him and gathered him up and held him in her arms, rocking him.

"He said," she said in a whisper, "that William would always do something about something that bothered him. Sometimes he did it very badly, he was very bad about raising you, but he never neglected it. And he said you were like that about madness. He said," she said, "that you were like William. Not neglectful. It was one of your strengths. I didn't think you would neglect Gilbert."

"Jouvet is not about William," he said.

"Gilbert is about us."

He didn't know what to say.

"I *have* to go back to America," she said in a flat, quiet

voice. "You live here, your life is here, your job is here, but they only hire me to play in the States. So I have to go back, not all the time, but—" She held Toby to her, his head on her shoulder, and kissed him; he was asleep, and she got up and put him back in his bassinet. She got up, facing him, naked too, pushing her long hair back onto her sweaty shoulders. "And I was going to leave Uncle Gilbert there in the middle of it," she said, still low-voiced. "I was going to do that, because I know what it means to you to get away from the Knights, and I hated myself for it, but I was going to do it. I hadn't seen him. I hadn't asked him why he didn't want to see me. Because I knew how you would feel, because no one had encouraged me to, not even you this time, Alexander; because I was going to be a good person and *go along*. And then, the last day—"

She told him the story of the concert: the cancellation of the original concert, the impromptu concert on Commonwealth Avenue. What impressed him was that Harry had gone as far as to cancel one of her concerts, and she hadn't spoken about that egregious act of meanness; she had talked about Gilbert. Family love is a dreadful thing, he wanted to tell her. Harry wants Gilbert's attention and is willing to do anything to get it. What Harry did is wrong, dead wrong, but it doesn't change anything else. She told him about the meeting, about the Woolworth's teardrop Gilbert had given her.

"He told me," she said, "you had told him a story. When you left Vienna with Tasy, you bought her a pin to celebrate because you were going to escape. It was a cheap pin, but it was a thing to celebrate, he said, because of the escape. So he gave me this—" She put her hand to her neck as though she were still wearing it, although she was not.

Reisden had put the necklace on the nightstand; he picked it up by the chain. The pendant swiveled in his fingers.

"And I hated it. I hated the very idea that he was something to escape. That we could escape and he couldn't, that we *wanted* to escape him the way you wanted to escape Vienna—"

The strong July sunlight brought out every detail of the tacky little thing, the irregular base-metal bumps meant to stand for pavé rhinestones, the uncertain edges, the glue at the edges of the stones. And the clear hard spark of the stones themselves. The pin he had bought Tasy had been an enameled blue flower with a red glass center, another vulgar thing—

"It was a ruby by the time we ran away," he said. He had sold everything he had to buy it. "We lived on it for months after we got to London. Do you know what he's done?"

"I know," Perdita said. "It's diamonds. That doesn't matter. He—escaped, too, Alexander. He's not in Boston. Look out the window. He's here."

Chapter 33

Cyron's special train for Arras, which Reisden had been supposed to be on, had already left; Reisden drove to Arras in his car. The back was loaded with luggage, his newly altered costumes, a tricorne hat borrowed from Dotty's attic, and his old fencing sword. And not his wife and son. They would come down by another train, Perdita said. Later. They had a great deal of washing to do. And unpacking. "Don't hurry," he said in a tone that made her flinch.

"What about Gilbert?"

"You brought him, you can d—n well send him back."

There might have been a person waiting on the street when he drove the car away from Jouvet; he deliberately did not notice.

He drove north through suburbs of Paris, through satellite towns and villages, up the valley of the Oise to Amiens. It is supposed to be pretty country. He crossed the marshes and bridges of the Somme, where France begins to blur into the old country of Burgundy, and came out onto the great hazy plain of Flanders, where the beet fields stretched from horizon to horizon and the only traffic was a horse-drawn mower clopping across the road from field to field.

At the edge of the road, where the mower did not reach, a farmer stood scything the hay. The stalks slumped and fell in ranks, glistening. At the top of the field they had already begun to wilt. He thought of his son's hand holding hard to his jacket button. He thought of himself in a rage against Thomas Robert; *don't take chances, don't go out in the boat, keep me secure.* Don't leave me. He should have turned back, but he went on.

He wouldn't think of what Perdita and Gilbert had done until he could think of it without rage. And he was taking it out on his baby, not because he wanted to, but because, whatever happened in the family, Toby was part of it.

Gilbert. Coming to Paris in the midst of Jouvet's money troubles. With diamonds.

About six, hot, dusty, tired, angry, discouraged, he drove through Arras and took the road northeast toward Montfort and the frontier. He saw the towers first, two black sticks in the sky, far away across the fields.

From Montfort hill, as he neared it, a cloud of dust rose. Wagons were heading up the hill, spiraling and circling upward. He followed them, coughing in the haze of dust. In the slopes between the walls, the sheep looked up to stare at the commotion of vehicles.

He drove through the Jerusalem Gate into the courtyard;

the area inside the castle walls was already full of people, boxes, luggage, horses.

"Where do I park the car?" he asked.

"Stay off the grass, we're filming on it," a man with a clipboard shouted. "Put your car in the garage next to Monsieur Cyron's Rolls. Costumes go to the old refectory, ground floor, north wing, New Buildings. . . . Did you see the caterer's wagons?"

The New Buildings were through the Lion Gate, worn-down animals rampant; he fit the car between them and drove down the chalk path to the two brick-and-sandstone wings of the abbey guesthouse. On the ground floor, the old refectory was crowded with metal pipe racks hung with soldiers' or peasants' costumes; piles of clothes were scattered on the floor. The costume manager was standing in the middle of them, clutching his hair, while his assistant leafed frantically through a notebook. "Are your costumes ironed? Keep them with you. It's the only safe thing." The costume manager sent him back to the lawn outside the main buildings. From a folding table set up in the entranceway, the production manager's assistant, harried little Guix from the Necro, thrust at him a rehearsal schedule, a red ticket, and a room key. "Don't lose your catering ticket, you only get one."

His room was 13, according to the brass ticket on the key. Why not.

He had rehearsal for the first scene in half an hour. He went up to his room, unpacking himself and hanging up the eighteenth-century clothes first. On the top of his own clothes was the picture of Toby in Central Park that Perdita had sent from New York. He sat on the edge of the bed, head down, looking at his boy.

He'll wake up and he'll want me and I won't be there.

It had already happened.

And he thought of Gilbert too, the figure on the other side of the street. *Gilbert came to reassure us he's all right,*

Perdita had said. Gilbert had always been afraid of boats. Reisden could picture him, peering over the rail at the hull of the ocean liner, urging Perdita and Toby to wear lifejackets to bed.

"Dr. Reisden, time—"

They were filming the first meeting between Mabet and the witches on the south slope of Montfort hill, where the light was good; orthochrome film is greedy for light. They rehearsed in street clothes first, without the witches. It was Cyron's scene; he directed himself, stalking from stage left over the uncertain ground toward the box that was standing in for the Holy Well. "Stay back," he instructed Reisden, "don't move, don't try to put an expression on your face; just stay out of my way."

The camera equipment was still being set up. Reisden cleared his mind of anything but Méduc. Méduc stood behind Mabet, hesitating while Mabet grasped the chance to make history. Mabet held the middle of the stage, gesturing, pointing.

André was behind the camera with Eli Krauss, the photographer, oblivious to everything.

Back in the refectory, the company barber cut Reisden's hair shorter so it would not show under his wig. The rear of the ballroom had been made into the men's dressing room, with makeup tables, lights, and mirrors. The makeup supervisor greased Reisden's face an all-over yellow, the institutional yellow of the walls of an asylum, outlined his eyebrows and eyes in black, and painted his mouth ochre. Reisden closed his eyes. He wanted to lose everything but Méduc; loss had always been one of the pleasures of acting, emptying out oneself, being someone else. A sane thing. But he could think only of his son.

"Have I time to make a telephone call?" The Montfort telephone was in the main house of the château, the Vex-Fort, in a telephone cabinet off the Great Hall. He captured the telephone from André's production manager, who was dictating to the Necro staff a long list of things that had been forgotten, and asked the operator for the apartment number at Jouvet. In the glass of the telephone cabinet he saw himself, yellow-faced, his shirt dyed a garish pink because white was too dazzling for the film stock. A clown.

"Ici la famille Reisden—" Perdita.

"Hello."

A long silence. "Hello."

Perdita, you were wrong, he thought, and said nothing. On the other end of the line she would be thinking he was wrong. "Come here," he said. "Please." He didn't mention Gilbert, then thought better of that. "Only you and Toby. Aline, of course."

Another silence. "Is there a train?"

He covered the transmitter and talked to the production manager. There was one at 10:30 tonight; it got in at 3:46 in the morning. There was a sensible one at ten tomorrow, when a load of missing items would be coming for the film. He told her about both trains. It made sense for Toby to have at least one night's sleep in his own house. Reisden said nothing for a moment, and they listened to each other breathe over the line.

"He misses me," Reisden said.

"He does. We'll come tonight." She said it as though it were her decision.

He rang off and sat in the telephone booth a moment taking deep breaths. He felt, not securely Méduc, but lost between lives, vulnerable, angry, deserted, hurt, deserting, confused.

Guix knocked on the door; the Arras witch had arrived; they were being called for the full run-through.

The hill slope had been transformed. According to the script, the scene with the witches was supposed to occur by the Holy Well, but Cyron had forbidden everyone to as much as go down into the cellars. Instead, a backdrop painted with stalactites and moss had been set up and the ground had been covered with sandcloth and plaster rocks. A white canvas diffuser, a big screen, had been set up to the sun side of the set. "We still got that bump on the backdrop," Tripod Krauss said in his flat American voice. "You got those Kliegl lights ready?" It was too far from the castle to use the generator and electric supply; they were running the lights from the engine of Cyron's Rolls. Krauss' assistant cranked it and it started with a roar.

Sabine was standing with Cyron. Cyron, in full eighteenth-century costume, was explaining something about the filming. He looked equally bizarre; his face was yellow, his wig pink. Sabine was looking up at him and giggling.

On this day of transformations she had dyed her hair.

Or, judging from the results, some Parisian professional had. Sabine had been a determined chestnut brown; she was now a blonde. And not just any blonde, but the sweet, wistful, Victorian blonde who plays the second lead and marries the hero's best friend. Not as sensual, not as potentially threatening as a hot-blooded brunette. A sweet young girl. Cyron was an expert at making over other actors.

It was hot on the slope, but Sabine was wearing a modest robe in pastel shades, buttoned to the throat and to the ankle. Underneath the robe she was dressed in black, the Second Witch's costume. The Third Witch would be André himself, who was consulting with Cohen now. André was dressed as an eighteenth-century version of Necrosar, skull makeup and all.

The Second Witch's costume was a bodysuit, thin and tight. In a very few minutes, André would know that his wife was with child.

"Turn off the generator." The racket died, leaving isolated sounds. The wind snapped against the canvas diffuser. Cyron and Sabine talked together. Reisden took his coat and wig off and stood with his arms away from his sides to keep from sweating into the costume shirt. It wasn't only from the heat that he was sweating. He looked away, off into the hazy distance. He could see, grey in the distance, the pyramidal artificial hills of Sabine's coal mines.

The First Witch arrived, the old man from Arras, Omer Heurtemance, mangy and magnificent; his grey hair and beard were tangled into elflocks and, in the July heat, he was wearing a vest of grey mouse fur. André looked down at him with lively interest.

"Actors, places," André called through his megaphone. His eyes moved over the group without stopping at Sabine. They kept going, looking for someone.

He didn't recognize her. Was that good or bad?

The girl with blonde hair huddled off her kimono, but under it was a thin black robe. "That's not—" André said, and squinted, and then said nothing, then, "Who is that?"

Sabine took her place by the witches' pot. The wind blew her blonde hair against her robe and her robe against her body.

André stared at her for a minute. Then, deliberately, he turned away, noticing nothing or pretending to notice nothing.

He began to explain the filming process to the actors.

"At the beginning of each scene, I will read the scenario, the description of the scene. We'll rehearse the action. Then we'll film." They would shoot this scene twice, he explained, to calibrate the lights against each of Krauss' two cameras. To get the actors used to the lights, the set would be fully lit during rehearsal.

He opened the scenario to the first scene and began to read. "WITCHES discovered in cave. WITCHES stir pot, perform curse. MC, AR enter stage left and react. OH tells MC his fate, then tells AR his . . ."

"What's that mean?" Omer Heurtemance asked. André explained it all again to him, spreading his arms and making cabalistic gestures over the pot, while the witch scratched at his beard. Heurtemance made an objection to the form of the curse. Ruthie Aborjaily, holding a clipboard, came forward to negotiate with him. André took another look at the Second Witch, surreptitiously, out of the corner of his eye.

Krauss' assistant cranked the Rolls. The lights flickered, crackled, and came on. Immediately, under the lights, with the breeze cut off by the canvas diffuser, the already sultry afternoon turned stovelike, and the fug under the lights took on the sharp cheesy odor of unwashed old man.

"All right, Mabet," André said. "Méduc, behind him." André walked into the camera-field and stood as far as possible from the Second Witch.

". . . Three, two, one . . . *On tourne!*" André said. Krauss began cranking. "Iris out!" The First Witch spread his arms and gestured widely over the pot. The Second Witch stirred it. André skulked around the edges of the scene, grinning like Fate. Mabet strode in from the left, reacted, and halted magnificently, drawing his sword. Méduc half-drew his. Heurtemance waggled his beard and pointed, giving Mabet his doom: he would reign like the king. But not his sons—he pointed at Méduc—*Méduc's* children will rule here, but not *yours*. Mabet and Méduc looked at each other in confusion. André raised his arms; his skull-face tilted back in a fleshless laugh.

"Stop and hold it." Krauss stopped the camera. Mabet and Méduc held it, living statues. An assistant put the pot on a wheelbarrow and pushed it bumping out of the scene; Sabine, Heurtemance, and André followed; a second assistant brushed the wheel-marks out of the grass; Boomer O'Connelly, the armorer, carefully set a flash-match on the ground. O'Connelly struck a match on his thumbnail and lit the flash fuse; Krauss cranked his camera; the flash went off, and Mabet and Méduc jumped back, astonished. The witches were gone.

"Cut."

Sabine wrapped her kimono protectively around her. Cyron smiled at her, patted her hand, told her she'd done very well. She gathered the robe over her stomach; it was only her concealing it that showed there was something to conceal.

André paled and said nothing. Just "Again."

André, Reisden thought, André, *see* it—

"In a minute," Cyron said, gesturing at his most magnificent, "when your wife is feeling restored." He couldn't wait any longer to boast. "After all, André, we must think of Sabine's child!"

André went absolutely white and still for a moment, and then— It was as if something enormous and black and from another dimension had manifested itself on the set. André watched while the object appeared, and grew larger, filling his world, slicing through what André called reality. André's shoulders squared, shuddering; he shook himself, like a rabbit that has seen an auto in the distance, a rabbit to be sacrificed; and then he was the theatre director again. But for a moment, the man who had been on the film set had not been André du Monde, theatre director, but someone Reisden had seldom seen, staring with a willed indifference that was the other face of anguish.

We've reached him, Reisden thought. And he wants to deny it. "Congratulations, André," he said into the silence.

"Makeup," the makeup man decreed. In the heat the actors' faces were blurring; they submitted to being touched up and powdered. "Places. *On tourne.* Iris out!" The First Witch spread his arms over the pot; one could see sweat stains under his arms. Mabet strode in, drawing his sword. The Second Witch stirred the cauldron, but—"André? Cut! Where's André?"

André had disappeared.

Chapter 34

When Reisden had been a bad young man, he had hit upon the golden rule of moral cowardice: When you say something no one wants to hear, say it in a restaurant. Wait until just after the first course.—The middle of shooting the first scene of a film will do quite as well.

Cyron had made sure that André had listened to him.

The lights were turned off, the generator turned off, leaving the scene suddenly windy and silent. The technicians cleared their throats and congratulated Sabine on her good news. "I'm going after André," Reisden said.

"Take off your makeup and costume," Cyron said. Doing anything else would signal André that they were concerned.

By now it was the end of the light anyway; the shadows were lengthening over Montfort. Most of the cast and crew were queueing up by the main entrance of the castle; meals would be served in the Great Hall, and the professionals knew not to be late. André wasn't with them. Reisden had had years of experience chatting up the Montfort kitchen staff; he got bread and cheese and wine, for bait, and went looking.

André wasn't in the kitchen garden, beyond the Lion Gate, or in the walled garden with the roses and the old immense globe-shaped bushes of lavender. He wasn't in the ruins of his father's scientific greenhouse or in the drying room of the laundry. Over the fields, veils of rain drifted, pink in the evening light. The shadow of the abbey towers stretched across the hill, across the chalk road, into the fields. Reisden looked up and saw a candle flickering in the more ruined of the two towers.

The top of the tower was half-overgrown with weeds and flowers. André was sitting on the cracked stone floor, barefoot, ankles crossed, staring at the candle. The breeze that always rose at night tugged at the candle flame.

"She looks like Mama," André said, turning frightened eyes toward him. "Mama was blonde."

Reisden said nothing.

André said nothing.

Reisden sat down, near André, in the shelter of the tower wall. The wind whispered around them, damp and chill. Eventually he pushed the bread and cheese over to André. André unpeeled the butcher-paper and examined the food with the air of someone who was not going to eat it. He was frighteningly thin; the candlelight picked out the joint at the corner of his jaw and a fold of skin by his mouth.

"When I think about my own son," Reisden said, "I think: not a life like mine. I want better for him."

André nodded.

Reisden said nothing, providing no resistance.

"Elle faisait toujours le petit bec, tu sais," André said suddenly. "Mama was picky, Papa said, picky about everything. It bothered her that her dresses were out of fashion. She didn't like to hoe in the garden or pick weeds. She would always wear gloves. I remember she had boxes of gloves, hundreds of pairs, every color, a pair of plaid gloves, red and green. She had gloves with frills and embroidery. She didn't want to wear them. They were for when we went back to live in Paris." André closed his eyes and leaned against the wall. "Papa had been a cavalry officer, that's what we do. She had met him in Paris during the war. She thought he was rich because he had a title and a castle, and romantic because he had been wounded. One time, I remember, it must have been the

worst of the winters after the war. We ran out of wood. Papa broke up a big old oak chair. She piled the pieces in the fireplace and burned them all at once, and she said that in Paris there were houses that were always warm and always light. And Papa shouted at her because she had burned all the chair at once."

He opened his eyes and stared into the candle. The sun was gone; the wind had come up strongly. The candle flame ripped away from itself and the candle went out. In the darkness André's voice was almost a child's. "They were always fighting," André said.

He's going to talk about it, Reisden thought wonderingly.

"It was summer then," André said. "The sickness came. Papa was a doctor, you know." Suddenly he was Necrosar. "He wasn't a doctor," he said in Necrosar's overprecise voice. "There simply needed to *be* a doctor; the Count pays for the village doctor; and he had no money so he doctored them. He gave his patients tea, *grass,* whatever he had. The horses usually lived but the people died." Necrosar paused, perhaps waiting for a laugh from the audience of the Necro, but it was too terrible for that. Reisden held his breath, didn't even look at André: and when he spoke again, miraculously André was back. "Papa meant very well," he said with the insistence of a small child. "Papa did his best for everybody. There wasn't anybody else. But Mama was afraid that he would bring the sickness back to us."

André stood up, blond hair and pale face visible in the crescent moon. "There were more people in the village then," he said, looking beyond the wall where blocks of darkness slumped: the ruins of tenant farmers' houses. "But the sickness came. One day everyone was dead, or gone. Papa buried them in the graveyard, there." He sprang up and leaned against the crumbling wall of the tower, pointing downward. On the graveyard side of the tower, the walls had fallen away, leaving nothing but a crumbling edge of floor. Bits of mortar gritted under their feet. Reisden looked over the edge, seeing stones and crosses in the iron-railed yard below the tower, the graveyard of the commune of Montfort.

"Here he is, then," said André. "He comes home. Papa." Suddenly he was acting it out. He put his hand to his forehead, then his stomach. " 'My head aches. My belly aches.' " He turned his head to the other side; now he was looking back at himself, pressing his hands together, biting his lips in a frozen smile. He curled his hands into fists and brought them up to his mouth, big-eyed like a terrified Necro ingenue. "Mama says, 'I'm so afraid. It's the fever. We'll die, Henri. You've brought the sickness to us!' " He dropped his hands and pointed at the air, shouting in a deep, rough, pained voice. " 'Foolish woman! Bring me my medicine bag!' And the mother doesn't do it," André said, "so the little boy has to. Papa is sick, very sick; he's throwing up. 'Aren't you ashamed, Henri, to send your child where you think there's danger!' "

Reisden said nothing; he was André's audience.

"She sends the boy outside," André said. "He goes into the graveyard. He sits down." André sat down. "There are new graves in a row, six, seven, ten. Some are big ones but some are little." André put out a hand to pat them. "There are no names and he wonders whose they are.—Can you imagine?" It was Necrosar again. "She *sends him outside*, where he's *safe*. Except from his *imagination*." Necrosar whispered. "The *dark* comes. The dark ought to *protect* him, but he can hear his father crying out from inside the castle. He shouts— he *shrieks*—and the little boy sits in the dark, between two mounds of dirt, and wonders, who is dead? Is Papa dead?

"He falls asleep, crying, and when he wakes up he doesn't hear his father anymore. It's dark. Quiet. So quiet. And his mother comes out of the castle with a candle in her hand."

André smoothed his long blond hair back, tilted his head to one side, knelt, and picked up the candle. He was calm suddenly, composed, half-smiling, the movements of his hands as delicate as though he were wearing frilled gloves. " 'Your father is asleep. Come with me. We're going to sleep too, and then we'll be safe forever.' "

He led the way down the stairs, barefoot, holding the unlit candle high. Reisden followed. The steps were soft with dirt; grass grew in the cracks of the stones. They came out the door and crossed the moonlit grass toward the graveyard gate, and there André stopped. The chalk path into the churchyard intersected the path toward the main part of the castle. At the crossing, the paths had been widened and straightened, and an area had been cut out and filled with gravel or concrete. In the faint moon the cross shone chalk white, but the grave below it was darker, starkly visible.

"See?" said whatever spirit or role inhabited André's body. "Here I am. They found me in my husband's arms. I loved him, after all. But what a fate for a girl from Paris! Buried in the country! Right there, see, in the moonlight. X marks the spot. People walk over me. Consecrated ground would spit me out—"

André's mother was buried at a crossroads, three hours by train from Paris. Why? Suicide? Murderess?

"Walk on her to keep her down," André said. "That's what the people say."

"And she poisoned you," Reisden prompted. "But you—threw it up? What?"

André jumped; some spell was broken; he moved away jerkily, holding up his moonlight candle, past the wooden crosses and rusted iron of the churchyard, through the ruined abbey door. Reisden followed, stumbling in the rubble. One of the side chapels, in better condition than the rest, had been re-roofed. Inside, rows of rush-seated church chairs faced the altar. The rear of the church was a stone wall, blank except for an iron door and inscriptions. André put his hand on a name.

"It doesn't happen in real life," André said earnestly. "Only in the theatre.—I'm a very imaginative boy," he added as if it were someone else's words. André leaned his cheek and the flat of his hand against the stone with his father's name.

"Nothing happens like I think," André said, "because I'm odd, like my mother. Odd. Like the flowers. Sweet peas; do you remember you told me about them? Red and pink. Red parents make pink children. But we don't like to talk about it, because we can't talk about how odd I am."

Reisden said nothing for a moment, because he couldn't. Think of the ways parents desert their children. Fighting with each other, playing at doctor and farmer and mistreated wife; killing each other or just dying, leaving the boy to say *You were murdered* and not to be believed; and leaving him to think that, whatever she had been, he was too, *but we don't talk about that;* no; we encourage André to become a cavalry officer like his father and to marry and have children.

André reached up above the door and, with Necrosar's teeth-baring grin, offered a key to Reisden. "We keep the key above the door for visitors!" He laughed; above them, in the ruins of the abbey roof, bats shrieked and flew. And then he said earnestly, even politely, "*Please* let's dig my parents up soon."

Chapter 35

By then it was past eleven at night. Perdita and Toby would arrive around four in the morning. Reisden wasn't going to drive them to Montfort; he drove into Arras and booked a room for them at the only hotel in Arras that, at midnight, was answering the phone.

The Grand Hotel de Commerce, off the Grand'Place, was unfashionable and comfortable: dining room with one long table already set for breakfast; lounge with a gramophone and a shelf of railway novels. Tonight it was crowded with wool-factors and tradesmen who had come for the Saturday market. Reisden did the necessary negotiations for a long-distance call to Paris.

"Becker? Would you come down here for an exhumation?" Eddie Becker, alias Eddie Profane, was the best exhumation man in Paris. "Thirty-five years ago, maybe cholera, maybe poison, just your thing." He switched to English, which the operator probably would not know, assuming the operator was listening in. "Do you mind its being a bit unofficial? The son has authorized it." Becker agreed to come Sunday night, for discretion getting out at Vimy and bicycling to Montfort. Reisden hefted the key André had given him. It weighed a pound at least and was flaking with rust. "Bring machine oil. And a burglary kit."

He washed off the Montfort chalk-grit in the bath. (It was already obvious that Montfort didn't have enough baths.) He had dressed again and lain down on the bed to get a few hours' sleep, before he thought about getting Perdita and Toby from the station to the hotel.

There were no taxis for hire at four on Sunday morning in a provincial town.

He went down and sat in the Renault, which was parked in the plaza. After ten years, he could still see and feel and hear the accident that had killed Tasy. He had been driving, back in the days when the world was full of experimental cars and any fool drove them. He got out and checked the Renault, shining his electric torch carefully into every part of the engine, lying down on the stones to look at the undercarriage.

Nothing ever finishes. A little boy sees his mother give his father medicine, and no one believes him that it's poison; so thirty-five years later he is still saying it, this time about his wife. Alexander Reisden crashes a car and kills his first wife. Years later, he won't drive Perdita and Toby. It makes one despair of cures.

He drove the car to the station and parked in the forecourt, by stacked crates of vegetables going to Paris. A wagon waited for freight; the horse was asleep in the shafts. In the station, the grilles were down on the ticket window and the coffee-seller, and the green plush benches were almost deserted; one commercial traveler was stretched out, newspaper under his shoes and over his head. A middle-aged woman was sitting under the light, taking notes on a clipboard. He blinked and recognized Ruthie.

"Hello, Dr. Reisden!" She smiled her shy smile and laid her work aside. Some vital forgotten thing was coming for Count André, she said; she was making sure it got to Montfort safely. He said he was meeting his family. She asked after them, then folded her hands in her lap and asked him directly: "How is Count André?"

In need of whatever comfort she could give him.

She nodded, businesslike; anything having to do with food,

tea, or comfort was Ruthie's preserve. "I'll make—" She corrected herself. "I'll teach his wife to make my special chicken soup."

"Not yet. He still thinks she's poisoning him."

"He won't forever—will he?—and I mustn't put myself forward at her expense when he does. I don't want to do anything wrong, he is our greatest friend," Ruthie said simply. "And Madame Sabine I think is very kind. Do you know, she gathered ashes from the Saint-John's bonfire for the production?" He remembered; ashes from the St.-John's fire protected those one loved. Ruthie looked in her bag and came up with a bulky envelope. "She gave me some for Jules."

"How is he?"

"Worrying about Count André and the production. He'll be here as soon as he won't be more trouble than he's worth."

"Sprinkle ashes on André," Reisden said.

They sat in silence for a while; she tucked the envelope in her purse, finished with her notes, and brought knitting out of her bag. He leaned against the back of the bench and closed his eyes, hearing the even ticking of the needles, as soothing as hearth fire. She should have been somebody's, he thought, perfectly conscious of what Perdita would make of that *somebody's*.

"Was it dreadful," Ruthie asked, "what happened to him?"

"It seems so. He told me a bit of it. His parents died. That alone would be enough."

"That's dreadful. It does get better," she said, knitting away steadily.

"You lost your parents early?"

"When Juley and I were seven and ten—that was far too long ago!—almost everyone was massacred in our village." She counted stitches, her round face as calm as if she had been talking about the weather. "Our parents, and our aunt and her son, and our neighbors."

He looked at the scar of grey in her hair. She had always

had it. "How do you—?" He hesitated. "How do you bear that?" he said.

"It would be impossible to live without forgiving," Ruthie said.

"You don't blame them?"

"I blamed myself," Ruthie said, "for a long time."

"I'm always afraid it'll happen again," he said. Ruthie nodded. "Perdita goes out on the street, with her eyesight. I think, don't do that. . . . What can one do? Nothing. Worry. Be afraid. Nothing. There's no one to forgive."

Ruthie put down her knitting and rummaged inside her purse as if she were giving a child throat lozenges, and put the envelope into his hand. He opened the envelope and looked at an aspirin tin, closed with tape.

"It won't do any harm," Ruthie said, smiling. He felt like a child; he distrusted being a child, holding this little tin of magic protection.

"Witches, Ruthie?" he said, putting it down.

Ruthie took the box and pried at the tape with her fingernail, pulling it away, taking off some of the paint, too. She opened the box, took a bit of the grey powder on the end of her finger, reached forward, and lightly touched his forehead, as if she were changing his mind. "There, Dr. Reisden. Now you do the same to Madame Perdita and your baby." She clicked the box shut again and gave it to him, suddenly blushing and smiling shyly, helplessly. "Heavens! I'll go back to my knitting.—I think," she said, "I think it is only that one does the best one can."

As it grew time for the train to arrive, he waited outside by the car. He laid the box with the ash onto the seat. The train pulled in, late. He hung back, watching Aline get off, then Perdita with his Toby slumped in her arms. Her shoulders were round with tiredness. Aline went off to make sure the luggage was unloaded. He crossed the pavement to meet them.

"Alexander!" she said. She leaned against him. "Have you had any sleep?" Yes, he lied. "Then you hold the baby."

"I have a hotel for us," he said, and went on before he could think any more about it, "I'll drive you there if you like." *If you like* was cowardice. It was all cowardice. He helped her into the car. "What's this?" she said, feeling the little box; she handed it back to him, and as she did, it opened, spilling ash onto her. He had not precisely meant it. "Nothing," he said, and closed the box again. The ash was on his fingers too; he smudged her cheek and marked his son's sweaty forehead. He would have done that anyway, touching them for tenderness' sake because they were there.

The mile took him fifteen minutes to drive. The motor clattered and choked in first gear. They could have walked to the hotel faster. They pulled up in front of the hotel; he set the brake very carefully; he helped them all down. Perdita, who had heard him say time and again that he absolutely would not drive her, said not a word. He wasn't sure whether he would have liked to be praised for his courage or whether it would have irritated him. But Toby snuggled into his arms. The concierge let them in; they dragged upstairs to their rooms—Aline to hers, the baby and Perdita to share the bed with him.

Neither Perdita nor he got undressed; she took off her hat and shoes, laid the baby down on the bed, lay down next to him, closed her eyes, and was asleep. He lay beside them, looked at Toby sprawled over most of the bed, got up, took one of the drawers out of the bureau, put a folded blanket and a pillowcase in it, and gently laid his son in it. "Sleep well, love; Papa and Mama are here." He lay down again. "Perdita?" She made a sleepy sound. The ash was still on her cheek. "Hold me," he said, and he held her, and sleep wrapped them all round like arms.

Chapter 36

Gilbert saw Alexander leave Paris. The green porte cochere of Jouvet opened; the car eased into the street; Alexander closed the door and got in the car and left without looking in his direction. Perdita's maid came out five minutes later, when Gilbert was still debating what he should do. Madame would speak with him later, Aline said. But now— *"Elle pleure!"* Aline said, making tear-tracks with a finger down her plump cheeks. Gilbert left a note and went away, feeling to blame for everything.

He walked miserably with Elphinstone through the strange city, and eventually found himself hungry and near a restaurant. He hesitated outside, looking at the menu. Elphinstone thumped down under one of the tables on the terrace.

Father's ghost hovered, faint in the sunlight. *You could never do anything right,* Father accused. How could a grown man, an *old* man, walk out of his house and leave his city with nothing but his dog?

He would go home. . . . The ghost across the table nodded vengefully.

But first Gilbert had to eat something. He worked through the names on the menu, consulting his pocket dictionary, looking for a dish that would suit both him and Elphinstone. In the middle of it he remembered that Father had always eaten the same dish every noon. Meat loaf on toast.

He looked in his pocket dictionary.

The French have no word for meat loaf.

Gilbert looked at the menu in wonderment. It was a very elaborate menu, with a colored picture on top and the dishes written below in purple ink. Perhaps there would be meat loaf tomorrow, but there was none today; he consulted the dictionary until he was quite sure of it. And perhaps there was no meat loaf in all of Paris. Gilbert had a picture of Father sitting furious over an empty plate, clashing his knife and fork and calling for his dinner, but there was nothing in Paris to feed Father.

Gilbert was always rather surprised when anyone had heard of him, but at the American Embassy they had heard of him. They sent a nice young man out with him. "Are you sure I am not giving you difficulties?" Gilbert said.

"No, sir, it's an honor."

By that afternoon he had rented a furnished apartment. Father roared at the waste of money.

But it is my money now, Gilbert thought. It is mine. It is my life.

For the second time in two weeks he used a public telephone. It worked quite differently than in Boston, but Gilbert persisted and prevailed. A voice rumbled over the phone from Jouvet. *"Elle n'est pah ici. Elle est pahtee pour l'instant."*

"Mr. Daugherty?"—for Roy Daugherty came from Boston too; Roy Daugherty had retired to Paris.

"Bert Knight! Well, I swan! Perdita was just leaving to come find you."

"Uncle Gilbert?" Perdita was breathless. "Alexander wants me to come to the country with him."

"Of course you must go, dear. I am not going away for the present."

"Oh, thank you," she said. "I shall work on him."

Work on him, Gilbert thought. Why must she? He should go home; he should not bother them. He thought of Perdita's face, pleading as she threw down the necklace she didn't know was diamonds. *You must tell him yourself!* "I will speak with him," he said to the vacant telephone line, though he did not know how or what to say.

Gilbert went out to Courbevoie for dinner with Roy Daugherty and Roy's pleasant French landlady, and during the course of the evening he spoke with Roy about Alexander and Perdita. Jouvet was in financial difficulties. The company was not recovering from its expansion as quickly as it ought. "If Alexander were not bothered by the money," Gilbert said.

"Druther eat his own guts than take Knight money." Roy Daugherty snorted. "He got his pride. Y'ask me, Bert, he got it screwed on tailwards and upside down."

"He has reasons," Gilbert said, thinking, All the same, it is not Father's money anymore; it is mine. Am I only what Father was? "Is there anything I can do for him?"

"Well, you can help me go lookin' for this file of André's."

So that was how Gilbert spent his first few days in Paris, at Jouvet.

He knew a great deal about Jouvet already. For four years, until Toby had been born, Alexander had written to him about it, enough to make him curious, and now he saw all of it. It was imposing, almost stern, but there was kindness in it. There was never any dark corner to frighten someone who might be frightened. In the past few years, Gilbert had seen many places where people worked and money was made; he liked Jouvet as well as any he had seen. Downstairs the nurses and doctors treated their patients kindly. Upstairs, in the testing rooms and the labs, they burrowed after medical mysteries with Elphinstone's persistence and celebrated their victories with jokes and beer. They sent a daily report to Alexander and put the jokes in. He has friends here, Gilbert thought. Roy Daugherty took Gilbert upstairs to Alexander's private office, and Gilbert saw the new books with Alexander's bookmarks in them, Alexander's notes spread over his desk; Alexander educating himself about madness.

"You think he's workin' too hard at it? Bein' obsessive, they call it round here."

"No, no, I do not think so. Father was overwhelming," Gilbert said. "You cannot imagine how—overwhelming, how—wholly Father ruled one— And Alexander is not overwhelmed."

"Well, I wonder if he ain't at least bothered some."

Roy showed Gilbert the secret door. On the stairs Gilbert saw his own picture, overexposed and huddled down in a corner, a shameful thing. He saw the red doorknobs, evidences of care and love. Alexander was a good man, doing a good thing. But he had driven past Gilbert on the street and turned his eyes away.

Alexander was not overwhelmed, but Gilbert wondered whether Alexander too did not sometimes see Father's wild eyes in the mirror, and he thought of Alexander turning his face away on the street. He has Father in him, Gilbert thought, and he sees Father in me.

And every day, while he was at Jouvet, one or another of the technicians, or the office clerks, or even Alexander's secretary looked at him, speculating. They see Alexander in me, Gilbert thought. This is exactly what Alexander fears.

Chapter 37

On Sunday evening, when everyone at Montfort was supposedly asleep, Reisden, Eddie Becker, and André broke into the crypt. In the theatre, grave robbing takes no more than prying off a coffin lid. Hah. They had to find the right coffin, of which there were far more than needed: X, Count of Montfort, and Y, Count of Montfort, and countesses and sisters and aunts in their crumbling boxes. André's father had been buried in a crude chalk sarcophagus and the lid had been mortared down. They chipped around under the lid, which took several hours. Then they sent André outside, ostensibly to stand watch. Becker half slid off the lid, looked inside, said, "Oh bugger," put on gloves and a disinfectant mask, lay down on the coffin lid, reached inside, and began taking samples, another process rightly glossed over in the theatre.

In theory you can test for arsenic forever; it's a metal and doesn't decay. But in acute arsenic poisoning the metal hasn't had time to settle into the tissues, so if one finds it at all, it's in the stomach contents or the intestines. Reisden tried not to let his imagination loose on the scraping sounds from inside the sarcophagus. "Oh *gloriously*-buggerit," Eddie Profane muttered, "reach me that light, won't you?" Cholera, on the other hand, does not persist at all; it is readily killed by drying out, or by burying the body in a shroud wetted with bichloride of mercury. So rummaging through the remains of the intestines, if Becker could find them, would be relatively safe.

If Henri-Julien de Montfort had died of cholera, and not, say, of something that happily wets up and becomes virulent again.

André was waiting under the broken arches of the abbey, looking up at the moon-sketched outline of the towers. They collected him and silently went inside, where all three of them scrubbed down with carbolic soap in the bathroom. Eddie Becker lacerated the outside of the steel specimen case with soap and a heavy brush. André looked at it with a face Hamlet would have envied: sorrow, fury, just a little repulsion. Murder most foul.

"How long will it take you to do the testing?" André asked.

"Becker's taking it to Paris." The Marsh test for arsenic is easy, but André wanted to test for a list of poisons a foot long.

They went out into the Great Hall. André took a last look at the specimen case, then looked up, behind the banners, to the scars of a disappeared staircase and the mark of a bricked-up room.

Chapter 38

My dear Mr. Daugherty—Perdita wrote to them. *I am translating for Mr. Krauss the cameraman, who doesn't speak any French. I go about with him from morning to night. There is nothing that could be mistaken for a laundry closer than Arras. We ferry mounds of diapers there. Alexander is even more busy than I, since he has been given some of the jobs that Mr. Fauchard would have done. So you can imagine our days. We barely see each other and have hardly spoken.*

Under the best of circumstances, Perdita learned, a film crew on location is a barely controlled mob. This was not the best of circumstances. The Vex-Fort had eight bedrooms, of which André, Sabine, and Cyron used three. The two New Buildings, which had been the abbey guesthouses, had thirty rooms between them, but there were many more than thirty people here. Wardrobe had a wardrobe mistress, five laundresses, and three full-time seamstresses including the harried Mademoiselle Huguette. There was Boomer O'Connelly, the Irishman who made the explosions, and Mr. Krauss and his assistant, and the men who worked the lights and the men who painted the sets and the men who took care of props.

And that was before the actors.

Citizen Mabet was full of actors: banquet guests, witches, soldiers, judges of the Revolutionary tribunal, a physician, an executioner, and crowds upon crowds. Monsieur Cyron had many friends, all of them distinguished, generals, political persons, important Conservative hostesses, who came to do a cameo and stayed the night. They brought valets, secretaries, and friends; some of them brought their horses. Every one of these amateur actors had to be rehearsed, fed, flattered, and got onto the set at the right time.

"Every nob's got a diet," the caterer complained. "He can't eat celery, she can't eat beef; this one has to have a cup of chicken soup exactly at ten o'clock, and the soup can't be too hot, but it can't be cold. . . . They're worse trouble than your baby."

"The *horses* have diets," Zeno Puckett's French assistant said.

"Not one of those women is the size she should be," Mademoiselle Huguette spoke up in her trembling voice. "Taking two inches in, letting two inches out, it's nothing to them."

Reisden, Perdita, and Toby were evicted from their bedroom in the main château as soon as the important guests began arriving. They had one cell in the New Buildings, with
two small rolling iron bedsteads with straw-stuffed mattresses. They slept a different way every night: beds pulled together, beds roped together, mattresses on the floor. Perdita
sent for Toby's bassinet from Paris.

There weren't enough dishes, forks, knives, glasses. The
tiny commune outside the wall was too small even to have a
boulanger. The bread, the milk, the meat but for mutton, and
the vegetables came from Arras. The house staff washed
dishes and changed linens from morning until bedtime. The
Holy Well pumped constantly—at night the pump from the
New Buildings woke Toby—but there was very little water
supply when spread over so many people, and much of it was
saved for washing the film during developing.

And all day they worked, every day, and what went on film
had to be perfect. The world isn't perfect. "Cloud," someone
would warn just as they were preparing to shoot, and they
would have to wait, looking up, while the cloud drifted by
overhead. A kitten wandered into the shot just as Cyron was
condemning an aristo to death. They filmed a scene without
noticing that a sheep was doing something private in the
background, and filmed and developed another before they
saw André's shadow falling over it.

If everyone had been calm, it would have been bad enough.
But tempers were very short. Germany had started a war.

It was not *the* war between France and Germany, at least,
but it was a test, everyone said. Germany had sent a warship
to Agadir in Morocco, which no one had heard of before but
now seemed important, a center of finance and trade for the
whole southern Mediterranean. The German warship was sitting in Agadir harbor with its guns trained on the town.

The war was not only in Morocco but between Cyron's
army friends and the set crew. Two young cavalry officers and

three infantry officers were helping to stage the big battle scene. They swaggered around boasting of what France would do to the Boche. "It's you lot who'll start the war," one of the set builders said, "but we'll have to fight it. Instead of sitting on your round pink arses—"

"You dirty Boche-lover—"

"Shut your mouth," said one of the laundresses. "What about that treaty? Who broke that first?"

"Franco-German cooperation, hah! That was a farce from the beginning—"

"The capitalists make money and the workers die!"

There was one bar in the half-ruined commune of Mont-fort, and it was too small for the factions that developed. The army men drank at one end of the zinc, the tech crew at the other. "Bloodsuckers!" the union men said. "Cowards!" the soldiers said.

On July fourth—the Fourth of July; her American soul missed fireworks—Spain officially declared that it supported Germany in Morocco and England that it supported France. The bar discussions got out of hand. Bottles crashed. In the yard behind the bar, men grunted as they hit one another. The fights woke Toby, who cried and woke everyone on their part of the floor.

"What does it mean?" she asked Alexander.

"Diplomatic maneuvers," he said. "Germany wants concessions in Africa. The whole war will be fought over a mahogany table in Berlin."

Alexander was avoiding her. He got up before dawn, to practice for the big battle scene, and then was always doing something. He wasn't in all the scenes; she and Aline and Toby kept track of when he was acting, but there were whole days when he wasn't, and he wasn't with her either. He came in late and fell into bed, hardly speaking to her except to say good night.

Toby, who was usually such a happy baby, fussed. He was

getting a tooth; he missed his house and his toys; there were too many people here and he didn't know any of them. When Alexander left early in the morning, he would wake Toby and Toby would shriek. Perdita walked him, held him, comforted him, "it's no worse than being on tour," but he sobbed and grizzled and sweated against her neck, and just when she thought he had finished he burst into howls again and people began pounding on the walls.

"Don't leave so early," she asked Alexander. He had to, he said; he was the star of the battle scene. "Don't wake the baby, then!"

"I don't mean to wake him!"

"But you do! You should go live in a tent in the fields!"

Of course she had to apologize to him afterward, which didn't help her temper at all; and she had hurt him, which didn't help his.

"Your little boy's sick," said Count André, noticing Toby crying. "He'll *die*," he added hollowly.

Perdita snapped. "I should think even you would be sick of your nonsense, Count André."

My dear Mr. Daugherty—Half of Citizen Mabet is in the can, as Mr. Krauss says. She wrote him and Uncle Gilbert a note at lunch. On one side of the hill, horsemen were practicing for the big battle scene, which, she was told, would be the largest scene of its kind ever filmed in France. Horses thumped up the hill in a geyser of dust; someone was banging a drum. On the other side of the hill (the invaluable sun side) a party scene was being filmed. A string quartet played with a tinny plucked-string instrument; it must be a harpsichord, a real eighteenth-century survival rescued from someone's attic. She longed to have the leisure to explore it. Pink clouds danced, heels thumped on a wooden floor; people laughed and chatted on the sidelines, filling up the scene. Below everything the camera clicked and whirred.

Count André's wife is doing well. Sabine was the center of every scene she played in. She wasn't an actress as Perdita understood acting; actors had beautiful voices, Sabine had a tiny nasal breathy one. But she was one of those people everyone looked at; Perdita had been at the center of things and knew what it sounded like. "Put that spot behind her head," the American cameraman said. "Okay, honey, smile, don't move your head, right? Ya look great. Ya look gorgeous." Perdita had to translate all this. There is no doubt, she thought. I miss the audiences. I miss being the center of attention; I miss being a person and not just the baby-minder and the cameraman's translator, the useful woman who speaks both languages and doesn't have anything else to do. *I* shall go live in a tent in the fields. And I shall take the harpsichord and a piano.

Star of the battle scene indeed. She was furious with *him*, the anger of the real performer for someone who hogs the spotlight without having done the work to deserve it. She didn't have enough practice time, which always made her nasty.

The one sensible suggestion that anyone had had was providing entertainment in the evenings. There was a terrace outside the old main building, with a nice flat green lawn on two levels, and every night the actors put on some kind of amusement. General Pétiot, who came frequently, told funny stories. The American horse-handler, Zeno Puckett, played the banjo. Monsieur Cyron performed magic tricks; a chauffeur did comic songs; three of the maids did a chorus line; everyone wanted to do something. Sabine told fortunes. Perdita played "The Maple Leaf Rag," "The Bow Wow Rag," W. C. Handy's "St. Louis Blues."

It was her protest, to play American songs: the only way to say what she was feeling. She wore Uncle Gilbert's necklace because it was too valuable to leave around. Wearing it, she thought of the money it represented. Money to go to America. She thought of America in shockingly concrete terms. An apartment, a place of her own. She even knew where in New York she would live.

She didn't want to leave him. She only wanted to talk to him about Uncle Gilbert, to have him talk with Gilbert, to have them all at peace with each other again. Until they were, she felt breathless, as though there were a storm coming.

It is a good thing at times like this to be close, to have breakfast together, touch hands, kiss, love, remind oneself how precious the other person is. "Alexander," she would ask him, "do you have a moment? Let's talk. Let's just sit together."

But he avoided her.

Chapter 39

Sabine told fortunes.

Apart from seeing death, she had thought she had no talent for fortunes at all, but last winter her treasure of a father-in-law had taught her how to force cards. Sabine could put the Last Judgment or the Emperor anywhere in a deck she pleased. And fortune-telling is only telling people what they want to hear—the sort of thing girls are trained for, whether they are witches or no.

She turned up art, harmony, and music all together to please Dr. Reisden's wife. For Papa Cyron, she dealt a full ten cards of good luck; he knew what she was doing but it pleased him all the same. For a maid, she dealt a journey ("to a big city! Paris?"); for a young lieutenant, glory.

A real witch tells her clients their dreams.

Sabine could tell fortunes with Voyage of Life, the new Waite tarot, straw in water, Chinese bamboo, herbs, any one of a dozen ways; but her favorite was the Oracle of Napoléon, because of two cards in it, the Bear and the Nesting Storks.

The Bear was the Prussians. " 'An enemy sly, here is the Bear. Treachery's nigh, so watch and beware!' " And the Nesting Storks meant Alsace. The soldiers laughed to see the Storks. "I'll get to fight in Alsace, it looks like! Three cards away from the Gentleman, that's not so far."

Sabine made sure the Storks were near the Gentleman. She surrounded them with the Star, the Key, the Tree, the Castle, the Tower, and the Mountain: "You will have great luck and long life! Go on a journey, seize your luck! Strike hard, strike first!" She gave the Gentleman allies: the Dog, the Cavalier. She sent into faraway exile the Dark Clouds, the Robber Mouse, the Cross, and the Grave.

The Russians came in officially on the French side. "You're a marvel, Madame Sabine, didn't you say that France would have more allies? The Dog, that's the English bulldog. The Cavalier must be Russia."

Everyone adored her. Everyone believed her. Even while the Paris papers said the situation was only a diplomatic crisis, the fighting would be in Morocco at best, the officers believed their fortunes and dreamed of war in Europe.

Chapter 40

Jules arrived only three days after everyone else, leaning on two canes, gritting his teeth, needing to be helped to sit down and to rise; but he had had to come. He had heard from Gehazy. They had both got postcards. Reisden's was of the crypt of St.-Vaast Cathedral in Arras. There was a message, *Donnez-le-moi*—"Give me it"—and a date and a time, typewritten in purple ink. *16/7 11h.*

The sixteenth of July, the Sunday of Bastille Day weekend. Eleven in the morning was High Mass, when the church would be crowded. A place for spies to meet.

Jules had his own, identical but for time and place. *Donnez-le-moi,* Saturday afternoon the fifteenth, by the obelisk in the Place Victor-Hugo.

"He wants the secret from both of us," Reisden said. "And he bloody well doesn't tell us what it is."

Gehazy didn't intend to spare Jules, even after what he'd already done to him.

Reisden sent a letter back to Gehazy. *We don't know. Tell us where we're looking.*

He didn't tell Perdita about this threat. He was ashamed of it, where it had come from, the way he was ashamed about Richard and Leo.

With a Kodak he bought in Arras, Reisden climbed up into the abbey bell tower; he clicked a panorama all the way round, showing the base of the tower, the ruined abbey, and the maze of Montfort castle. From the air the walls of Montfort looked like the ruins of a city. Around it, roads, woods, hedges, farms, bits of village at more or less regular intervals along the main road to Arras. To the east, the same flat land, the rutted road to Neuville-St.-Vaast and Vimy, the woods along Vimy ridge; farther east still, the artificial pyramids of the Wagny coal mines.

Ruthie, Jules, and Reisden spread out the photographs and divided the castle into sections. Each of them had a list of places to search.

The abbey: nothing. Jules spent a night looking for secret hiding places, shining a torch down into the tumbled stones and leaning forward stiffly to peer at them. The abbey crypt, the abbey towers: nothing. The Marconi aerial was conspicuous but not connected. The walls of the castle, the towers, the outbuildings, the seventeenth- and eighteenth-century New Buildings: nothing. Reisden searched white chalky walls, rooms without doors, stairs leading nowhere. Potting sheds, gardens; the outhouses behind the New Buildings; the generator; the apple orchard and the farmers' barns at the back of the hill; the stone-dump of broken chalk. The Lion Tower. The little towers scattered in the grass, some no higher than a man's knee, scratched with their patriotic slogans. Nothing.

Reisden drove the Arras road, looking for some signs of military activity. No. At Arras, factories for farm equipment and fertilizer. A big chalk factory with a sign like a school slate. Farther north and east, farm country. He passed Mademoiselle Françoise's isolated house, standing out yellow against the woods. Toward the village of Vimy, the road climbed. He let a bit of air out of the tires, for traction, and drove up on the ridge by Vimy, where he could see all over the valley from Montfort to Sabine's mines.

Rich land. Coal mines. Sugar beets; most of France's sugar came from here. Rich Flanders farmland, land worth taking. Not protected by anything but the Citadel at Arras.

He decided to look at the Citadel. The key to doing that was the battle scene.

Méduc's attack on Montfort castle would be the most difficult sequence of the film. Squads of men would charge up Montfort hill, battling Mabet and his forces. Cannons would fire into hundreds of men in hand-to-hand combat. It was as large a scene as had ever been filmed; it would use two cameras at once and take three days to film; and it would use conscripts from the Citadel in Arras.

Fifteen men were needed to coordinate the attack and train a group of soldiers each. Reisden volunteered to be one of them. So every morning before sunrise, he left his son crying and Perdita asking him to stay, and practiced the scene.

Reisden was leader of Méduc's group, Group A, which would be twenty-two men. In the dark he would stumble out of the New Buildings and make his way to Group A's rallying point, a patch of bushes behind the sheepcote. Once in place, he would swing his torch over his head to let André, on the abbey tower, know he was there. From behind the wall, from the edge of the sheep field, from the apple orchard, the gate at the wall, and the churchyard below the tower, men raised electric torches and lanterns.

"Everyone ready!" André was using a megaphone; his voice carried brassy and clear in the darkness. "Three, two, one . . . *On tourne!* Iris out!" And, from the Abbey tower, a trumpeter would begin to give them their cues.

First four notes of "La Marseillaise": that was Reisden's cue to scramble up the hill, Méduc leading his army. Torchlights sliced the darkness; Groups B, G, and F (Puckett and two of the officers) ran up the hill, slipping, scraping their boots, coughing in the dust they raised. Boomer O'Connelly strode up and down where the row of cannons would be, banging a drum. Up at the New Buildings, lights went on and servants leaned out windows to swear at the actors. From somewhere to the east, toward Wagny-les-Mines, a cock answered the trumpeter.

After a week of practice, they were ready to teach the soldiers.

The Citadel was like provincial army barracks everywhere: rules and regulations were posted on every wall, guards snapped to attention at every door. Conscripts drilled on the huge parade ground, their figures wavering in the heat. Only the horses, switching their tails in the long brick stables, allowed themselves to look bored.

The "aggression" had cast its shadow here too. The commandant took Reisden into his office and interviewed him personally before letting him go inside. Puckett had to go through none of this; he was an American, either neutral or on the French side.

They met their men in the dining hall. "This is your flag," Reisden told his recruits, showing them a banner from the Necro props room. "This is your cue. When I wave the flag and you hear your cue—if you hear it, the scene will be noisy—you'll charge up the hill." The men nodded eagerly, sitting straight on the hard benches, grinning at being soldiers on film.

When the recruits went off to be measured for uniforms, the commandant gave Cyron and his guests a tour of the Citadel. Certain doors were left closed, as the commandant looked meaningfully at Reisden; but Leo had taught him how to guess from what he saw. Long rows of seventeenth-century barracks testified to the size of the garrison. Underground, the chill arsenal gleamed behind bars; Reisden instinctively counted rows of guns.

They were let see only parts of the arsenal; behind a barred door, a tunnel lined with more doors led into the distance. Reisden wondered what they were hiding. Not simply more weapons, but something that needed ventilation, men or horses; in the distance he could just see the light of a ventilation shaft.

He had been too well trained to linger at something interesting. Leo would have sent a second person to look into the Citadel.

It wasn't his business. Gehazy had no interest in the Citadel.

The younger men walked the long circumference of the brick-and-granite walls. They sat on the top of the wall, with the parade ground on one side and the long green slope of the moat on the other, and watched soldiers replanting flower beds and whitewashing outbuildings. It was a humid, hot, lazy July afternoon; the grass smelled sweetly damp. The soldiers waved up at the film people.

"Look at 'em, poor little vermin," the Citadel horsemaster said, taking his pipe out of his back pocket. "Wanting to get into action."

"Will they go to Morocco?" Reisden asked.

"Unless this Morocco thing comes home to us. What do you say, Austrian, is this Wilhelm's excuse to invade France?"

"I hope not."

"Me, too. Victory, glory, that's for the films."

Reisden looked out over the city to the northeast. He could see the old stables and the cattle market, somnolent in the sun. "Why did Vauban build this fort south of the city?"

The horsemaster puffed at his pipe and grinned. "You know what they call this place? The Beautiful Useless."

"Why not refortify Montfort? Isn't it a better location, closer to the frontier?"

"What for?" the horsemaster said, not even needing to think. "It's got no armory, no stables, no barracks, no place to practice your drill nor put your firepower; no town, just two or three farmhouses by the walls, one bar, and no whores to speak of. Montfort 'castle'? Germans don't want it any more than we do."

Merde de merde. What was the secret of Montfort?

It was hot continually. They worked all day on the sun side of the hill. The canvas diffusers stank, and the fresh paint on the sets, and the car engine that powered the lights; and the actors perspired and stank because there was only one bath at Montfort. At the end of scenes they whipped off their wigs, which were hot as fur hats, and drank bottled water, and sweated. The carbon flaked off the arc lamps and irritated their eyes. They wore dark green glasses against the glare.

They rehearsed and rehearsed again. They waited for the light to be right, and caught it sometimes and sometimes not. André diffused the sunlight with curtains he ripped from the windows. He directed it with mirrors. He reacted to Sabine's presence by overworking himself and his actors. He had had a reputation for being a considerate director. Not now. "Faces are only an excuse for shadows," and he worked Reisden and the other actors until the ochre ran down their faces and their shirts sweated to dark rose.

As far as Reisden could tell, André was not sleeping at all. At night sometimes Reisden would sit with him while he worked on cutting the film. André had new ideas about that, too, and he would not trust the cutting to anyone else. "What about your wife, André?" Reisden asked. "What about yours, Reisden?" André said. Reisden would go back to Perdita and Toby to find them asleep, uncomfortable on their straw mattresses. In the dark he would lie awake, itching from the straw, then get up, take a lantern, and explore yet another tower.

Gehazy had picked up Reisden's letter. But Gehazy didn't answer.

Reisden was supposed to find the secret. He was supposed to send André to Katzmann. He'd succeeded at neither, and he began to be afraid he'd fail. He did not talk to Perdita about the consequences of failure, he could not.

Reisden wanted Perdita and Toby with him, eating picnic lunches on a white rampart or against a white wall. He wanted to talk with her, the talks they needed to have; he wanted to enjoy his son. But there wasn't enough time, and he didn't want to be with them when he was— Say "spying," it was what he was doing.

"What are you thinking of?" Perdita asked him. "You're very quiet."

"Nothing, love."

She was very quiet, too. She wore Gilbert's teardrop; he hoped because it was too valuable to leave around, and not to remind him of unfinished business, but he knew Perdita. They had a little time together, never enough. They played with Toby; they talked about filming.

They didn't talk at all.

My dear Milly, Have you ever met someone who thinks she is perfectly right? Sabine does.

"I can't wait until the movie comes out," said Sabine to Perdita. "What's it like to be famous? Do people take pictures of you? Do you go to a lot of parties? Do they ask you to sign autographs?"

"I'm not famous," said Perdita. It was hard work, she said: hours of travel, days of travel, finding the theatre, checking the piano, practicing (never enough!), performing, smiling and shaking hands and heading for the railroad station again.

"It's much nicer for *movie stars*," said Sabine. "I'm going to have a private car and flowers in my room every day and people are going to *love* me because I'll be a movie star."

"With a baby it's very much harder," Perdita said.

"Somebody else will take care of the baby."

Poor baby, Perdita thought, juggling Toby on her knee. Sabine seemed to think her baby would just disappear except at convenient times. She and André were alike; for them family was all about themselves. If Sabine and André ever made peace, Perdita thought, they would fit beautifully together; both were complete monsters of egotism. They would grow old together, sitting on either side of the fireplace, André talking about death and Sabine about herself, and neither one of them listening to the other.

She was beginning to be cynical about marriage, she thought, to think the best it offered was two egotists ignoring each other. What were she and Alexander going to do that was better?

You're jealous, her friend Milly wrote. *Wouldn't you love to have her money! And her—obliviousness! She'll be one of those old women with an inch of makeup and a young boyfriend. The boyfriends will use drugs and have nervous breakdowns. And if anyone dies while she's talking she'll say, "But you're not paying attention!"*

Reading this with her magnifying glass, Perdita smiled in spite of herself.

One thing Perdita didn't like at all about Sabine. Every night, when other people entertained, Sabine told fortunes. The young officers flirted with her and she dealt out the cards for them. The cards made a whisper like soft slippers dancing on a ballroom floor. *Glory, fortune, fame.* And then the officers would drink on the terrace and talk about Cambon and Kinderlin-Waechter negotiating in Berlin.

"Let them fail! We'll march into Berlin."

Sabine was encouraging them to war, and only because she wanted to be the center of attention.

Chapter 41

Cyron asked Sabine to tell Dr. Reisden a particular fortune. "Tell him he'll have good luck," Cyron said, smiling and pulling the end of his nose, *"if—"* And he told her what to say.

"Well, all right, that's not hard."

They grinned at each other conspiratorially. "You're a good girl."

"I know!"

That night at the entertainment she found Dr. Reisden and dealt him cards before he could object. "You've had a run of bad luck." She had dealt him all the worst cards across the top row, the Book, the Cross, the Catafalque. "Oh, my, there you are just below them. But everywhere except *above*, you're surrounded by luck." He was looking away from her. "Pay attention to me! The Tree and the Key next to each other, that means you're close to your goal. Look, the Ring to the right, between you and the Lady; you'll have success in love."

He looked back at her and half-smiled: good news that he wanted but didn't believe in, because it came from cards.

"The Château, the Bright Clouds, the Friend, the Child, the Cavalier, the Road, those are all good cards. You're going to have great prosperity. Fortune will smile on you. A friend will help you, a stranger will give you good news. You're going on a journey. *Look below,*" Sabine said.

She wished she knew what it was all about. Up and down

were important for only a few cards in the Oracle of Napoléon. What was Dr. Reisden supposed to understand?

One night, during the entertainment, something happened,
something that disturbed Sabine. Papa Cyron, whose turn it
was to entertain, came out onto the terrace with something
that looked like a feather duster. He unfolded it and it was a
puppet, an ostrich with long legs and a long feathered neck
and a tiny head that waggled absurdly. He held it by its sticks
and paraded it up and down and made it bow and then, as he
whistled a soft little tune, he made it begin to dance. Step to
the right, kick, step to the left, kick, the puppet-bird and Papa
Cyron pointed their toes together, as serious as two priests
dancing.

And then André got up from the little wall where he had
been sitting and came forward, and he began to dance, too,
step and kick so that there were three of them in line, man and
puppet and man, all in rhythm together. Everyone looked at
them; only Dr. Reisden whispered to his wife what was going on.

And Sabine understood something uncomfortable, threatening; André and his stepfather shared something that was
not about her. It disturbed her. It was something they had
done together as a family, without her. It was as if a frame that
had held only her picture now held a second one.

Sabine jumped up and danced, too. The rhythm was broken, André retreated into the darkness, and she and Papa Cyron danced instead.

Chapter 42

The trick guillotine for the film was delivered to Arras on the tenth of July, Monday. It was set up on the stage of the Théâtre d'Arras. Charles De Vere, who had designed the trick, was there to train the actors.

Sabine had seen guillotines before: In Paris, the one that had actually beheaded André's great-grandfather was now a decoration in the garden of André's and Cyron's house. The real one wasn't large; the space under the blade was no wider than a narrow door, and she had to duck under the blade's rusted edge.

But this one— It stood on a massive red platform, which one had to crane upward to see. The guillotine posts were painted dead velvety black and were scrawled with Revolutionary graffiti: DEATH TO ARISTOS, LONG LIVE DEATH, and a skull whose neck spurted blood. Swags of tricolor bunting draped the platform. The upper half of the circular lunette into which the victim's neck fit was painted with a red-and-black half-bull's-eye. The steel blade gleamed like Necrosar's blue eyes.

The guillotine blade was terrifying, it was fascinating, it made one want to lie down on the plank, looking up at its edge. Sabine felt intensely alive.

The director of the theatre, who was playing the King's tax collector, was green with terror; he looked as if he would throw up. André looked up at it as if it were Sarah Bernhardt. "Beautiful," he breathed. "Beautiful."

"Thank you, Monsieur le Comte." Charles De Vere was a kindly, grey-haired man with a magician's spade-shaped beard. "Monsieur Jules, how glad I am to see you're better. You're playing the Executioner? Good." Jules Fauchard bowed stiffly from the waist. "Monsieur Krauss, Monsieur de Reisden . . . Ah, Madame! Ah, Monsieur Maurice!"

"One problem with it," Papa Cyron said. "I don't want anyone to see the mechanism." He walked across the stage to peer underneath the platform. "Can we make this bunting longer?"

They negotiated and measured for bigger swags. Then Papa Cyron and Sabine were escorted to chairs shaded by potted palms. The rest took their places on the guillotine platform. The photographer stood on a tall stepladder in the orchestra pit, at the height at which he'd photograph them.

"Now this is very dangerous equipment, madame, gentlemen," said the prop-maker De Vere. "This is a working guillotine. The blade weighs thirty pounds." An assistant was taking props from a long, narrow wicker basket. The assistant handed his master a section of peeled pine trunk, about the diameter of a neck. De Vere balanced it on the lunette. The half-circle outlined it, drawing attention to it. De Vere fitted the top of the lunette over it.

The second assistant hauled on a rope to pull the blade up to the top of the posts. The blade slid upward in jerks. It was almost too heavy for the assistant; he had to wind the rope around his wrists.

"You aren't frightened, are you, Binny?" Papa Cyron said, leaning forward. "I wouldn't want to startle you, in your delicate condition."

It was just in her stomach, in her womb, she felt the guillotine most.

"When the machine is to be used," De Vere said, "the executioner pulls the blade up to the top of the posts. The victim kneels with his body resting on a small wooden platform behind the machine." He showed them the platform. "His neck rests on the lunette. We place a wicker basket next to the guillotine to receive his body; a square wicker hamper stands in front of the guillotine to catch his head." De Vere moved the narrow wicker basket a bit closer to the platform.

"Now. Are we ready? Monsieur le Comte, if you would do the honors?"

André came up the stairs to the guillotine.

"Everyone stand away, please. No one close to the front of the machine. Thank you. Now, Monsieur le Comte, when you're ready, pull on the rope."

André looked up at his machine, and Sabine looked at him. The blade hung above them, its edge a line of fire from the stage lights. André pulled. The thud jarred the whole stage. Sabine heard the blade ripping the air.

"The executioner releases the blade," De Vere said, "which falls and slices through the victim's neck. The decapitated head falls into the hamper. The body rolls into the larger basket." He tilted the long, narrow wicker hamper, and the sheared remnant of the pine trunk rolled out.

"Now I hope I have persuaded you that this is a very dangerous trick. Monsieur Boufils—?"

The director put his head on the block, closing his eyes tight. "You're not going to die today, monsieur!" Sabine called; she knew.

"You are kneeling," De Vere said, "yes, yes . . ." He fitted the director's chin onto the bottom half of the lunette. "Put your head between those two long dowels."

"Can I see?" Sabine said.

"Yes, of course, madame, but be careful."

Papa Cyron and she both climbed on the platform. The dowels were painted black, the first sign of trickery. "Executioner?" De Vere said. "Make sure that the victim's head is securely held."

Jules thumped the wooden collar and nodded.

"Now, our Executioner must have a costume. A black cloak," the assistant handed it to Jules, "and a black hood," De Vere produced one from the air. Jules laid his canes aside and put them on, leaning against the guillotine post. The hood caught on the cage on his jaw. "Marco, make a note, a bigger hood for Monsieur Jules."

The blade gleamed grey like death's veil. Sabine felt momentarily dizzy.

"Now, Monsieur Boufils, we want no trickery, so the Executioner will secure your wrists. Monsieur, your right hand—good—" With his cloak and hood, Jules could hardly see to help them. They snapped handcuffs around Monsieur Boufils' wrists and secured them to the guillotine frame. He could move neither his head nor his hands. Sabine smelled sweat on him, like a sacrificial victim; he looked as if he were about to cry.

"Can you get out, monsieur?" The director braced himself and tugged backward, doing nothing but scraping his chin and wrists. "No. You're caught, immobile. Now, Monsieur Jules, you are going to come across here to pull the rope. Step just in front of him," De Vere demonstrated, "on this plank. Where *that* stain is. No, don't pull yet!"

Jules made his way across the platform, using one cane. Suddenly, as Jules stepped on the plank, the lower part of the lunette fell away. The poor astonished little director slipped backward and found himself safe, looking at the back of the lunette. His hands were still cuffed to the frame but his head was free and out of the path of the blade.

"Move the dowels a little with your head, Monsieur Boufils," De Vere said, "but don't move your shoulders. That's good. Twist your hands in the cuffs, pull.—Now, Monsieur Jules, here is your part of the trick. You have this mask under your cloak. You have blocked the audience's sight of Monsieur Boufils as he frees himself. You quickly fit this mask over the hole in the lunette, like this, and hook it onto these hooks.—Are you ready, Monsieur Jules? David, the rope; unhook it and pull it up the rest of the way."

It was only an illusion after all. Sabine moved around to the front of the guillotine to see it. It was a rubber head painted to look like the director. As the director moved the dowels, the rubber head writhed and silently screamed, showing white teeth and a red tongue. The hooks were large to catch the mask but painted black against black. The director's hands writhed on either side of the mask, out of the path of the blade. Mask and hands together looked like a living victim.

Tricks are disappointing, Sabine thought.

"After Monsieur Jules crosses the stage and before he pulls the rope," De Vere said, "we see the mask for perhaps a half a second, just enough to give an impression. The bands are attached to the mask near the mouth. Wires ensure that the skin also stretches around the glass eyes." He unhooked the mask and showed them the wire bracing behind the rubber. The photographer came onstage to look.

"Now the aristo is about to be beheaded. Monsieur the Director, I'll ask you to do a little business with your hands. Just as the blade comes down, clutch your hands, then let them go limp. Perfectly limp, like that. Ready?" The photographer retreated down the stairs and back onto his stepladder. "Ready, David? Ready, Monsieur Jules? Pull the rope."

Jules pulled. The platform thudded like a drum. The still-writhing head suddenly went limp and expressionless, gave a ghastly hop forward, and fell into the basket. The Executioner threw a cloth over the "victim," unfastened its wrists, and let the body fall into the big basket.

"That's all you need to do, Monsieur Boufils—Monsieur?"

The "body" lay still for a moment, then sat up hurriedly. "I'm feeling a little—" Monsieur Boufils scuttled offstage.

Sabine put her hand on her stomach. She leaned back against one of the supports of the guillotine. "Madame, are you all right?" De Vere asked.

"Oh, yes—yes—"

She was frightened of that guillotine. And the fright was beautiful. She felt like a sacrifice, helpless, chosen, with Necrosar's blue eyes looking down on her. She imagined herself lying on the plank, in a flowing white gown, her hair glowing light. The camera approached her.

She had so close a sense of death that she looked into the shiny blade to make sure she was not grey. But no, there she was, blonde, beautiful, alive, alive, alive.

Chapter 43

"Your mother didn't poison your father. He died of cholera."

Reisden had got Eddie Becker's report from Paris. In the evening he went to see André. André was gluing bits of film together; lengths of film were clipped to strings, like laundry drying, and more bits were spread on the table, which was covered in clean white paper. André was wearing white gloves. He laid the film down and stripped the gloves off, took the paper, and read it through.

His face didn't change. Ever since the news about Sabine he had had a stare when no one was looking at him, a stare partly angry, partly afraid: a man trapped. "I don't feel different," he said now.

"Give yourself time."

"*She,*" André said. "She *did* try to poison me."

"She poisoned herself at least. This will make a difference in how you feel," Reisden said. He hoped.

André drew the gloves on again. He held up a piece of film against the light for Reisden to see. It was a close-up of Sabine. Krauss had backlit her and lit her face with a mirror; she glowed. "I don't like to touch her," André said. "Not even with these." He spread his fingers in the gloves. "Not even this."

Reisden nodded, not reacting, letting him know he was heard.

"Am I—different?" André asked.

Oh, André. "Than what?"

"Different. Like they say Jules is different . . ."

"Are you?"

"Perhaps I'm nothing." André did this as Necrosar, pulling his lips away from his teeth. "Nothing."

The two men sat together for a while. "I love my son more than anyone else in the world," Reisden said finally. "More simply than I thought anyone could love anyone. That may happen to you. If you work at it."

"With her?" André turned his face away like a man flinching.

"Sabine tells me my fortune is below," Reisden said dryly.

By now Ruthie, Jules, and he had searched everywhere they could think of but for one place, the lower cellars of Montfort. The uppermost cellar was in use, but the two levels below it were supposed to be dangerous and were locked. Cyron kept the only key; Reisden had asked him for it and been refused. "There's nothing down there," Cyron had said, "it isn't even a proper basement. There's bad air and no ventilation. You'll get lost and never come out."

Ruthie contemplated their photographic map and put her fists on her hips.

"Count André can get us into the cellars," Ruthie said.

Until about halfway through its length, *Citizen Mabet* is about revolutionaries taking power. But after that it is about the death of a family, the struggle between a father and a son. Mabet quarrels with his son; Méduc flees to Paris, leaving his wife and son behind, counting on his father to protect them. He is wrong. The Revolution has grown larger than Mabet. Mabet makes a terrible, tragic mistake, ordering the arrest of his son's family. A mob goes to the Méduc château.

On Wednesday the twelfth, in the cool, early morning with the mist still rising from the water, Krauss filmed Méduc's wife and son fleeing from the mob and drowning in the moat at Olhain.

The rest of the film would all be big, difficult scenes. In the Ball of the Dead scene, Mabet and his wife would receive the news of the deaths. Madame Mabet would go mad. In the "He has no children" scene, Méduc would get the news, curse his father, and offer to lead an army to defeat Mabet. In the big battle scene, Méduc's army would defeat Mabet. And finally, Mabet and Madame Mabet would be guillotined at Arras.

Most of the actors would be leaving on Thursday to spend the fourteenth of July, Bastille Day, with their families. But before they did, Cyron wanted to get them well into rehearsing the Ball of the Dead. "I don't want you lot coming back hungover on Monday afternoon; I want you here Sunday night, begging to work."

Groans and cynical laughter.

André took over, standing on the platform at the top of the Great Hall, focused and in control as he always was when he worked with theatre, though he looked half-starved. "This

will be our most technically difficult scene, and we have actors from the Necro here to help us learn it. Two things to remember." André held up long fingers one by one: "Marks and
timing. Keep exactly to your marks because we'll be filming over 'ghosts' that are already on the negative. Timing
has to be exact. You'll rehearse to music. When we film, the
same music will be playing. Think that you're dancing your
part. —I've put together a demonstration. Cazenove, come
here."

The shutters were closed and a stagehand set up the projector behind a sheet. While other stagehands set up the demonstration, the projector showed bits from the magician Méliès'
films to warm the audience up. Seven ghostly Mélièses
played in a band; Méliès blew up his own head to huge pro-
portions. Meanwhile, onstage, two stagehands wearing
gloves brought out a tall sheet of plate glass and set it up at an
angle to the audience. Another arranged a black folding
screen. Krauss the photographer set out Arnaud lights, bright
focused spotlights. Some of the extras, recognizing the illusion, began to laugh and applaud. "Pepper's Ghost, of
course," André said. The actor Cazenove stood behind the
screen, reflected in the glass. André stood in the center of the
stage. From the audience, it looked as though André were
standing next to Cazenove's ghost. André "saw" the ghost
and gestured to it like Necrosar. The ghost recoiled in fright.
Meanwhile, behind them, the films had changed. A woman
was turning into flowers; a man's head floated in midair. With
perfect timing, André turned and batted at the onscreen head;
it drifted away.

"We will throw special effects at them," André said, turning back to the audience. "Pepper's Ghost, filming through
glass, double printing. We've done the special effects already
at the Méliès studio. And they won't catch what we're doing
because," André dropped into Necro-voice, "they'll be scared
to death. Lights."

The lights went on and André twitched the sheet away. Half the audience screamed.

The dead were standing behind him in a row, grey-faced, swathed in shrouds or dusty pre-Revolutionary dress. Méduc's dead wife curtsied and her head jerked forward sickeningly. A man offered her his severed skull like a bunch of flowers. The royal tax collector tried to hold his head on with his hands; a collar of blood circled his neck and his eyes were upturned, white and staring.

"We'll scare her," said André. "We'll scare them all. This afternoon we'll block the scene. Before dinner, ghosts get their makeup and costumes and practice the head-jerk." He clapped his hands for attention; the actors playing the ghosts were already trying it. "And this evening, after the end of practice, we'll have a party. We'll go down into the cellars and the ghosts will try to scare us."

We'll scare her. Cyron and Sabine were sitting together near the platform. Reisden went over to talk to them. "I don't think you should be here tonight," he said to Sabine.

Sabine sulked resentfully and crossed her arms. "I don't have any fun here!"

"I'll take you to a nice dinner in Arras," Cyron said. "We'll talk about your role."

Which got rid of both of them and opened the way to the cellars.

Chapter 44

For this evening, all the electric lights had been turned off at Montfort. The kitchen was blackness; the candlelight flickered off barely visible crescents of saucepans and plates. A black-veiled figure stood by the entrance to the cellar, handing out flickering candles and brown, obscure maps. "What scares you?" André murmured. "What really scares you?" Extras hung back, giggled, made faces; the younger ones poked each other in the ribs. "Merde! Paris folks get scared at nothing." From deep in the cellars came groans and, very faintly and far away, the planging of a ghostly harpsichord.

André had outdone himself. Perdita had spent the afternoon being turned into something rotted and cobwebbed, and had only just drifted down the stairs; the caterer's men and the cooks had been disappearing toward Makeup, Wardrobe, and the cellars. The extras had got into the spirit of the thing; half of them were whey-faced and dripping with blood, trying on their makeup for the big scene. Even Lucien Pétiot, here to consult with Cyron about something, had been persuaded to stay and to sport a fatal gash across his forehead.

Reisden, who wasn't in the Ball of the Dead scene, had spent the afternoon at Arras, in the heat of the Municipal Library. In 1804 a Danish traveler, Flores Rosenkranz, had visited Montfort, which was then deserted. He had explored "the dungeons" and copied his map of them for a local antiquary,

208

whose papers had found their way into the *fonds municipal*. Reisden had copied the map this afternoon.

The stairs to the first cellar were wide and whitewashed. Ranks of candles lit it. The cellar was squared-off, classical, with flat Corinthian columns carved into the walls. Cadaverous waiters were serving, from cobwebbed tables, wine and punch with "witch's herbs." In some of the empty wine bins, Props had stacked false wooden cannons and hollow piles of cannonballs for the big battle scene. A few ghostly soldiers guarded them.

This evening, food, drink, and dancing would be on the top level of cellars. On the second level, open for this evening only, were the Torture Chamber, the Mysterious Tunnels, and the Haunted Crypt. Reisden found these on Rosenkranz's map: prison, subterranean passages, and storeroom. On the third level, off limits even tonight, was the Holy Well.

Jules and Ruthie were meeting him at the Ghostly Harpsichordist. He found Perdita at the back of the first level, near the stairs, working happily through something of Vivaldi's. "Hello, love."

She stood up to kiss him. He kissed her carefully on grey lips, ducking the cobwebs in her hair. The makeup had worn off her finger-ends, leaving them pink. He kissed each one.

"I'm off in an hour," she said. "Come for dinner, Alexander; let's have dinner together."

"I'm doing something for a bit. Wait for me."

Jules and Ruthie arrived, Jules still limping but making his way with his cane over the uneven floor, Ruthie with a knitting bag full of supplies.

With them was André.

"So, Reisden, you're finally going with me into the *cellar*." André was in full Necrosar tonight; his ice blue eyes glittered underneath the monk's hood. "And it's dark," he murmured gleefully.

Reisden moved them away from oblivious Perdita.

"I'll go with you," André said.

"You have things to do," Reisden said firmly.

"I have the keys." André held them up.

"You could be very helpful, Count André," Ruthie said, "if you *would* be, and not simply try to scare us." She took out of her bag an electric torch and a ball of string. The men looked at her in amusement. "We might get lost," Ruthie said.

The barred gate to the second cellar stood open. They went down a narrow, dark set of stairs. There were no lights except near the stairs. Medieval arches extended far into the distance; Ruthie tried a tentative *hello?* and got back echoes.

"Look at this." André led them away from the lights. "You can't miss this." André's torch showed a narrow corridor. André went first; the Aborjailys followed, Jules limping; Reisden, who disliked dark narrow places, took a deep breath and followed. The tunnel narrowed, then opened into an echoing blackness. "I'm usually not allowed down here," André said.

"Are there bats?" Ruthie said nervously.

"No," said André, taking the torch and shining it into the dark: and out of the dark sprang a heap of black eye sockets and ivory grins. "Skulls."

Ruthie screamed. But the skulls were ancient, half-crumbling, piled in a mound next to a broken paving of leg bones; it was the remains of an ossuary, which had escaped even the Revolution. They must be under the ruins of the abbey. Reisden felt the weight of towers over their heads.

"My house," André hissed. "Do you wonder my mind is a little odd, Reisden?"

"Could you apply your mind toward looking for this secret?" Reisden said.

"Yes, Count André, or you might as well go back."

They retreated to the château cellar. From far away they could hear the actors, hollow voices echoing among the arches. The voices faded as André led the way through low-ceilinged chalk rooms toward another barred door.

Worn stairs led downward. A smell was seeping up from below, something unidentifiable and unpleasant. Jules mimed sniffing and fanned his hand in front of his nose.

"Count André, if you are trying to scare us with a smell, that is not proper." Jules' competent sister looked a little pale.

André laughed under his breath. "That's not mine, Ruthie. It's drains."

"Finest medieval engineering," Reisden said. "Ruthie, stay up here if you like."

Ruthie shook her head, no; she would come.

Grown men are not afraid of the dark, Reisden thought. He went down the stairs toward the chill blackness of the lowest cellar, ducking his head. His candle guttered and marked the ceiling with smoke stains. Jules, with the electric torch, negotiated the stairs painfully behind him.

Whatever was down here, it stank, and not of drains. They moved forward into the cellar. It smelled of cemeteries, a powdery putrid sweetness, the smell that comes with something staining the wall or blocking the chimney.

Jules tugged at André's sleeve, then Reisden's. He rolled up his eyes and let his mouth go lax, looking dead. He was a Necro actor and even with his neck brace it was dreadfully convincing.

"Dead animal," said André. "In the spring we fish them out of the pond."

It smelled enormous, but that was only the dark—

It was not only the smell that bothered them; it was the dark itself, lurking at the corners of their eyes, and the oddness of the place. The third cellar was not a single level at all, but a set of tunnels. Stairs went up and down; thick pillars supported the weight of the castle above it. Reisden lifted his candle and saw arches, thick white bony tree trunks, looming out of the dark. This place had been a mine; the stairs were steep miners' stairs.

Ruthie unfolded the map prosaically, holding it up to check

their way. "Here, Count André, tell us—" But her hands were trembling. Reisden held the candle for her.

They were to count eighteen of the primitive columns, turn right, count sixteen, and they would be near the Holy Well. But the columns were not in straight rows, nor at equal distances.

Jules shone the torch beam on three columns that seemed grown together. He signaled in the torchlight: one or three? The space in front of them suddenly had no columns at all; Jules limped forward into the dark, scything the beam to find where they were. The smell had got much stronger. Reisden took out his handkerchief and gave it to Ruthie, wishing for camphorated vaseline. Where was the Well?

Jules stumbled and dropped the torch.

It hit with a *clink* and went out. Reisden knelt to look for it, holding the candle. The candle flame trembled; the flame was balancing at the very end of the wick. Jules stood, pressing his hand to his jaw—the stumble must have hurt. Reisden found the torch and picked it up, clicking it to make sure it still worked, and handed it to Ruthie.

The smell was too bad; Jules began to cough, which was obviously painful for him. Ruthie took him by the shoulders and pushed him back toward the stairs.

That left Reisden and André to continue alone.

In the guttering light, in the dimness, the columns wavered, moving, blue-shadowed. The Well was supposed to be straight ahead, but nothing was straight. In the dark, past the columns, shadows seemed to be moving.

"It's not an animal," André said, and grinned.

"Don't do Necro," Reisden said sharply.

They saw the bars almost by running into them, parallel darknesses in the dark. The candle was burning blue, a wavering near-lightless vertical line. André turned on the torch. They could see nothing but bars, and behind them a man-high wooden box and some pipes going up the wall.

André moved the beam of the light. In the darkness it showed a circle of chalk floor behind the bars, and the edge of the box; and behind that, a shadow. It was long and thin and humped on the ground, not recognizable, but at the end of it, moldy and twisted, was lying one of the pointed-toed boots that American cowboys wear.

If this is another of his effects, Reisden thought. André shone the torchlight on that terrible thing, through the bars, then put his hand with the torch through the bars and leaned his forehead on them to look at it better. The light spilled back onto his white face haloed by his untidy light hair. His mouth was wide open, the corners pulled away from the teeth.

"Mama and Papa. They were just like this. You see?" His eyes were wide bright blue and expressionless as glass. "Papa said I have to stay."

Chapter 45

Getting up the stairs felt like climbing a mountain. Reisden half-dragged André, Ruthie supported Jules. They staggered into the brilliant candles of the first cellar and found themselves in a circle of concerned faces. Reisden shook his head and pointed to Jules, who was flushed bright cherry red, dragging air in painfully through his nose and his wired jaw. Ruthie was crying. André tried to go back downstairs. A cook and under-cook manhandled Jules up the last flight, out through the back door and onto the paved terrace, under the stars. Reisden followed them. When the night wind hit his face, he sat down abruptly against the side of the kitchen wall, his chest heaving.

"Get the police," he said as clearly as he could.

Cyron was shouting at him. "What's happened to André? What is wrong with André?"

Reisden lay down on the terrace flagstones, put his arm over his eyes, and gasped.

When he got back in focus again, finally, he was not looking at the clouds but at an electric light; it was almost morning, he was lying in one of the château bedrooms—not his and Perdita's in the New Buildings. The windows were wide open. An oxygen apparatus stood by the bed and he had a rubber taste in his throat and a headache so fierce that it hurt when he blinked. Perdita was sitting by the bed. "How is Jules?" he managed. "André?"

"Jules is all right," Perdita said. She was holding his hand tightly; her voice was trembling, her face tear-streaked, and she was furious. "Alexander, *what* happened down there? What is going on?"

"Later." Much later. "André?"

"The third cellar is *full* of carbon monoxide," she said. "From the well pump. It isn't vented right."

"There's a dead man. Blantire, I think."

He didn't know if he remembered this, or dreamed it, or told her about it: André hadn't wanted to leave. *I have to stay,* he had said, holding tight to the bars with both hands. *Papa says I have to stay.* The candle flame had been burning blue, a thin string, flickering, gulping for air. *Papa said I'll never be a man if I don't stay,* André said. He sounded like a child. *Turn this way, André,* Reisden had said, and André had turned, and Reisden had hit him hard enough to loosen his hold of the bars, and then hit him again with the torch. It had been the necessary thing, but he felt as though he had been hitting a child.

He woke up definitively in midafternoon, hoarse and headachy and bone-exhausted. Perdita was gone; a servant told him the police wanted to see him in Cyron's office downstairs.

Baltazar, the Sûreté detective, was a tall, thin, morose man with a pockmarked face. He wandered around Cyron's office, looking at posters and props, answering no questions, taking Reisden methodically through the events of Wednesday evening.

"You reached the Holy Well."

"Two of us, André and I. We saw the body. Was it Blantire?"

"Did the Count of Montfort say that it was?"

Reisden shook his head, and regretted it. "How is André?"

"What did he say?"

"He said, 'Mama and Papa were just like this.' " Go on, Baltazar indicated. "He wouldn't let go of the bars. I hit him," Reisden said, "with the torch, to get him moving."

"That explains that," Baltazar said, writing.

"How is he?"

"Just a little bruised."

"How is he mentally?"

"There have been a number of—unfortunate incidents connected with this production." Baltazar consulted his notebook. "The murder of the costumer. And of this Blantire—"

"The costumer wasn't murdered," Reisden said. "Was she?"

"The costumer was poisoned by belladonna," Baltazar said. "Belladonna that the rabbit had eaten. Rabbits eat belladonna. It doesn't hurt them. But how did the rabbit get the belladonna, that's the question!—You've been here before, yes? You've stayed here often. You never went in the cellar before? Why not? A young man, almost a boy— Didn't it interest you?"

"No."

"Monsieur le Comte says he was always asking you to break into the cellar with him."

"André likes to frighten people. Is he all right?"

"He's helping us in our inquiries."

"He hasn't done anything."

When Baltazar let him go, Reisden went outside looking for information and his family, and found Zeno Puckett. The cowboy was sitting on the terrace, yellow under his tan, looking out over the view. Reisden sat down beside him. Down below, two policemen were discussing something, pointing at the vent set into the side of the hill.

"Danged thing to happen," Puckett said, shaking his head. "T. J. breaks broncos and rides trail and dodges husbands for near fifteen years, then he just up and dies in a cellar."

"How did he die?"

"Carbon monoxide poisoning off the pump," Puckett said. "They say."

Not that one could tell, after this time and before an autopsy. Perhaps not with one; probably not. Another case for Eddie Becker.

Puckett took off his hat, held it by the brim, and flicked dust off it with one finger, rotating the hat slowly. "That gal he was seeing. She died. Mighty peculiar, two accidents in a row."

"So I'm told."

"I'd guess he passed away about the time he disappeared. She died maybe two weeks later, huh?"

"The Saturday André and I were here."

"T. J. liked his ladies and they liked him and all, but I don't see any gal taking poison over him," Puckett said, then cleared his throat as if he were changing the subject. "What kind of gal was she?"

"I met her only once."

"Was she political?"

"Political? Was Blantire?"

"He was Russian."

"So," Reisden said, surprised.

"Family come from Russia when he was a kid," Puckett said. "Oo-cry-eeny, he said, someplace like that. Family was sodbusters, but not him. He was cowboy." Puckett tried to explain. "They ain't no cattle drives any more, noplace for boys like T. J. They ain't nothing but Carver-Whitney's Wild America and horse-wrangling for the movies. T. J. missed the high stakes. There was always someplace bigger'n where he was and he was lookin' for it."

"In Russia?" Reisden said.

"He just sort of angled into Russia. A newspaper in Chicago, I disremember the name, they started off to print things he'd writ about the drives. You know all them Schmidts and Hinkeydoofers round Chicago, they love them Wild West stories."

"It was a German paper he wrote for? They sponsored him?"

"Yup."

"Why did he come here after Russia?"

"Dunno."

"Did the Germans send him?"

Horsemen's hands are marked with a rein-line of callus under the thumb. Puckett rubbed at his uneasily. He had the thumbline, but also a callus on the first joint of the middle finger of his right hand.

"How did you get to Russia?" Reisden asked. "Were you writing too?"

"Me?" Puckett grinned. "I was making Westerns in New Jersey, drifted east from there. I mean to get to Africa someday.—Heard *you* was supposed to be working for the Germans."

"No. My job is André."

Puckett looked at him shrewdly, with slitted eyes.

"Why should you believe me, no one else does. But there is

rumored to be a military secret here at Montfort, in which the Germans are rumored to be interested. I wonder if Blantire found something," Reisden said. "I wonder if he and Françoise Auclart found something. And now they are both dead."

"I be danged," said Puckett. "Well, that would be interesting."

The two men looked at each other. Puckett stood up, unfolding himself in sections. "Don't you go away. Might be I could say something more about T. J."

Perdita and Toby were coming round the corner of the terrace: Toby in a red jumper in Perdita's arms, Perdita wearing her yellow-tinted glasses to make sure she could see him. Puckett touched his hat and took his leave.

Chapter 46

"**Y**ou should be resting," Perdita said.

"No, I'm fine." He looked at his son's bright red sweater. "I'll watch him." She put Toby on the ground; he crawled briskly away. She took off her glasses; she hated them, hated every inconvenience of being blind.

"*Why* did you *stay* down there?" she asked, sitting by him.

What is the secret of Montfort? If he knew it, his family would be safe. But even Thomas Robert could not have been more stupid, he thought; the candle had been visibly going out.

Toby had discovered some potted plants on the terrace, had

pulled himself up to investigate them, and was happily grabbing a handful of mulch to stuff into his mouth. "No, love," he shouted, and ran to scoop him up, and panted, to his annoyance. Perdita, panicked, turned her head from side to side to understand what was going on.

"Just something he'd got that he shouldn't," he said, bringing Toby back and putting him down on the flagstones. Aline came round the side of the château. Toby was crawling off toward the plants again. "No, love; here."

"Alexander, if someone has to chase him, give me my glasses back because I'm going to do it."

"I'll get him, monsieur, 'dame," Aline said.

"Sit down, Alexander. You're out of breath," Perdita said accusingly, her voice trembling.

"I'm all right. Really."

But he did sit down. She sat beside him and held his hand like someone at a sickbed. He caressed her hand with both his. If things had gone badly, he thought, today Perdita would be trying to deal with a funeral. And he wasn't insured; no one sells insurance to a man with his history.

"Don't be kind to me, Alexander," she said, unforgiving and at the edge of tears.

Aline had retrieved Toby, who was an unspeakable object, face covered with brown stuff, giggling happily. What would happen to you, my love, if I were dead? "Give him to me," Reisden said. Toby chuckled and reached out a little goo-covered hand, smearing his father's face and shirt with muck. "Vile child, such mischief. Here—" Reisden swabbed at his son's hands with a handkerchief. "Papa will look after you."

Papa hopes he will. Papa's doing a G-dd—n bad job of it just now.

If he were to die, as things were now, the Jouvet situation would go bad instantly. The corporation he had set up owned both the business and the building. One mortgage covered everything. If he were dead, the whole mortgage would come due at once and there wouldn't be money to pay it.

If he died, Gilbert would be her only resource.

So don't die, he thought, holding his baby boy, who was already wriggling to get down. Much preferable. Don't leave your baby to be fathered by a photograph.

And tell Perdita what's wrong.

Tell her about Gehazy? In two days, if I don't find the bloody nonexistent secret of Montfort, Gehazy will tell the world I'm a spy. Meanwhile André has gone off the rails and there's a body in the cellar.

He kissed his boy on the top of his head, pressed his cheek against Toby's hair, and handed him back to Aline. "Look after him for a bit. Love," he said to Perdita, "let's just sit. I'm tired."

This time Toby crawled off in the direction of the chalk wall around the terrace, pulled himself up, and began inching along the wall, holding himself upright by clutching at Aline's skirt.

They sat together, holding hands, looking out over the pasture and the beet fields, not facing the things neither one of them wanted to talk about. He thought of what he should do for her, to guard against anything happening to him. He should write her a letter, detailing who could advise her financially, whom she should avoid. Tell her to take advice from Armand Inslay-Hochstein or Dotty but never anything from Sigi. Diversify to such-and-such stocks if there's money to do it. (At the moment there wouldn't be.) Sell Jouvet before it's sold from under you.

Or before it's sequestered. They do that with the property of traitors, especially in times of political uncertainty. Cambon wasn't doing well in Berlin. Germany wanted part of West Africa in return for giving France a free hand in Morocco. France didn't want to give it up. G-d help Europe if the

Africans ever got the idea they should be consulted; Europe was tense enough fighting its wars on African soil.

Cyron and Lucien Pétiot came out of the house, through the French doors from the dining room. "Reisden!" Pétiot called him. Cyron looked ill with fury.

"Excuse me a moment, love.—How is André?" Reisden asked, going to meet them.

"He's gone mad!" Cyron said. "He doesn't mean anything he says.—This is Jouvet's fault, your fault—"

Pétiot laid a hand on Cyron's arm, but Cyron shook it off.

"He says he killed them both," Cyron said. "Blantire and the Auclart woman."

Oh L—d. "Why?"

"Why? What do you mean, why?"

The Arras coach, Cyron's coach, had been making its way up the hill, more quickly than usual and swaying emptily. Everyone had left for the Bastille Day weekend; no one should be arriving.

"Why," Reisden repeated, "when he met Blantire only once, if that, and wasn't here when Blantire died?"

"He says he poisoned them."

"He's not talking about Blantire."

The coach stopped and let out Roy Daugherty.

He came round the side of the château toward the terrace. He was rumpled and disheveled, like a man who has been working all night and traveling all day, and he was holding a file, a thin brown Jouvet file tied with tape. He squinted, saw Reisden, and held it up, waving it.

"Found it," he shouted, and lumbered toward them.

"Where? Never mind." Reisden took the file. The knots in the tape were stiff, thirty-five years old; he cut the tape with his pocketknife and opened the file.

The handwriting was the last Dr. Jouvet's. Interview notes with the five-year-old Count André de Montfort; with Maurice Cyron, actor, not yet of the Théâtre Maurice Cyron; with two detectives. A photograph fell out from between the pages: André's parents, taken by Reutlinger, probably a wedding photograph. André's father in his cavalryman's uniform, too sloppy to be a desk soldier, too much smelling of the actual horse. André's mother, very young—she might have been sixteen, fifteen—smiling tentatively into the camera. She looked startlingly like a small feminine version of André, with white-blonde hair, big cheekbones, and big wrists. To Henri-Julien, the scientific farmer, she might have looked like a small but sturdy draft horse, but there was a nervous fragility about her, an edge to the smile.

Reisden turned the pages and read what André had to say about his parents. When he had finished, he closed the folder, leaned against the wall, and shut his eyes.

"Son?" Roy. "I got to get goin' back to Paris. 'Zanne and I are goin' dancin' for Bastille Day. You all right?" Reisden nodded. "Bad stuff in there?"

"Very bad, and useful. Thanks."

Daugherty nodded. "Well, I could have been fishin' and paintin'; you remember you owe me." He strode back over the terrace toward the courtyard and the Jerusalem Gate, grumpy and hurrying, a man who has been taken away from his family.

Family, Reisden thought, and looked down at the lines of steady writing, the hopeless story of André's family. Jouvet had written down everything; so here it all was, the first of the Necro stories, the one that had fathered all the rest.

"What does it say?" said Cyron.

"Sorry. I have to talk with him."

Chapter 47

They had tied André up. He was in the bedroom with the angel bedstead, roped to one of the pillars, his wrists behind him. Above him the slant-eyed angels smiled enigmatically. It was as if he had been tied to a tomb. If he hadn't been tied he would have been rocking back and forth, the short, choppy, mourning rocking of the desperate in spirit, and perhaps they had tied him to stop it, but his head could still move and he was banging it against the pillar as if he wanted to smash the thoughts out of his head. Someone had tied a pillow between his head and the pillar. His eyes were closed; his head thumped rhythmically against the bedpost.

Jules was watching him. Reisden caught his eye, nodded at the door: leave us alone. Reisden dropped into one of Sabine's Olde Medieval chairs and opened the folder on his lap.

"You told Julien Jouvet that you killed both your parents. True?"

The creaking stopped; André opened his eyes. Blue, wide, stunned.

"How did it happen?" said Reisden.

"I was supposed to stay," André said, half stupidly, as though whatever he was thinking got in the way of speech. "Reisden. You hit me."

"I'm sorry. You wouldn't let go of the bars."

"I was supposed to *stay*," André said with a childish insistence.

"I know. Your father took you to deathbeds."

"I told you that," André said.

He had, once. One doesn't put it together; one doesn't remember that André's father had died when he was five. Or one doesn't want to believe it. André's father had started taking André to deathbeds when he was three or four years old.

"I *told* you. I'm never supposed to leave until he lets me. I have to stay."

SCENE I: THE GREAT HALL, MONTFORT.

André can't tell Reisden what happened because he can't tell anyone, he can't even think of it himself, and Reisden won't believe it. Reisden avoids the dark, he has a wife and child, he tries to believe the world is better than it is. There is no happiness, there is no security; André knows that and Reisden doesn't. That is why André writes plays, why he makes films, lies that tell the truth. So he thinks now, out loud, not about what happened to him but a safe lie, shadows on a white sheet. Working title: *Never Leave a Deathbed*.

THE GREAT HALL, MONTFORT. FULL SHOT. NOON. Poverty-stricken ruins of old gentility. Cupboard in background. At a table by the fireplace, the COUNT, his wife the COUNTESS, and his son ANDRÉ are discovered eating a bowl of vegetable soup. The COUNT, a big solid man, wears glasses, reads as he eats. It could be soup or hay he is spooning in, he doesn't notice. The COUNTESS eats with exaggerated Parisian manners. Little ANDRÉ imitates his father, spooning carelessly. His mother raps his fingers. ANDRÉ looks dubiously from his father to his mother.

NECROSAR enters from right, points over COUNT's shoulder at book.

CLOSE-UP of book, a shabby secondhand textbook of veterinary medicine.

CUT BACK to FULL SHOT of family eating. FARMER enters from left, distraught, carrying a sick child. COUNTESS shrinks away. She is afraid of the sickness, which is obviously communicable. COUNT examines sick child on table, takes shabby medical bag from cupboard.

COUNT gestures to little ANDRÉ to come with him, while NECROSAR takes out of the bag and holds up for the audience a syringe so large it is obviously meant for a horse or cow.

COUNTESS, hysterically: *Villain! How can you expose your child to such horrors?*

COUNT: *There is nothing to be frightened of. . . . André must not be afraid of death.*

NECROSAR, still clowning with the syringe: *There's nothing to be frightened of, is there? It's death. It's only a joke, André.*

It's a play, a film, not a memory. André takes particular care over the next shot, a complex track-and-pan in the village outside the walls of Montfort. The village street is deserted. The camera pans over the street, tracks forward to the brick wall and wide doors of a particular farm, and continues tracking into a courtyard. It pans around the walled farm to the stables where the cows low, waiting to be milked. No smoke drifts from the farmhouse chimney. The farmhouse door stands open.

INSIDE THE FARMHOUSE. FULL SHOTS of a farm family lying on their stained pallets in the main room. An old man lies sobbing for someone to help him, someone to change his soiled clothes, to give him a drink of water; then he vomits yellow bile onto his pillow. An old woman has been dragged into a corner. Her mouth has fallen open and a fly sits like a black-and-green teardrop at the corner of her half-open eye. The fly rubs its head with its front legs. And there is the boy lying on the bed, in close-up, his eyes sunk so that the insides of the eyelids are visible, his face like a wax mannequin's left too long in the sun; all the color is bleached out of it. His tongue looks yellow and dusty and the end of his nose has drooped a little to one side.

Nothing moves in the frame. Will the boy look too much like a mannequin? A fly enters the frame left, alights at the edge of the boy's mouth where there is something like a bit of brown soup. The fly crawls into the mouth. *Ah,* says Necrosar, squatting down by little André, *that will make them believe.*

FULL SHOT of little ANDRÉ among the dead people. NECROSAR takes him around the back of the set, shows him how the gaslight is turned down and the filters are changed to make twilight. NECROSAR adjusts the lights. It is twilight. The old man is dying. The others are already dead.

COUNT, sitting by the dying old man, to ANDRÉ: *Never leave a deathbed. Your people need you. Remember you are a Montfort. You aren't frightened, are you?*

ANDRÉ, lying: *No, Papa. No.*

COUNT: *Good boy! That's my son.*

The film breaks for a moment, and André becomes conscious momentarily of himself, hungry, his wrists chafed; ashamed, ashamed.

Reisden is watching him from the depths of one of *that woman's* ugly chairs. "What did André feel?" he asks.

Reisden doesn't understand. André doesn't feel. André only watches. With Necrosar.

The fact is, though, if it were not for Necrosar, André would be afraid like Mama. It is only Necrosar who comforts him.

Papa takes him to deathbeds, where death sneaks in; to a mine explosion, where the bodies are black and red; above all to the cholera victims. If all this were real, the broken bones, the red intestines, the blood, the smell, above all the smell . . . but Necrosar shows him the lights and the stage sets behind.

Then something happens. One day, at a cholera victim's house, Papa drinks water.

Papa is sick.

And the film breaks again. André is ravenous, tired; his arms are on fire from being tied behind him. "Let me go," he says. "Untie me."

"Tell me the rest."

"I don't remember." They are all gone now, the last thing he can see is Papa drinking water from the pond in the village; his tongue is dry and cleaves to the roof of his mouth. "I'm thirsty," André says. "There's no beer, no cider. Give me water from the pond." Papa has forgotten that no one is supposed to drink from the pond.

Papa is sick.

"I don't want this," André says. "I don't want to see this. Stop the film. Stop it." But it won't stop. Close-up, Mama, with a wet towel in her hand, hesitating, still afraid of touching a cholera victim! Close-up, Papa, his eyes sunken, breathing hard. Mama says, *Go outside.* Papa opens his eyes. Be a man, André. Don't leave. *Go away!* says Mama. *You shouldn't see this.*

He wants to leave.

Mama has a bottle from Papa's medical bag. She stares at little André as she pours out a dose. Her hands shake; the medicine spirals and drips from the spoon in thick strings like witch's hair. *I don't want you to see this.* Papa's eyes are open; he watches André. She pours him one dose, slides it into his lax mouth; then she pours another.

Mama loves you, she says. *Go outside. Please go.* Mama's hands shake, her breath is hot and sour, he can smell her perspiration as she hugs him. Behind Mama's elbow he can see Papa's eyes, fixed, watching him. *He doesn't see you,* Mama says. *Go outside.* Her eyes are wide, frightened. The bottle is half-empty; she picks it up again, and pours again.

And he goes outside. He is not a man. He has run away. It is getting dark; at the foot of Montfort hill, shadows chase light across the fields. He sways back and forth; he makes little sounds in his throat. Papa wanted him to stay; Mama wanted him to go.

Finally there is nothing left of the light but deep blue at the top of the sky, and then that darkens, too. There is no moon. An owl shrieks, and from inside the Vex-Fort Papa begins to cry out. André makes the sound himself. He has practiced this sound for years in secret, because he knows one day he will need to frighten someone terribly, and he makes it now, the raucous monotonous shriek of a man in agony. Papa is not dead. Papa knows André has deserted him.

He stumbles away from the noise, toward the abbey towers, through the Lazarus Gate. In the churchyard he huddles against the side of one of the new mounds. The soil smells sharp and clayey. He thinks of the dead boy's brown mouth and the boy's lips fallen away from his teeth.

Where is Necrosar? Who will tell him that this is all a play? His mother is coming from the house, holding a candle. She is calling to him. *It's all right now, darling, come! Come inside!* She looks young and she is smiling. Her blonde hair is down, and a strand of it catches in the candle, flares and sizzles, but she doesn't notice that it is burning. *Your father is asleep! Come inside, we'll sleep, too, and we'll be together, safe! Forever!*

She looks around; she can see no farther than the circle of light around her candle. *Where are you, my darling? Come to Mama!*

She waits for him. Then, all alone in the courtyard, she begins to cry. Because she knows she is deserted; because she is angry at him for not coming when she needs him so much; because she is alone in the dark, and afraid. She drops the candle onto the stones; she sobs, and sobs, and André cries with her, but silently, pressing his face into the clayey soil so that she won't find him and take him back to the house with her, digging his thumbs into his ears so he won't hear her, so she will not take him back into the house where they will sleep forever.

My darling! Where are you? Don't leave me alone!

A long time after she has gone, he unblocks his ears. He listens for her as if he believes she could still be there. Then, from the house, she begins to scream; and he shrieks too, sobbing, dashing his head from side to side because his arms are tied behind him, he has no hands to wipe his eyes, no thumbs to put in his ears to press away the screams.

Oh, Mama, Mama! Oh, Papa!

And he screams and cries forever. He screams all the time they think he is only silent. When the man comes to buy Papa and Mama's house, he cries; and when the man tells him stories, he cries while he listens; and when he goes to live with the man and calls him, punctiliously, *Papa Cyron,* not *Papa;* and when he goes to school and when he becomes a man; in the cavalry, on the parade ground. The only way to stop it is to tell stories, dreadful stories, and to be with Necrosar, to be Necrosar. Then it's safe. Then he can stop for a while.

But Necrosar is gone. "There is no Necrosar," André cries out. He makes the dreadful sound again, he bangs his head against the bedpost, but there is no Necrosar, there is no Mama, there is no Papa, they are all dead.

There is only André.

André sags against the bedpost. The inside of his arm chafes against an edge of wing. "Let me go," he says in a whisper, "untie me; I won't do anything. I have to piss." They untie him. He moans while the blood comes back into his arms. Then he pushes the chamber pot behind the screen, puts the lid on the pot, sits on the floor like a puppet without strings.

"I'm hungry." They take him downstairs. It's the middle of the night, no one awake but him and them. He fits names to his two guardians. "Reisden. Jules." Saying their names reminds him that he knows them, and this for some reason makes him cry again. He is good for nothing but crying. Jules brings him an egg and toast. He cries as he eats.

He is sitting where Papa and Mama and little André sat, at the table near the fireplace. He looks up into the shadows behind the banners.

"There," he says, pointing with his swollen fingers. "The stairs were there, and that was their room. I came back, finally—I waited till the sun came. And they were dead. It was too late. I was supposed to stay, and I stayed *then*, but it was too late."

He straightens up and brushes something like cobwebs away from his face. It is his own long hair. Necrosar's hair. Not Necrosar's. "I remember," he says. "I remember before I was safe." He remembers before Necrosar was here. He stands up, bracing himself for a moment by leaning on his knuckles on the table. There is a tray on the table, a silver-plated tray sent by some admirer of Papa Cyron's. He turns it over and peers at himself in its rippling surface. But it is as if he has been drinking from a pool or a trough and then has tried to see a reflection. He can see Necrosar's blond hair, Papa's height, Mama's pale blue eyes, but the ripples have to clear before he can see himself.

He remembers before Necrosar was. Now he feels as if he were newly born, or born long ago but only just conscious, some huge baby thing, grotesque, still with the egg-sac meat on him. He flaps his aching swollen wings and laughs and cries.

Chapter 48

"He remembered everything," Katzmann's voice said tinnily from Paris, "with all the feelings associated, just as it happened? Then I forgive you for waking me at this hour."

It was dead night. Reisden saw himself reflected in the phone cabinet glass, jaw rough with whiskers. He leaned against the wall phone. He was so tired the receiver felt too heavy to hold. "I never want to do that again."

"Isn't it wonderful when you see their minds changing?" Katzmann said. "You know, the betting at Jouvet is that you'll be a psychiatrist someday."

"Never. Come down and take him over. Please."

"First train this morning. Will there be fireworks at Montfort? And girls to dance with? I want a girl."

"What?"

"It's Bastille Day," Katzmann said patiently. "Bastille Day. Fireworks. Dancing in the street. With girls."

When Reisden hung up, he went into the *lavabo* to wash. The tap-handles spun uselessly: no pump, no water. Oh H——l, he thought, good H——l G-dd——n. He went back out into the Great Hall, thinking of all the things he wanted and didn't have: sleep, security for his family, a shave, a good relationship with Perdita, the secret of Montfort. Hot water. Any water. A bath. He slumped down into another of Sabine's

231

uncomfortable medieval thrones, propping his elbow on the arm and his chin on his hand.

Someone had taken the old banners down. They were spread on the table, old battle ensigns and flags, stained with cooking-smoke and mousy with dust. He was tired enough to think of sleeping on them. But, he knew, wherever he tried to sleep, even next to Perdita, he would simply end up staring at the ceiling. He looked at the wall where the flags had been. Behind their pale shadows he saw the shadow of the stairs and the sinister bricked-up door that had been André's parents' room.

André came through the door to the kitchen, followed by the ever-patient Jules and two frowsty, sleepy techs dragging a long ladder. "Set it up there," André said, pointing at the wall. He went out and came back with a pickax.

Jules looked at Reisden pleadingly.

"Let him do it." There was no question of letting him do it; André swarmed up the ladder and attacked the bricks as though he were axing enemy skulls. Bricks and parts of bricks smashed down on the floor around them, hitting the table and Sabine's new medievalesque chairs. The techs ducked; Jules pulled chairs out of the way. All four of them moved the table.

Cyron arrived in a red bathrobe and Moorish slippers, his thin hair sticking in all directions. "What's happening *now*?"

André turned around and saw him. "I didn't *poison* anybody," he said. "You don't need to tie me up. I'm harmless. I don't *kill* people. I didn't kill *them*. I'm just a coward." Another great smash.

Cyron looked up at him, scowling at *coward*.

"Just go away," Reisden said to him. "Go." For a wonder, Cyron actually went.

The mortar gave way suddenly. An irregular chunk of chalk cracked out of the wall and crashed in pieces on the floor, starring everything with grit. The tech holding the ladder swore and patted at his clothes. André carefully began knocking the rest of the mortarwork back into the room. The hole was big enough; he scraped through it and disappeared.

The two techs looked at Reisden. "Get me a light," he said. One of them brought an electric torch. He climbed the ladder too.

André was sitting on the floor, back against the wall, knees drawn up. Reisden fit himself through and sat down near him.

The torchlight showed cobwebs on a beamed ceiling, stone walls, a bricked-up window, an ancient hillocked floor. The air smelled like stone.

"They're *not here*," André said. Reisden shone the torch beam toward him, half-covering it with his fingers to dim the light. There were fresh tear tracks on André's face, but he had stopped crying; he wiped his nose with his knuckles, a gesture part childish, part brutal. "I wanted to be frightened. It isn't frightening," André said, "just—sad. I feel sad."

His voice made echoes in the empty room.

André tried to do Necrosar: "I'm *harm*lessss," he cackled, making a face. He bared his teeth. Above them, his eyes were sad, the eyes of a caged great ape, speechless and questioning. "Don't shine your light on me. It's like being onstage."

Reisden turned the light out, reluctantly. They sat together in the dark. André sniffed a bit. What Reisden heard, in the dark, was a child who had been frightened, had been crying, but was coming out of it. Sometimes, when Toby woke in the night, Reisden sat with him like this.

"I'll go to bed," André said finally.

André struggled back through the hole in the wall. Reisden got up to follow him but sat back down. Let Jules take care of André. He clicked on the light but found it distracting; he turned it back off and stared into the dark. *I am sad.* André had never said those things simply; he had always been an actor in his own mental theatre, Necrosar, the horror in charge.

Do I frighten you, Reisden?

I'm frightened. I remember before I was safe.

He leaned against the wall, worn out, a little sick at heart from all that emotion. The old stone surrounded him, and the dark. He clicked on the light again, shining it around the empty room: fragments of a wall, broken out of the darkness by the light; nothing else. André was right; there was nothing frightening here. All the fright had been in André himself, and he had kept it with him for thirty-five years.

And now he's going to let it go, Reisden thought. And that frightened *him*; he didn't know why. He turned the light off and closed his eyes, but now the uneasiness that lurked in the dark was here for him.

I must go to sleep, he thought. With my wife and my son. I must talk to Perdita. We must work out our quarrel over Gilbert. If André can face his parents, I can face down Gilbert.

But thinking that, with his face toward the light from the door, he fell completely asleep and woke up what seemed like hours later, sprawled on the stone. Someone had put a blanket over him; someone had left a lantern burning low so that he would not be in the dark. Ruthie? Perdita? But she had gone. He was alone.

Chapter 49

I t was barely dawn. He descended the ladder stiffly, blundered into the washroom, swore at the pump again, and went into the kitchen. There was coffee. He got a cup and sat down at the kitchen table, a massive thing almost as old as the table in the Great Hall. Its surface was scarred into hillocks with knife cuts and butchering. He moved his index finger back and forth along a deep cut, tracing it.

"Reisden? I've been looking for you."

It was Lucien Pétiot, up and fully dressed at four in the morning, bandbox-fresh in his blue general's dress uniform, the color of a perfect sky. Reisden felt grit down the back of his neck. He touched his unshaven jaw and shrugged apologetically.

"No, no, no, quite all right," Pétiot said, sitting across from him. "I've seen André. He actually seems better. What's more to the point!—I've seen Maurice. Maurice is preparing to apologize. We both are."

"I don't know that I've done anything for André."

Lucien Pétiot tented his clean, manicured fingers and smiled over them at Reisden. "Apologize for the trick I have played on you."

"What?" The coffee was bringing his headache back. "I'm completely confused, I'm afraid."

"Yes. You were meant to be. I confused you." Pétiot beamed at him. "I had better start from the beginning, hadn't

235

I? You see, I know what Gehazy's looking for. At least what will content him. Come outside."

They sat on the chalk wall, looking west toward Arras. The moon was full, low in the southwest, but in the east the sky was tinted with rose, blue, and a few white clouds: a beautiful Bastille Day morning.

"Maurice has always thought you were an enemy of France. One of von Loewenstein's spies. I have less ambiguous enemies in mind, the ones in the German government, and in France. A faction in both governments wants the negotiations to fail."

Reisden nodded; someone always wants war.

"Some Germans are exploring an invasion of France. One of their routes"—Pétiot drew a finger delicately along the plain below—"is the Arras road. They want to know how well we are fortified. They think we're perhaps like the Alsace-Lorraine frontier, with the Rivière line of forts.

"Of course we have no forts but the Citadel," Pétiot said. "A terrible oversight. But suppose that we did have"—he smiled—"a secret of Montfort. Some sort of fortification along the Arras road. In the French government there are also factions. One believes the—secret—should be a complete surprise to the Germans if they invade. The other"—he bowed slightly—"suggests a fortification is no use unless it is known about."

"Don't tell me secrets." A fortification at Montfort?

Pétiot took out his cigaret case and offered it to Reisden, who shook his head. Pétiot lighted his and blew smoke. "I couldn't simply send a love note to Berlin. I had to let them find it. Fortunately our new allies were curious too; Ambassador Izvolsky wanted assurance that we could stop the Germans. And he sent a spy."

"Blantire?"

"Thomas Jefferson Blantire, the innocent American working for a German newspaper, riding across Russia on a lark.

Thomas Jefferson Blantire, picked up several times by the Cheka on suspicion of being a spy. Clever. Even if he were really working for the Russians it would get to Berlin, which would satisfy me."

Half the Russian Secret Service worked for the Germans.

"The trouble is, he didn't find it."

Pétiot stood and began to pace up and down the terrace, looking toward Arras. "Blantire was overcome by carbon monoxide in the cellars, completely by accident as far as we can tell."

"And what happened to Mademoiselle Françoise?"

"She had given Blantire hints, pointed him in the right direction. Perhaps someone—perhaps I'm wrong. It could have been an accident. The point is," he continued, "I had no spy. Until Gehazy appeared."

"Is Gehazy also working for Izvolsky?"

"I should say for the Germans. Gehazy approached Jules, who could be blackmailed. I was delighted. But Jules approached you, and by the time you had come to Maurice, you had advised Jules to give Gehazy a false secret. When I wanted him to give them mine! I was indignant."

"I was helping Jules," Reisden said. "To help André. Just as Cyron had bloody well asked. Did I know you wanted to give away French secrets?"

"Perhaps you wanted to be sure it was the real one. And then you came to Montfort in May."

"Why did Gehazy have Jules beaten?"

Pétiot nodded reluctantly, as if Reisden had said something he had to agree with but didn't want to. "We thought you arranged that. To get yourself here."

"So you thought I was a spy. You intended to let me find your secret and pass it on."

"But you didn't!" Pétiot objected. "We let you have your head and run your course, and where did you lead us? Did you spy? Did you find our secret and send it to Sigismund von

Loewenstein, or the Germans, or even the Russians? We would have known if you did. No. You told André and Jules and his sister and even the American that there was a secret. You looked for it, elaborately, with diagrams and maps. But you didn't find it. You've been down in the cellars once, just once. Did you," Pétiot said thoughtfully, "did you want to find it?"

Reisden went over to the stove and got another cup of coffee. "I'm not in that game."

"Or you are immensely clever and want us to think you aren't."

He turned to face Pétiot. "I'm not a spy. I'm not clever, I'm not playing games, I only want to do my work and protect my family. You could threaten me and intrigue me and flatter me till I did it. Leo came as close as anyone has. But it wasn't my game, it wasn't my work, and I turned on him. Ask anyone who was around then. You will not get yourself a pet Austrian spy; you will get all the trouble I can give you. I promise you."

"Reisden," said Pétiot, "you've won."

Reisden looked down at Pétiot, breathing hard.

"Someone else has told Gehazy the secret of Montfort." Pétiot put his finger on the side of his nose. "Gehazy has a good new informant. Someone he doesn't even have to blackmail! A Socialist clerk in the government who wants to pass him secrets. Tonight, in his hotel room when he comes back from the Bastille Day dancing, Gehazy will be arrested, he'll be sent to the Belgian border, but it won't matter to him because he has enough information to pay off everyone. I think he'll take up his residence in Switzerland. He'll spy on Russian dissidents." Pétiot lit another cigaret. "He'll be Ambassador Izvolsky's best friend."

"Gehazy has the secret already?"

"And not from you. Or Jules. I shall bribe you to forgive me." Pétiot rummaged in his tunic, under his beard, and brought out two papers. "Here."

Reisden unfolded them. He looked up to see Pétiot beaming interestedly at him. "These are copies, of course," said Pétiot. "I'm sending the originals to Paris. There'll be paperwork to get through, everyone's leaving for vacation, I imagine these'll sit on someone's desk until September. No trouble with that? Glad to be working with Jouvet."

Two letters on Pétiot's office stationery. *A man of integrity, soon to be a citizen . . . no further obstacle to Jouvet. I recommend Jouvet for the contract.*

"You're not a spy," Pétiot said. He wasn't a spy. He was a fool. Reisden felt flat, powerless; he had failed to see everything and had been let off.

"I hope you still want the job?" Pétiot asked innocently. "You must admit I did well enough. I fooled you."

Papa Pétiot, who do you really work for? Boring administrative work was the perfect cover. Buying supplies for the army. Leo would have said he should have known.

Yes, Leo. I should have.

"Do you want the job?"

He swallowed his pride. "If we both understand what the job is."

"My only regret," said Pétiot, "is that you won't give me secrets either."

"Oh? This is not simply step one of fourteen to look at our German files? If so, you have my promise as before."

Pétiot spread his hands. "I simply like to know my suppliers."

Well, thought Reisden, you know me. "Bribed to take a test," he said. He might never have spent time in Leo's household, he had been so thoroughly taken. "Was Cyron in on this?"

"Maurice simply believes you're not sufficiently French.— D'you know what decided me?" said Pétiot. "Two things. First, you actually do care about André."

"He is Jouvet's patient," Reisden said. "That is my job."

"If you cure André, Maurice will be happier than he has ever been. And the second? The Americans trusted you."

"Americans?" Reisden said, at a loss.

"D'you remember that story you told me? The American millionaire, the one with the missing boy? The one you look like. I saw the picture, but I didn't know what you meant until I saw the man himself. The most extraordinary thing. *They* must have trusted you, his people, to let you near him when you looked like his image."

"You saw Gilbert Knight?" Reisden asked. "In Paris?"

"No, no," Pétiot said. "Here. Yesterday."

Chapter 50

Reisden woke up Perdita. "Where is Gilbert?"

Gilbert was in Arras.

"He was *here*?" Reisden said.

Perdita sat up in bed, hair rumpled from the pillow, beautiful and defensive and as stubborn as a rock. "He did what you would have done if he were sick; he came. He went away when he knew you were all right—"

"Only staying long enough that Lucien Pétiot got a good look at him, d—n it!" It had helped, not hurt, but that wasn't the point at all.

"It doesn't make any difference what he looks like," she protested. She was not even able to see him in the dim light; she was looking past him.

"You've no idea," he said. "None."

"Will you see him?" she said. "Please?"

"I'll send him back to Paris," Reisden said. "Back to America. Since you won't."

"You're right," she said. "I won't, Alexander."

They were perfecting the art of fighting in whispers, but they'd wakened Toby. Reisden picked him up. "There, darling," he whispered, rocking him. "There, dearest Toby; dearest, dampest Toby Belch." He laid Toby down on the bed, put a towel under him, and unpinned and wiped and pinned efficiently.

"I want to tell you something," he said. "I've won. Jouvet has the contract." How he'd won stung him. Clever enough to delay? Hiding until the bad men left, more like.

"I'm glad for you," Perdita said. But she didn't care. This was their security, and he'd fought hard for it, and nothing mattered to her quite so much as his going to Arras to see Gilbert.

"I'll see him alone."

He bathed, as much as he could with a washcloth wetted in drinking water, and shaved painfully. In Cyron's coach, going to Arras, he fell asleep, too exhausted to dream.

Gilbert's hotel was the one at which Reisden and Perdita had stayed, the commercial hotel in the Grand'Place. It was early; the sunrise hardly had made its way into the square. All along the arcades, the red in the tricolor bunting caught the pink light. The shops in the arcades were closed, but rows of booths had been set up in the square: toys, balloons, trinkets, and games. The cheesemaker at the corner of the square was hanging flags from his iron signs; his apprentice steadied the ladder and yawned. Gilbert was sitting in the open-air café by the hotel, at one of the front tables, with a cup of coffee—no, it was probably tea. Gilbert thought coffee was dangerous.

Reisden smiled at his uncle's foibles, and then just looked at him.

Gilbert looked old. Not unhealthy or fragile-boned; he was still what the Irish would have called a lovely old man, straight-backed and with thick white hair and grey eyes that, even at near seventy, needed glasses only for reading. The sense of his age was only that he was sitting up straight in the way a man will do who, if he doesn't take care, will slump over in defeat.

He had brought his dog.

A year or so ago, when they had still been corresponding regularly, Gilbert had surprised them by writing he had acquired a dog, not *too big* a dog, nor one of those *little nervous* dogs, indeed he seemed *quite intelligent* and affectionate and not at all cast down by his afflictions. Reisden and Perdita had laughed and looked forward to hearing more about Elphinstone, and then Toby had been born.

It was clearly Elphinstone sitting patiently by Gilbert's café chair, with his muzzle affectionately on Gilbert's knee and his eyes on Gilbert's croissant. He was brown-and-black, with a smooth coat and alert ears, and a hunting dog's patience somewhere in his background. Gilbert's hand patted his dog's head absently, but Gilbert was looking apprehensively out into the square, and Gilbert's book lay neglected by his plate. He knows I'm coming, Reisden thought. Of course; Perdita had phoned him.

Elphinstone nuzzled Gilbert's knee. Gilbert called over the café waiter and they consulted over Gilbert's book, which must be a phrase book. French cafés do not often serve breakfast to dogs, but the waiter went away and came back with something magnificent on a plate and water in a coffee-bowl, and Elphinstone got to his feet and put his head down to it, wagging his tail.

The cheesemaker had finished hanging his flags; the

cheesemaker's two children came out to admire them and to wave their own flags. A passerby gave them coins. The Four-teenth of July is a day for families, for parades and picnics, for candy and toys bought at the street market and for fire-works in the evening: for children. Gilbert waved the children over to him. They came, shyly, dubious about foreigners. He held out his hand with coins on it, in the tentative way that a man would hold out breadcrumbs for a sparrow. They came close, holding to each other's smocks for security. They gog-gled at the coins and shrieked in alarm, running back to their papa's shop.

Gilbert put the coins carefully down on the tablecloth, at the edge of the table, as if he hoped the children would be lured back.

"You gave them too much," Reisden said, sitting down by him. "You frightened them."

As if this were the most appropriate thing to say, after eight months of silence. He felt suddenly terribly shy and awk-ward. Why was he giving Gilbert advice about what to do in France, as if he approved of this visit?

I'm demonstrating who the expert on French children is.

A deliveryman crossing the square looked at him and Gilbert, looked again. Elphinstone had cleaned his plate and bowl. "Come away from here," Reisden said. He considered the saucers and the coins on the table, left two—still generous—and gave the rest back to Gilbert, who put them down on the chair for the still-watching children. "We'll go for croissants where we'll not be seen by everyone."

Elphinstone limped along behind them. A long scar riffled the fur of his flank. Here we both are, Reisden thought, friends to the damaged.

At the bakery, on the Place de la Vacquerie, the walls were covered with mirrors. The two of them chose their breakfast breads, and the mirrors reflected them back at each other.

Gilbert was slightly shorter, a bit heavier, with the Roman face of all the Knights: a grey-haired man in a grey suit. Reisden was taller, thinner, black-haired, in a black suit, and not as cleanly shaven as he should have been. They moved alike. They both deliberated like chess players over the choice of croissant; not out of greed, but because they were deliberate over everything. They had the same expression on their face, as if they were about to be thrown to lions. In the mirror, each was looking at his mirrored other. The dog looked from one to the other of them. Something about them puzzled him. Perhaps they even smelled alike.

Arras is a green city, full of little parks. They found one and sat down on a bench, Gilbert tentatively at one end, Reisden warily at the other. Elphinstone settled at Gilbert's feet.

"You came to France," Reisden said in a low voice. "You shouldn't have. I want Toby to be free of all the Knights. I want him never to know what happened. Never to be affected by it. You couldn't stop what happened then, but you can at least take care of him now; you can take care of the rest of your family; and you're not doing it."

"Alexander—" Reisden heard the little hesitation before *Alexander*. "Harry has written me. He—he and his wife have decided to have a child."

"Fine," he said, denying its relevance to him.

"Yes. After Perdita's visit," his uncle said. "They decided."

"Good. I'm glad." He was not entirely. He was surprised; he felt the kind of emptiness one feels when an impossible situation has suddenly been solved by other people. He'd just felt it with Pétiot. "Yes. That's good."

"You are glad?" said Gilbert.

"Of course."

Neither said anything for a moment. Reisden ate some of his croissant, which was dry. "You'll have an heir," he said.

"You don't mind? That the money goes—"

"No." It was more true to say that he didn't mind now, with Pétiot's contract in prospect.

"You'll be free of all of it," Gilbert said.

"Yes."

He looked at the dog, who had laid his chin against Gilbert's foot.

"You'll have a child to love," he said. He thought of his Toby. "Children save the world, Gilbert. Another generation. Someone who won't care about William or Richard; someone to give the money to quite innocently."

Gilbert looked up at him stricken. "Do you want me to forget you?"

"Forget Richard? As if he had never lived."

"Then I am keeping you from being forgot?" Gilbert said. "Is that what I am doing?"

The dog looked up at the tone in his master's voice.

"Don't," said Reisden. "Please don't. You know what I mean."

"I do," said Gilbert. "Richard, do you think that having another child, having Harry or Harry's child, is the same as—as caring for you? Do you think Harry and you are just alike?"

"You have never been good enough to Harry," Reisden said.

"I cannot make him you."

"Richard is dead," Reisden said.

"You are not, Alexander."

"Think of Toby!"

Gilbert got up and headed blindly across the park, almost walking on the grass in his haste. Gilbert never walked on the grass. The dog looked after him worriedly and then got up and limped after him. Gilbert stopped at the other end of the park, near a stone tub of geraniums set next a wall. He was waiting for the dog, perhaps. Reisden stood up, suddenly feeling that he should be the dog, should go after him and catch up to him and say something; that it was inconceivable that this should be their last moment. Gilbert looked back and saw him standing, and they stood with the length of the park between them, seeing each other, hesitating.

Reisden walked toward him, certain that this was wrong, too, and Gilbert turned and walked back toward him. They met in the center of the park, by a bench and a bed of flowers.

"What can I do?" said Reisden. "What else can I do?"

"No," said Gilbert, "you are right— It is only—"

The dog looked from one to the other of them, distressed. Gilbert sat down on a bench and put his hand over his eyes. Reisden knelt down on the gravel and soothed the dog by patting its head and ears. The dog sniffed his face; he put his arm around its neck, holding on to it. Gilbert's dog. The gravel cut into his knees. He stood up, dusting it off, turning away.

"I killed your father," he said to Gilbert, "and now I have to get rid of you. Isn't it odd."

Gilbert drove his fist into his palm, cupping his fist with his palm, helpless against the past.

He sat down, on the other end of the bench from Gilbert again. In the middle of the bed of flowers was a smiling copper bust of some local worthy, put up, according to the inscription, in 1892. The copper had verdigrised to a streaked mid-green, and dark streaks had run down the stone plinth, in less time than William and Richard Knight had been dead. Above them, in the trees, the birds were singing and chirping and getting along with their lives. It was time they did the same.

"I've told Perdita what this is about. She doesn't understand it. I'm glad she doesn't. She loves her whole family. Including you. But will you please go home?"

"I shall miss her so."

"She will miss you." He ventured, because he knew Gilbert would understand it, "We will all miss each other. It's not that. She could visit you. But she'd bring Toby, out of some misguided—I don't know what; honesty; she can't see. In two or three years Toby will notice that you look like me. And that's the conversation I don't know how to have with him. Not at the age when he'll notice. I don't know how I'll ever have it."

"We will all miss each other," Gilbert said, and called him by his name, "Alexander."

And for a moment all his care seemed so unnecessary. Never mind, he wanted to say to his uncle. Buy an apartment in Paris. Come to visit. When Perdita goes to America I'll visit you in New York. We are all we have.

"If you should ever need me," Gilbert said, "*I will be there.* At any time. If we have not spoken in years, Alexander, if you should ever need me, promise to call me; I will come."

"If you need me I will come, too. If ever—" He thought of the gas in the cellar, the dismal Moroccan situation. "If ever I need to call on you, I will; I promise. And if there's ever a time Perdita and Toby need someone and I'm not there—"

Gilbert's eyes widened; he shook his head.

"Listen. Please listen. You know what happened yesterday. If there's need, make sure that they're all right."

"Yes," Gilbert said. "I will take care of them. I promise."

"But until then—"

"I understand," Gilbert said.

Reisden had left his croissant somewhere; a concentration of pigeons around the other bench suggested where. Gilbert tore his in half and they ate in silence. Gilbert fed the crumbs to birds while Elphinstone watched patiently, motionlessly, with his head between his paws. Reisden scattered the crumbs from the baker's paper wrapping for the birds too, feeling awkward, not something he had done before. The birds flew away. The paper must have looked like a hawk to them. You do it better, Reisden told his uncle silently. You're better with the birds. Better at being kind.

They walked back toward Gilbert's hotel, where there was a telephone. He called Perdita, who would be up by now. "Hello, love." He was here in Arras, he said, with Gilbert. Yes, they had been talking. They had gone out for breakfast. No, not to a restaurant.

"And what will he do now?" she asked. "Must he go away?"

He heard what she wanted. "Yes, love, he must go away." She had heard the answer in the silence before he spoke.

"Without my seeing him?"

She had to understand. Gilbert had understood; between the two of them they had to explain the necessity to her.

He covered the transmitter with his hand. "She'd like to see you. Will you stay here today with us, for Bastille Day?" And help me talk to her?

Of course he would. Gilbert had promised to help, anytime, for anything.

"Yes," Reisden said into the phone. "Today."

I want my boy's life to be different from mine, Reisden had written to Gilbert just after Toby had been born, and in the middle of it, still writing, he had realized that the very last person he could bring into that process was Gilbert, and he had put the pen down, and so the silence had come between them.

But he had been wrong. He needed Gilbert. Only Gilbert could help make the silence lasting.

I was not trying to cut off communication with him, Reisden thought. I was trying to put off the end.

Chapter 51

No one had thought to tell Ruthie Aborjaily that her brother was safe. From the walls of Montfort, she heard Boomer O'Connelly's cannons firing to celebrate the fall of the Bastille. One more day until Jules had to meet the blackmailer at the Place Victor-Hugo and tell him the secret of Montfort.

They had looked everywhere, and finished looking every place but one.

The police had left Montfort and the actors were gone. From her window, Ruthie saw the Rolls puff out the Jerusalem Gate with Monsieur Cyron, General Pétiot, and Count André. The coach returned and left again with a load of upper servants, and the young maids and servingmen left in groups, arm in arm, for the eight-mile walk to Arras. No one would be in the cellars but Ruthie.

She dumped the knitting out of her knitting bag and put into it Flores Rosenkranz's map, the electric torch, two candles, a tin candlestick, a ball of string, and a box of matches. On second thought, she added her extra pair of glasses, her largest ball of yarn, and her only bottle of perfume, a present years ago from Count André. She put a kerchief over her hair to protect against bats.

Count André had not only got the key but copied it; Ruthie took the copy and ventured into the cellars. She shone her light down the Mysterious Tunnels, which were practically collapsing. The torch lit crumbling chalk ceilings and beams stained with white-rimmed damp. In some places, chicken wire had been stretched between the beams because chunks of stone had fallen from the ceiling, but the wire was rusting through. She looked at the Torture Chamber and the Haunted Crypt. She looked at everything, until all that was left was the Holy Well.

Engineers from Countess Sabine's mines had pumped out the carbon monoxide in the cellar, but Ruthie was taking no chances. She lit a candle at the top of the third stairs and watched the wick carefully. If the flame were starved for air, it would climb to the very end of the wick.

The candle flame burned calmly. Ruthie set the candlestick down in the hollow of the cellar steps and squared her shoulders. An old wrought-iron torch-stand stood at the bottom of the stairs; she tied the end of her ball of knitting to one of its legs and, paying out the yarn with one hand and taking up the candlestick with the other, set out among the ghostly white columns.

The pumping out of the bad air had helped, but near the Holy Well the air still smelled of death. Ruthie took her perfume out of her purse and dabbed it under her nose fiercely. *Poor Mr. Blantire,* she thought. For a moment she was back in her own past, a girl of ten, fleeing toward the border with her seven-year-old brother. All along the road there had been bodies, and the smell. She took a good deep breath of *Violettes de Valois* and thought of Count André giving it to her; she touched the carved flowers on the stopper and thought of putting it back on the dresser in her bedroom, when she was upstairs again and safe. Mr. Blantire had died here, but he had just been overcome, it was nobody's fault, no one had meant him harm, there had been no Turks, no murder, no—

Mr. Blantire's body had left a stain by the door. She stepped over it carefully, shivering a little. She stood the candle on the top of the wooden box—she had to stand on tiptoe to reach it—and shone the torch around the enclosure of the Holy Well.

Iron bars around the Well. Thick chalk columns holding up the roof. A wall. She took her yarn in hand and followed the wall. No tunnels. No bones. She felt the frustration her brother and Dr. Reisden had: what was she looking for?

She made her way back to the Holy Well, winding up her yarn. She circled round the iron cage, examining it from outside. What could be here? Some wonderful flying machine or bomb, like in a story by Jules Verne or H. G. Wells? No, it was a well in a cellar, with a cage around it.

The beam of her torch fell on the dusty floor, and on the dark irregular stain that Mr. Blantire's body had left. Just by the door of the cage.

She wondered why he hadn't tried to make his way to the stairs. The door to the cage had been open; the police had mentioned that.

But why would he have died? He would have had time to stagger up the stairs, as Count André and Dr. Reisden had.

If the door had been open when he died.

Men always have a pocketknife. Mr. Blantire would have had a pick to take out stones from horses' hooves. Ruthie opened her eyes, stood up, and looked at the lock. It was bright with scratches.

"Mademoiselle Françoise locked you in," Ruthie said, and felt poised over her the nightmare scimitars of murder.

She knelt down by the stain, not touching it, but close. The stain curved as the door did. She saw him, pressing his body against the door. She folded her hands, closed her eyes behind her glasses, and prayed as she had when she was a little girl; it had done good later, but it hadn't stopped the Turks, and it didn't help her now.

She reached down her candle, and as she did something fell from the top of the Well enclosure and clinked and glinted in the corner.

A button. Ruthie picked it up and held it on her palm. An old-fashioned dressmaker's button; little girls had worn them on their dresses in rows when Ruthie was first in Paris. It was a distinctive design, a pink rose in clear faceted glass. Mademoiselle Françoise would have liked such a thing; she had loved frills and her uniforms had always had twice as many buttons as necessary.

Mademoiselle Françoise had seemed so harmless, always flirting and vain of her looks, but not a bad woman. Not bad like that.

Had he put the button where someone could find it, proof she had murdered him? Perhaps he had tried to protect her. Perhaps she had only meant it as a joke—had locked him in, for a joke, and then had come back to find that the pump had killed him.

Ruthie shivered and put the button in her pocket. The woman was dead now. Forgive; forget.

She climbed the stairs tiredly. She had found nothing, no secret of Montfort, nothing to help her brother or Dr. Reisden, only a love story that had ended terribly and mysteriously. She went into the washroom to wash her smudged hands and face. There were no towels. She pulled her handkerchief out of her apron pocket—

And the button clinked into the basin and fell down the drain. Let it go, she thought. But she remembered what it had looked like, a glass button with a rose, which might have been one of a row on a dress.

Chapter 52

Reisden had to meet Katzmann when his train arrived, which would be a little after one in the afternoon, but his family had the day until then, the only day they would ever have together.

"I will help her understand," Gilbert said. "She does understand, you know. . . ."

They met Perdita and Toby at the railroad station. The sun was shining, and in the paved courtyard outside the station the workers' bands were practicing. Toby giggled and wriggled, wanting to get down and play with Elphinstone.

They walked slowly down the green Boulevard Carnot toward the Citadel, taking turns pushing the baby carriage with its load of diapers, extra clothes, and baby food, and Toby sitting up and crowing and occasionally throwing his socks over the side. Elphinstone trotted along behind. Other families were also heading toward the parade ground, on foot or in carriages. Perdita leaned into the baby carriage, bumping it over the cobblestones. Reisden took over. I should have taken the car, he thought, but he'd been too tired, and Gilbert fit with Perdita and Toby into the category of people that he would rather not drive.

Toby didn't want to sit in the carriage, he wanted to explore; he tottered along, almost walking, holding to both of Gilbert's index fingers to keep himself up. Gilbert had to walk bent over to keep up with him. Reisden knew that position, which was backbreaking. It was like watching himself with his son.

"Aah*aah*," Toby said, wobbling along at breakneck speed.

"Ah-aah!" Gilbert agreed, puffing to keep up with him.

Perdita stopped to listen to them, silent on his arm, holding him as if to tell him to stop and listen too. Perdita had brought Toby to Boston and let Gilbert come to Paris, to show them all they could be happy together. But you're wrong, love, he thought.

"Pétiot is pushing forward our French citizenship," he said. "He has written our *juge d'instruction* a really fulsome letter, saying that I am a paragon of integrity and that he won't rest until we are French."

"Oh," she said. "Good." She smiled at him, bravely, but like a person who is deciding to have an operation. Being French wasn't for her what it was for him; he had never been more than half an Austrian. As good as we shall have, love; the country we can belong to together. We can't have America. Not together.

Four women in white marched past them, holding up placards and wearing green-and-white sashes. LA PARTIE FÉMINISTE, he read, and WOMEN WANT THE VOTE. He told Perdita that the Feminists were there. "Next year you'll march with them."

She smiled at him, but faintly, sadly, distractedly.

The highlight of Bastille Day in any French town with a garrison is an army revue. At Arras it was held on the *Petit Champ de manoeuvres*, the big open field just outside the Citadel. The grass was crowded with families. *Pères de famille* shepherded their wives, wives' sisters, mothers, mothers-in-law, sisters-in-law, and incredible crowds of children. Proud mothers held twins in arms, pushed babies in prams over the bumpy grass, or expostulated with school-age boys and girls. On the picnic ground, the grass was bright with white dresses and soldier-blue school uniforms. Red-white-and-blue flags fluttered everywhere. Every old man wore his lapel ribbons or his medals from the Franco-Prussian War; the younger men, with nothing but colonial wars to decorate them, looked envious, and the little boys jingled their school medals and agitated their flags. Reisden watched the fathers, proud and worn down, with the lines of responsibility in their faces.

They found a spot for their picnic, spread a tablecloth, and sat on it. Toby plumped down on his behind, put his fingers in his mouth thoughtfully, then grinned, fell forward onto his hands, and crawled toward Gilbert. "Ah-aah!" he crowed triumphantly, pulling himself up by Gilbert's shoulder, and planted a wet, dirty baby slobber, somewhere between a kiss and a hug, on Gilbert's face. They have the same smile, Reisden thought.

The cannons fired, startling Toby; the bands began to arrive on the field, playing "The Marseillaise." The crowd waved flags and cheered, *Vive la France!* Reisden bought all four of them flags from a man with a tray of them. Perdita and Gilbert waved theirs with the air of Presbyterians at high mass, trying to fit in. Reisden did not wave his or shout *vive la France* either; he was not that sort of man. Toby tried to put his flag in his mouth.

"Oh, dear boy, you must not eat that—"

"Aaah!"

"The dye is full of horrible poisons, and you will stick the point through the roof of your mouth—"

Toby blinked at Gilbert and kept gumming the flag. Reisden took it away from him. Toby wailed, beginning to be tired or hungry or overwhelmed by the crowds. Reisden walked him up and down, jiggling him to distract him. "Come to years of discretion, Toby, don't put things in your mouth." Toby needed changing again. One wants children but one doesn't always want them.

A reviewing stand had been set up under a green awning, and all the dignitaries of the town were gathered under it. From a distance Reisden saw Pétiot, Cyron, and, improbably, André, pale but irreproachable in morning dress with his hair clubbed back. Pétiot made a speech; Cyron made a speech, which was enthusiastically clapped by everyone close enough to hear it. *Vive la France! Vive la République!*

The scarlet cavalry burst out of the Citadel and caracoled down the field. Behind them came the infantry in lines of sky blue and red and the artillery pulling wheeled cannons. Reisden had been to Austrian and German revues and to one Bastille Day parade at Longchamp, out of curiosity. In peacetime it was the showy cavalry who got the loudest applause; today it was the guns.

The *Figaro* was predicting confidently that there would be no war in Morocco. But that was Paris and this was Flanders, land fought over since Roman times. Beefy old men with moustaches whipped their flags back and forth and shouted *To Strasbourg! Vive l'armée! To Alsace!* A girl ducked under the ropes to kiss a blue soldier. A very old drunk with a decoration swayed by their picnic blanket, weeping and singing "The Battle-Trumpet" as he headed off to vomit against a tree. Row after row of soldiers wheeled, marched in close order, and knelt to fire blanks toward the east.

Gilbert's worried eyes followed the clouds of gunsmoke.

When the revue had finished, they walked back toward the city center. They found an open-fronted café in the Place de la Vacquerie and had a long, leisurely Flemish lunch under the awning. Toby single-mindedly transferred the contents of his plate to his bib, his clothes, and Gilbert's lapel, then sprawled angelically in his pram, asleep in the heat, while Elphinstone licked the flagstones under their table and lapped water from a bowl. Around them, in spite of the noon sun, Arrageois burghers drank beer and forked up *flammenkuechen*, flatbreads fried with meat and cheese.

Gilbert asked questions about the countryside. What was the history of this area? Reisden, yawning in the heat, left them for Perdita to answer, but she didn't know. She would have known the answers to questions about New York. They fell silent. Perdita was wearing Gilbert's teardrop necklace, tucked into the neck of her blouse. She tugged at it and ran her fingers along the length of its silver chain.

"I must go and meet Katzmann," Reisden said. *Talk to her,* he mouthed to Gilbert. From the other side of the square he looked back at them, his wife and his uncle talking, heads together, now he had gone. He fought a sense that he should go back, that nothing he could do was as important as being with them today.

"André's here in town," he told Katzmann at the station. "With Cyron. If I know my country towns, they're at a lunch hosted by the mayor. It'll be out by two-thirty; there is a puppet theatre in the street fair; conclusion, by three you should find André backstage at the puppet theatre, re-carving the puppets into figures of horror."

"Tell me everything that happened," Katzmann said.

Reisden took a deep breath. "No," he said. "I don't want you prejudiced. Look at him; talk to him. You've seen him before; tell me what you think has happened. If anything."

Katzmann nodded. "See you at the fireworks?"

He didn't really want Katzmann seeing Gilbert. "I'll find you." He went back to his family.

He found them at the hotel. Perdita and Gilbert were in the parlor murmuring about friends in Boston. Had Gilbert convinced her? Gilbert shook his head silently, no. Reisden went in to see his boy, who was asleep in the bedroom, pink-cheeked, with his black hair fuzzing out in every direction. He lay down on the bed next to Toby and half-heard Perdita and Gilbert talking.

He doesn't talk to me, she said. He talks to you. He needs you.

Reisden laced his fingers behind his neck and stared up at the ceiling.

They went to the street fair. They watched the juggler and the wild animal man, who was giving rides on a terrible-tempered old camel. The camel spit at them and sidled away on elephant feet. They shared gingerbread pigs. They strolled through the fair stalls, admiring fresh fruit and potted plants, garden forks and rolls of wallpaper, idling away the afternoon before the fireworks like persons who would be together always. They had nothing to say; they were too far apart in what they thought; they were too close to say it. They went to the puppet theatre, though not at three o'clock, and watched wooden soldier-puppets attack each other with clacking snippets of swords.

In Mademoiselle Françoise's now-closed shop, the publicist from the Necro had set up a little advertisement-cum-museum. "See the terrible history of Citizen Mabet! Visit the haunts of witches!" Next to easel photographs of Cyron in costume, Guix from the Necro was telling a crowd of shepherds and shop boys that they could earn good money in the pictures next Sunday. Photos from *Citizen Mabet* hung in the window. A male and female mannequin wore costumes from the film, and Guix's assistants were handing out tin buttons, Cyron's picture in a tricolor cockade, to those who signed up as extras. "Tell your friends! Next Sunday! Skip Mass and impress your girl!"—which made the boys grin and the women scold.

Gilbert saw a picture of Reisden in one of the first scenes of the film. He frowned over the model of the guillotine. "I do not see the point of fright."

They stood outside Mademoiselle Françoise's old shop, looking out over the plaza. A group of men in rough white jackets and pants and round felt hats came round the corner all together, holding a sign: they were the *orphéon*, the miners' chorus, of Wagny-les-Mines. "Look," said Gilbert. One of the *orphéonistes* was carrying his son on his shoulder, a little boy dressed in white like his father and wearing a miniature round hat.

Reisden put Toby on his shoulders too. A passerby looked at Reisden and Gilbert curiously, and looked at Toby crowing above his father's head, and smiled.

Chapter 53

There is a saying in the Jewish scriptures: We do not see what we see, we see what we are. Today André does not know what to see. Everything seems to be as distinct as if it is in strong sunlight. He looks at the black-and-white clothing laid out for him, the weave of the fabric, the complicated up-and-down of the threads. He sees the black pores on the nose of the waiter who serves him breakfast, the swirl of milk in black coffee. With Necrosar, everything had meaning. Coffee was poisoned; a tie was to strangle with. Now everything is distinct, flat, and flavorless, like a bad photograph. Nothing he touches seems to belong to him.

He walks through his morning role as the Count. The guns fire only blanks. No one is poisoned at the luncheon. Sabine is not there. Papa Cyron explains that Sabine is in a delicate state. *My* stepfather, *my* wife, *my* child? Sabine and Papa Cyron belong to André, Count of Montfort. There is another André, who is new.

Without Necrosar's stories to fill it with meaning, the world is dull and strange. Papa Cyron is in love with Sabine. Perhaps that is just a story to substitute for the ones André can no longer quite make up. André disappointed Papa Cyron. Today he ought to have worn his old uniform or had a ribbon in his buttonhole. There are fragments of a story in this, but nothing to go on with, nothing André knows how to give a shape to. The mayor is sick; André sees the sharp yellow angle of his cheekbone. The *directrice* of the Institute for the Aged is a slattern; her wineglass is a clutter of lip-rouge and fingerprints. Perhaps she drinks alone. But these are not stories.

After lunch he is let loose to wander on his own (but Papa Cyron's chauffeur follows him; Papa Cyron must think he is not only mad but stupid). He goes to the Grand'Place to look for his film, but he cannot see his guillotine and the crowd screaming for blood. There is only a street fair. Fisherwomen in stiff-starched lace hats sell hake and whiting; hawkers show him candy, cheeses, and pictures of St. Barbara and St. Isidor. There is a puppet theatre, but there is no life in it, only sticks of wood.

He is looking at a stall of cheap rugs when he recognizes a man at his elbow: Philippe Katzmann, whom Reisden sent him to see earlier this summer. The psychiatrist.

"Something has happened to Necrosar," he tells Katzmann. "Necrosar is gone." Katzmann thinks this is good news. He questions André eagerly. "No, I have no hallucinations," André says sadly. He looks at Katzmann, a balding man with brown teeth who wheezes as he smokes his cigars. Necrosar would have had him killed by a vengeful patient. Katzmann will only get older, frailer, his teeth browner, his eyeglasses thicker. "I can't see anything that isn't there," André says.

"Congratulations," Katzmann says. "You're proving a point for me. This is extraordinary."

André thinks, I want Necrosar back.

He walks through the fair and it is a horror in a way that Necrosar's horrors have never been. Who are these people? What does he know about them? Everything is strange. What do the rug-dealer's flat eyes hide? André does not know, he does not know at all. Katzmann tries to talk to him, but he doesn't listen.

It is a relief to see someone he knows. Reisden is sitting at a café table with a grey-haired man, whom at first André doesn't notice.

"Where is Necrosar?" André strides across to Reisden. "I don't like this."

It's then that he really sees the other man, and for a moment, *blazing* through his blood, Necrosar is there again, the meaning of the world. Because the other man looks like Reisden. Not only in a general way but in hundreds of specifics: the lean bones of the face; the long Roman nose; the photographable cheekbones; the grey of their eyes.

"Who are *you*?" says Necrosar. Reisden and this other man turn and look at each other as if they are deciding together who he is.

"You're Reisden's secret father," André says. The resemblance is that close.

"Don't be an ass, André, this is Gilbert Knight."

The uncle of dead Richard Knight. André knows the story. "Remarkable," says Katzmann.

"Oh, Gilbert Knight," André says. "Come stay with me. I want to look at you. To use you in my film. I need you." If there's no imagination in the world, if he cannot make up stories, there is nothing. He needs to surround himself with monsters of nature, with guillotines and fear. "I am lonely. Necrosar is gone. I am so sad."

If this is sanity, André can hardly bear it.

The hotel door opens. Reisden's wife comes out, holding their baby. Reisden's eyes turn toward her: no, to the baby, and then to the old man. And *there* is a story, André sees out of the corner of his eye something interesting, something more complex than the obsessions of the engineer Henri, who wanted to kill his son. "André wants you to stay, Gilbert," Reisden says in English. "He wants to use you in his film." That's all, but the group becomes four-sided; Reisden's wife holds the baby more tightly, she reaches out toward the older man. Reisden's eyes never leave his child. He stands up and goes to her; the dead boy's uncle stands up, too, as if following Reisden's lead. Light coming through the archway of the arcade isolates him, making him bright and grey: Reisden's mirror, Reisden's ghost.

The old man looks at André. *"Je suis très désolé que— de—"* He speaks French as if he is looking it up word by word. He turns to Reisden.

Katzmann comes up behind them. Reisden puts his arm around his wife and child. The old man looks at them for a long moment, and then he turns to André and smiles.

"No," he says in English. Even his voice is Reisden's. His smile is not Reisden's rare smile, though; it is someone else's, he can't think whose. "I am sorry, my dear," the old man says to Reisden's wife, and puts his arms around her. "We will see each other in America," and then he and Reisden clasp hands for a moment. André's theatre eye catches hold of their gestures, like the eternal parting at the foot of a scaffold. Reisden and this man do not want to leave each other. Each is afraid of what will happen to the other, to himself, to all of them. The old man turns back to André. "You must not make your moving picture *frightening*, you know," he urges. Then he is gone, a pair of bowed shoulders making his way through the market, followed by a discouraged, tired little dog.

Chapter 54

E ven then, even until that moment, Perdita hoped that they would work something out. She would not take it, not understand it. "Please," she said. "It is wrong." She stood in the middle of the crowd and had had no more of a goodbye to Uncle Gilbert than a press of the hand. "No, Alexander, you can't," she said, "you can't—"

"You know I must. We must."

"You *cannot*," she repeated. "Please, let me talk."

So they walked Gilbert to the train. Halfway down the green boulevard there was a bench. She sat them both down.

"Oh, my dears," she said. "You tell each other things you can't tell anyone else. We need one another. *I* need you both."

"I will write you," said Gilbert.

"I want more than that," she said. She had said it. "I know, I know, you look too much alike. You sound alike, too. But— but—!"

"What will I say to Toby?" said Alexander.

"Perhaps he won't care."

"I want him to care." He had never said this. It deeply surprised her.

"Alexander." She was really furious. "Alexander, yes it's important, but never in this life will that secret be the most important part of you unless you make it that way. And you are giving up your family for this."

"Am I giving up you?" he asked.

She didn't know how to answer. Who am I, she thought, what am I to him? What does he want when he wants me?

"Gilbert," he said, "I am sorry that we're quarreling in front of you."

"You need each other," she said to both of them.

"Apparently you need him," Alexander said. "Do you need me?"

"Alexander! Don't!"

They said nothing after that but only walked together awkwardly. Forsaking all others, she thought. Her marriage ceremony had not contained those words. It had been in French.—She thought about the thousand possibilities for prevarication in a foreign country.

Uncle Gilbert said nothing. She walked between them, cuddling Toby, who began to cry.

The sun would not set for a long time but it had sunk behind the trees. In the station, the train was streaks of red against black. Uncle Gilbert got on the train. She saw him, a white blur, and then after a while a flash of white—he was waving. She waved back with her free hand and then thought, what am I doing? What should I do? Once she had run for a train and caught it. That had been for Alexander. But this time she was Toby's mother, holding her boy.

Then she and Alexander walked back through the streets, which had gone grey. Somewhere ahead she could hear music, but she hadn't the heart for it, and Alexander turned away, too. "Let's just walk a bit," he said.

"You shouldn't have done this," she said.

They walked down the grey streets, silently. Toby fell asleep and lay a heavy weight on her shoulder.

They came out on a vast dark square, where their footsteps echoed against the cobblestones; a French square, too large, too regular, smelling of horses and French bread. From far away a first rocket bloomed like mildew against the black. Do I belong? she thought. No. I want to go to a ballpark and listen to the bat crack against the baseball. I want to cook hot dogs on a stick. Perhaps I only want to be American again.

I'll leave Alexander, she thought, because I can't speak with him or he with me. I'll go back to America. He expects it. Toby will grow up speaking English. We will see Uncle Gilbert. And we'll all be miserable, because we all adore Toby; because no one Alexander can talk to will know he's Richard, or care; because no one will make me red doorknobs anymore. Because I love him.

They walked through the dark, saying nothing to each other. This will be our epitaph, she thought: Even at the last we had nothing to say, as if we had our whole lives to say it.

And Gilbert Knight sat in the train thinking about Father. Richard was right, Father was with them when they were together. He had been with them in the bakeshop, while Gilbert, appalled, hesitated before choosing his croissant. *Obey me, go back to Boston, run my companies!* He had been in the film office by the guillotine. *I shall show you fright, Sir.*

When Gilbert looked back at them from the train window, Father had been by Richard's elbow.

Chapter 55

On Saturday, the fifteenth of July, Ruthie's brother Jules had been scheduled to meet Gehazy at the obelisk in the Place Victor-Hugo. But Jules had come back last night with wonderful news. He was safe, and André, and Dr. Reisden and his family. Ruthie was almost giddy with happiness.

Jules went off in midmorning by the coach to Arras—not to be blackmailed but to oversee costumes being sent back to Paris. Ruthie rolled up her sleeves and sat down to the work for the Ball of the Dead and the battle scene next week. Did they have enough film stock? Black powder and lard for bombs? Kliegl and Arnaud bulbs? An extra sheet of plate glass on call in Arras if the Pepper's Ghost glass was broken? Costumes, wigs, chocolate syrup for blood, sausage and cheese and wine to feed the extras, enough extras to fill the Grand'Place? Ruthie hurried from Boomer O'Connelly's shed to Eli Krauss' storeroom, checking off items on her list. Mr. Krauss was off at Olhain with the Reisdens and Madame Sabine, filming part of the ghost scene; she left him a note to count light bulbs.

As she crossed the Great Hall, she noticed that the door of Monsieur Cyron's office was closed. She knocked and opened the door a crack. Count André was sitting inside, screening his film against a wall. His head was down and he was looking at the film through his disheveled hair, running his fingers through his hair, tugging it in desperation. "Oh, it's terrible," he moaned, "it's terrible, Ruthie. *Look* at it." Everything was going just as usual. She smiled, closed the door, and went off to make him a salad.

After lunch she put on a sun hat, pinned up her skirt, and bicycled to Mademoiselle Françoise's house to count the uniforms for the big battle scene, which were being stored there.

Inside Mademoiselle Françoise's house the air smelled of damp and shadow. The parlor and workroom were crowded with costumes, hung on iron-pipe racks to shake out their wrinkles. Ruthie counted dutifully, thinking how profound the silence is in the house of a person who has died; and then she looked up at the stairs to the second floor, where Mademoiselle Françoise's bedroom was.

Nothing had been touched in Mademoiselle Françoise's closet. Ruthie looked at her elaborate ruffled Sunday dresses, her blouses, even her narrow shoes. One blouse had glass shoulder-buttons with stars, not a bad effect, but none matched the button that had been in the cellar, the clear glass button with the rose.

In the attic, Mademoiselle Françoise had hung a dress here under a sheet—but it was a ballgown fifteen years old, black satin crusted with stars and spangles, its skirt drooping over its hard bustle. Too beloved to alter and too ugly to wear. Ruthie had a dress like that herself.

But there was no dress with rose buttons.

She went out thoughtfully into the garden. The house still looked as though Mademoiselle Françoise was just round the corner, but in the garden she had been dead two months. It was a jungle. Sage sprawled drunkenly under an overgrown rosemary bush; the chalk-gravel paths were whiskered with grass. Among the bolted lettuces by the well, the weeds grew so thickly they looked planted. In the sunny south exposure by the garden shed, white funnel-shaped flowers were being strangled in flamboyant stalks of purple bloom.

They were not only weeds, but noxious; thorn apple and foxglove, poisons both. Ruthie went back into the kitchen and found Mademoiselle Françoise's garden gloves, long and narrow and with an embroidery of a little girl watering flowers. They were too small for Ruthie's capable hands. She wrapped one around the stem of the foxglove and pulled. The plant came up whole with its roots, and in its shade she saw another plant growing. A small, slender one, with small dangling fruit. She knelt down to see it and pushed her glasses up her nose to look more carefully. Delicate, soft, hooked bristles.

She had researched witchcraft for the film. She was looking at enchanter's nightshade.

Ruthie dropped the foxglove plant on the garden path and backed away, brushing her hands against her skirt. Carefully, bed by bed, she looked at all the plants in the garden. Close by the house, near the rhododendrons, she found a large-leaved plant with little lemony fruit. Mandrake. Around the corner of the garden shed, on the rubbish heap where it often grows, sprawled the tangled dark stems of henbane.

In the kitchen, on a shelf by the stove, Mademoiselle Françoise kept her cookbooks: four handwritten black-bound books spotted with grease. Three were in various women's hands; one, in a man's. Among the mixtures for killing bed-bugs with chrysanthemum petals and removing red-wine stains with salt were ones that disturbed Ruthie deeply. Ruthie wrapped all four books in her apron and dropped them into her knitting bag.

She looked around the kitchen. Table and kitchen chairs, shelves in the chimney-corner, stove blocking the old fire-place, door to garden, stone sink with a window over it, painted wooden cupboard. It looked so ordinary. On the shelves were ranged canisters of flour and sugar and coffee, jars of preserved green beans and tomatoes, jams and spices and condiments. She stood on a chair. Behind the nutmegs and pickling salt were two or three small unlabeled tin canis-ters. One held rose hips, one ashes; the third contained some kind of salve, rancid like mutton fat and smelling of green herbs and mint. She dipped the fingers of her right hand into it and brought her fingers to her mouth, touched her tongue to the salve—nasty! It almost numbed her mouth. She wiped her fingers carefully clean on the hand towel, but to her over-heated imagination, the skin of her hand tingled. She dropped the tin of ointment into her bag, too. Dr. Reisden could have it analyzed.

The noon bells were clinking from St.-Laurent Blangy and with a deeper boom from Arras. She locked the gate behind her and pushed her bicycle away from the house. She had errands at the film office; then she and Jules were going to have dinner, celebrating their first completely carefree moment since the blackmail.

She pedaled her way along the road toward Arras. The sun pounded down, the light bouncing off the road up under her hat. Her mouth was dry; she should have drunk some water in the house. Her right hand tingled where she had touched the ointment. Then it was as if the hand were going to sleep: It went numb entirely, and flopped. She was using one hand to keep her knitting bag in the bicycle basket. She tried using the numb hand but she could not steer the bicycle.

She got off and let her bicycle fall into the tall grass at the side of the road, by a tree. She stood against the tree, dizzy, thirsty. I shall take off my hat, she thought, and keep my head cool, but with only one hand she could not untie the strings. Her heart was pounding. She slid down the tree and lay in the grass and wildflowers, her hat tilted over her face and blocking her view. She could not feel her body at all; she felt as if she were floating, or flying.

Chapter 56

André had stayed at Montfort to edit the film but he had sent Eli Krauss to Olhain with the Reisdens, a wagonful of children, and detailed instructions. In the same location by the moat where Eli had filmed the drowning of the Méduc family, he was to photograph a crowd of laughing children. Against a black scrim, he would film Reisden, in old-man makeup, sitting surrounded by his grandchildren.

They did the scrim scene first. Reisden, in grey crepe whiskers, had to look patriarchal, the children as worshipful as if they were in church. Reisden was uneasy with it and got a bad case of actor's laughter; as soon as the camera began cranking he broke up. Of course the children did the same; under the hot sun they began to giggle and poke one another.

"We're starting to get shadows on the scrim," Eli Krauss said diplomatically. "I gotta move it, so I'm thinking I should do the long shot, on account of I gotta reframe anyway?"

"Yes, let the children run around a bit."

Reisden took off his patriarchal dress-coat and padding. Perdita and Toby were extras in this scene, Perdita in a coal-scuttle bonnet and bell-shaped skirt, holding a wriggling Toby. With the other extras, they moved off toward the moat. Reisden sat in the shade, watching his wife and son.

Last night Perdita had cried in her sleep. She had wrapped her pillow around her head, in the heat, and turned away from him. She had pretended she'd gone back to sleep, and he had lain awake and pretended to believe it.

What happens to Gilbert now, he thought. He goes back to Boston, to Harry and Efnie. And we won't know what happens after that. But my son will be safe.

What happens to us?

Zeno Puckett hunkered down beside him. "Heard I'd find you here. You got a couple minutes?"

Puckett was wearing a rusty black suit of French cut, made for a man somewhat heavier and very much shorter. "Blantire's funeral was today?" Reisden asked.

"Yep," Puckett said, "we boxed up old T. J. and sent him off.—I hear you're old Pétiot's best friend now."

"What is that supposed to mean?"

"I wondered what he was doing, is all." Puckett took off his hat, sat it on his knee, and flicked the brim with his finger, stirring little puffs of dust. "My land, he's taking a casual attitude. Old T. J. up and dies, and a couple weeks later his lady friend dies. And the po-lice just don't seem to pay it no mind, it ain't no more to them than drowning kittens.—Your friend Pétiot talked 'em into chuckin' the investigation."

Pétiot turned off the investigation? Reisden thought, and said nothing. If Blantire were a spy, Pétiot would have had it taken away from the ordinary run of Sûreté cop.

"S'pose you don't know why."

"He thinks it's an accident; Cyron's making a film; Cyron doesn't want police." A good enough explanation.

Puckett scratched at his long nose. "I guess I'm going to tell you what else I know about Blantire. You ever heard of the January Manifesto?"

This at least did not sound like the secret of Montfort. He shook his head.

"The Amiens Congress? The Educational Society? Bureau of Investigation?—What d'you think of the labor movement?"

Reisden wondered where this was leading.

"The January Conference," Puckett said, "it was in Chicago, January 1905, and it was a conference of miners like your Amiens Congress. Some folks say the Germans was behind it, using the labor movement to weaken Americans. Most of the folks at the January Conference were Germans, 's all I know, and there's been more strikes in America since then, mining strikes, which ain't good for the country, same as it ain't for France." He took a breath. "So the U.S. government got together some guys, ex-Pinkertons mostly, to find out what it was about. The Bureau of Investigation."

"Do they break strikes?" The Pinks did.

"They investigate," Puckett said. "They got regular agents,

and then there's special agents, like deputies, who go round
and—investigate."

"And what was there to investigate about Blantire?"

"Well, that German newspaper? It wasn't just German. It
was Wobblies."

"Blantire was in with the labor movement?"

"To my mind he wasn't serious; I think it was just T. J. get-
tin' into the biggest saloon fight around. That boy wouldn't
just hang round with any other man's wife. It had to be the
sheriff's.—But turns out he don't come back to the U.S., he
comes here."

"To the mining country."

"You betcha. And I would think," Puckett said, "now I
would think, that the French would be real interested in what
he was doing an' who sent him."

"And instead," Reisden said, "Pétiot tells the police to wash
their hands. Are you saying you think the government had
him killed?"

"I'm just a friend of T. J.'s."

Reisden considered it. "Pétiot thought that Blantire was a
Russian spy, looking for something completely different, and
he wanted to use him."

"Is that so," Puckett said.

"That's what he said," Reisden said.

"Well, you're goin' to believe him, you're Pétiot's pal. I
don't suppose it's no matter, T. J.'s dead now." Puckett gave
his hat a final slap against his knee and jammed it back on his
head. "But he was all right, you know. Spite of his politics. He
was all right. It gravels me nobody cares what killed him."

"Why not carbon monoxide?"

"Oh yeah? Ain't that supposed to build up when folks use
the pump a lot? How many folks was staying here when T. J.
disappeared? None, I say." Puckett unfolded himself and
stood up.

"Busloads of guests come every weekend," Reisden said

sharply. "This is Montfort. The Friends of Montfort are distinguished old men with bad bladders; they come to visit, they dig, they drink, they get their hands dirty, they use the W.C. Meanwhile a Socialist cowboy is spying on them from the cellar? No wonder Pétiot wants a quiet, controlled investigation. I presume your investigative bureau lot are not actively trying to embarrass French security."

Puckett knuckled his jaw, thinking about it.

"I am tired of spying and rumors of spying," Reisden said, "and second and third and fifty-fifth motives. Blantire died. People do."

He felt he was being Pétiot's dog, but only because Puckett thought he was.

"T. J. told me one more thing," Puckett said. "And I'm going to tell you because I can't make sense of it. T. J. told me about this girl he was seeing here. You ain't read his book? T. J. couldn't never resist a superstition. And he wrut me in this one letter I got? He said he'd met this girl. She was a witch. That's what he said. She'd showed him tunnels, under her house, where the other witches met. And he'd took part in a witch ceremony.—You're Pétiot's nearest an' dearest. You tell him about that," Puckett said. "Maybe he ought to investigate that. 'Cause that was strange."

Eli Krauss called Reisden back to filming. This time he sat Toby on his knee. After the filming he let Toby pull off his crepe whiskers (*ouch,* dear Toby) and sat Toby on his lap while he took the spirit gum off his face with rubbing alcohol.

Grey hair: the face in the mirror was Gilbert's, of course. He washed his hair fiercely.

He thought about Pétiot. Cyron's friend, Cyron's protector. Had Blantire simply died? Pétiot hadn't had him killed, had he? "I want him to have simply died, my love," Reisden murmured to Toby. "I was bought. No doubt of that. I want to stay bought."

He drove his wife and child back to Montfort, very slowly and carefully, conscious of being distracted. Perdita, who had eaten lunch, took Toby up for his nap. Reisden took bread and cheese and a drink into the library—which was no more than the ancient and worm-eaten shelves lining the billiard room. Among the scripts and the popular novels that might one day be scripts, he found what he had hoped for, the familiar grey back of *Through Russia on a Mustang*. He took the book up in the abbey tower. And, looking up sometimes at the Arras road and the mine-tailings, he read about T. J. Blantire's trip through Russia.

Blantire had not liked the Russian peasants; he would have preferred prosperous, industrious Germans. He had loathed Russian officialdom; every country officer wore "short jackets with the pockets well uncovered" to make bribe-taking easy. And officialdom had not liked Blantire. He had been arrested four times for spying and had once had to telegraph the American ambassador at St. Petersburg to get himself released.

But more often he had been taken for a supernatural being.

Blantire waxed eloquent about Russian superstition. Holy pigeons, werewolves, house-spirits, soul-witherers. Bread inscribed with messages to the dead and given to the ikons to eat. St. Elias the weather clerk making thunder with his chariot. Blantire had them all, and a few more that Reisden suspected the peasants had made up on his behalf. In his outlandish ten-gallon hat and decorated boots, Blantire had frightened the girl-ostlers at the inns, who would sometimes refuse to touch his horse. Clearly he had enjoyed the attention.

Why had he come to Flanders? Why to Montfort? But once he was there, he would have heard the witchcraft stories. And, according to Puckett, he'd got involved with a witch.

Far down the Arras road, Reisden could see a yellow speck, the wall of the Auclart farm.

Chapter 57

The Auclart garden door was locked. Reisden parked the Renault off the road, out of view of passersby, and scaled the garden wall.

The house itself wasn't locked. Its cellar was little more than a pit reached from a trap door below the kitchen. It held root vegetables, preserves and pickles, and a witchcraftly supply of cobwebs. He looked in the kitchen and found nothing sinister; no cauldrons, just an iron pot to cook a spinster's stew. Most of the house was filled with costumes.

He went out into the neglected garden. Someone recently had started to weed, then given it up. He tossed the weeds on the rubbish heap.

A long brick-and-sandstone storage building formed one wall of the garden. The empty rabbit hutch backed up against it, flanked by bush-size weeds. The shed was half roofless but still substantial, with an oversize Greek portico in the center. In the seventeenth century, when the French, the British, and the Spaniards had all been fighting along the Arras road, it had perhaps been a posting house for some army.

The door was a replacement tin sheet with a bright new lock. But the lock was merely for discouragement; the key was above the door. Reisden tugged the tin sheet back.

The inside of the building had been stripped to its stone walls. Sunlight streamed down from the rotten roof onto the floor, which was simply the chalk bedrock, covered in parts by grassy dirt. Along all the walls were piled chalk blocks and fragments of rock. More rock was scattered across the floor. And there was nothing else to lock up but a hole in the ground.

It was a capacious square hole with crumbling edges, about five meters to the right of the door, sheltered by the remains of the roof. Steps led down into darkness.

Under the shelter of the roof, hanging from pegs on the wall, were three ordinary kerosene lanterns.

Three, Reisden thought, for one Mademoiselle Auclart? He took down one; it sloshed heavily, full. He lit the wick. In the sunlight it gave no light at all.

The stairs were built for shorter men; he ducked. At the bottom of the hole a worn floor stretched away into darkness. He held up the lantern and looked, astonished.

The room looked like the dugout shelters, half pit, half mound, that men retreat to during a siege. Under a primitive chimney near the wall stood a portable stove, not very old, and on top of that, an industrial-size cast-iron pot. The walls were living rock, carved into benches and shelves, dark with centuries of resinous smoke. Heavy beams supported the ceiling; herbs hung from nails pounded into them.

On his left the floor slanted up like a ramp. But it ended in a wall, a thick and ancient wall of irregular chalk blocks and the remains of timbers. The beams were enormous— how long since trees that large had grown in any forest in Flanders?—and they were almost rotted away.

At the far end of the room was the entrance to a tunnel. It was narrow enough to brush his shoulders and low enough to make him half-crouch. He shuddered, checked the lamp again, and pressed forward. The tunnel led a little way downward and diverged into three branches like the root of a tree. In the left branch a blanket had been spread on the ground. Reisden shone the lantern at the crumbling roof. It was not shored up and was low enough to reach; he brushed it and a little avalanche of pebbles fell on his head from a seam of soft rock.

The right-hand tunnel was wider and looked much newer. It led to a storage room, also with shelves cut in its rock walls. Spades and pickaxes. A box of blasting caps, which Reisden looked at respectfully and did not touch. A roll of fuse. Miners' safety lanterns, with wire gauze over the lamps. In a corner, on a low shelf, he found sleeping sacks and the long-dried end of a wheel of cheese.

There was a box of compasses, not the Peigné compass-sextant that the army uses, but miners' brass compasses with a sliding indicator to mark direction. Taking one, he went back to the middle tunnel, sighted down it, and slid the indicator to mark its direction. Roughly northeast, in the direction of the frontier. He explored the tunnel for about a hundred yards. Still it stretched away farther than the lantern beam reached.

He locked the door of the stone shed and washed up with water from the well. Upstairs, on the wall of Mademoiselle Françoise's bedroom, was the photo of her uncle in his uniform; he stared at it for a long time. He scaled the wall of the farm again, the compass in his pocket, and stood in the middle of the deserted Arras road, holding the compass.

The indicator pointed straight down the road, toward Montfort. In the same direction as the tunnel.

Chapter 58

Back at Montfort, Perdita and Toby were still asleep. Reisden climbed the crumbling steps of the abbey tower for someplace to be alone and think. Sitting in the sun, with his back against the heavy irregular stones, he looked out on the fields and the countryside and Montfort, spread out like a map below him.

When he was fourteen or so, at one of the numerous military schools Leo had hoped would improve him, he'd read Caesar's *Gallic Wars*. Caesar had fought here in Flanders and had described his enemies' fortifications. Stone blocks and timber, *murus gallicus*. That stone-and-timber wall in Mademoiselle Françoise's cellar was *murus gallicus* and was newer than the rest of the room.

Below him, the little Vex-Fort sat at the top of the hill. Bits of ruined wall and lines in the grass marked abbey buildings now disappeared. The New Buildings barred the drive, serene brick relics from the Age of Reason. Behind the Vex-Fort was Cyron's nineteenth-century kitchen, gabled and gargoyled. And around everything Cyron had built his new fancywork-Montfort, his maze-walls and white towers and winding chalk road. In the stifling July afternoon, the sheep grazed on the green lawn. Montfort, 1911.

If the dugout at the farm was older than Caesar, he wondered how old Montfort was.

St. Eloi was supposed to have founded the abbey, and St.

Eloi had died in 660. But that was the abbey. Christian churches were built on the sacred spots of other religions, as Christian ikons ate pagan bread and saints drove Jove's chariot.

When had Montfort's Holy Well first become holy?

The word *boves* isn't French. The closest French word is *bauge*, which means a muddy place for animals, such as a pig-wallow, and *bauge* is the Gallic *balc*, which means both a fort and a patch of waste ground. In Latin the closest word is *bovile*, a stall. The boves in Arras had been chalk mines; so said the Romans, who had mined them. Most chalk mines in this area were no more than a trench into the earth, a man-made cave near a beehive limekiln. The disused mines would have been a place to keep the cows warm and store the hay in rainy winters. A place underground, a mine, a storehouse. A bove.

The boves would have had other uses. In times of war, they would have been hiding places from which to strike back at the enemy. The Romans were unfamiliar with tunneling. Caesar had written that the Gauls seemed to come from nowhere.

Through the centuries the armies had changed. At Agincourt, the field had belonged not to tunnelers but archers. When the Spaniards had fought the English on the fields of Flanders, cannon and cavalry had carried the day. There was no more place in warfare for little bands of men popping out of the ground.

Until 1870.

In 1870 the Germans had invaded France, annexed Alsace and Lorraine, and conquered Paris. In the north, a soldier named Maurice Cyron declared his own private war. Cyron had only a handful of men, but he seemed to possess the secret of invisibility. In the middle of the flat land, Cyron's men could appear and disappear like Gauls.

The Roman road, the road from Arras to Belgium, ran dust-white through the green fields, straight as a ley line, marked by the red moving dots of roadside poppies. A road worn into the chalk from two thousand years of marching men. On the horizon was the bell tower of Arras, eight miles away.

Reisden thought of the Germans, marching down the temptingly straight Roman road toward Arras, between the beet fields on a steaming August morning. They would be cautious, of course, but there would be so little to fear. They would have already subdued the little villages and farms, locked up the inhabitants or sent them to the rear of the column. They would have captured Montfort, off the road as it was. They would have men in the tower, watching for the telltale dust of soldiers gathering over the flat fields. But there would be nothing; no snipers in the hedges, no sharpshooter in a bell tower; nothing; and they would be tired, off their guard a little, looking toward the capture of Arras and its all-important railhead; and Arras, they thought, would be relatively easy, because Vauban had built the Beautiful Useless on the wrong side of town. They would march along the road. Perhaps some of them would be singing.

What use is Montfort? No visible use. It is a joke; it is an actor's folly. It is even more of a folly than it needs to be. Ridiculous chalk walls and little stonehenge towers among the sheep, Friends of Montfort, Sunday char-a-banc excursions, the annual dinner and the speeches. A half-restored medieval castle with a garage, a gas-powered generator, André's coat of arms on the chamber pots, and Cyron on the ramparts orating and huffing as he mortars another chunk of chalk. Ridiculous; Paris had laughed for years; and almost no one remembered what had been Cyron's chief claim to attention before Montfort, that he had been a guerrilla soldier.

Reisden thought again about those German soldiers on the Arras road, and because he was a bit German himself, he could see them very clearly, blond and round-faced, not unlike the men from Flanders; not unlike André.

And under the road there was a tunnel, which followed the road.

There is a spectacular military maneuver called sapping. One digs a tunnel that dead-ends under the thing one wants to blow up. One packs into the end of the tunnel several hundred-weight of dynamite, a stick at a time. One lights a long, long fuse. The mortality among sappers is horrifying, but a well-sapped piece of ground does not simply blow up; it explodes and dissolves in upon itself as if hit by an inconceivably large shell. No one in the area survives.

Sapping the Arras road—if that was what Cyron had done—would not stop the Germans, except for those blond boys marching to their deaths. But one would not have to stop them, only delay them, narrow that six-week window in which Germany must conquer France.

Was that the secret of Montfort? Sapping the Arras road? It was interesting. Not exciting. Not quite worth the fuss that was being made over it.

Not the secret that Pétiot had passed, the one that would prevent the Germans from attacking at all.

What could be that large? *Suppose,* Pétiot had said, *we had some sort of fortification along the Arras road, like the Rivière line of forts.* Rivière's forts were all underground; even their size was unknown. Reisden imagined a fort in Flanders. Gauls with machine guns. French troops appearing like stage devils in fields the Germans thought empty, scything the road with guns.

He thought of Cyron. Indomitable, unstoppable Cyron. Young Sergeant Cyron, with his big Gallic nose and Gallic curled beard, had known all the crypts of country churches, the old cellars and the old mines.

What could a man do who knew all the underground holes between his house and Arras, if he had friends with picks and shovels and thirty-five years to dig?

More tunnels? A fort?

Not likely. The excavated chalk would make a tailings like the pyramid at Wagny-les-Mines. Where would they put it?

And Reisden looked down from the Montfort tower, and saw the white road that spiraled up the hill, the roofless white towers, the stonehenges in the sheep fields, all the mazy white useless chalk walls of Montfort.

Chapter 59

He wanted to talk with someone about it, but he didn't know whom to speak with. He could have talked to Leo; sometimes he missed Leo. But he was alone in this. He went over to the New Buildings. Perdita and Toby were up from their naps. He could have talked to her if he had told her everything from the beginning. They negotiated around each other in the small room, talking about nothing in a fragile half-silence.

He tried apologies in his head. I believe you love me more than Gilbert.—He didn't believe it. He believed what she said; she wanted both him and Gilbert, as if she were still the little girl in Gilbert's house in Boston.

She took Toby away. He threw himself on the bed. The pillows smelled of her hair. He laid his cheek against them. He was sick of love and sick for it. Despicable.

He would never have to tell her. Pétiot had already arrested Gehazy, and Gehazy was on his way toward the frontier. With him would go the secret of Montfort—whatever it was. Reisden was a curious man but he didn't want to know about forts.

He fell asleep and dreamed. He was with the Friends of Montfort, digging somewhere subterranean. From ahead, Cyron was urging them on. "God loves the French soldier! The Germans shall not pass! Show them no mercy!"

The sound of the pickax got louder, echoing. Someone was knocking at the door.

"Reisden!" André.

"What?" Reisden said crossly.

"Have you seen Ruthie?"

"No." And don't bother me, André.

"She went to the Auclart farm," André said, opening the door. "She was to come right back. I have things for her to do." He added uncharacteristically, "I'm—" He groped for a word. He was looking for some emotional word that he knew how to apply to himself. This was new. "I'm worried," André said uncertainly.

"Shall we go look for her?"

They drove all the way to Arras and looked for her at the film office; Ruthie hadn't been there. Jules was there, concerned. They brought him along and returned along the Arras road, driving slowly, looking for her. Necrosar would have made up some dreadful fate for her. André half-stood in the car, holding on to the windshield, examining the tall grass at the side of the road.

It was André who saw the bicycle.

Neither laughter nor fright will help her; Necrosar is no use here. While Reisden drives the car at top speed back toward Arras, André sits in the back seat with Ruthie's head on his lap, willing her to breathe. She is dying and he has to face it without Necrosar. The pupils of her eyes are dilated. She is breathing slowly, shallowly. (*Barely breathing,* he thinks.) Her face is pale, her lips are pale. *Ruthie has been poisoned.* He cannot help thinking that. Jules sits by them, holding Ruthie's hand.

In the hospital, Ruthie's hands lie lax on the sheet. Jules and Reisden talk with the doctor. André sits beside her bed and holds her hand.

Heatstroke, the doctor thinks, possibly a heart attack. *But Ruthie has been poisoned.* An alkaloid. Perhaps a combination of them. André knows these things. He is a little mad but what he knows, he knows.

He gazes into her face. It is strange to him, so faraway, so profoundly asleep. He stares at her, willing her to wake, to be Ruthie. And little by little, as he gazes, he begins to think, not of all the things that need doing, but of her.

Ruthie. When Jules joined the Necro she was still working at the grocery. She was useful, good with figures. She would tell him how much he could spend on an effect. She could mend a costume, make tea. He had always thought of her as older because she wore glasses and there had always been a streak of grey in her brown hair. Now her hair is sprinkled with grey. He gazes at her face, relaxed by the poison, smooth, remote, soft-edged. Her hair is spread on the pillow.

He can see her story as he sees Katzmann's. She will be kind as long as she lives. She will be kind to him. She will never marry. André does not know how he knows this, but he does.

He is crying again. Water stars his hand, holding hers.

The straight chair where he is sitting is painful. He gets down on his knees, by the bed, and lays his head and arms on the sheet by her shoulder. His loose long hair falls among hers. The brown hair and the blond both have silver in them. André stirs their hair with his fingers, mixing them together.

"André, what are you doing?" Reisden, sharply.

"Nothing." André sits in the chair again.

"Come home."

"I'll stay here." Reisden looks at him as if he'll object, but he doesn't.

Jules comes in to watch, too. He sits in the chair by her bed, he takes her hand, but he falls asleep, exhausted. André helps him to the more comfortable chair and sits again by the bed.

Ruthie's knitting bag is on the table by the bed. It feels heavy. It is perverse and tender to look in her bag, to see her private things, her handkerchief, her change-purse. In the bag are four books and a little covered tin canister.

He opens it. He only sniffs at it, but the tin is greasy with the rancid stuff. André wipes his fingers on his handkerchief. They tingle a bit. He rubs his fingers together, frowning.

He opens the first of the books. It is late and his vision is blurred, he is sleepy, but he reads. When to plant hardy vegetables and tender. A recipe for sausage.

How to call upon Vapula.

How to fly.

André blinks, wonders whether he is dreaming. His head falls helplessly against the chair-back. His body is numb from having sat so long. But he feels, because he has been reading about it, that he is flying, a strange, innocent, happy sensation; he is climbing through the air on huge wings. He looks at Ruthie and remembers, with hallucinatory clarity, the first time he saw her. She was in the grocery sweeping the floor. When he came in the door she turned with the broom in her hands, stopped, blushed, smiled at him, her beautiful shy smile.

André closes his eyes and dreams of her.

Chapter 60

Reisden arrived back at Montfort exhausted, stumbled down the hill from the garage to his own pallet in the New Buildings, and took off no more than his shoes before clearing a place on the bed by his wife and son. He actually fell asleep, and dreamed that he was sitting in a café in Paris with Gilbert.

"Reisden."

Pétiot's voice woke him. "Get up. I have to talk to you."

It was three in the morning. From her side of the bed, Perdita half-woke. Toby began to wail. "Is it Ruthie?" he said, his heart sinking.

"No."

They sat in the kitchen again. Reisden made coffee. He saw his unshaven, rumpled self in the bottom of a copper pot. Why was it that every time he talked with Pétiot, he looked like he'd slept under a bridge?

"Gehazy hasn't got the secret," Pétiot said. "We went to arrest him. He wasn't there. Judging by the amount of mail, he hasn't been home for days. My clerk's letter was there, unopened. Jules didn't go to the Place Victor-Hugo, I made a mistake there. And Gehazy didn't show up, or he didn't show himself because he didn't see Jules. . . . Has Gehazy got in touch with you?"

"No."

"I have to pass the secret. Jules has failed. I want you to meet Gehazy."

The water was boiling on the gas-ring. Reisden poured it into the filter, wetting the grounds, then poured again. I thought I would get the contract without paying for it. He poured them both cups of coffee, and sat down, and passed Pétiot his cup of coffee.

"You'll meet him in the Sainte-Barbara chapel at Saint-Vaast," Pétiot said. "Eleven o'clock today. You'll pass him the secret. We'll arrest him as he gets on the train."

"No," he said. "You know what I will and won't do."

"This is not about the integrity of your d——d company!" Pétiot exploded. "This isn't about your good name! I'll guarantee your name. Your country needs you, if France is your country—I didn't come to argue with you. I came to give you this." He pulled an envelope out of his jacket. "Give it to him."

He slapped the envelope onto the kitchen table and left.

The envelope lay on the table. One sheet of writing paper, perhaps two, in a long envelope. Reisden picked it up and held it to the light. He could see the grey blur of typewriting inside the envelope, but not what it said.

He didn't want to know what it said, even though he thought he already did.

He thought of those German soldiers marching along the Arras road toward Paris. Whatever Cyron had done, if the knowledge of it was enough to stop them—

Pétiot was outside. Reisden handed the envelope back. "All right. Give this to me at Saint-Vaast. I'll pass your secret but I will not know it."

Pétiot shrugged impatiently.

St.-Vaast was cream-colored, enormous, and echoing, filled with a cool Dutch light. In the side chapels, old women knelt at their private devotions. A priest was mumbling Mass at the altar. Reisden waited in the Ste.-Barbara chapel, reading the plaques and epitaphs on the chapel walls. SACRED TO THE MEMORY OF FORTY-TWO MEN KILLED IN THE EXPLOSION AT PORTAS, APRIL 20, 1878, he read; ST. BARBARA PROTECT US. Women in the rough clothes of miners' wives and in the caps of coal-sorters knelt, prayed briefly, dropped their centimes into the money box and lit a candle, in memory of a disaster or to prevent another, until the candle-rack in front of the altar was a mass of flame.

He moved away from the chapel of St. Barbara, into the aisle and the next chapel, trying to look like a man whose wife was at Mass. He didn't fit in; he felt conspicuous, too tall, too pale. The coal-smudged miners' wives and widows looked up at him suspiciously.

The bells tingled as the Host was exposed on the altar. The smoky sweetness of incense drifted back to the chapel. The faithful queued to take Communion. Reisden's eyes searched the recesses of confessionals and the rows of rush-bottomed chairs. He didn't see Gehazy.

He remembered Gehazy coming to the back door of Leo's house. He'd always been early. A man who is early for an appointment is never surprised; one of Leo's maxims too.

Gehazy wouldn't come here either. He'd scented a trap. Reisden strolled down the aisle toward the ambulatory, a religious tourist, and looked into each of the chapels behind the high altar. Funerary monuments of abbots and bishops. Behind him the priest intoned prayers for the sick and all those who had died in the Lord.

He went back to the Ste.-Barbara chapel and stared into the candle flames.

He was a Catholic—not a believer, but Catholic. For something to do, he lit candles. For T. J. Blantire and Mademoiselle Françoise. For William Knight. For Leo, whose teaching was getting him through this. For Ruthie and Jules, to prevent more accidents and disasters.

For Ferenc Gehazy.

Nunc dimittis . . . The Mass was over. The priests and altar boys glittered down the aisle, a mass of red, white, and gold. Behind them, churchgoers gathered their hats, genuflected, and moved toward the doors, murmuring to one another.

Reisden took the envelope out of his pocket, twisted it, and fed it into the candle flames. Fire flared and gnarled along the envelope. The fire almost burned his fingers; he dropped the blackened envelope on the floor and stamped on it. He could see the Ferret with unusual clarity: fat, chinless, with his pointed nose and grey curls, ridiculously lifting his pinky as he drank coffee and waited for Leo. He had had a weakness for fast women and slow racehorses, but the women he'd loved best had been opera stars. He'd actually been a journalist. Once he had given Reisden a copy of a review he'd done. That was all Reisden knew about him.

Except that he wanted the secret of Montfort, and would have been here if he could.

Pétiot met him on the steps. "He'll contact you yet—"

"I don't think so."

The two of them stood on the steps for a moment. Blantire is dead, Reisden thought. Françoise Auclart is dead. Jules, Ruthie . . .

"I think something has happened to him too," Reisden said. "Another accident?"

"I shall have someone find that letter from my clerk," Pétiot said resignedly. "Someone who will believably pass on secrets. Which you will not, I really think you will not. You have caused me an immense amount of trouble, Reisden."

"Five of them so far," Reisden said. "The only connection is that all of them were looking for the secret of Montfort."

"I wish one of them had found it!" Pétiot snapped. "Don't exert your imagination where it isn't wanted. Jules Fauchard caused his own problems, his sister has heatstroke, Blantire and Mademoiselle Françoise died by accident, and we don't know Gehazy is dead. There are no murderers here."

"Whatever you say," Reisden said with irony. But he was not going to challenge Pétiot. Gehazy's death was too much a relief for him: for him, Jules, André, everyone. He thought once of Gehazy, proud of his opera review, and then consigned him, with Blantire and Mademoiselle Françoise, to the spreading silence.

Chapter 61

Sabine went to visit Ruthie in the hospital. She found Ruthie still asleep, still pale, still drugged—Sabine knew with what—and beside her, sleeping in a chair, with his hand stretched out across the bed and his fingers tangled with Ruthie's, was André.

He was drugged too, though not so profoundly. Now they were in a dream together. Sabine glared at them, narrow-eyed, uncertain. She felt as she had when André had danced with his father.

She looked carefully into both their faces. She wanted to see grey. She wanted them *out of her life*. But Ruthie was only pale and André's ugly cheekbones and big lips were as red as ever. She wished them fractured dreams full of monsters.

Ruthie's knitting bag was on the metal table by the bed. Sabine looked inside, hissed with annoyance and surprise, and brought out Mademoiselle Françoise's bibles and her tin of concentrated ointment.

What! A thief! Ruthie a thief!

Sabine took the whole knitting bag back to Montfort, telling the nurse she was keeping Ruthie's things safe for her. She left the bag in Ruthie's bedroom but hid the books and the ointment in her own room.

Downstairs she found a tin of the right size among the cans and bottles and old newspapers in the larder. For ointment she mixed some of Papa Cyron's muscle liniment with cow-balm from the stables, dried mint, and a little of the beef fat the cook saved for soap. In the library, on a bottom shelf, she found some dusty old recipe books; one was green-bound instead of black but they would do. She put the replacement tin and books in Ruthie's knitting bag.

She went out and stood on the terrace, thinking.

Ruthie had found Mademoiselle Françoise's bibles. What to do?

Sabine had known what to do before—but then she had seen the grey on their faces. They were going to die anyway.

The incubus, the horseman, hadn't gone away, that had been the trouble. She had tried to explain to him. His work was done. It was time for him to have other lovers and for her to get back to the task of conquering Necrosar.

If he had been a demon, she could have banished him. But he was a man. Everything proved it. He was sunburned and used a camera. His toes were squeezed and knotted and pointed together from his strange boots, but he had no hooves nor horns. He was going bald in back. All demons can speak French—it is their natural language after Latin—but he could hardly speak French.

She had taken holy water from the font in the chapel and flicked it over him. He thought it was a game. Powers of the Underworld, Sabine prayed, he is only a man; banish this man from my life. But spells runneled off him like water off slate.

He had always wanted to go down into the lower cellars.

She took the key for him. They found a roomful of bones, a series of crumbling dangerous tunnels. Are there more tunnels, he asked her, *de plus,* like this?

She had shown him the Well.

She had shown him it, she had even drawn water for him from the tap that came out of the box. Exorcised water, which drives off demons. He had tossed off the cupful without hesitating. She had been standing outside the well cage looking at him, with the keys in her hand, and from inside where he had been poking and tapping he had looked over his shoulder at her and she had seen his face dark grey in the lamplight.

For a while Mademoiselle Françoise had been almost the only person to notice he was gone. She had kept asking about him. "What has happened to Mr. Blantire?" she had said in that cracked, sharp little voice of hers. "I'm so worried about him." Her arms had been full of costumes; as she was turning to hang the uniforms on the racks, Sabine had seen pale grey flow across her face.

It had been awful about the cat.

Now Ruthie had found the bibles. Ruthie read books. She had studied witchcraft for the film; she would know what she'd read. She hadn't turned grey, though. Not yet. It was no use poisoning her yet.

But there were things Sabine could do.

The breakfast dishes were still in the dining room. (She would have to speak to the maids about that.) Sabine got a small, sharp fruit knife and took it down to the first cellar. In one of the disused wine-bins, in the dark, she spit across the back of her hand, turned clock-backward three times, and poked the tip of the fruit knife into the ball of her left thumb, squeezing the blood to drip out onto the living stone floor.

"Oh, Great Master, turn your attention to your servant Sabine. Thank you that your power has delivered me before from people who might harm me. Now Ruth Aborjaily threatens me. Curse her in all ways, curse her in her coming and her going, curse her in her speaking so that no one will believe her if she speaks against me. Do not give her *anything* she wants," Sabine added, because what Ruthie wanted would be André.

She took the knife upstairs again, washed the blood off, found a piece of sticking-plaster for her thumb, and went off to speak severely to the maids.

Chapter 62

By Monday afternoon Ruthie felt not only well but restless and disturbed. She thought she knew what had happened to her. Books about witchcraft spoke of a "flying ointment," which witches smeared on themselves to be transported to sabbats.

The witches had not flown, of course. They had merely drugged themselves.

Ruthie had not dreamed of sabbats, of orgies and misty lovers. She had dreamed she was in the last scene of the film, about to be beheaded, and rows of costumes were chasing her up the guillotine stairs, throwing sausages from the caterer's van. Both cameras had grown wings and perched like gargoyles on the Dutch roofs of the square. Then it had begun to rain pink buttons that gleamed like blood.

To her astonishment, when she awakened, Count André was asleep in the chair by her bed. He had been sleeping softly, smiling, as though in a happy dream, and her heart melted for him; not in the old familiar way, but with a pleasure in the shape of his lips and his hands. That was the drug, she told herself shamefacedly. And he had awakened and had looked at her as confused, as red-faced, as she at him.

And there she was, in bed with her hair down, and both of them blushing and speechless. "Are you well?" he asked. "Quite well," she said and felt herself being short with him, impolite. "I am embarrassed to have you see me this way—" Really there was nothing she could say. "Everything will be back as it was as soon as possible." She was not going to explain to him that they had both been drugged.

He combed his disarrayed hair out of his face with his fingers. All the time he was looking at her, questioning.

"Go, go, go," she said. But when he had gone she pressed her hands against her mouth, disturbed by the nervousness that had made her speak so strongly to him. Even drugged she knew better. He was a married man. What a thing even to say to herself, *he is a married man,* he was just her best friend and Jules'. She felt profoundly embarrassed, shaken to her core, disturbed by something deeper than embarrassment.

"I must walk to our office in the Grand'Place," Ruthie insisted. "To see how many extras we have for the last scene. I dreamed the costumes had to wear themselves." She wanted to be again the competent, helpful Ruthie whom she knew.

Sister St. Placide, her nurse, had the brown face of a woman who likes the sun; she allowed herself to be persuaded. "But if you feel the slightest out of breath—"

Slowly and shakily, leaning on Placide's arm, Ruthie made her way to the Grand'Place. At Mademoiselle Françoise's old shop was Mademoiselle Huguette, Mademoiselle Françoise's old friend. The woman signing up extras was just going out to lunch. Ruthie offered to cover for her and asked Mademoiselle Huguette to stay with her.

"Did Mademoiselle Françoise own a dress with red-rose buttons?" Ruthie described them. Mademoiselle Huguette considered.

"I've seen them somewhere," she decided.

"Could you look for them?"

One whole wall of Mademoiselle Françoise's shop was lined with drawers of buttons. Mademoiselle Huguette pulled out drawers one by one, talking as she went. She had been offered the lease of the shop, she said, did Ruthie think it was too much for a single woman? She would have to find an assistant. She wasn't sure she was up to it. "Françoise was so strong-minded, and I'm not, perhaps it's because I don't eat meat, but the dear little calves and bunnies, it just doesn't seem *right*. . . ." She found red celluloid roses with green leaves, red velvet buttons with rhinestones, and big garnet beads.

"No, pinker than that."

"These," said Mademoiselle Huguette finally.

There they were, half a box left of them. "I think she put them on a yellow blouse," Mademoiselle Huguette thought aloud. "Yellow . . . some color like yellow. Coral stripes perhaps. Or checks? Perhaps it was a dress. Violet? Blue? Françoise always had the eye, not me!"

"Was it a dress for herself?"

"I suppose . . . I don't know . . . She was always changing the buttons on her dresses, she said it was almost the same as having a new one. But she didn't sew much for herself." Mademoiselle Huguette's bulging eyes overflowed with tears. "She was too successful, too much in demand!"

Ruthie remembered Mademoiselle Françoise's clothes cupboard very clearly. Mademoiselle Françoise had had one checked dress, an old red-and-green Sunday silk—you would not wear it with rose buttons. The rest of her clothes had been dark, blacks mostly, a widow's clothes with ruffles, unusual

for a spinster whose business was fashion. *Witch's clothes,*
Ruthie thought, startled. Nothing yellow or coral. Mademoiselle Françoise had been a sallow blonde; she would never
have worn yellow.

"I will take one of these buttons," she said to Mademoiselle Huguette.

On Monday, Reisden heard from Pétiot that someone had
burgled Gehazy's room in Paris. "In his mail, they found a letter from an informant," Pétiot said, brushing his moustache
with a finger. "The same informant who was going to trade
Gehazy French secrets for Russian ones."

"So you've passed your secret."

"I hope so," said Pétiot. "The news from Berlin isn't
good.—But you're safe, you and Jules."

Chapter 63

Monday they filmed the Ball of the Dead scene, and
Sabine just couldn't do it. It frustrated her terribly.
All morning she practiced with Papa Cyron. "You're not giving me what I want," he complained. Sabine hated to do anything badly; it was like being back at school.

She was a good actress, a wonderful actress, Papa Cyron
said, but this scene, she was fluffing it.

She was supposed to see ghosts in this scene. Méduc's wife
and child had been killed; her husband had condemned hun-

dreds of others to death; she had encouraged him. Now she was supposed to be suffering the torments of conscience.

Hadn't she ever suffered the torments of conscience, Papa Cyron asked.

"No, Papa Cyron." Sabine had never done anything to be ashamed of. (Well, she thought privately, poor Merlin.)

Couldn't she be scared? Couldn't she imagine it? Blood, guts, gore, Papa Cyron said; he had seen some terrible things in the war, he could make her hair stand on end, André's ghosts were nothing. He told her about a friend of his, one of his soldiers, who had been blown apart, both his legs and one arm gone. She thought about when the sorcerer had been run over. Papa Cyron must have been so happy to be alive.

"Blood and guts don't frighten you, Binny?" Papa Cyron held her hand. "You're a good, brave girl," he sighed. "Let's break for lunch. We'll think of something."

What frightened her? She thought about it in her sitting room with the terrace doors open, eating her omelette meditatively. Nothing had frightened her but being a little girl in Lalie's cut-down skirt and orange blouse, and since the sorcerer had given her his powers, everything had gone right. What could she be afraid of? Demogorgon or Lucifer himself? They would come with gifts for her.

Even Ruthie didn't frighten her, not really; something would happen to Ruthie. Only Ruthie and Necrosar together made her feel wrong, made her feel like the little girl in the cut-down skirt who was missing her destiny.

To be a witch is like being a mill wheel, Sabine thought. You have power, but only in the direction the millstream moves. She was young and pretty and rich and good in bed and she was making André a sorcerer baby; what else can you do for a man? A spell only works for what a man wants.

"I thought this movie would make him *see* you," Papa Cyron said. "But the filming's nearly over."

"Don't worry, he's liking me better." Lying is the sort of thing girls are trained for and men are trained to believe.

Papa Cyron went off to talk to the extras. The extras had behaved just as he'd thought they would and had arrived back early, all full of questions about the body in the cellars, as if it were still there. Dead people bored Sabine. She opened the windows of the ladies' retiring room and sat all by herself, with her feet up on a hassock, before she went off to be made up for her role in the Ball of the Dead scene. From her windows Sabine had a good view of the Lazarus Gate and of her husband, who had been sitting by his mother's grave during lunch, sometimes looking through papers Jules had given him, sometimes just sitting.

Sabine got up and examined herself in her full-length mirror. Her hair was still down. She loved it now it was blonde. She pulled it up over her head and let it cascade down. Her breasts were big, her belly just beginning. She could feel herself ripening, gathering power. Now there, she thought, there; I am just what he should want.

Outside, on the long terrace, the pigeons were strutting and cooing. She put down her cup of tea and went outside in the sun, barefoot and in her embroidered Japanese dressing gown. Below the terrace, the sheep drifted across the green fields like clouds. A gull hung in the sky. The bull-pigeons huffed up their peacock-colored necks and swept the flagstones with their tails, making their mating call, *roucoule*. She raised her arms and spread them wide; one of the pigeons, startled, rose lazily and perched for a moment on her outspread palm. Translucently, behind her, her Japanese sleeves spread a multicolored shadow. She felt as if she were giving off light.

André looked at her, but dully. If he doesn't love me now, in this moment, he never will. His expression did not change; he still shrank away from her.

Fate is fate. She had tried her best. She saw the two of them as if she had spread cards out on the flagstones of the terrace: Necrosar and herself far apart, black clouds and coffins between them. She watched herself instead, her shadow coloring the pigeons, as if she were a tinted film projecting herself over them.

Let fate deal with him. Whatever happened would not be her fault. And she knew what she could do to hurt him.

Chapter 64

When Reisden and Perdita went to pick up Ruthie, they were told they'd need to wait at least an hour; the doctor wanted to check Ruthie's heart again. Perdita suggested they have a cup of tea and talk. Reisden suggested they tour the boves. He had brought an electric torch and the compass he had got from the Auclart farm.

The official entrance was through the Hôtel de Ville. They found their way through the low vaulted corridors and rang for the guide, who shuffled into view still holding the mop that indicated his usual duties. Reisden paid him to take them all the way through the tunnels under the two squares.

With the compass it was relatively easy to navigate underground, if one did not think about the dark mazes one was passing through. The compass-needle danced in the torch-beam, and the bronze indicator pointed which narrow tunnel to go down; from the Hôtel de Ville the Grand'Place was just a little north and east. They found themselves safely first under the airwell in the Grand'Place, then, finding it by smell, at the cheesemonger's cave at the southeast corner of the square. Reisden bought one of the heart-shaped, foul-smelling Coeur d'Arras cheeses for André, to inspire him, and a heart-shaped tin box so the cheese wouldn't asphyxiate them on the way back to Montfort.

"What is this about, in the boves?" Perdita asked him.

"Orienteering."

I could tell you, he thought, but then I'd have to tell you more. The conversation ended there.

At the hospital, Ruthie looked tired and shaky. They had to admit that the Ball of the Dead scene hadn't gone well yesterday. Sabine hadn't got her mad scene down. "We were all very worried about you," Perdita said.

"Oh, *I'm* fine," said Ruthie. "But I am so worried about the number of extras for Saturday. I looked at the Grand'Place yesterday; it is so *large*. I think we must ask General Pétiot to keep the soldiers past Friday, so they can fill up the scene. And we must ask the market men not to take down the stalls."

They talked like this, superficialities, all the way back to Montfort. But when they arrived, Ruthie drew Reisden aside.

"I believe I know what made me have that fainting fit, Dr. Reisden. I'd like you to have something analyzed."

She sent a servant upstairs for her knitting bag. They went into Cyron's office, off the Great Hall where everyone was trying to film the Ball of the Dead. Scripts were piled on every surface. A set of magician's linking rings dangled from the back of the only chair, and the cane-stand held two property swords. Reisden sat Ruthie in the chair and sat on the edge of the desk, moving away Cyron's belongings: three playscripts, a dog-eared pack of cards that had the air of not being quite complete, a pair of reading glasses, a Chinese finger trap, a magician's stalk of artificial flowers, two pen-holders (one with no nib and one with a splayed one), and a single usable pencil.

Ruthie looked round the room with the air of someone who would like to clean it. The maid came back with Ruthie's bag. Ruthie closed the door behind her.

"At Mademoiselle Françoise's farm I found a very odd thing. Mademoiselle Françoise—grew poison plants." She had found several books with very odd recipes, and a tin of ointment.

"I've read about flying ointment in my research," Ruthie said, her cheeks going pink. "The Romans used it, and so did the witches. They rubbed it on their feet, which paralyzed them and made them feel they were flying above the ground. I felt as if I were flying." Ruthie paused and went on bravely. "It gives some people hallucinations of *romantic pleasure*. But I'm afraid I only dreamed of costumes."

"Mademoiselle Françoise made this ointment?" he said.

"It was in her kitchen. I'm afraid I *took* it. And her *books*. I really should not have done it; it was stealing. But here they are"—she rummaged—"right in my bag."

She set out on the desk four battered books and, very carefully, holding it in her flowered handkerchief, a tin labeled Denti-Frais Pearlescent Tooth Powder. "I dipped my fingers in it and touched my tongue to it. I shouldn't have."

He could have told her about the room under the garden shed. He didn't. "What is supposed to be in flying ointment?"

"Aconite and digitalis principally—" Contact poisons. Reisden used his own handkerchief, doubled over, to open the tin. "Could you have it analyzed—?" she asked.

"I think you should give it to the police," he said. "Or to Pétiot. He's been investigating Blantire and Mademoiselle Auclart." Let Pétiot have the difficulties.

Ruthie was looking through the books. She leafed through one, then another.

"Why," she said, "I cannot find anything of what I saw before. This is only—a recipe book. This is a printed book," Ruthie said, distressed, holding it open. "It is a recipe book, but printed." She put it down and stared at the tin in his hand. "And I am almost sure that the tin had no label." She put her hand up to her forehead. "Could I be that confused? Could these be different books from what I had before? I am almost certain that they were all handwritten."

Ruthie even remembered recipes, but they were all recipes that she had read before in her research on witches. The flying ointment she knew from the same research. She watched while Dr. Reisden daubed the flying ointment, very carefully, with a stick, onto a hen. The hen clucked and pecked at worms, ducking its long supple neck, completely unaffected. He tried it very carefully on the end of one of his own fingers. "Does it tingle?" she said.

He shook his head.

"Oh, this is so embarrassing. I never—never anything like this before. Could I have had heatstroke?"

"I'll have the ointment analyzed," he offered. She shook her head; they both knew what he would find. She took the books and the tin upstairs and sat in her room, defeated.

"How could I have thought of it? Dreamed it?" The ointment would have explained everything. Mr. Blantire would have used it (her cheeks pinked) *for its intended purpose*, and died. Mademoiselle Françoise could have used it to commit suicide out of grief— No, she must have poisoned herself by mistake. Or when she was making more. And the cat had licked her fingers, poor puss.

But, she thought with a chill, Mademoiselle Françoise wouldn't have made such a dangerous thing in the middle of sewing, when her friend Huguette was in the house.

Had she been using it? Mademoiselle Huguette said she had been sewing. Mademoiselle Huguette might have lied— perhaps she was a witch too, Ruthie thought.

No, not Huguette Giroufle. Witches sacrificed rabbits, witches used beef fat; everyone knew Huguette had been a vegetarian since the age of twelve.

Then what had happened in that house that night?

She felt in her pocket; she brought out the button. She held it on her open palm. Mr. Blantire, Mademoiselle Françoise. She loses a button. He puts it on top of the well—

But he would have been paralyzed. If it had been flying ointment, he would have been lying on the ground.

She looked at the button in her hand, quite distressed. But—there could not have been— He would not have been paralyzed from anything in *this* tin, which had not even affected a hen.

She must really stop doing this; she was no good at it and there were things to do. She put the button in her pocket and opened her bedroom door—to find Count André.

"Ruthie," he said, and cleared his throat. "Mademoiselle Ruthie—"

"Monsieur le Comte—" Oh, she would say *vous* to him in a minute, as if he were not her old friend.

"You seem distressed," Count André said. He must think that her distress was due to—At least he did not say he was sorry for it. Her cheeks burned again.

"It is nothing, nothing at all," no embarrassing and unexpected moment between us. "But only that I have somehow made a great mistake in some books I brought away with me. They are only recipe books." She was holding them. "From Mademoiselle Françoise's kitchen," she admitted.

He opened his mouth and closed it again, opened it. "Let me see them."

He turned them over, looking not at the contents but at the binding. He opened them and looked up at her wordlessly, as if he were waiting for her to say the next thing. Confession trembled on her lips, confession of she didn't know what. She was miserably conscious of the open bedroom door behind them. He could see her sheets from here.

"I looked in your purse," he said. "These books aren't the same." He opened a book. "Look, this is my mother's handwriting. Why would my mother's books be at Mademoiselle Françoise's?"

"They're *not* the same," she breathed. He was sure of this, as sure as anything he did on stage. She trusted him.

"Look, too," she said. "This tin." She brought it out of her pocket.

"Not the same."

"Do you think so?"

"It had no label."

"They are not the same," she said. "I thought I was mistaken."

"No," he said. "Never."

She put her hand into her pocket again and brought out the rose button. "This," she said. "This too. A button like it was in the cellar where Mr. Blantire died."

He stared at it in her palm. He looked up at her, and she saw him as she never had before. He was Count André being driven back into Necrosar's shell.

"Don't look!" she said, but it was too late.

Chapter 65

The mirrors stood in their places on the floor. The lights were blazing on their iron stands. The floor of the Great

Hall was covered with chalk marks and X's. They reminded Sabine of the cabalistic marks Françoise had drawn on the floor of her workroom, but everything was much grander. And around them, all around them, stood the party guests and the dead, swathed in their rags and their grey shrouds.

"We're right here," Cyron said, drawing Sabine toward an X on the floor. "We can both see these ghosts. Mabet tries to bluff it out—" He glared around him. "But Madame Mabet, who has a good heart, is horrified. Binny, do us horrified."

She rolled her eyes and cringed the way Papa Cyron had showed her.

"Horrified? Eh? Never mind, that's good enough. You, there, you're toasting the Revolution," Cyron said to an actor. "We raise our glasses, and, Binny, that's when you see Madame Méduc. Right over—" Cyron peered at the floor. "Right over here, where's our ghost? You, into position. You don't have your baby, where's the baby?" A stagehand tossed the actress a bundle of rags. "She's here, Binny, and you see her and your eyes bug out, you round your shoulders, you let your glass fall and put your hands out in front of you, like this—"

There was a pop and a shower of sparks. One of the Kliegl lights had gone. A technician swore and went off to get another.

Eli Krauss was adjusting the lights on the other side of a huge sheet of glass. "Stand here, Binny, we need your light values." The hairdresser, Claude, moved in to touch up her makeup and hair.

Ruthie had come into the hall behind her. Ruthie was standing with her hands over her mouth, one hand open and one fisted, her face pale over her flowered blouse. André was behind her; and he looked at her, Sabine.

It was as if there had been a noise in the air; it was as if there had been a shot or some great pressure in her chest. It was too early to tell what had happened to her. She was far

away from him, but she saw his blue eyes, she felt him looking at her, she felt it everywhere.

She had got his attention at last.

He came across the Great Hall to her; he spoke to her, for
the first time without sullenness or restraint. "Buttons?" he
said. She looked up into his eyes; she was seen, felt, lost in
them.

His icy eyes burned her like flames. "You poisoned Blantire."

"No!"

She retreated toward the camera, stepping over cables on
the floor. Lights were shining everywhere. "Stand just here."
She looked through the glass toward the shrouded ghost, who
was joking with an electrician.

And for a moment she saw two ghosts, two veiled grey
presences in the blackness, and she screamed.

The second one was herself.

Chapter 66

Rows of pink eyes. André remembers them, pink eyes
winking at him on her shoulder. Eyes of albino animals, ghost eyes; eyes that would be red in the dark. Monster
eyes on a violet checked dress.

And now she is afraid. Just now, there, looking into the
glass, she has remembered where she wore the dress with the
eyes, and who saw her. She turns pale, she shakes her head in
protest. Yes, murderess, I saw you! You were standing next to

Mademoiselle Françoise in the Grand'Place. Had you just poisoned her? How did you give it to her? Candy, like me? Apples, bread? The rabbit?

The rabbit.

He grabs her by both wrists. "You poisoned Françoise Auclart," he says. "And you poisoned Blantire too, didn't you? Because he was your lover?" He feels Necrosar wrapping around him. Ruthie, he thinks. What did you do to Ruthie?

She tugs away from him, eyes wide. "You're crazy!"

"Oh, yes, yes, I am, but I know what I'm saying."

"You're going to kill me!" she shrieks, pointing at the reflection of the ghost.

"Why not?" There is only one reason why not, and that is Ruthie, shaking her head beyond the sidelines, mouthing *No, no.*

He takes a step away from Sabine, still holding her hands, almost as if they are dancing. And at this distance he sees something that inspires him. "See, Papa Cyron!" he calls out. "I can direct her better than you can. Now she's frightened. She's sorry because she's going to die."

He drops her hands and moves behind the camera.

"Places," he says. "Camera. Iris out. Music."

And the ghosts move in on the horrified Sabine.

Chapter 67

"Forget him. You were marvelous," Papa Cyron said. "Marvelous. Binny, you were perfect! Binny, you'll be the toast of Paris. Here, we're going to have champagne.— Go, go, get off your makeup, we're all going to have champagne."

While Claude creamed her makeup off, she looked into the mirror. She was grey, grey; her lips were purple. Her blonde hair looked dry and garish.

But, she thought, I'm only eighteen. Look at how healthy I am. Hear my heart. How could I die? But her fingernails were blue-purple, like bruises.

"Come on," said Papa Cyron, "come on, Binny, we want to toast you!"

Claude splashed cologne on her face and made her up. "There, you've never looked better!" She went out into the Great Hall. Corks were popping; even the technicians were cheering her. And what good is it, she thought despairingly. Every person she had seen covered with the grey shroud had died. It was a matter of two days, four, a week at most.

"Come on, Binny, it isn't so bad." Papa Cyron laughed. "You look as if you were going to your own funeral! If I'd killed every actor I said I'd kill—"

"He really means it," she hissed.

André watched her with blue-acid eyes.

She excused herself and shut herself into her rooms. But he's only a man, she thought. I'm a sorceress. There must be some way out.

She took out her cards and spread them on the tablecloth. This was a serious matter, a matter for the Tarot. She took the Empress as her card. The Ten of Pentacles covered it, a card of family matters and the home. The Two of Swords crossed it, a terrible card: danger, fatality. Around her, the Six of Cups, a card of children, and the Ace, Two, and Three of Wands. All of them together, what did it mean? Strife, danger? Cards of great fortune or misfortune. She put her chin on her hands and looked at the future. The Hermit, the King of Cups reversed, the Two of Pentacles reversed, and the Four of Cups. The Hermit might be Mademoiselle Françoise. The King of Cups, a fair man, an artist, but badly disposed to her and treacherous: André.

Her husband, whom she loved, wanted to kill her. She saw that in the mirror even more clearly than in the cards.

But in the end— Where was her death? The Tarot should see it. The Two of Pentacles she did not understand clearly; a long uncertainty, perhaps. The Four of Cups meant she was in for a time of messy unhappiness. But there was nothing about dying.

She did the Oracle of Napoléon to make sure. The same fortune: the dark clouds facing toward her, the treachery, the fights. The Ring was far left of her, her Gentleman as far as he could be. Her troubles came from her marriage. But still no death. There were the Ship, the Tower, and the Cloverleaves. She would go on a journey; she would have long life and good luck.

It was a good thing that the Oracle of Napoléon didn't depend on reversed cards. Every card but the Cross was upside down.

So, she thought, and took a good long look at her mirror.

André hadn't gone grey, which meant she couldn't fix him a rabbit and have it over with. And she didn't intend to die.

What did the sign of death mean? In the Tarot it meant transformation. Transformation, a journey, good luck. What she had planned already, to hurt André.

She found Papa Cyron in the Great Hall and pulled him aside. "I'm going to leave him. I'm finished with this. I'm going to divorce him and move to New York and I'm going to be in the movies *there*. It's more than not letting me go to Paris, he wants to kill me."

"This is only rehearsal nerves—"

"It's not, I know. He threatened me! I can't stay around here, can I, and let him murder me? You heard him."

"I'll take care of him," Papa Cyron promised. "You'll be safe."

Chapter 68

Reisden was making himself up for Méduc's great scene, his renunciation of his father.

He has no children. Find Méduc in the phrase. He has no children. It is the worst thing one can say about a man who actually has a child. You are not worthy to have a child. Your child says so.

He has no children: It makes no sense. Once you have children you are changed. If Toby were to renounce him utterly, he would still be Toby's father.

So it is a child's curse, the curse of someone who has never been a parent.

Reisden put on Méduc's tattered uniform and his long sword.

No. It was the curse of a child who had grown into a man, a father cursing another father. You killed my child. You are not my father. You are not worthy; my father could not kill my son.

At the edge of his mental vision, he thought of William Knight. *You have no children.*

He thought of Gilbert.

Cyron's wrong, he thought. Méduc won't end up grey-haired and happy among his grandchildren. He won't know how to speak to them.

Destroying his father will destroy his family.

He'll do it anyway. He has no choice.

André didn't show up for the shoot; Krauss reported some big fight over the Ball of the Dead scene. They motored a little way up the road until they found a field where the hay had not yet been cut. Montfort was visible in the distance. The farmer took money for his hay and called his family to watch the filming.

The shadows lengthened. They were ready. The Messenger came in shot and told Méduc that his family were dead. Reisden could show nothing in his face to express what Méduc would feel. He turned away from the camera, thinking of Toby.

He looked out on the tall wheat stalks, brown and ripe, but living. Nothing should live if his Toby were dead. He lifted his sword and brought the sharp edge down almost gently at first. The stalks fell and died. He swung the sword like a scythe. The stalks fell, and fell, and the wheat ears crunched and broke under his feet. The scene went on too long. He waded into the standing grain and cut at it until his shoulders were on fire, his knees and arms were shaking from weariness, until there was not a sound but his breath. He raised his arms high, holding the sword over his head, its edge trembling and turning down, and he fell to his knees and stabbed at the ground, the broken grain, destroying everything.

"Cut," finally, Krauss said. "I got it."

"Good." He couldn't have done it again even if he'd had the field.

They took close-ups. The farmers stood round silently, out of shot, staring at the waste of hay.

He drove Krauss back but afterward simply parked his car by the New Buildings and, without taking off his makeup or removing his costume, went to see his boy. Toby was playing with Aline and looked up in delighted consternation at his father, yellow-faced and in strange clothes: How did you get that way, Papa? Reisden was filthy with sweat and chaff and field dust; he swung Toby up, hugging him. Toby picked hay off his face.

I have a child, Reisden thought, I have a child and he has a father, and nothing is wrong. We can build something on that. I can give what I did not have.

He held Toby until the sick hollowness the scene had roused in him was eased. Toby was wriggling to get down. "All right, love." He left Toby with booty, a goose feather that had got in his hair from the field. He hoped he hadn't done the whole scene with it plastered to his face.

"Alexander?" Perdita said.

"We did 'He has no children,' " he explained.

She opened her arms to him and held him. He held on to her, suddenly breathless with grief. "I'm sorry," he said. "For speaking to you that way in front of Gilbert. At all. I had to send him away, but— I'm sorry."

"You're wrong," she said, but she held him.

He took convulsive breaths. "Don't leave me. Never leave me. Never die. I never want to feel like this."

Chapter 69

André goes looking for Reisden and finds him in the bathroom, waiting for the tub to fill. He is still wearing his costume and makeup and he is leaning exhausted against the wall.

"We've canned 'He has no children,' " Reisden says. "Without you."

"Did it go well?" André says automatically, but doesn't wait for the answer. "I need your help."

He explains. Ruthie, the Auclart farm, witches' grimoires, flying ointment, Sabine's child, Blantire. A button. "I *knew* what she was, I sensed it from the beginning." André is exalted, afraid. "I am not mad, Reisden. She poisoned him when she was done with him. Françoise Auclart too."

"Why?" Reisden asks flatly.

"Blantire was her lover. The Auclart woman *knew too much*. I don't know why," André says impatiently. "Does it matter?"

"André—"

André digs the button out of his trousers pocket. "Look, look, look." He turns it and makes it glitter. "Rows of pink eyes. Rabbit eyes. On her dress," André says patiently. "*She* went down in the cellars with Blantire; *she* poisoned him. The Auclart woman found out." André waves his left hand, filling in the blanks with whatever motive Reisden likes. Motives

313

are Reisden's business. "And so she poisoned her, too.—You know. You *saw*."

"What have I seen? What eyes?" The ruins of Reisden's makeup make his face into a brown-yellow mask patched with dust, black around the eyes. A clay man, half-finished, a golem.

"You saw the buttons," André insists. "You were there. In the Grand'Place. She was wearing a purple checked dress with pink rose buttons. She introduced us to the Auclart woman. 'This is Mademoiselle Françoise.' " He imitates *her* breathy nasal voice. " 'I've just poisoned her.' "

Reisden remembers it. André sees.

"Where did you get this?"

"From the cellars. Ruthie found it by the Holy Well. It's Sabine's. You remember it." Reisden says nothing. "You are going to help me, Reisden?" André says. "Aren't you? You remember this?"

"I remember buttons something like this—"

"No, this one, this! It came from the Holy Well, Reisden! From the Holy Well! Right by Blantire's body! From where he died!"

"Why didn't anyone see it before?"

"It was on top of the well box."

"This button," Reisden says. "You're sure."

"This button," André says, but he has to add the rest. "A button exactly like it. The first one went down the plumbing."

"André," Reisden says, and oh, André knows the tone.

"You know it is the same," André says. "You saw. You were there with me. She was wearing the dress with these buttons. You saw. You tell Papa Cyron. She has to be arrested."

He takes Reisden's hand and drops the button into it. Reisden looks at it and up at him. It might be the makeup. But there is something hard about his face, something closed-in, self-protective, rejecting.

"This time I know," André says. "This time I'm not making it up. *This is real*. I know I've said things about my parents, I was wrong, but I'm all right *now*, I know what I'm saying *now*. My wife is a witch and she has been poisoning people."

"André."

André, André thinks.

"Ruthie hallucinated everything," Reisden says. "There's nothing to this. You're acting mad."

"So reasonable, Reisden." For a moment André can summon Necrosar. It is a relief; Necrosar can help him deal with the creeping terror that is invading him. It can't be that Reisden won't stand by him, Reisden has always stood by him.

There is a crashing from outside. "I've been looking for you," Papa Cyron roars, slamming the big oak door open. They are now all three in the bathroom. "What've you been saying about Binny?"

A great hopelessness comes over André as if he will be made to go back into the cavalry. "Listen to me," he says, but now Reisden and Cyron are talking to each other.

"You've heard what he's saying?"

"I've heard."

"I've had enough! It's too much! Good G-d!"

"She's a murderess," André says.

"Be quiet, André," Reisden says.

Papa Cyron points his finger at Reisden. "Don't make excuses for him anymore. Don't say you've cured him. He threatened her. He said he would kill her, don't you understand?"

"I never said my mother was a witch," André says.

"I want him locked up," Papa Cyron says. "Bring me the papers. I'll sign them."

There is a terrible silence, and instead of Reisden saying what André knows he should, he says, "Cyron, André is forty years old."

"He is a danger to others. She's ready to run away, she's so frightened."

André looks at them, not quite believing what he's hearing. "Papa Cyron," he says. "Reisden."

Papa Cyron turns on him.

"What do you want? I've done my best for you. I found you a wife who'd have you, and it wasn't easy. You've spoiled that, boy. You've spoiled everything. I—" Suddenly Papa Cyron is helpless, a magician who has tried to transform a stone into a dove, but the stone won't fly. "I don't have anything left for you, André. It's gone. You made me choose between you and her." Papa Cyron looks at him, from far away. André reaches out his hand. Papa Cyron pulls back. "I choose her," he says. "Reisden, I want him evaluated for insanity. What I have to do, I'll do. And there's only one answer you can give." He turns his back and walks away.

For all André's life they have been a family. He cannot imagine this betrayal. They borrow each other's pocket hand-kerchiefs. It is unimaginable. He looks over at his friend, Reisden, who is suddenly in charge of his future. Reisden is pale under his yellow makeup. He is still holding the button in one clenched hand. The bathtub is nearly overflowing. André turns the tap off. Suddenly it's very quiet.

"Reisden, are you going to say I'm insane?"

"André," Reisden says, pleading with him. Always with *him*. Be well. Be perfect. Be happy. *André*.

"Are you going to put me in an asylum?"

"I have to have someone look at you," Reisden says tiredly. "He asked. It's the law.—Don't say this, André."

"Look in your hand."

Reisden throws the button on the floor angrily.

"You want to fix me," André says. "Make me well. But I'm not sick. She kills people."

"Stop it."

André sees it all, all the betrayal. "I get in your way. The way of your precious Jouvet, your family, your baby. You can't fix me and you need to fix all the crazies. Oh, Reisden, you don't like to worry, you don't like to be frightened, and you don't want Papa Cyron against you; how will you help me?"

"André, listen to me."

"When you put me in the asylum, what will you do to resign yourself? Give me a puppet theatre to play with? Stage blood and detachable heads? Will you come to see the plays? Don't do this."

"Then stop all this," Reisden says. "This is a story. It's Necro."

"What about Ruthie?" André says. "Ruthie won't betray me."

Chapter 70

Reisden went to see Ruthie just as he was, dirty and in his makeup. "*What* is this?" Ruthie was in tears. She thought she had seen—she thought she had read—

"You didn't," said Reisden.

She held her handkerchief over her face and wept openly.

"I must have him formally evaluated. And you know he won't pass for sane.—There's more happening here than you know."

How would one prove André wrong? Blantire had died

because he was spying. But the authorities wouldn't allow that story to be told, not if there were some tunnel or fortification actually to be spied on. They'd rather say André was mad.

The trouble was that he might be. Reisden called Katzmann, who was about to leave for Scotland and fishing. "I'm disappointed," Katzmann said. "The theory's perfectly clear! The talking cure works! It's worked before," he conceded a little defensively.

"He was doing better," Reisden said, "and then—" He told what had happened during the Ball of the Dead scene. "Ruthie set him off," he said. "She'd found a button," he added finally, "one of Sabine's buttons, in the cellar." He did remember the button. Yes, it had been Sabine's. There were a thousand explanations for it. "He made up a completely mad story around it."

"Do you think he'd harm his wife?" Katzmann asked.

Reisden thought of the poison bottle, of André describing the guillotine scene. "Yes," he said finally. I'm sorry, André. "Yes."

"Then I'm coming."

Reisden went to see Cyron.

"Katzmann will come tonight or tomorrow," Reisden said to Cyron.

Cyron scrawled on a piece of paper: the request for evaluation. "You find him a place," Cyron said, handing the paper over. Suddenly he looked a thousand years old. "A good place.—How long will—it—all take?"

"That depends on whether André goes willingly. I think he won't. He doesn't think he's insane. It could take weeks."

"I'm a public figure," Cyron said. "These things are bad. Sooner."

"I'm doing what I can. Don't push me."

"Will he finish the film—?" Cyron said.

"You're putting him in an asylum," Reisden said, "but you want him to finish the film first?"

"Don't get on me, boy. This is harder on me than it is on you."

He saw Cyron's face. Of course Cyron wanted to finish the film; there was a huge amount of money in it. There was, he thought less bitterly, a lot of André in it. "I'm sorry."

"*I'm* sorry. I've been sorry for years." Cyron cleared his throat. "Saturday. The last scene. With—the guillotine."

"Cancel it. Don't let Sabine put her neck in a guillotine with André there."

Cyron nodded. "We'll cut away as Sabine kneels. Cut to my face; I'll react."

Chapter 71

The soldiers gathered early the next morning for the start of the battle scene. The air was full of banners. All the costumes that had been ready so long were manned, their buttons glittering, their colors bright. The soldiers from the Citadel ran up the hill, shouting and charging and falling. Smoke obscured the battlefield. The hot sun beat down on them. Men fell at the sound of the trumpet. Eli Krauss filmed them from above the Jerusalem Gate, from the slope by the stonehenges, in the fields where the soldiers swept forward and beat down the hay. He filmed them from Reisden's car, moving along the Arras road with them as they charged. The soldiers bivouacked in the fields that night, enthusiastic for more war the next morning.

By the next morning André had changed everything.

The soldiers found new makeup numbers with their uniforms. When they lined up at the makeup stations, they were given wounds. Bloody stumps for hands. Bloated faces. Blood-soaked uniforms. André marched them down to the fields past Montfort commune. When they joked, he told them to be quiet, because they were dead.

André filmed the dead for two days.

They lay in piles in the hot sun, among the ruined fields. They lay where they had fallen, tangled in hedges or face-down among the wheat and beets. The sugary blood drew the birds, which pecked at their hands and faces. "Stay still," André said. He filmed the wounds, the blood, the birds. He filmed the sky through the ruins of the commune roofs. He set a track through the field and moved the camera along it; he set the camera on Reisden's car and had it driven along the road filming nothing. Motionlessness, silence, bodies, broken hay.

A very few soldiers he kept alive. He had them drag bodies from the field, one by one, until the living soldiers dropped in real exhaustion.

The script called for Mabet and Méduc to have a sword fight as the culmination of the battle. But there was no battle and there was no sword fight. André filmed them in a few minutes of unchoreographed fighting, clumsy and unshowy, until Cyron tripped and Reisden pointed his sword at Cyron's sprawled body.

"What are you doing?" Pétiot said to André. "My boys came here to fight."

"You're not using that piece of film?" Cyron said. "I stumbled. He didn't win. I stumbled. Don't even develop that piece."

"It's not about fighting and winning," André mumbled. "We've all come here to die."

On Thursday, Katzmann arrived and followed André through the hot day of filming dead men in the fields. In the afternoon he spoke for a long time to Cyron. On Thursday evening Reisden drove him back to Arras, and they sat on a bench in the park in front of the station, at the edge of the electric lights, waiting for the train.

Katzmann grunted. "If Cyron weren't pushing us so hard I'd feel better about it," he said frankly. "She has money. And Cyron doesn't want to let the money go."

If Cyron were making something under the Arras road, he'd need money. Pétiot doubtless funneled money to him through army procurement, but tunnels are fearsomely expensive to build and more expensive to maintain.

He thought of Cyron and Sabine dancing. Cyron didn't want to let Sabine go. "Andre's troubles don't come from Sabine."

Katzmann pulled the papers out of his jacket pocket and scribbled in the portion of the form marked *Reason for committal*, then signed them. Reisden tilted the paper toward the light and read it. *Believes his wife is a poisoner and has threatened her life.*

He went back to Montfort. Cyron was in his office, not working or reading scripts; playing solitaire with the dogged late-night persistence of a man who would rather put the black eight on the red nine than think about what he is doing. All the cards were up but Cyron couldn't find one to move. Reisden dropped the order of committal on his desk. Cyron stuck his chin out and inscribed his signature on the line for *Next of Kin*.

"I'm asking Pétiot to guard the machinery on Saturday." Pétiot would have men available.

"You watch him, too."

"Ruthie and Jules and I."

"He'll—go—that night?"

"Katzmann will find him a place."

That evening he didn't sleep at all. He lay in the heat with Perdita and Toby asleep beside him and stared up at the ceiling.

The button meant nothing. Sabine had simply gone to see the death scene, later. She had known him, after all.

No.

He remembered that afternoon in the Grand'Place: Mademoiselle Françoise's hot hands, Sabine's brooding eyes, the missing button. The chemical smell of the dress. He wouldn't have noticed it if he weren't married to Perdita. New dye, a new dress.

According to Puckett, on the day Sabine had worn that dress and lost that button, Blantire had been dead two weeks.

Reisden thought, She looked at his dead body.

For a moment he convinced himself completely. If Sabine killed Blantire, she must have killed Françoise Auclart too. But Sabine? Sabine, who sat in the coach afterward reading about movie stars?

André was dangerous. Katzmann had said so. Reisden wasn't being Pétiot's dog; he wasn't abandoning André for the army contract. He could reassure himself of that. André was dangerous.

But Reisden couldn't sleep.

Chapter 72

On Friday Perdita learned something terrible.

She had two letters. The first was heartening, a note from Uncle Gilbert. *My dear, it is wrong. I feel that I am leaving him to deal with everything again, and this time you and Toby are involved. Come to see me when you return to Paris.* She shook her head. *You* must talk to Alexander, she thought. She felt hopeless.

But the second—The second was from Milly. *I have heard a story about that Wagny girl. Do you know she ordered mourning before her father was dead?*

Perdita, Aline, and Toby went to Arras. Mademoiselle Huguette had all of Mademoiselle Françoise's order books. The new assistant, a good brisk girl, found the entry for Sabine's mourning, three days before her father had died, and marked *Rush.*

"She murdered him!" Aline exclaimed in a whisper.

"No, how could she?" Perdita said. "Her father died of a heart attack."

"Oh, heart attack, heart attack! Like they thought for a while Ruthie'd had!"

"Perhaps she sensed he was ill," Perdita said. But what sort of woman, apprehensive for her father's health, went off and ordered mourning?

They went off and collected laundry, and by that time Toby needed changing. "Aline, let's beg Mademoiselle Huguette to use her washroom." While Aline dealt with Toby, Perdita sat and gossiped idly with Mademoiselle Huguette.

How terrible that Mademoiselle Françoise had died while she was there. Had they done anything unusual that day? No. Eaten nothing unusual? No. Anything from someone else?

No. Just the rabbit.

"And that was one of her rabbits?" said Perdita.

"It must have been," Mademoiselle Huguette said.

"But—" And Perdita asked her question.

Chapter 73

André knows what is going to happen to him. On Friday night he edits the film as usual. But this will be the last time. They don't let inflammable film and sharp knives in madhouses.

For a moment, as he pieces the film together, he escapes his troubles. He has always thought of himself not as a play-wright or actor but someone who simply puts together effects for the audience, a little laughter next to a shiver of horror. Film is all about putting things together, shadows next to light, motion against motion.

Reisden always said that he couldn't stay in the madhouse because they wouldn't let him do chemistry. André can't go because they won't let him do film.

Katzmann asked him questions. *Do you think your wife can cause harm to other people?* There's only one true answer to that. But André mulls over his answer, tries to say it sanely, waits too long, and Katzmann writes in his little book.

André has written plays about being mad. Just before the madman cuts the visitor's throat in *Dr. Wardrell*, he says earnestly, "I am not mad."

André is not mad.

He tries to see Reisden, but Reisden has managed to disappear. He goes to see Ruthie. She and Jules are making up paypackets for the extras tomorrow.

"Am I mad?" he asks them.

"No," they answer loyally.

"Would I kill—someone? Her?"

No.

"The scene tomorrow, the guillotine scene," he says. "You're sure she's not going to put her head in the guillotine? If it chops off her head, I will never see you again. They'll lock me up. They'll cut *my* head off."

You wouldn't do it, Jules says. *You never hurt an actor. Never.*

But André can't escape thinking of the huge, heavy blade and Sabine's plump neck. It is like Henri the engineer thinking of strangling his son, the play Reisden can't watch anymore. "Keep me from killing her," he confesses in a rush to them. "Keep me away from her tomorrow. Don't let me do anything, nothing stupid, you understand, nothing insane."

Ruthie says "You wouldn't," but Jules doesn't. The two partners look at each other. Jules has a scar by his eye and a scar on his mouth; the bruises have almost faded but Jules has changed. He knows what it's like to be cornered and beaten. Jules raises his hand slowly, yes: Jules will stop him.

"I want to ask Ruthie something," André says. Jules leaves them alone.

"I," he says. "In the hospital. Do you think it was flying ointment? I dreamed of your hair. You smiled at me."

Ruthie says, "You mustn't dream of me, Count André."

"I am going into the asylum. May I dream of you there? Will you come to see me?"

"Of course."

"Every Sunday, in the afternoon," André says sadly. He has written too many plays about madhouses. "Come during the week," he whispers, "when they don't expect guests. They'll treat me better.—Can you keep my theatre going?"

They both know the answer.

"Perhaps they'll let me write plays there." This is wishful thinking. André knows all the interventions by which doctors try to rip the madness out of men. "The theatre won't work without me. The audiences want Necrosar. I can still do Necrosar," he says. "Look. 'They are taking him away. But he isn't mad enough. He knows what's happening to him.' "

Necrosar would laugh but André's throat is dry.

"They'll take me tomorrow. After the last scene. Papa Cyron pulled strings.—I want to ask you," André says.

He is a madman, he has been one all his life. Motives have never meant anything to him; in André's world people do things because they are mad. "I don't know about people," André says. Other human beings are fragments to him. "Ruthie, do you love me?"

She takes a step away from him. "I would do anything for you."

"No," André says. "It's important to me to know these things. I know I trust you and you would never poison me or hurt me. I like you. I know that." He thinks of laying his head on the bed near her hand. He can be comfortable in her presence. What does that mean? "I need to know."

She looks at him in agony and confusion. "Of course I would not hurt you."

"Tell me, then."

"No, no, I cannot."

He takes her hands. "Please. Please."

"Count André, you do not know what you ask. Let go my hands, please, let them go."

She pulls her hands away. She walks away from him, into a corner. "We must count the pay-packets yet," she says, wringing her hands. "There is so much to do." She turns. She has to look up at him, he is so much taller than she. *"Tomorrow?"* she says, bringing her clasped hands up to the level of her heart, her throat. "Tomorrow? How could it happen so fast?"

André stares down at her, his wide mouth open in an *O* of grief. "I'm frightened," he says.

She looks up at him. There is nothing she can do for him now, nothing, she who prided herself in doing for him. "You—are all my life," she says. "Working for you is all I want." It is not enough. She unfists her hands and holds them out to him. "You are loved, Count André. Believe me, you are loved."

"Do you love me?"

She reaches out for him; she touches his sleeve. He puts out his other hand and touches her arm, lightly as a butterfly.

"*I* love you," she says. "I'll pray for you. You'll be safe tomorrow."

Chapter 74

Sabine, too, knew what would happen to her. All afternoon she read the movie sections of the theatre magazines and cried. All the beautiful girls—she had been a beautiful girl, too. Now in the mirror her face was dark and decaying. She was going to die.

She put a scarf over the mirror.

Papa Cyron had told her she would not have to put her head in the guillotine. But instead of the guillotine it would be a railroad accident, a fire, a shipwreck on the way to America. It would be the button that Ruthie had found.

"André will be nowhere near the guillotine," Papa Cyron had told her. "Pétiot's men will watch the guillotine. No one can hurt you."

The sun had set. Would she see the sun again?

That night, like every night, there was entertainment on the terrace. The soldiers wanted Sabine to tell their fortunes. She dealt the Gentleman, the Storks, the Bear; but her hands were grey, the fingernails purple with a white moon. She started to deal her own fortune. The first card on the table was the Tomb.

"Everybody, everybody, they're showing the Ball of the Dead in the Great Hall."

She didn't want to go. Papa Cyron made her. She didn't want to see herself; she closed her eyes.

"No, no, Binny, you're beautiful, I've never seen anything like it!"

She opened her eyes.

She was beautiful.

She was grey, but everyone was grey. On the screen she moved through the crowd of ghosts. The decapitated heads swooped at her, the roughly jerking dead people bowed to her. She was frightened. But she was alive.

Look, Sabine thought. I will always be alive.

A witch is flesh. She dies. But to be in the movies is like being burned alive young. It is a death no one forgets.

She looked up at herself, like a flower on the white screen. This is how they'll look up to me, she thought.

"Papa Cyron!" she whispered. "I'm not afraid anymore. Tomorrow I'll put my head in the guillotine."

Chapter 75

Perdita heard the news about André late in the afternoon, when she arrived back from Arras. Until after supper she tried to think how to tell Alexander what she had found. But there was no way but the direct way.

She was wearing the necklace with its four "rhinestones." She touched it nervously. She gave Toby to Aline to put to bed and went out to find her husband.

He was at the entertainment, which had not started yet. "Come away with me," she said. "I have something I have to tell you."

She took him all the way past the stables, to the drop-off of eroded hill above the road. They stood with their backs against the stables, on the little half-moon of uneroded land. No one went here. Perdita sat in the prickly dry grass; Alexander dropped down beside her. The sun was dusky orange. It would be a fine day tomorrow for the guillotine scene.

They talked for a moment about André's going into the asylum. Alexander didn't want to talk about it. "I as much as signed the order," he said.

"It wasn't you, it was Monsieur Cyron." Dotty would have handled that better. *Darling, how terrible for you.* What

Perdita wanted to say was *If you stopped blaming yourself for things, we'd be happier all around and you could help.*

If André were telling the truth about Sabine, Alexander would have to say so, and he'd go up against Cyron. And if he fought Cyron, he would have to fight General Pétiot. Who had just given Jouvet its big new contract. *I've won,* Alexander had said. Perdita knew she was not bringing her husband good news.

But he would fight for André.

She moved her fingers nervously through the crackling grass. "André might be right," she said. "About Sabine. Did you know Sabine ordered mourning before her father died?"

"Where did you hear that?"

She told him.

"Get Milly to check her facts."

As if Milly were an idiot for finding out an inconvenient thing. Well, now she would be inconvenient, too. "Did you ever wonder who cooked the rabbit?"

"Rabbit?" her husband asked.

"Mademoiselle Françoise's rabbit, the one with the poison in it. Where did it come from?" she said. "I do know French cooking. There are different kinds of rabbits, Alexander. The ones that are best for cooking come from the South. The rabbits from around here aren't very good, so Mademoiselle Françoise would have marinated hers all day before she cooked it. But she didn't cook it that day because she was at her shop. Mademoiselle Huguette didn't because she's a vegetarian. And she didn't have it left over from the previous day; she would have died the first day she ate it. So who cooked the rabbit?"

"She bought it at the market," he said.

"She didn't," Perdita said. "Aline and I went all around the market trying to find prepared foods. That's for Paris and rich people, Alexander. This is a country town; people cook their dinners at the public ovens but they don't buy cooked rabbit from shops. And even if she'd bought half the rabbit, who bought the other half and why aren't *they* dead?"

"Don't of all things strengthen André's delusions. He's done that well enough himself."

"Does Sabine do any cooking?" Perdita said. "I mean ordinarily, when the caterers aren't here?" She answered her own question. "André wouldn't think she could poison him if she never took an interest in the food."

"Sabine sends parcels of food to Paris from Montfort. Blackberry jellies, preserved beets, legs of lamb. But they are not poisoned, and of course she doesn't cook them herself."

Perdita knew better. "She does the pretty parts. After someone else has picked the fruit and hulled it and done all the work, she stirs the jam and says it's hers. She would flirt with the cook while someone else skinned and gutted it and took the membrane off. And then she'd do a sauce."

He didn't say anything. She'd thought he'd say something like *Now André has a chance*, or swear and say *Why now?*

"I think Sabine came to see Mademoiselle Françoise that Friday," Perdita said. "She said a button had fallen off her dress, or something, or just came to say hello. She brought some rabbit from Montfort as a present. Mademoiselle Françoise didn't eat the rabbit on Friday, because that's fish day; she saved it for Saturday, market day, when she would be too busy to cook."

He said nothing for a long time. "You sound like André," he said.

She shivered. It was one thing to put together clues, like Sherlock Holmes, and to use Sabine as an excuse for André's behavior. But suddenly she was talking about a girl younger than herself, who had done this—"I think I might believe André," she said.

"She'd visited the dressmaker," he said, trying to dismiss it.

"Mademoiselle Françoise would have sewn the missing button on."

"No, because it's bad luck to sew a dress someone's wearing. Mademoiselle Huguette told me. Mademoiselle Françoise would have given the button to Sabine ... And Sabine—" She stopped, thinking about T. J. Blantire the cowboy, who had died in Sabine's cellar. "She killed Mr. Blantire."

"No," he said.

"Yes. And Ruthie found a button in the cellar and then something happened to her too." Perdita had not thought everything through, the button and Blantire and Ruthie; it struck her only then, as part of the great terrible surprise of what Sabine might be. "The button," Perdita said. "*That* button. In the cellar, by Mr. Blantire. Sabine lost it there. She came to get another from Mademoiselle Françoise, who had made the dress in the first place. But when Sabine realized where it had gone, she knew that Mademoiselle Françoise would know who'd murdered Mr. Blantire. And she— Sabine, she just—"

She shook her head. She could not think of it.

"In other words, Mademoiselle Françoise died because she knew too much. People who know too much don't get murdered, Perdita, they get confessed to."

"But you believe it, don't you?" Of course he would in the end; it helped André.

"No. You haven't got the point. The point is that André, who's very lightly balanced at best, said in front of fifty witnesses, including his stepfather, that he would kill his wife. Therefore he is being put in protective custody. Full stop. It's too late to help André. He's threatened to kill her."

"But you have to tell Monsieur Cyron," Perdita said. "It will make a difference. And someone, Alexander, someone should watch her."

"It'll only make him think I've gone insane, too. A button that Ruthie says she saw but dropped down the drain. Which might or might not match buttons on a dress that is probably now on the back of a deserving poor woman in the Balkans. A button that wasn't sewn on because of superstition. Grimoires and a canister containing an unknown substance, which Ruthie blames for her heatstroke, and which no one else but André saw. A cooked rabbit. A cooked rabbit, Perdita."

A cooked rabbit, as if it were nothing. Cooking is important, as taking care of the baby is important; there is a whole world of housekeeping that men don't see. "Mourning for her father when he wasn't dead. I don't know why we're fighting about this, because you're going to support André. Unless you think I mind your fighting with his father. I know it'll be hard; we'll get through."

"You don't understand. I'm not supporting André. Say André's sane because Sabine is a murderer—on the evidence of buttons and rabbits? Cyron will be our enemy, and Lucien Pétiot will back him and be our enemy, too. With evidence I may be able to do something. I am not able to do anything now. And I want to support my family, Perdita; I want to support you."

She was tired of this. "You don't need Lucien Pétiot."

"Why?" he said. "Because I have Gilbert? No, Perdita."

"Because you're Richard Knight," she said. "You have money of your own. Your father left you all his money.—Uncle Gilbert told me. Do you know what he's been doing in the last five years? He learned about money. He took the money you'd got from your father. He bought two companies. He's going to leave them to you, and if you don't take them he's leaving them to me and Toby." One of them was a medical-supply company. Gilbert had thought it would please Alexander. They had waited to tell Alexander until he was used to

Gilbert. But that had never happened. "I didn't mean to tell you until it would make you happy—" She tugged at the chain and brought out the awful diamond pendant. "I don't care if I don't make you happy. He didn't buy me this; you did. Uncle Gilbert says it's about a month's profit from one of the companies. He told me it would help us escape—It was a sort of joke. He doesn't need to wait until he's dead to give them to you. You can have them now. You can have Jouvet; it won't matter if you show a profit. We'll be as secure as money can make us, which will be pretty secure even if there's war. And Alexander, you can spit in General Pétiot's eye and tell the truth. And you should."

"You want them?" he said. "You take them, and Gilbert, and explain to Toby why I don't want them. Thank you, Perdita, for making it so clear to me that Gilbert can buy and sell me. I do appreciate that."

"Alexander—!"

But he got up and went.

She lay back on the dry grass, clutching at her hair in frustration. Some people, she thought, some people are proud of their families. We are his family. We are your family, she said to the air where Alexander had been. Gilbert was haunted by that money, Alexander, he didn't feel right keeping it; William's money was one thing, but this was yours from your father.—This was about claiming each other, belonging to each other, taking a part in each other; it wasn't about money, and it wasn't about Alexander's pride.

All right, she thought, if he doesn't take it I will. And he'll be about to lose Jouvet and come crawling to me and—

And he won't, she thought. And he's doing all the wrong things. He can't let Sabine get away with murder. He couldn't possibly do that.

Reisden found Sabine at the entertainment. The sun was an edge of gold on the horizon. She was setting up her table to tell fortunes. One of the cavalrymen was talking to her, flirting, but Sabine was looking at the sunset.

Reisden went into the Vex-Fort and turned left into the kitchen. The big main room bustled; the harried cook-maids were washing piles of dishes. The caterers' staff were packing boxes with sausages, cheese, and *ficelles* to feed the extras for the guillotine scene. He could have asked the castle cook-staff whether Sabine had cooked a rabbit on the first Friday in May. But who would have remembered?

He could have asked them. Tomorrow, he thought. They were busy.

He went outside again. Now Sabine was alone. He went over to her and sat on the low wall beside her.

"Do you know how to cook rabbits?" he asked her.

"I have a good recipe."

He didn't want to ask this. "Have you ever sent food to anyone but André?"

She was idly dealing the cards as they spoke. A girl fell on the table, then a smoky black mausoleum. Sabine pushed the cards together and laid them down. She looked up at him, her chin high. Their eyes met.

"Sabine?" he said.

The entertainers were setting up their lights for the last show. She watched them. "I didn't do anything wrong!" she said. "I didn't."

"What did you do?" He didn't want to hear what she had done—he was sick at what he was going to hear—but he had to hear.

"People don't understand," she said. "They never do."

"I will." He took her hand. He was unconvincing. He knew and she knew that he was looking after André, not her.

"I'll tell you tomorrow," she said. "After the end of the film." She smiled sadly.

"If you tell me now, you'll be safe," he said.

But she said, "What kind of safe is that? I won't be safe. Nobody really understands."

"Sabine," he said.

She was watching the light fade out of the sky. She held his hand tightly; her hand was warm. "Everything's the last thing," she said, her lower lip trembling. "This is the last sunset. The raspberries for dessert tonight, I've eaten raspberries for the last time. And I'm frightened." She bowed her head. The wooden table with her cards was dusty with pollen from the hay; beads of her tears splashed the table and the cards. He gave her his handkerchief. She wiped her eyes and then wiped the cards; she put his handkerchief on her lap and picked the cards up and squared them. She smiled up at him. "You were always nice to me," she said.

The actors were arriving; the three-piece orchestra was warming up. "I'm going to tell my last fortune now," Sabine said, "and it's going to be for you."

"No," he said.

But she was dealing the cards. "There you are," she said after a moment. "The Serpent, the Garden, the Road . . . And here's the Lady, and the Tomb, and the Cavalier. Someone's going to die, someone close to you. It could be change but it's death."

Her finger moved over the cards: the Cross, the Scythe, the Waning Moon, cards of pain and sadness; then she swept them all up together, wrapped them in his handkerchief, and offered them to him.

"You'll miss me," Sabine said. Then she jumped up and went to find her place among the actors, moving from one to another, talking, laughing, kissing on both cheeks, embracing; and if she seemed a little sad and brittle, it was no more than most of them were on the night before the last scene.

Chapter 76

Saturday, July 22, 1911.

In the marketplace at Arras, Edythe and Arthur Bernhard Abraham, from New York, are standing in front of a market stall looking at chalk swans. The sun's heat bounces from the cobblestones and up under Edythe's hat. In spite of the heat, Edythe and Arthur Bernhard are holding hands.

Today is their fiftieth anniversary. Edythe is fifty years away from the dreamy Jewish girl who loved Tennyson; the waist-length hair she was so proud of is short and white, and life has turned her sensible, a woman whose hat folds for packing. Arthur Bernhard never built moated castles for her, but he has done well enough. They love each other; they are romantics in a beautiful summer, in Arras, a magical city with its ancient arcades and great squares. So Edythe is buying souvenirs, little Arras chalk swans with gracefully heart-curved necks: two swans for her daughters, one for her best friend and across-the-hall neighbor, and two, perhaps three, to glide on a circular mirror somewhere in her friendly and cluttered apartment.

On both of their lapels are little Stars-and-Stripes pins.

It has not been a peaceful summer. When Edythe and Arthur were in Paris, they saw a German waiter beaten up; they walked past smashed sausage shops and broken kegs of beer. For weeks the papers have been full of the deteriorating situation between the French and the Germans in Morocco.

The Abrahams are Americans, neutrals, protected, but still they are Jewish, with almost-German last names. Arthur Bernhard has taken to signing his name Arthur B.

The humid, barely stirring air has a feel that Edythe remembers from the New York draft riots, as if someone is about to shoot. The crowds on the plaza are waiting for something. There are crowds of strange men on the plaza, short, muscular, grimy men, pale as though they never feel the sun. There are policemen. There are soldiers.

In the middle of the square, the technicians are putting together the huge guillotine that will dominate the scene. It's blood red, enormously tall. From it hang blue-white-and-red bunting and fluttering tricolor flags. Steps lead up the side. On top of the platform—the Abrahams must step back and crane their necks—two workmen are hammering together two narrow, high beams connected by a crosspiece.

They unbox the enormous slanted blade. The bunting on the guillotine seems dreadful to Edythe, as if someone should put flags on an electric chair.

But it's only a movie. Making his way through the crowd by the platform, a man is shouldering a mahogany-and-brass box on a tripod.

Edythe and Arthur Bernhard know the movies. The roofs of New York are covered with glassed-in movie studios, and just across the river, in the New Jersey streets and fields, cowboys fight Indians and policemen chase burglars, and men with tripods film it all. Anybody can be in the movies, especially if they know the rabbi's nephew who makes them. Arthur, with his crooked smile, was the preacher who married Our Hero to His Little Girl in *A Cowboy's Love*. Edythe has played any number of nurses and grandmothers.

"Maybe they need a couple extras," Edythe says. "For our fiftieth, Arthur Bernhard—!"

The cameraman, who's American, points at the casting office, a shop in the arcade. They change clothes in the back of the shop. Tall Arthur Bernhard becomes a gigantic soldier guarding the guillotine, and shorter Edythe, with her white hair and big grin, is in rags at the foot of the scaffold, brandishing a set of knitting needles and cackling, "*I* want to catch the *head*!"

She is perfectly placed to watch the mechanism of the guillotine, which is below the platform.

Edythe talks in bumpy French with another extra, a big plump lady's maid from a local château. Most of the pale men are miners, Edythe learns; they've been drinking all day, and in the crowd are also real soldiers, who are worn out from dying on camera for the past half-week. It hasn't been an easy production, the maid Aline says; everyone's unhappy; there have been deaths.

"Real deaths?" says Edythe, startled.

But no time to find out about that now, the actors are arriving. A stern, strong old man and a bright-haired young girl are drawn into the square on a rough wooden cart. The crowd recognizes the old man and begins to cheer him: "Cy-*ron*! Cy-*ron*!" But Edythe and Arthur Bernhard look at the girl.

Anyone would who knows films. She has a face that captures hearts, huge-eyed in a cloud of yellow hair, beautiful and frightened.

"That's Countess Sabine," the maid Aline says. "Her husband hates her. And that's her husband, the director."

From outside the shot, a blond man with a megaphone is shouting at the extras, lashing them into a frenzy. If the girl is a heroine, this man is a villain. He is tall and thin, pale and terrifying, with long, tangled, yellow hair. He moves like a snake. The megaphone turns his voice into shrieking and hissing, a voice out of a nightmare.

"That man's crazy," Edythe says.

"He hates his wife!" says the maid.

Another actor has been standing on the stairs leading up to the guillotine. Now he descends all the way and begins to talk in a quick undertone to the maid. "Watch André," Edythe hears him say. The actor is dark, handsome, and young; as he smiles briefly at the maid Aline, his face lights up almost to his careworn grey eyes.

"He's going to rescue the girl?" Edythe guesses.

While the crowd scenes are being taken, and afterward, while the platform for the camera is being pulled into the square, men come to make sure the machinery is working.

Later the police will ask Edythe who checked it. She remembers Charles De Vere, who built the machine; he is with the old actor, Maurice Cyron, and the lovely girl, Sabine. Edythe gets to talk to Cyron, says that she has acted in films, and charms the girl by asking for her autograph as well as Cyron's. "You'll be famous in the films! Believe me, I've seen stars."

The girl smiles heartbreakingly. "Do you think so?"

More people come; people come back. At this point Edythe loses track of who comes before whom. A French general, who talks to the soldiers. The actor Cyron again. The girl again. She just looks at it.

Next comes the man she thinks of as the Executioner, the man in the black cloak, with the handsome actor, Baron von Reisden. They both watch while a woman checks the mechanism from above. It drops with a thud; it works.

Because there is no wind, the filmmakers are using an effect Edythe has never seen before, an enormous fan like a ceiling fan, but mounted vertically on a cart. It is taller than a man, perhaps nine or ten feet high; Aline says it is a ventilation fan from one of the local mines. Men in the crowd take turns cranking its engine to start it, and then the big vanes moan and reluctantly begin to turn, moving faster and faster, whipping and threshing the air under the scaffold and bringing some relief to the sweaty extras in the square.

"Be careful of those blades. Stay away."

All the extras are waiting. And waiting, and waiting. The director wants a particular light effect and hasn't seen it yet. These aren't trained extras, used to the delays of the movie business. They get restless and begin to shout. The director takes his megaphone and shouts back. Edythe doesn't understand what he says but it doesn't help. The square is almost in shadow; Edythe worries that it is too late to film. But the technicians bring out more scaffolding and lamps; they pay out wire from a roll. People are jostled aside and there's more muttering, then a cry of dismay as the lights go on and add to the grilling heat.

Now the whole square is unbearable. The extras are crowded elbow to elbow, broiling, thirsty, faint with the heat. The shadows of the Dutch-roofed shops are eating the buildings on the other side; the shadows look like menacing giants. The evening wind stirs the flag on top of the guillotine, but it's only a tease, making the crowd more restless. The technicians maneuver the big fan's cart to point it at the guillotine. The flags become alive, the bunting stirs.

The girl climbs the stairs to the scaffold as the cameraman films her. Edythe steps back as the cameraman shoulders his tripod and makes his way through the crowds toward the platform from which he is going to film the guillotining scene.

Edythe and Arthur move back to get a better view. They are standing between the guillotine platform and the small camera platform, almost underneath the camera platform. By craning they can see all the actors on the scaffold. The Executioner is now standing on the scaffold to the right of the guillotine, a frightening character, wearing an iron brace around his neck and dressed in the black cloak and hood. The enormous fan is still going and now the evening breeze is rising by itself. It ripples the Executioner's cloak. The girl stands by the guillotine.

The shrieking director is on the platform with the cameraman. They can't see him but they can hear him instructing the actors. Then "Three, two, one— *On tourne!* Iris out!" The camera cranks with a sound like cards being shuffled, which Edythe can hear through all the other noises. The girl looks around her with an air Edythe always will remember, dignified and astonished and somehow final. For a moment she takes the old man's hand and says something to him, and then she fits her neck into the gaudy lunette of the guillotine and her thin wrists into smaller holes in the board that holds her head.

The executioner moves across the front of the guillotine, blocking Edythe's view for a moment. But she can see the girl. Her wrists are twisting inside the holes in the board. As the executioner reaches the lever, his cloak blows aside and Edythe can see the girl's face.

The blade hangs trembling against the sky.

Chapter 77

André had filmed the beginning of the scene, but now, he insisted, they were too early, the shadows weren't right yet. The square must be in darkness; the buildings must show the shadows of giant men; the girl and man, and the blade of the guillotine, must be in light.

The heat was appalling and André added to it. The techs brought out lights and André climbed up to the camera platform while Krauss' assistant adjusted them. From the edge of the square, Cyron's Rolls gargled and sputtered. Krauss had taken off his eternal cap; under the lights, his hair was soaked with sweat.

"Don't step on the wires," the techs yelled at the crowd.

Reisden and Jules were on the scaffold, in costume, by the guillotine. Jules abruptly sat down and took off his hood. Under it his face was slack and translucent, like too-warm wax.

"Give us our money!" a group of drunken extras were yelling under the camera platform. "Look, it's the end of the day."

"There's a woman fainted here!" someone else yelled.

"It's inhuman!"

But André was waiting for the shadows—one shot, no cuts. When the shadows were right, they would be right for only two or three minutes. No one could move, he yelled. Anyone who left the square wouldn't get his wages. The lights flickered for a moment. "Stay away from the wire, idiots!"

Ruthie came up the stairs with cold lemonade in a pitcher. She took one look at Jules and started pouring out some for him, but he stopped her, pointing down at the extras. Lead actors don't get cold drinks when the extras can't.

"Jules," Reisden said, "have you checked the guillotine machinery? We'd better." He wanted Jules out of the heat.

They went down the stairs and looked at the levers while Ruthie worked the machinery from above. The ventilation fan from Sabine's mines gave André his breeze but didn't help; under the lights at the base of the scaffold, one could barely breathe. They went back up on the scaffold instead, in the sun. Reisden persuaded Jules to take off his executioner's long black cloak and hood. Ruthie gave Jules her fan to fan himself. He did so for a moment, then stopped and closed it quickly, handing it back to her. It was a pink fan with flowers and one of the extras had sniggered.

The shadows were beginning to touch the platform. Eli Krauss used his second camera to film Sabine climbing the stairs, from darkness to light. He very nearly filmed the cloak and hood as well; Ruthie whisked it away at the last minute.

The late sun was red, rose, yellow, like a fire; the lights hit the guillotine like steel explosions. The shadows had begun to pool around the arcades at the far side of the square. André began to warm up the crowd. They were hot, restless, exhausted, hungry for the ten francs and food and free beer they had been promised, and André taunted them. "Film companies have no money! What makes you think I'll give you wages?" The extras snarled in fury. The yellow raking light from the west turned their mouths and eyes into black holes. Perfect. Next to André, Eli Krauss was cranking his camera.

Jules gestured to Ruthie to get his costume. There was a moment of panic; someone had moved it, it couldn't be found. Jules went even more pale. "No, here it is—" Ruthie handed it up; it had simply fallen. Jules shrugged his way painfully into the cloak and hood. Under the cloth, his breath puffed in and out; he was panting.

André, being André, was playing to the crowds. "Look at my wife! She's a poisoner!" The miners shouted, shook their fists, threw offal from the market at André; André was misbehaving shockingly and Sabine was one of theirs. Eli Krauss' backup camera was catching it all.

"Now!" André turned his megaphone and shouted at them on the scaffold. "Places!" Eli moved over to his principal camera, already set up. "Three, two, one, *on tourne!*"

Sabine took Cyron's hand just before she knelt to put her head in the lunette. Reisden was behind the guillotine, watching Cyron as Méduc should: watching Mabet, the butcher of Arras. Mabet's eyes turned from one betrayal to another, his wife being executed, his son on the scaffold watching. He turned helplessly toward the crowd, toward the camera and

André, looking for some help. He has no children. No one will help him or pity him, no one will forgive him for having done his best—

Jules, the Executioner, moved from one side of the guillotine to the other. He jerked the rope, and the blade fell.

The crowd cried out.

One woman screamed first, then there were ragged cries, and then a scream, a universal scream from a thousand hoarse thirsty panicked throats, a shriek of horror and fear. The crowd surged toward the scaffold. They think we've really killed her, Reisden thought, knowing better because he had checked the guillotine himself—

He saw curls of blonde hair, cut, tumbling and drifting across the platform floor.

Sabine looked up at the guillotine. The blade hung against the sky like a sword. It was the moment of her death and she could give her powers. She gathered them all, her life, her riches, telling fortunes, seeing death. None of them would go now to her son. There will be no more sorcerers in the North, she thought oddly, because there would always be sorcerers as there would always be shepherds and blacksmiths and priests in the little villages around Arras. But there would be no more Sabine. I give my powers to— And she took his hand and grasped it hard and looked into Papa Cyron's eyes.

Peur té seuc', she said. Because you were sweet to me.

She laid her chin and neck down on the smooth wood. It will not be long, she thought, trying to console herself. The lights darkened but it was only Jules' cloak passing in front of her. She tugged back, hoping, trying to get free, but her chin was caught.

And then it was as if all the powers she would have had in her life came upon her at once, and the lunette fell away and she was free. She had escaped! Escaped! Astonished, delighted, full of life, she opened her mouth to laugh.

* * *

André knows audiences, and it's never happened to him before but he knows the difference between an audience and a riot. He stops the cameraman's hand and tears the film across, snaps the screws that hold the magazine, gestures to Krauss to put the magazine of exposed film under his coat, safe, safe, you understand? Now get away from here. Krauss looks down at the crowd, terrified. André leads him over to the ladder and almost pushes him down. The crowd isn't paying attention to Krauss, it's pushing toward the steps of the scaffold. A man in the lead points at Jules. André picks up his microphone.

"She's not dead!" he yells through it. "It's a trick!"

For a moment it works. They stop, they look at him. But the man in the lead shouts something, points at the guillotine.

And below, in the crowd, a woman starts to scream.

The crowd draws back and leaves an empty space and a woman is in the center of it, all alone, a white-haired old woman under the spotlights near the camera platform. And she is holding something, something pale with blonde hair that drips and drips in the light. What an illusion, André thinks, what a marvelous illusion, the lips move and the eyes blink.

And he begins to laugh. He drops the megaphone and puts his hands over his mouth and begins to giggle like a child, because it is such a marvelous illusion. Sabine's head, Sabine's severed head, the woman is holding it, carefully, tenderly in her two hands like a salad bowl she is bringing in to dinner, and screaming, screaming, it is perfect, everything has gone right at last, so where is Krauss to film it? And his laugh is like screaming because he is so frightened, because he doesn't know who has created this effect.

The face of the mob turns toward him.

Policemen's whistles shrilled, but it was Pétiot's soldiers, the men detailed to watch André, who moved in on the men on the scaffold. The soldiers took Jules away first, jostling him through the crowd. "He's under arrest! Make way there, we're taking him in!" The police moved toward them, batons at the ready.

But everyone was trapped in the square. No street leading to the Grand'Place is wider than a seventeenth-century carriage, and the streets were shoulder-to-shoulder crowded with people, some pressing forward to see, some recoiling.

Cyron stepped to the front of the platform. He shouted but even Reisden, next to him, could hear nothing; the mob was shrieking, crying, roaring. From above, the movement of the crowd was braided and confused like eddies in turbulent water, heads bobbing, turning toward them on the platform, toward Jules, above all toward André.

Pétiot's men arrowed in a wedge toward the camera platform. André was up there all alone, laughing with his head thrown back, laughing or shrieking or sobbing, impossible to tell, and the crowd could not bear it; the crowd was pushing at the platform, trying to pull it over. Two men climbed on others' shoulders, but the soldiers pulled them down and they melted into the crowd. André swayed at the top of the camera platform; an officer held up a hand, trying to help him down.

"Get out of here," Pétiot shouted. "We don't want you in this." He tugged at Cyron's elbow.

"We can't leave André," Reisden said.

"Go, go, we'll take care of him!" Pétiot shoved Reisden into the circle of soldiers around Cyron.

As they elbowed their way down the scaffold steps, the lights flickered and died. The soldiers moved them through a muttering obscure shadow. The crowd stank of gin, sweat, and fear, a sharp rank animal odor like goat or fox. The soldiers shoved and the crowd shoved back, a terrified herd ready to stampede. Shudders in the crowd pushed them back and forth like undertow through thick liquid.

The soldiers who had arrested Jules were in front of those guarding Cyron and Reisden. They had got as far as the wide rue de la Taillerie, but the street was blocked with people, and as the soldiers faced them, an ominous murmur rose to shouts. The group turned toward the rue du Noble and the rue des Trois Marteaux, but they were blocked, too.

Between them was Mademoiselle Françoise's shop. "Inside, 'sieurs." The door was open. For a few seconds it was completely dark in the shop, then by the dim reddish light they could see blurred rectangles of film stills against the dark of the button drawers. Through the window they could see the backs of the soldiers in a double rank between them and the crowd.

Garbage splattered the window glass. The rank of soldiers writhed and André was pushed inside the door, sprawling on the floor. André lay next to the counter, curled up into a ball with his arms over his head. His shoulders shook. His face was splashed with garbage.

Stones hit the windows and the door. One crashed through the window glass and hit André on the arm. Jules was standing between two soldiers; he tried to tug himself away, to stand over André. Reisden took André under the armpits and dragged him backward, into the inner room where Mademoiselle Françoise's shawl was still hanging. The soldiers shoved Jules in with them, and the techs crowded in, too, white-eyed. "Get them downstairs," Pétiot said. "Into the cellars."

The cellar of Mademoiselle Françoise's shop was bare; there was only a costume-rack built of pipes and a curtain hung along one wall. This was the stars' changing room. The kerosene lamp smoked against the ceiling. There was a folding chaise longue here and, dropped carelessly over it, a Japanese kimono embroidered with insects. *Sabine,* Reisden thought. André, half-collapsed on the floor, opened his eyes and stared at the colors. Cyron was nowhere to be seen. From above they heard breaking glass and shouts.

Jules was leaning against the wall. The hood was still over his head. Reisden pulled it off. The fabric was wet and came hard. For a moment Reisden thought that Jules had been hurt, and then he saw the dark sprays and stains across Jules' shirt-front, his trousers, the cloak, and knew where all the blood had come from. Jules stared down at the floor, his shoulders bowed over, pulled in, his face pale.

"They aren't after us," one of the techs said tightly. "Just them. I say send 'em back up."

Jules raised his right hand. *Yes,* and touched his chest: *Me.* Only me. "No," said Reisden.

"We're trapped, monsieur."

"We'll go out through the boves." Reisden found his own jacket on the rack and felt in the pocket the weight of the compass. "To the Hôtel de Ville. I know how to get there—" A good solid building; not even mobs would break into it. He was cold; he put the jacket on over his costume and jammed his hands in his pockets. "You"—he nodded at one of the techs—"take the lantern; you"—the other—"bring André."

"I'm not going in them boves."

Mademoiselle Françoise's entrance to the boves was behind the red faded curtain. Reisden twitched it open.

And then they heard, from very far away, the sound of voices.

For a moment it was impossible to tell from where the sound was coming. They might have been from above, the boves echoed so; but it was the mob, in the boves, coming through the tunnels.

"They're breaking into the boves! They're going to catch us here!"

One of the techs broke and ran upstairs.

"André." André looked at him woozily; he was like a drunken man. "Do you really know the boves?"

"She's dead," André muttered.

"*Pay attention.* Can you take us to the northeast corner of the Grand'Place and toward the Arras road?"

André's head bobbled, more or less a nod.

"Then do it now." The other tech was wide-eyed, standing back against the wall. He broke and ran too. Reisden took the lantern and pushed André.

The cold of the boves hit them immediately. André straightened up and walked first, too slowly, holding himself up by leaning against the wall; he was half in shock. Reisden came second with the lantern, Jules behind. The darkness pressed in on the circle of light.

There was no pattern to the tunnels. Within a hundred feet, three branched off. Reisden kept his eyes on the needle, dancing on its pin. André was going northeast.

"I did it," André said in a half-asleep voice, stopping. He had brought along Sabine's dressing-kimono and was clutching it around him as if for warmth. The insects' wings fluttered, the garish colors catching the light.

"Don't talk now." Over the scuffle of their shoes he could hear a ragged muttering in the tunnels behind them.

"I'm not going to the asylum. I'm going to be guillotined.— This tunnel," André said.

The tunnel was wide and worn, and on the walls were initials in candle smoke, dates a hundred years past, and iron rings for rushlinks. The tunnel opened up into a room, and Reisden knew where he was. The floor was slippery with wax. Under the chalk idol were new offerings and candle-ends, held upright by melted wax. Reisden snapped the candles loose and dropped them into his pockets.

From the dark in back of them they heard, quite close, the echo of voices. André looked backward, behind them, suddenly realizing what was following them. Wordlessly he pulled Reisden and Jules off into a side tunnel, into the dark. He led them into a narrow, descending cul-de-sac. They all crouched under a rocky shelf, hardly big enough to hide the three of them. Jules pulled his black executioner's cloak over André's blond hair; the smell of blood gagged them. Reisden turned the lantern down to a red wick-line of light, and then, reluctantly, blew it out.

"Get the bastard—" From their hiding place they saw the shadows of torches, very faint and far away, like a hallucination in the eyes. "—gone this way?" "—can't be far—" "Wish I'd brought my lamp." "And a pickax for the bastard's skull!" Miners. A hand thrust a lantern almost over their heads; the light hammered around them. Reisden held his breath.

"Ssh!"

But nothing crashed at them out of the darkness, no one turned on a torch and shot at them as if they were trapped rabbits. The light withdrew, and finally the voices fell away into mutters and deepening faraway echoes.

"Reisden?" André whispered finally. "It's all right."

He got matches out of his jacket pocket, spilled them on the ground, and for one terrible moment thought he couldn't find any of them again. He felt along the ground as painstakingly as he had ever done with any experiment, felt a match, picked it up in clumsy careful fingers, scraped the matchhead along the box, and lit the lantern.

He simply stared at the light for a minute, grateful for every bit of it, the line of light crawling along the wick and the yellow and blue flame rounding above it, comfortable and sane. But he could feel the darkness, the weight of rock above them.

He counted the matches as he picked them up. Twenty-two, more than half a box. He counted the candle-ends, nine, three of them as long as a thumb, the rest shorter. The lantern was half full of kerosene. The end of the Arras road should be close; they had a compass; they had light. They had André, who knew the boves.

"Northeast," Reisden said.

Chapter 78

Perdita and Toby had not gone to be a part of the mob scene; small babies do not mix with mobs. She had been packing. By eight in the evening, she and Toby were ready to go to Arras. She brought Toby's things downstairs, put them in his perambulator, parked it and Toby and herself by the Jerusalem Gate, and waited.

The coach didn't arrive. No one came back from the shoot. It grew full dark to her eyes, and then dark to anyone's. The château should have been lit up but no one was there. She wondered if she had been forgot. She could only imagine the scene there might have been when André was taken away to the asylum.

No one arrived until near midnight, when the police came.

They took her to Arras in a car. She brought Toby, and realized only halfway there, when he needed to be changed, that she had left everything behind, his diapers, his food, everything. In the Grand'Place the crowd had dispersed, but she could still smell a stink like skunks and garbage. "They chased Count André and Jules into the boves," she repeated after the policemen, to make sure she understood it rightly. "And my husband went with them."

Alexander had taken a compass; she found out that much by talking to the technicians. It was so much like him; he would have had all the litter in his pockets, his watch with the stopwatch built in, a penknife with extra tools, string, a compass, matches, someone's business card. But he wouldn't have remembered food or water; he would have worked all day without stopping for more than coffee.

She listened quite calmly to the searchers talking about the men's chances.

They had had lights, that much she knew. She heard the story of Alexander taking a lantern. She didn't have to think of him in the dark.

He is keeping Jules and André in the boves until the danger is over, she thought.

"My brother was dehydrated," Ruthie said tearfully.

Extras whispered to one another. André had threatened his wife and laughed when she died.

"Alexander always lands on his feet," Perdita said. "He knows what he's doing. He has a compass."

Monsieur Cyron led a party into the boves; he knew them as well as anyone. Monsieur Cyron would find them. But the party came back at sunrise, tired, hungry, and unsuccessful.

All Sunday they waited for the men to come out of the boves. By the late afternoon Toby had run through all the diapers and clothes Perdita could borrow. She took him back to Montfort.

At dusk Sabine's body was brought home to lie overnight in the Great Hall. Aline went down and reported that people from the country and the mines were standing in line to see her. Some of them were crying; most were curious. Monsieur Cyron had had her dressed in her beautiful pink costume from the film, Aline said, but she had a thick scarf across her neck and her jaw looked wrong, small somehow. Perdita shuddered. And there was a pail of water by her feet, very strange, an ordinary pail, as if the washerwoman had left it.

In the early morning, when Toby was asleep, Perdita went down to the Great Hall to sit by Sabine and pray for her. No one else was there but Monsieur Cyron, who was weeping in a corner. She said "I'm so sorry" and he talked about Sabine, little things Sabine had done and said to him. She said, "I'm sorry about your son," but he said nothing about André. She sat with her hands folded, in the silence, with Monsieur Cyron's shuddering breathing and the drip of ice, and tried to think about Sabine. But all that came into her head was the shush and click of cards, Sabine laughing and flirting with the soldiers and promising them war in Alsace, and a cooked rabbit. She had not known Sabine at all.

She thought of Sabine's baby. The baby had been a subject for a fight, an accessory to Sabine's triumph over André, but it had never been the center of anyone's universe the way Toby was, the way Sabine herself had been to Monsieur Cyron. It had never been really loved, but it had died. She wept for the baby. She went upstairs and held her own little boy and wept for the baby, and that helped for the moment to keep her thoughts away from the men in the boves.

Sabine's funeral was the next morning, from the chapel at the château. Perdita went for as long as she could, but she couldn't stand being at a funeral. She went back into the house, into the kitchen, and found Ruthie filling bottles at the sink.

"I'm taking bottles of water to Arras," Ruthie said. "To every man who goes into the boves to search, I'll ask them to leave bottles of water in the boves . . . so that our men will find them. It's water they need above everything."

"Yes," Perdita said. It was absurd to take a cartful of water bottles all the way from Montfort to Arras, but now the men had been in the boves a day and a half and would be desperately thirsty. She rolled up her sleeves and filled bottles with Montfort well water and corked them. They ran out of empty bottles and she pried out corks from unimportant bottles of wine and poured the wine down the sink. And only then when she was contemplating what a waste it was that the grapes should have grown and been pressed and barreled and fermented, and the wine bottled and left to grow ripe in Monsieur Cyron's cellars for years upon years, and then poured away, did she think that Alexander might have been poured out and wasted too.

A man can die of thirst in only three days.

When she and Ruthie went to Arras she took all the money she had and went to the cheese shop. She bought all their stinky cheese, the Coeur d'Arras, and cut it in pieces and wrapped each piece in cheesecloth. "Put one with each bottle," she told the men who were searching. And with the water and cheese she left candles, so that Alexander would have light.

"Hurry."

After the funeral, she and Ruthie moved out of Montfort and shared rooms in Arras. Every day they went to the film office on the Grand'Place and waited. The film office was being closed. They helped to pack up the photographs and the costumes. It gave them something to do. Ruthie was given the clothes Jules had left. No one picked up André's, so Ruthie folded them up and took them too. "For when he comes back," she said in a firm voice. Perdita was given Alexander's clothing, his shirt and trousers. His penknife was in his trousers pocket. He had always kept it with him. She folded up his clothes; they smelled of him. His penknife she put in the pocket of her skirt. At night she put it on the nightstand and in the morning she put it in the pocket of her skirt.

Three days. They passed that mark on Tuesday. "There must be water underground," Perdita said.

For a day she drank as little as possible, trying to convince herself that he could live without water too.

Wednesday. Thursday. Friday. The searchers still persisted. On Saturday, a week after the men had disappeared, Omer Heurtemance, the First Witch, brought some of his friends and made a special effort. The searchers were very kind to her and Ruthie. They were apologetic. But on Sunday there were fewer searchers, and they were quiet, grim, not happy with going down into the boves. They had long ago searched the tunnels they knew.

Uncle Gilbert and Mr. Daugherty both had wanted to come out from Paris. But Perdita put them off. She didn't want them yet. She did not want to feel as if she must be taken care of.

On Monday, Mademoiselle Huguette officially took over the shop that had been Mademoiselle Françoise's and had the painters and the glaziers in. Ruthie and Perdita sat at a table in the Grand'Place, making their coffee last all morning.

On Tuesday, for the first time, no one showed up to search.

What day do you choose to stop hoping? What hour? Men had been lost in the boves for a week and survived. But they had had water with them. Ruthie and Perdita waited in a parenthesis of silence, but on the eleventh day it ended. Alexander's secretary, Madame Herschner, wrote from Paris, asking whether she should begin to refer business questions to Madame Reisden. Urgent questions needed resolving.

"I'll come back," she told Ruthie. She wanted nothing more than to sit at the café within sight of the place where he had disappeared.

She could not bear the last moment at the station. The train jerked and started and it felt as though she were leaving Alexander, as if her staying there could bring him. Hope is a terrible form of mourning. She closed her eyes and the train picked up speed and she went on, toward Paris, into a world without him.

He had always done all the business of Jouvet. He had signed the checks; there was no one with the power to do it now. Madame Herschner explained to Perdita that there was very little left in the bank. In September Alexander would have signed General Pétiot's very good new contract. But he hadn't lived to do it.

That was the first time she thought it, that first day in Paris. She went upstairs to the apartment, where Aline was playing with Toby, and she thought: He did not live to do it. It did not feel like death yet, only an absence, a perpetual and unexplained absence like his silence earlier this summer. She hung up his trousers and shirt in his part of the armoire—she would not let Aline hang them up, nor have them laundered—and when the shirt was on the hanger she pulled the fabric to her and breathed the smell, already growing fainter, the smell of the twenty-second of July, in which he was still alive. What shall I do, she thought. She wondered if she should wear black. Not yet. She got from her own closet another of the dark skirts and plain white blouses she had worn since that day. But it felt Pollyannaish now, as though she were refusing to admit what everyone knew.

She washed her face and straightened her hair and went downstairs. She sat in the office that had been Alexander's and one by one she called the people of Jouvet in to talk to her. Madame Herschner, Alexander's secretary. Each of the doctors. The technicians, from the head man on down. We do not know for certain what has happened, she said to each of them. But we must fend for ourselves in the meantime. Tell me what you are doing, how your part of Jouvet works, what you think we must do.

Then she sat in his office alone except for memories of him and the terrible ache of his absence. She had thought she wanted to leave him. How sure she'd been of that.

It would have been easier (she faced this truth) if the searchers had found the bodies. Now, in law, Alexander had just disappeared. He had no insurance, there would have been no money from that, but he had owned the company; no one could act for it except him.

Exactly like what happened with Richard Knight, love. She could hear him say it, exasperated. *How could I have done that? How could I have been so stupid?* She agreed with him. After Richard had disappeared, no one had known whether he was alive or dead. Uncle Gilbert had insisted he was alive. It had been chaotic for years.

Uncertainty is another way to hope.

She finally let herself understand how she must behave. She couldn't do it alone.

"Now, Uncle Gilbert, I must see you."

She dressed in black for their meeting; for the first time, all in black. Alexander had always dressed in black, and she had a wordless sense of being close to him. They met in Alexander's office. She put Uncle Gilbert in one of the leather chairs and she sat in the other. Elphinstone lay on the floor.

"I've talked with Alexander's lawyer," she said. "He left Jouvet to me. The will isn't in force yet, and it will be a long time before we can officially apply to have him declared," she hesitated and said the word, "dead." It was the first time for that. "But in the meantime there are decisions to be made. We will need a loan."

"Of course," Uncle Gilbert said. "It is not even my money, it is his."

"But I need more." I need you, she thought. She could not put that weight on Uncle Gilbert, as if she were still five years old and had fallen and skinned her knee and asked him to fix it. But she had to. "General Pétiot wrote me and suggested there should be a committee to run Jouvet. If the judge agrees, that's what will happen. But I can't be on it. Not until I'm thirty." She spared a moment's halfhearted indignation for French law toward women. "I've asked for Madame Herschner to represent me, but how could she speak against General Pétiot? I want someone I can talk with, someone who would know what Alexander would have done. Uncle Gilbert, I want you."

She felt his astonishment, his hesitation.

"I'm asking everything of you," she said. "It would mean living much of the time in Paris. I don't know how I can ask it. But I need you.—Uncle Gilbert, it's not only that you can speak for him. You're American. I'm still Austrian. That's another thing that I can't change because we can't prove he's dead. I'm going to be Austrian for another seven years. Jouvet will be owned by an Austrian, when the war comes." She held up her hands, warding off his concern for her. "I don't only want you to stay. I want you to stay when there's a war. America's neutral so far. Both sides want the Americans on their side. So they're treating the Americans very well. Be our American. Be wild and horrible and wave dollar bills in the air and go to the embassy and say you've loaned money to Jouvet and you mean Jouvet to be treated right, like an American company." There was not a word from him, not a sound. They loved each other dearly, but she was asking him to change his whole life, himself. "It's only," she said, "I can't do it on my own; no one can do this but you."

"Yes," Uncle Gilbert said. Just *yes*.

Then she could cry. She put her elbows on her knees and her face in her hands and she cried, horrible retching tears that she tried to keep silent because outside the room people from Jouvet were probably listening. The tears ran down her face and out of her nose, ran through her fingers. Uncle Gilbert gave her his handkerchief, and it was like Alexander who had always had a clean handkerchief ready for anyone. He knelt beside her and put his arm around her and she cried on his shoulder. She cried until her nose hurt and her throat hurt and her stomach.

"When Richard disappeared," Uncle Gilbert said, "I missed him day by day. Alexander—Richard— When the children went to the first day of their schools, I missed taking him, buying him notebooks and pencils. I missed reading to him at night; every day I missed that. And when—Harry came—I read to him because I knew Richard would have liked it, and it was always somehow, and Harry knew, that I was trying to find again something that had never been."

"I enjoyed your reading to me," she said. "He would have liked it. He read to me."

"Ah, my dear, you were different! You were yourself! I was cruel to Harry."

"Uncle Bucky isn't, and Efnie isn't. We aren't as much Harry's family as they are."

"Oh, yes," he said, and sighed. He was thinking of Harry, and might be thinking, too, of sitting on committees and confronting General Pétiot, who was cheery and kind but, Perdita had seen already, very, very interested in having his way with Jouvet.

"I will not this time— I know what he wanted. He would not want me to say he was alive."

"I want to say something Alexander never did," Perdita said. "He didn't mistrust you more than anyone else. It was him quarreling with himself; he didn't put much trust in anyone. Nothing was safe enough for Toby, no one could take enough care. He always wanted me older, and more capable, and not blind— Well. We're what he's got. What Toby has, and Jouvet, and we *are* going to be up to it."

"Of course, my dear," Uncle Gilbert said softly. "Of course. I do not mean *of course* I shall be up to it, but—I shall be."

"Thank you," she said.

She gave Uncle Gilbert dinner. They fed Toby in the dining room upstairs, with all the windows open because of the heat. She let Uncle Gilbert do most of the spooning-in. In the middle of dinner she put her fork down. "Toby," she said. "Your father wanted to tell you something and he never did. He killed someone once. All his life he was sorry he did it and angry at himself, but he loved you so much, and he was such a good man. He wanted you to know he was that bad. I want you to know he was that good. You can be proud of your father."

You are orphaned, dear Toby, she thought. We'll do our best, Uncle Gilbert and you and I, baby, and we'll be brave. But we won't be what we were.

She sent Uncle Gilbert home to his apartment and played with Toby, gently, because she was afraid of giving way again. She got him ready for bed and read to him; she was learning the French version of Braille by reading children's books. When he fell asleep, she went up to her own room, only her room now, and took off her clothes, got into her nightgown, and sat by the window on the window seat Alexander had had made. She went into the music room, touched the piano; went into his upstairs office, next to the music room, and felt the surface of his desk, still scattered with the notes he had been making, the books he had been reading; went back to the piano. She sat down at the piano and began to play, the long sobbing shivers of the Brahms she was learning, trying to make her grief teach her fingers gentleness. But he was gone, he was gone. You didn't die giving up on André; you tried to save him. Alexander was good to all his friends, she thought, to everyone at Jouvet, to Toby and me, and I did nothing but tell him that he'd failed in one thing, that he still had to deal with Uncle Gilbert, which he knew. And when I'd said that, I just kept on going, thinking where he might fail; I had no faith in him.

She wanted him so much that it frightened her, so much that he must be there. She wanted to be able to tell him she had thought he was so good she had wanted him perfect, and what a burden that had been on Alexander, who wanted himself perfect. Oh, my dear, my dear, you were far from perfect and so was I, and neither of us had any faith in you. Let us talk now. Let me just tell you I love you; then let us go from there.

Let us have the rest of our lives to talk, and listen, and love each other.

She thought she was going mad, she wanted him so. *Alexander,* she whispered, *Alexander,* and she held out her hands to the empty air as if she could draw him to her. She knew all the time she was deceiving herself. But she wanted him so.

Chapter 79

M ost of all, Reisden distrusted tunnels that felt too easy; those were the ones that slanted down. They turned their faces in the darkness, trying to feel a breath of moving air. André led them toward the northeast. They found a wide tunnel, but it petered out; then smaller tunnels, mine workings, curving and branching off in all directions. At first, whenever the tunnel forked, they carefully explored each alternative, but there were too many, and after a while they conserved energy and simply chose the one that went northeast, or the one that felt a little more difficult and would not lead them farther into the earth.

The most promising ended in a crumbling downward slope into black water. From the ceiling, water dripped onto the tunnel floor. "We must be underneath the Scarpe"—the river at the north of town. They drank some water—they were already thirsty—but they had brought nothing to take the water away with them, and the place was too dangerous to stay.

They retraced their steps to what André said was the last branch they had taken. None of the other branches led in the right direction.

So they retraced farther, back down the tunnel André said they had come from. But now that path seemed suspiciously easy. Nothing was marked. André muttered to himself unintelligibly like a parrot. Reisden kept his head down, fighting terror. Beyond the lantern light, the darkness was absolute, like a missing sense.

The circle of light dimmed and grew yellow. The wick began to spark. Reisden lit the first of the candles from the last of the flame. They left the lantern because it was heavy, using it to mark a tunnel.

They had ten candle-ends, then eight, then five. Reisden held the bits of candle. They lit mostly his palm and fingers. "Hold it up," said André, "I can't see." The hot wax burned his palm and he dropped one inch-long stub that they never found again. He drilled a hole in the side of one of the candles with a match and held the candle by the match-end. When the candles were almost burned out, they dripped off the match-end like softened ice cream.

They had four candles and eighteen matches.

To save the light, they did something that turned out to be wrong. The tunnels were narrow; in this area of the boves, wherever they were, the passages went on for some distance without branching or turning. It made sense that they should conserve the rest of the candles and go on in the dark. They found their way by touching the walls. They groped; they stumbled over rubble. They found new tunnels by the difference in the smell of the air, or by a sudden disorientation when they reached out and could find no wall. Then they would strike a match, light the candle, and look at the compass to see which way they should go.

They had three candles and ten matches.

In a damp place, thirst is insidious. Water made a sheen on the walls; André ran his hand across the chalk and sucked at his dirty fingers. Reisden thought about drinking a glass of water: the cold mineral taste of it, filling his mouth with it, swallowing. He wondered if, by breathing deeply, he could get enough moisture from the air.

Above them, it would be a hot July night. Here the air had the chill of an icehouse. They were all shivering and Jules' clothes were wet with blood. Jules, dehydrated, staggered along, supporting himself with a hand against the wall. Reisden tried to help him but the tunnel was too narrow. He only realized how exhausted he was himself. He could barely support Jules' weight.

They found a branch tunnel and lit a match. One branch turned north, the other east. North, Reisden indicated, pointing down the tunnel.

The northern tunnel was blocked by old flinty rubble fifty meters on. The eastern tunnel led to air.

They smelled it from far away, a fresh breeze. Faintly, on the breeze, they could hear crickets. And they could smell hay, freshly cut.

Which meant hayers. People. Rescue.

They lit a candle to show them the direction. The flame tugged eastward. It jumped up suddenly, and Reisden held it high and saw in the ceiling a square black hole, a shaft for hauling up cut blocks of stone. It was as beautiful as the sun. A huge hand-forged pulley lay on the floor by the shaft wall. There might be ropes or a ladder in the shaft itself.

Reisden took out his pocket watch and held it near the candle. Midnight. Two and a half hours since they had gone into the boves. He was abashed at how long his terror had stretched the time.

"In the morning we can see."

They lay against each other to try to get warm. André took first watch. Reisden fell into a half-doze. He was sitting in the kitchen in Paris explaining to Perdita how they had climbed out of the mine shaft. She had made him tea with milk and sugar, just the right temperature. She was wearing Gilbert's necklace. Toby pulled himself up by his father's trouser leg. Reisden was exactly where he wanted to be, among his family.

Am I right, Reisden said to Perdita, *that I am being asked to choose you and Toby and Gilbert—and Elphinstone—all the people I love best? And on the other hand nothing; there's no choice. I choose you,* he said. *I want you.*

There was a plate on the table. Reisden had in his pocket the last of the matches they'd almost used up in the boves. Seven matches in a grubby cardboard box. He carefully piled six into a loose pyramid on the plate. He had treasured his secret like matches in the boves. *Here is everything that keeps us apart,* he said. *And here's what we'll do with it.* He lit the piled-up matches with the last; they flared up all at once. Not even much of a fire. With the ashes he marked her cheek.

And in the euphoria after that, they simply talked. He didn't remember what they said, only the closeness, how beautiful she was. She talked about music, about Gilbert. She was sharing her loves, he thought. With her love. I am her love.

"Reisden," André said.

For a moment he wondered what André was doing in the kitchen. He could still taste the tea—His throat felt sunburned. He groped for the idea he had had. He sat up and felt dizzy, disoriented in the absolute darkness. "My turn. How long—?"

Too long. He felt it in how thirsty he was. He smelled it in the breeze from the air shaft. It smelled warm; smelled like the sun over a field.

"I don't know, your watch has stopped. But I heard bells," André said, "the bells from Sainte-Catherine. It's nine o'clock. We ought to see light."

Reisden looked up, eyes wide, staring, trying to see a square of grey in the black. He could smell the hay. And with it, overpowering it, the damp stone smell of the boves, the chill of the boves.

Reisden could see the top of this shaft as clearly as if he were standing in it. A cave with an opening facing westward toward the prevailing breeze. A natural ventilation shaft. Not used by shepherds, because there was no smell of sheep, no sheep-bones at the bottom of the pit.

No light.

I am my wife's love, he thought. I choose her. She has to know it.

"Shout with me." They shouted raucously. The boves swallowed up their voices. Someone standing at the top of the shaft, in the cave, would have heard them. "Lift me up." He stood on André's shoulders, balancing unsteadily in the air shaft. *I burned the matches,* he thought for a moment, panicked, then struck a match and held the candle-end above his head. He was looking up at a narrow, endless, slick vertical tunnel.

No ladders. No ropes. A very small man, chimney sweep–size, might theoretically have braced his shoulders and feet against the walls and inched his way up the shaft. Reisden was at least a foot too tall to do it.

He tried. He almost wedged himself immovably. He half-fell back to the floor, scraped and battered. The candle went out. André re-lit it, using another match. He sat on the floor catching his breath. Jules, awake now, stared at him. Reisden touched the prickly surface of the old pulley. It was rust-eaten so badly that he could break off the edge of the wheel as easily as dried sand.

"No one will find us here." They had two and a half candles and five matches. "We can't waste the light. Let's go."

They turned back, away from the fresh air that smelled like life and had only been a waste of time.

They kept the candle alight, looking at the compass to guide them back. West, then southwest, then back through tunnels they had already explored. They thought they saw their own footsteps on the damp floor, but the marks could have been shadows or stains in the chalk.

Rocks littered the floor. They stumbled over them. It felt as though they had been doing this forever. Grope forward, stumble; find an opening, look at it, wonder if it was familiar. André sniffed at the openings, trying to smell ventilation again.

They should have moved faster. Jules, head down, staggered forward, leaning against the wall. The tunnels widened a bit, for a while, and so Reisden could help him. Jules gasped, almost dead weight, breath rattling in his dry throat. He was too far gone to apologize for being a burden.

When the tunnels narrowed again, Reisden felt phantom weight against his shoulder. It felt as though he were carrying Toby.

The tunnels grew more tangled, more confusing, branches dividing away from them. A long, promising tunnel opened up into a cave, stretching away beyond the tiny candlelight. Fallen rock hillocked the floor. André took Jules; Reisden led them across, over rubble from the half-fallen ceiling, following the compass needle.

In the candlelight Reisden looked at the compass. The glass kept the compass-needle on its pin. Without light they could not use the compass unless they broke the glass. Break the glass and they would lose the needle.

They had two candles and four matches. How could they use the compass without light? Keep the compass separate from the needle. At every branch, stop and balance the needle on the compass. . . .

They reached a wall, a tunnel. They lit the candle to look at the compass.

"Southwest," Reisden said.

"No. I think I know—I think I went here once. It's that way."

"That's north. Do you know what you're doing?"

André said nothing.

Reisden slid down the wall and sat on the floor. Jules nearly fell over; André eased him down. Reisden held the candle to look at him. In the candlelight, Jules was pale, his eyes unfocused. André's face moved into the candlelight, looking at Jules. André's inaudibly moving lips were cracked and his eyes looked dry.

Reisden blew out the candle. It would take one of their four matches to light it again.

He laid his crossed arms on his knees and his head on his arms and closed his eyes. It was not so dark with his eyes closed, but even then he could feel it, as black as if he were blind, black enough to dissolve in it. He felt as if parts of his body were breaking off, floating.

"Reisden." André's hoarse whisper echoed in the big space. "Light the candle."

"Not yet—"

"Yes."

The match scraped and caught; three left. The inch of candle guttered. At their backs the wall reflected it yellow; in front of them was only utter blackness. André leaned toward Jules. Jules was trying to say something. Jules gave up and took out of his pocket the little notebook and pencil he had used to talk with. He wrote something, fumbling, scrawling. "You aren't to blame," André said. "You couldn't see her." Jules wrote another sentence, then closed his eyes. André peered at the paper. Jules looked diminished, as if thirst were eating him from inside. The bit of candle on the floor sizzled windily and went out.

"He says to leave him," André said in the darkness, "but I won't."

Between them they tried to haul Jules to his feet. He was a sack of dirt, completely unconscious. They staggered a few steps with him, and then his weight brought them both to their knees. They laid Jules on the tunnel floor, in the dark.

André's breath rasped in the darkness. "You go. Take the candles. Bring help. But it's that way."

"It's the other."

Neither said anything for a moment. "Omer Heurtemance," André said. "Showed me the boves. When I was here in the summers. I never get lost." He was silent for a long time. "I don't know if I killed her," he said. "How can I know where the tunnels are?"

"I know the direction." But the compass hadn't helped. They were going to die here, within sound of the bells of an Arras suburb. I want my family, Reisden thought. I don't want to die in the dark.

"Did I kill her?" André asked.

"I don't know, I don't know," he said impatiently. "No. We were watching you."

"I couldn't have framed Jules," André said hesitantly. "I wouldn't fix the machine so he'd kill her, would I, no matter how much I wanted to?"

No. He wouldn't. "We have to go on."

"She was like a story," André said. "One of my stories. She was always telling my fortune, dealing the cards. She said she could make me do things. I wanted it to be like the Necro. I wanted to love her, like everyone else loves someone. Or poison her! Kill her, or get poisoned!—Something I could understand!—She was spooky, Reisden."

Reisden nodded, too dry-mouthed to talk.

For a moment, in the dark, André said nothing. "She gave me a charm. I finished my play, then I ate it. It stung going down. I knew what it was. But it had all come round again, I had been poisoned. My life had—do you understand, Reisden, a shape? It was like a story. It made sense. But it didn't work. I only got sick to my stomach, like being hungry, worse, so I ate some more, and then I threw up on my hands and there was blood. She looked at my face and said, 'You won't *die*.' I wanted to die."

Reisden closed his eyes.

"I wanted to die but it wasn't a story. It wasn't anything, it was just . . . I couldn't *bear* her. . . . It was all *wrong*. I didn't ever want to be poisoned," André said. "I should have known, I could have said she poisoned me, I mean I did, but—I could have said it and not made a play out of it, I could have acted less crazy. I didn't know what to do, I didn't know. Now we're all lost. Jules is dying and you won't see your son anymore and it's the end of the Necro. And it's all my fault." André thought aloud. "I wonder who killed her. What did she do to him? That would be a story."

Trust André to make a story of it even at the end.

Reisden levered himself painfully up against the wall. He opened the matchbox. His fingers had gone half-numb from the cold, or from simple exhaustion. He held the match against the sandpaper on the box, ready to strike it. His hands were shaking and he held the match tight; it seemed too small to feel. We are all getting to the end of our strength, he thought, even as he struck the match again and again against the side of the box. It must be damp. It would light. It had to. He gave himself a minute, and as he did he found himself saying something.

"Don't apologize for lying about it," he said. "One does. If you killed her I expect you'd lie about that too." He had spent all summer knowing what he could say to André to make him feel less alone. "One is ashamed of having such things in the family."

"I could have told you that," André said.

"You did." No, no, he thought, not to André, I don't need to say this to André of all people; but whatever he said, to whom, probably didn't make much difference now. "Murder in the family, no matter who did it, is like a curse. You asked me who Gilbert Knight is." He heard his own voice surprisingly steady and sure. "He's my uncle. My name was Richard Knight once, and when I was eight years old I shot my grandfather."

André said nothing for a moment, then, just as Reisden was going to try striking the match again: "What was it like?"

"André, we're past taking notes for a play."

"I write about this. Tell me."

"What is it like?" He shouldn't give an easy answer. "Everyone in the family feels it was their fault it happened. The people who forgive me, I push away. Something's missing. I lie a lot. I'm not quite real. Someone who was there said, *Don't say anything, Richard. Never tell anyone.* He thought he was protecting me. I said *I won't tell. I'll never tell.* He was wrong. I should have told everyone, repented with sackcloth and ashes. But I don't think it would have helped much, and I couldn't and I can't."

"Do you want to?"

No, he thought. "Do you know what murder's like? Really? It's that I have to be smarter than anyone else, André, and richer, because I have to outwit the world. Perdita asked me who cooked the rabbit that killed Françoise Auclart. I told her it wasn't important. If it had been Sabine, and I'd said so, I'd have been in a world of trouble with Cyron and we would have lost Pétiot's contract." He willed saliva into his dry mouth. "But none of us would have died. I went to see Sabine, and she told me, as good as, that she had done it. I knew the night before she died. I didn't know what to do. I didn't tell anyone until I could think of something clever. I let her do the guillotine scene. She's dead and here we are."

"It's all right," André said.

"No, it's not."

He tried to light the match. It scratched a red line across the matchbox and died. Two left, he thought. "Give it to me," André said. Reisden passed over the matchbox and André struck the match. It flamed; he lit the candle and held it by Jules' face. Jules was breathing so shallowly that his breath barely stirred the candle flame. He handed it up to Reisden. "Go."

They had not settled the question of the southwest tunnel. Reisden made his way along the wall to its entrance and held the candle high. "No, north," André said quickly. "Reisden—"

"Do you know the way?" Reisden asked.

"Somebody killed her. But I know I didn't kill her," André said, "and I think I know that tunnel."

He turned back and looked at André, at the two of them, Jules barely visible on the ground and André sitting beside him looking up into the candle flame like a sane child, for once in his life sure about something beyond the theatre, begging to be believed. You know the boves, he thought, not I. And still you're staying, because he's your friend, but also because your father told you you can't be a man unless you stay to the end of the deathbed. And I'm going because a murderer trusts only himself. "Do you really know the way?" Reisden said. "All right. I'm staying with him. You're going." He held out the candle. The tiny weight felt heavy in his hand. "Take it. Careful. If you're wrong I'll haunt you."

For a dizzying moment he was giving the candle to mad Necrosar. The dark, the dark, you're afraid of the dark. . . . *"Take it,"* Reisden said. "Don't waste the light."

André took it and turned away, shading the candle with his hand, and the hungry dark swooped in. "Wait," said Reisden. He ripped the stock off his shirt; he turned out his pockets. His handkerchief; Sabine's cards, which for a moment he didn't remember her giving him. Jules' notebook, which he took from Jules' lax hand. "They'll burn. They'll give you light."

"Keep something—"

"No."

The light moved away across the cave. It was a glow, then a spark; then gone. Reisden closed his eyes and laid his head on his arm, his arm across his knees, trying to keep warm, listening to Jules' breathing in the dark. "Jules?" Jules did not reply; and after a while he could no longer hear Jules' breathing, and then not even his own. His face was cold and numb, his hands were numb, he could not feel his eyelids or know whether his eyes were open or shut, or whether he had hands or arms or legs, except by the pressure of the dark against them. The darkness pressed in on him, with the weight of thousands of pounds of earth above him. He had been buried alive. He remembered every Necro trick André had ever played, and wished he hadn't, but remembering them was a trick to keep the worst of the dark away. And he ran out of them and there was nothing left but the dark, eating him down to the skeleton.

After an indefinite time, out of the darkness, something touched him.

A cane, the thick metal end of a heavy lead-weighted cane in an enormous hand. Poking into the back of a too-small closet where a child was hiding, jabbing, trying to make the child run like a scared animal. *Richard?* An old man's voice, harsh, demanding. *Richard, come out, or it will be the worse for you.*

William.

He saw what happened next. Not with the same feelings he had had then, as if he could know that. He saw William poking his cane into the closet under the stairs, and Richard finally being driven out, backed up, into the front room. He saw William cleaning his guns, looking up with his mad grey eyes toward his grandson, and the child, only a little less mad, seeing the little pistol, the child-size gun, the .22, knowing what would happen to him because he knew what he would do.

It wasn't happening to Reisden—Alexander von Reisden had a quarter-century's practice at not being Richard Knight—but it was happening to him because he was there. "Richard," he said, "you don't belong here now. Go." He saw the child turn and look at him. How much, how very much, he looked like Toby. He smiled. And then Richard—faded, or was simply not there.

He was making a play, Reisden thought, as André had. He must tell Katzmann this was how one could bear remembering.

You can have me, he told William. Stay with me if you want. Haunt me; I murdered you. You have a right to me. But you're done with that. You don't beat children around me.

William stood, shaking his lead-weighted cane; but he couldn't lift it, he couldn't raise his arm, and after a moment Reisden saw why; his arms were tied. Behind him, shadowy, stood André's slant-eyed angels.

I will have you, Sir! William cried out all the same. *You will obey, Sir! You will do my will!*

Reisden watched him, not taking his eyes off him. William was frightening. What am I doing, he thought, letting Richard go, letting William in my life?

Darling, said Dotty, is he a case?

He turned and looked at her in surprise. What are you doing here? She was dressed in the pastel silk and ropes of pearl that she had worn to face Gehazy.

You know I always come when you need me, she said, making a face.

I wonder what makes this man tick, said Leo, coming up beside her, examining William. I wonder what he means by what he does.

He wanted to see Perdita and Toby; those were the ghosts

he wanted to spend the next hours with. But Gilbert came next. Gilbert and Elphinstone. I promised you, Gilbert said. If you needed me I would come. They sat for a while, Elphinstone's head leaning against Reisden's knee. William, tied to the bedpost, shouted at them. They talked about him as if he were not there.

What did he want? Reisden asked. What does he want?

Us, said Gilbert. All of us. All our attention. Look, he is even jealous of Elphinstone. (*A dog, Sir? Any man may be a hero to a dog.* Elphinstone growled.)

He wanted to be everything to Richard, Reisden said. Everything to him, his God.

Was he?

Almost.

Reisden got up and helped Gilbert up. Dotty and Leo were gone. Gilbert, he said, we're going home. William's not going; he'll be here.—Elphinstone led them away, toward the light; but though Reisden went with his uncle, it seemed to him that he also stayed behind for a moment, putting a pillow between William's head and the bedpost, in case William should hurt himself when he was left alone.

Reisden went home, with Perdita and Toby, where he wanted to be. This time Gilbert was there, too, and of course Elphinstone. They sat round the kitchen table and toasted one another. Reisden had water in a wineglass; he could see the glass, beaded with water on the outside. They touched glasses—

And then he was back in the cave and there was a last ghost in it. André. André had brought light. André was holding a long civilized dining-room white taper, and over his wrist dangled a string bag such as women take to the market. In it clinked two corked wine bottles. Reisden could see the light, jagged on the rocks on the floor, the soft long curve of the candle flame, more candles sticking out of André's pocket.

André was grinning, a strange stunned half-laugh. "I found water," André said, holding up the bottles. "Someone marked a path. I'll show you."

Reisden took the bottle and drank, sip by sip, cold, sharp mineral water with an undertaste of wine. He knew it was a dream but it was a good one. André had given Jules water first; he was breathing more easily. They left him with a candle, one of blessedly many candles. André had marked the route with Sabine's cards. The Ship, the Mountain; the Serpent, the Garden, the Road; cards of betrayal, cards of journeys; the little colored pictures lay along the tunnels like fragments of life.

"Don't mind the smell. It's cheese."

The last tunnel smelled sweetly foul, like the path to the cemetery. The Tomb marked the path. But on the ground, in charcoal, someone had drawn an arrow pointing farther down the tunnel, and by it were a third tall green bottle of water, a tin box of matches, and a small cheesecloth-wrapped lump, the size of a teaball.

Cheese. Coeur d'Arras.

"Perdita," Reisden said. He knew who would mark a location by smell. He sank to his knees. He could not say any more, just: "Perdita." Oh, my dear. Here you are in my dreams at last.

"Reisden, are you all right?" said André.

"We're alive."

Chapter 80

The arrows led them back to the cellar of Mademoiselle
Françoise's shop. Their clothes were gone. The men
were all taller than the average, one with shoulder-length
hair, one with his jaw in an iron brace, all with frowsty short
beards; and Reisden and Jules were wearing the filthy ruins
of their costumes from the film. Pink shirts. They were not
inconspicuous.

"Shall we simply reappear?" Reisden asked. "I want to see
my family."

The floor of the shop was still starred with garbage, the remains of tomatoes, rocks. The broken windows were
boarded. "I can't," said André. "Jules can't. Not before we
know who really killed her."

He couldn't leave them, not yet. "I'll telephone her."

"From Montfort. We're going to Montfort."

How to get there without being caught . . . By stages. The
moon was waxing; until it set, the farmers were in the fields
stooking hay. But for a few dark hours the roads were deserted. They stole a wheelbarrow. In the starry dark they staggered up the Arras road to the Auclart farm, wheeling an
embarrassed and contrite Jules.

They were starved. "Half the plants in this garden are poi-
sonous," André warned. They dug potatoes. The three men
went to earth in the cellar below the garden shed. Over a slow
fire, using the small pot from the kitchen, they cooked a soup

of potatoes from Mademoiselle Françoise's cellar and flavored it with vinegary wine. It was terrible and made them half drunk.

"Who could have killed her?" André said when they were full. "I didn't," he spelled it out like someone needing reassurance. "But who would want to kill her except me?"

They put together their own confused memories of the afternoon. They had no idea where anyone but André had been. It had been confusion, waits and more waits, people wandering off to the toilets. For the end of the afternoon Reisden and Jules alibied each other. They had not left the platform after they had checked the guillotine.

"That leaves me," André said.

Who had watched André? Reisden, Jules, Ruthie. They might have banded together to give him an alibi. They might have broken the mechanism themselves, killing the murderess Sabine for André's sake. Reisden had a clear cold vision of himself and Jules and Ruthie, the last to check the guillotine.

"What are we going to do?"

"I have to tell Perdita I'm all right. Then I'll talk with Pétiot. You stay here with Jules."

In the heat, Jules and André stretched out in the cool room under the garden shed. Reisden, starved for light and heat, went inside the house and slept for a while in a shaft of sun. The heat woke him in midafternoon and he explored the house, one room at a time, sitting down when he was tired, which was disgracefully often. He did not even know what day it was. André looked skeletal, Jules worse; they were still dehydrated; they were filthy, covered in grime and dust. How long had they been in the boves?

He stripped to the waist and washed with water from the Well. It disturbed him to use drinkable water to wash. The costumes from the final scene had been brought back here. The wicker costume baskets crowded Mademoiselle Françoise's sewing room. He threw each of them open, looking for something in fashion later than 1795; no luck. His own clothes might still be at Montfort.

Proof, he thought. Proof not only to save André but to condemn Sabine. *I didn't do anything wrong,* he remembered Sabine saying indignantly. *But André's going to kill me.*

Jules and André were still asleep. In the cellar, Reisden took scrapings from the greasy residue in the big cast-iron pot. There might be belladonna in it, henbane, digitalis. Interesting if so, but it wouldn't prove Sabine was a witch or a murderess. There was nothing in the kitchen. Nothing in the parlor, the sewing room, the bedroom upstairs.

In the attic he found an old dress and books of patterns, but no reversed crosses or black candles. Mademoiselle Françoise's uncle's trunk was shoved into a corner. An army uniform and a black Sunday suit waited for the resurrection of the dead. Reisden shoved them aside to look underneath.

Books. Crumbling school notebooks, ledgers. Grimoires? Reisden brought them down to the living room.

Mademoiselle Françoise's uncle's diary. He looked through it for clues.

The earliest entries recorded Auclart's life as a young infantryman. *Punishment* frequently, and with more enviable frequency, *X Marie, X Lucette, XX Anne.* He wrote poetry, the last refuge of the inarticulate. Oddly enough, he recorded every time he took communion.

Reisden skipped ahead to 1870.

1 September: *Infamy!* The defeat of the Great Sortie: *It is all up to the countryside now.* The armistice of January: *No, we won't give up.* And on the day of the laying down of arms: *I have cast my lot with Sgt Cyron.*

Auclart had been one of Cyron's partisans.

February 3, *4 Germans.* February 20, *Munitions.* The

partisans hoarded every bullet and made them count. Reprisals and counterreprisals, raids and hostages. As the spring nights brightened, Auclart kept track of the moon phase; the partisans worked best in the dark. The summer brought frustration; at 10 P.M. it was still dusk, at 4 A.M. already dawn.

In the summer of 1871 Auclart first mentioned that they were working on tunnels.

The sun was fading from the room; Reisden brought Auclart's diary out into the garden and read on. The partisans had already used tunnels in early spring to blow up the munitions dump. Now, in the summer, they began to dream more grandly. Auclart drew pictures. At the center of each, like a spider in its web, were the Arras boves. Outward from them radiated various configurations as Auclart drew and redrew them. Four long, optimistic, Haussmann-straight tunnels in the form of a cross. A tunnel under the Arras road. A tangle of tunnels connecting underground barracks, concealed gun emplacements, kitchens, underground stables, everything the modern army would need. Fantasies, diggers' dreams.

Jules emerged from underground, shaky but standing, to offer him soup. Reisden gave him a volume. "Look."

The three of them divided the pile of diaries and read them by the light of Mademoiselle Françoise's kerosene lamps.

In the fall and winter of 1871 the partisans dug from a basement near the seventeenth-century caserne, under the *Petit Champ de manoeuvres*. By spring 1872 they had reached the Citadel, where the Germans were headquartered. The massive base of the Citadel stopped them until the fall, but in early October 1872, after a last massive effort, they succeeded in digging inside the Citadel wall, in the northeast corner by the gatehouse.

From there they dug into the Citadel's ammunition store. By the winter of '72, Cyron's men had armed themselves with German rifles and bullets. Every cannon in the Citadel was spiked. The partisans had keys to every prison cell. From St.-Vaast, the caserne, the Citadel, hostages and supplies were magicked away into French hands.

Reisden flipped ahead. "But now he goes away!" he exclaimed, annoyed. Auclart had done his three years' service; in the spring of 1873, he had gone to Amiens to study pharmacy, just as if he weren't one of Cyron's heroes. He had returned to Arras only in 1875, when he had opened a pharmacy in the Grand'Place. By that time Cyron had already gone to Paris; Auclart pasted into his diary a review of one of his early performances.

"Here's this farm," André said.

In 1875—and not with his own money—Auclart had bought this farm from his second cousin. For about a year the diary was full of references to "the plan," digging, and the difficulty of removing the debris inconspicuously. The Germans would come again. Auclart and unnamed others were digging a tunnel under the farm.

Reluctantly—they had had enough of underground—Reisden, André, and Jules took the lanterns and explored the tunnels. Going toward Arras, the tunnel ended in a cave-in, which they could date by the diary; in March 1876 four men had been killed here. The tunnel northward extended farther, far enough into the dark that they were all joking nervously about getting to Montfort, but then it ended, too, in rubble that slithered when they touched it.

In late 1876 the tunnel under the Auclart farm was given up in favor of "the new plan."

And there was not a word more about it. Auclart went back to his pharmacy. The economy was recovering, the pharmacy was flourishing, and Auclart moved to Arras (*XXX Martine*, two nights in a row, one can only envy).

"The new plan was another tunnel," Reisden said. They were eating the same potato soup as before, but Jules had made it today and it was palatable. Reisden told them what he had speculated about the chalk road and the chalk towers. Rubble from a project.

"Papa Cyron never let me go into the cellars," André said. "It's there."

1876. Reisden handed the diary for that year over to André, who sat with it, turning the pages in his big hands, looking for something that he didn't find. André put the book down abruptly and went outside into the garden. Jules got up to follow him. Reisden shook his head. No. Let me do this one.

André was in the garden. "The new plan of 1876," he said, jamming his hands in his pockets. "That was me. He needed a bigger area . . . He wanted Montfort."

"Yes. But then he liked you."

They stood for a while in the garden, not saying anything. He wanted you to be exactly what he wanted, Reisden thought, and I thought he was a demon. But then— And he thought of Cyron and André onstage, dancing with the ostrich puppet; father and son dancing.

The Orphans. Leo had collected them, rather as Dotty's mother-in-law had collected snuffboxes: many of them, but with discrimination. Leo's Orphans had spent the summers together in the *Schloss* outside Graz, where tutors drilled them in languages, diplomacy, strategy, the intricacies of Europe, a bit of modern science for garnish. Leo had genuinely wanted them to do well, all of them, pushing them, challenging them, and smiling with his brown eyes when they did well. What do you see? What does it mean? Even after Reisden had realized he would never fit into Leo's plans, some part of him still occasionally dreamed of being back in the gardens on some calm summer morning, being useful, being noticed, belonging, talking with Leo.

André had been sent to military school; André had been jammed into the cavalry; André had been as wrongly cast as

Reisden. But every man wants to be a good son, and some-times both of them had been.

"At least it's an important project," André said.

"Let's find the d—d thing."

They went back and read, skimming to find any mention of it. Nothing. Auclart's energies had turned to something new, something he referred to only as *A*. Some new part of the se-cret of Montfort? *A* included both men and women and met at various underground locations in Arras, as well as in the un-derground room at the Auclart farm. A secret society? A la-bor organization? *1C Martine. C Josephine.* Always female names. Was *C* the same as *X*? Was this the same Martine who'd already been *XXX*ed? Whatever *A* was, Auclart rose steadily in it, organizing events and providing supplies from his pharmacy (what union needed so much ethanol?). It was not until 1885, when Auclart started using a standard diary, that Reisden noticed that *A* always met on Thursdays, at the end of a quarter, or at the dark or the full of the moon.

A was a gathering of witches.

And try to prove it. Even in his diary Auclart wrote with the discretion of the persecuted. The group could have been accountants or pharmacy students.

Auclart's diary lasted until 1909 and was largely devoted to his pharmacy business, his garden, his declining health, and his coven. Auclart occasionally went to Paris. He had dinner once with Cyron, and several times went to plays in which "le Sgt" was starring. He was made an honorary char-ter member of the Friends of Montfort. His liver gave him trouble; he took the cure at Deauville. He became bishop of his coven. In 1895, *My niece Françoise made her 1C.* The Dreyfus affair split *A* as it did the rest of France; old members began taking their sabbats elsewhere. He lamented his bald spot. The *X*s became infrequent. Auclart was getting old.

After 1900, Auclart's eyesight began to fail. He closed the

pharmacy, sold the shop to his niece, and puttered around his garden, raising rabbits for sacrifice. He went nowhere but the annual dinners of the Friends of Montfort.

But Auclart was still bishop of his declining coven, and in 1907, two years before he died of emphysema, he recorded a new first communion.

On March 31, 1907, *1C Sabine*.

Chapter 81

At night, André, who knows Montfort best, goes to scout out how they can get into the Montfort cellars.

It's easy. Because the castle is almost deserted. The Rolls is gone from the garage; Cyron isn't here. "But he should be here," André mutters to himself, deeply disappointed even though he can't confront Cyron yet.

Everyone's gone, Eli Krauss, the lights men, the technicians, the extras, all Cyron's friends with their valets and their horses, all gone. No hammering or shouting or whinnying from the stables, no quarreling voices from the estaminet. In the dark main block of the Vex-Fort, no lights at all.

Papa Cyron has closed the house, in the height of summer when he should be in the country. Where is he?

By the front door of the house, André runs into something large and scratchy like a hay-pallet. Against the moonlight, above him, a great sheaf of wheat nods against the stars. The country people have made a door guardian, an effigy of hay

twice as tall as a man, tied into shape with bits of rag. Instead
of a head it has a sheaf of wheat, as if the chief of the house
has died. That is for me, André thinks wonderingly.

André circles the house and sees lights in the housekeeper's parlor. He stands on tiptoe to see inside. It's as he
hoped. Cyron has taken the house staff back to Paris, too, and
the gardener is off overseeing his farm; there's no one here
but old Roselle and her niece.

André crouches in a disused room off the kitchens and listens to the two women gossip. Oh, what a terrible thing, the
way Madame died! And the Count her own husband suspected. (André winces and nods to himself.) And he dead,
too, poor man. For a certainty they will haunt the house, the
niece says.

"Nonsense, girl!" says Roselle.

But André never disappoints an audience.

"Did you hear that?" the niece says nervously.

"What?"

"A scraping . . . a moan . . ."

Old Roselle marches into the hall, armed with the game-
keeper's gun. When the electrical system was put in, André
made improvements of his own; the lights flicker up the hall,
and in Sabine's dressing room they turn on with a white theatrical flare. Roselle marches up the stairs, the niece quaver-
ing at her heels like a shadow. Powder has been spilled on
Madame's dresser, as if Madame had been powdering her
face. "Her jewelry box is open, and one necklace gone—the
collar of pearls!" The collar of pearls is costume jewelry, a
couple of years out of date, the niece says; Madame would
never wear it *unless she needed to conceal her neck*.

"Nonsense, girl!"

But as Roselle marches downstairs she almost slips on
Sabine's cards, scattered on the stairs. Those cards disappeared when Madame died, and there is a slithering, sloshing

sound from the Great Hall. The niece bites the ends of her fingers in fear. Roselle marches forward, the gun trembling in her upraised hand. The furniture in the Great Hall is all disarranged, the table and chairs set against the wall as if for a funeral, the trestles ready to receive a coffin. Below the trestles stands a pail of water to cleanse the soul of the dead.

Across the dark room floats one lit candle.

"It's hooligans," old Roselle says firmly, recovering herself. "Nothing but vandals! We'll tell the police to watch the house. We'll report this to Monsieur Cyron, that's what we'll do. In Paris. Don't be frightened. Get my handbag, girl."

But Roselle's niece has already fled outside, and nothing will persuade her back; Roselle must get her bag herself. The two cut through the fields, sliding down the hill and stumbling among the little stones, taking the road to Arras. Roselle is still carrying the gun.

The coach and horses are gone, too; there's nothing in the stables or the garage but Reisden's car. André has never driven a car, never even started one, but he wrote a car crash once for the Necro. He cranks, he fiddles; the car hiccups and grinds and eventually moves; and André gets it nearly to the Auclart farm until the headlights show him Reisden and Jules, at the side of the road, waving him down.

"Could you possibly make more noise?" Reisden says, angry because he is tired. "Didn't Boomer have any bombs left?"

"No one's there. Not anymore," André summarizes. "We were right. They think I killed *her*."

"And when Cyron hears about floating lights and moving furniture," Reisden says, "he will send men to Montfort with guns and nets to catch you. And if you are very, very lucky, you will only be in an asylum for the rest of your life, instead of being guillotined at dawn for murdering Sabine."

It's true. The euphoria of giving the women a good scare has made André forget.

"He has been building a project in my house," André says. "He didn't tell me. He didn't trust me." Count André de Montfort, the cavalry officer, that was who Papa Cyron wanted. Count André de Montfort married to the rich, beautiful Sabine. "If we find the tunnel, and you tell him I'm not mad— Pétiot knows I didn't if he was watching me— Look for the tunnel with me. Then you can go to your wife; then you can talk to Pétiot."

And they find it, two days later.

Not near the Holy Well. Reisden thinks the tunnel is close to the stone-dump. They go down into the third cellar and, using strings to mark their path, work their way in the right direction with Reisden's beloved compass.

Reisden is better with the dark than he has been. André wonders about this.

Once they are close to it, the tunnel is obvious. The ceiling is heavily braced, the stone pillars have been cut away; a narrow track leads across a big cavern. There is a heavy iron wagon on the track, its sides battered, every inch of it ingrained with chalk dust. In the lantern light, metal gleams on the chalk walls: newly installed electric lights. "Off the new generator," André says. Reisden finds the switch and turns them on. Light underground. It is luxurious.

Everything is behind barred doors, the way it was at Arras. Behind the bars they can see a barracks-room with sleeping bunks, a room filled with miners' lanterns and pickaxes, and a roomful of wooden boxes stamped 1893 м. 1896—which is the model number of the French army rifle. And there are boxes of dynamite; there are thick rolls of fuse; there are blue boxes of ammunition.

Behind more barred doors, three tunnels, each with a track, lead off into the dark. André looks through the bars and can see electric lights illuminating heavy bracing beams, low dim passages painfully carved out by hand. In two of the tunnels the lights curve away to a tiny dim horizon of stars—a crossing tunnel. In the third, the lights are out, but he can see close to the bars another rail wagon half-full of broken chalk.

"He did it." For a moment André is simply proud of Cyron, proud of him as a Frenchman. He understands completely why Cyron wanted the Count of Montfort's support, Sabine's money. "What a great effort—an enormous effort." He sounds like one of Cyron's old men.

Jules has his mouth open in astonishment. He puts his hand over his heart and gestures expansively. "Yes," Reisden says. "Extraordinary. One wants to tell someone. No wonder Pétiot—"

What they are feeling is awe. For Papa Cyron.

They go up close to the bars and look through them. Reisden tries the doors, but they are securely locked.

They find a carefully camouflaged exit into one of the sheds—the same heavy concrete shed where Boomer O'Connelly stored his black powder. No wonder that no one found the exit, with barrels of black powder and lard stacked against it.

They go out into the day, closing the entrance to the tunnels behind them. André looks up at the white towers, the spill of white rock down the hill. Montfort was a nightmare to him, his mother's house and his father's. Now it is a new story, an extraordinary thing.

Reisden is frowning. "What's wrong?" André says.

"High stakes," Reisden says.

"Go see your family. Then see Papa Cyron," he tells Reisden. "Tell him that he can trust me."

Reisden looks at him and André knows what he's thinking. Can he?

Chapter 82

Reisden did not see a paper or know what day it was until he got to Amiens. They had all three speculated how long they'd been in the boves. It had felt like most of their lives, but based on how long their light had lasted, Reisden thought two days, three at most. A day at the Auclart farm, two days at Montfort. Three? He had left Montfort after dark and reached Amiens in the morning. He thought it might be Saturday, July 29, possibly Sunday.

Amiens was in the middle of its Thursday farmers' market. It was the second of August.

He hadn't telephoned Perdita from Montfort. Telephoning from a deserted house would have brought the police down on them. So far no police, so far no Cyron; he wanted to keep it that way.

Perdita would think he was dead.

Just outside Amiens the car hit a pothole in the road and the front axle broke. It would take a day to get or re-weld the part. He went to the post office then and negotiated the call to Paris. But when Aline answered, he broke the connection.

He might have called Ruthie, but he wasn't going to call Ruthie before his wife. He might have left the car in Amiens and taken the train, but beneath the car duster he was wearing a collarless shirt of André's and no jacket. (He had money; it would occur to him only later that he could have bought a ready-made suit in Amiens.)

He drove all night Friday and arrived back in Paris on Saturday, in the early afternoon.

He left the car parked two blocks away and reconnoitered Jouvet from across the street. On the front door hung a mourning wreath and a black-bordered death announcement. ALEXANDRE DE REISDEN, BELOVED HUSBAND, FATHER, AND EMPLOYER: Perdita had signed first, but all the employees of Jouvet had also signed, even Katzmann, who was only a consultant. All those mourners.

They would despise you, Sir, they would abhor you if they knew your true nature. Ah, William.

He let himself in by the back door and went up the private stairs to the apartment.

"Perdita? Toby?" he whispered. No one was there. It was as deserted as when they had gone to America.

In their bedroom, Perdita's closet was half empty. She had laid out on their bed all her light summer clothing, her whites and pastels, her Worth concert dress and the other dresses. She was packing, he thought. She was going back to America.

He went into Toby's room, expecting the same disarray of packing. But she had laid out only some light outer clothes, a couple of flannel baby frocks. In the piano room, she had not packed her music. There were no tickets tacked onto the message board where they kept everything important, no trunks in the hall.

On her reading desk, with the strong light and the magnifying glass, she had left an unusual litter of papers and books. Perdita hardly read; her sight wasn't good enough. Feeling like a spy again, he looked through the papers. Simple versions of Jouvet's accounts, written very large in Madame Herschner's hand. A Beethoven score. Under the others was hidden a thin maroon book.

He picked it up: what would Perdita read?

Little Lessons in French History. A child's primer of

France from the Gauls to the Third Republic. It was in English; the paragraphs were short, numbered, and factual; the print was large. There was a table of the French heads of government from Hugues Capet to Félix Faure, with the corner of the page carefully folded down for reference. She had got about halfway through the book so far; he knew because if he tilted the page so that the light raked across it, he could see the mark of her fingernail carefully keeping her place under each line. Her sight was bad; she read that slowly.

She had never shown it to him, never asked him to read it to her.

At the end of the book was a paragraph on Dreyfus; she had been reading that, too.

She was not trying to leave.

She could have run. He had run. He had expected her to go home (and it was only beginning to come to him how difficult that expectation might have been for her). People do run, or declare themselves mad and unfit, or wait paralyzed between choices, doing too little. And then there are those who don't, who attempt something very difficult and want to endure through it, for the sake of something they barely understand and have never experienced.

Downstairs the door slammed. He heard her voice in his office.

The other voice was Gilbert's.

He hid behind the closed portieres, but they didn't come upstairs. They were meeting in the office. Step by step, spying, he came down the stairs behind the secret door and listened.

He never trusted us enough, he heard. He sat and listened to them, with *Little Lessons in French History* still in his hand, his finger keeping the page. *Be our American,* Perdita asked Gilbert, and he heard Gilbert: *Yes.*

It was a bitter lesson, that he could depend on them and he

hadn't. *He would not want me to say he was alive,* Gilbert said. *It was him quarreling with himself,* Perdita said.

Perdita and Gilbert stood up, and he fled into the upstairs library and hid unceremoniously behind the portieres. Aline brought Toby back from the park. They ate with Toby in the dining room while Reisden heard them, listening to Toby pound on his tray and crow, and thinking about coming from behind the curtains, and not doing it. He would have frightened Gilbert too badly, he thought, but that was an excuse. *You are not worthy of anyone's love,* he heard from his own personal old man of the boves. He was inclined to agree.

And then, in the dining room, Perdita told Toby. "Your father killed someone," she said. And he had to listen to it, all of it, his wife's obituary on him. *All his life he was sorry and angry at himself. . . . He wanted you to know he was bad.*

He had to listen to it. And it could have been William speaking until he realized that, although he had listened, he had heard only half of it. He was a good man, he heard. He loved you. You can be proud of him. He forced himself to hear those things and understand that he had not really heard anything except that he loved Toby.

You are vile, the cellars whispered, but that wasn't what she had said. What would he teach Toby if he believed William? To loathe himself and distrust himself?

Through the curtain he could see a shadow of Toby. I will teach you, he told his son silently, that one can be wrong without being vile and right without being God.

He moved and looked through the curtain at Perdita, not knowing what vows to make to her.

Gilbert left. Perdita played with Toby; Aline took him off to put him to bed. It was Saturday night; Aline left for her Sunday off. Perdita walked away slowly toward their room. She closed the door behind her. He moved silently after her, through the corridors of his empty house.

She was crying.

He stood outside their door and listened to her. He opened it an inch. She was crying with so much abandon that she did not hear him. He had never wanted her to love someone who wasn't a hero. He had never trusted her much; she'd said so; she knew it. And still she cried like this, in pain, crying for an ordinary man. He was facing something much more serious than he had left, unbreakable, undeniable, which he did not comprehend at all, and he was afraid of it, less ready than he had been to have a son.

She dropped her hands and held them out. "Alexander," she whispered. He thought for a moment she had seen him and then realized she was only saying his name.

"Perdita," he said.

Chapter 83

S he shrieked and put her hand over her mouth; then she reached out to find him. She clasped her arms convulsively around him. She was still sobbing; he felt her ribs hiccup under her thin nightgown. They clung to each other, saving each other or drowning. He began shaking too. They both lay down, collapsed almost, on the bed, among the clothes she'd been sending to be dyed black. "Love," he said, "love."

"Where have you *been*?" she said, muffled against his chest. He could have taken it as accusation, though she didn't mean it that way. Perhaps he should have. He had obviously got all the way to Paris without letting her know he was safe.

Not that they were safe, he thought. Not as long as he had to tell Cyron to trust André. *I was coming back to you,* he wanted to tell Perdita. *I'm alive and everything is all right now.* No. He held her, held on to her convulsively, because this was what he'd wanted, being here.

"It was good, what you did with Gilbert," he said. " 'Our American.' He has enough resources to keep Jouvet independent, whatever happens. I've seen what Pétiot and Cyron are fighting for. It's important, not only to them. They will do anything they have to." *They'll sacrifice André for it. They'll gladly sacrifice me.*

"It was what I had to do; you weren't here," she said. "What are they fighting for?"

He shook his head. "Even with Gilbert's money, I don't know how to protect André. Or any of you."

He thought of the black-bordered *faire-part* with his name on it, still down on the gate. A temptation. *We have a chance,* he thought. *A choice.* "André's safe as long as he's dead," he said. "You and Jouvet are as long as I am."

"No," she said, holding tight to him. *"No.* Stop saying that. I've thought you were dead for two weeks, I won't have you dead, I won't."

He held tight to her. "I know. I know. But—" Was this the same old fear of family, time and again? "You're right. We will need Gilbert. And I complicate things. If Gilbert gives money to Jouvet because you ask him, fine. If I'm here, if we are using Gilbert's money, it's because of me. Because I'm Richard. Or because I'm taking advantage of a foolish old man, because I look like him."

"Then complicate things! I wish I had never talked to Gilbert!"

They said nothing, only lay in each other's arms, as close as if they were skin against skin, body to body. And then she said the thing he knew, in spite of his unworthiness.

"It doesn't work," she said. "You tried running away. You tried dying. It doesn't work, Alexander. It doesn't finish anything. It never did. But you always think so. Why don't you just stop?"

"What shall I do?" he asked her, his blind, almost hysterical, risky wife.

"What you think is right," she said as if there were no other way. "And not die and not go away. I won't have it."

"Saving André," he said without needing to think. "But here's what will happen. I say he's not insane. He's tried for murder, I imagine; perhaps Jules as well." Perdita nodded. "Cyron and Pétiot come down with both boot heels on Jouvet. We will be a scandal, like Dreyfus. Gilbert will be called a foolish old man, driven mad by my resemblance to Richard. I'm taking advantage of him. So are you. Harry will say that; not only Harry. It'll be like Dreyfus. It'll come down on all of us, love, and it'll come down on Toby. Is this what you want?"

She gave him the courtesy of not giving him a quick answer. He moved back from her and looked at her face. He could see the moment when she understood what it would mean to her: the whispers on the street, the snubs here and in America. What Ellis and the women who booked her concerts would think of her.

"There will be more than that," he said. He had to tell her. She looked up at him apprehensively. He wondered whether all this, this form of trusting her, was one more scheme to drive her away.

"What happened this summer," he said, and took a deep breath. "I was being blackmailed. And not about Richard. About something else, which will come out too."

He held her hand and told her. André and Jules, the original blackmail, Jules' beating. "Then they came to me." He told her about Leo, about how he had been chosen to be Franz von Reisden's son; about looking at his friends' fathers'

newspapers to see their opinions and opening the back door
for men like Gehazy. Her face was very still and white. She
closed her eyes. He told her relentlessly about spying on
Montfort for Leo. "Leo was a very decent man," he said,
"who believed in what he did. I didn't. It took me years to decide that.—Dotty was in with it too. In this climate I'll bring
her down with me." Dotty and Tiggy, he thought; Tiggy who
was eight years old now, like Richard, no more capable of facing such a thing than Richard. "Should I do this and have it
come out? Is it the right thing to hurt so many people because
I want to save one man? I want you and Toby, I want Gilbert, I
even want the money, but should I not care what chaos I
spread because of it? Is it what you want?"

She kept her eyes closed. She breathed raggedly as if she
would have been crying if he had not been there. It must have
been minutes before she spoke. I would say yes, he thought;
but he had been saying no and putting all the decision on her.
"I don't want things to come out that badly," she said slowly.
"I want them to come out easily right. That's what I want. I
don't want you dead—don't ever say that anymore. But I just
want things easier."

He nodded. "I'm sorry. I am more than you bargained for."

"It has nothing to do with you!" she exploded. "Not much.
It's—it's everything: France, the language, music, even Toby.
Sometimes I just want to run away, and it doesn't help that
you do. Oh, I'm sorry," she said. "I'm sorry, I missed you so
much, and here you are and I felt guilty because I had been so
angry at you and now I'm doing it again."

She burst into tears, deep wrenching sobs. She drove her
head against his shoulder as if she were banging her head
against a wall. He held her, being the solid thing she needed.
He realized he had reached one of the limits of his marriage.
If he left her on her own, or threatened to, she would find
some other anchor. "I am here," he said to her over and over
again. "I'm not going away. I'm here."

She finished, finally, and lay limp as Toby against his arm. "It'll be so bitter," she said, apologizing or explaining. "People can be so hard on each other. I didn't tell you about Boston. It was bad. They think they're so right, and we know we're right."

"Yes," he said. Right is on everyone's side. They call that war.

"Did you think you were right?" she said. "When you did—what you did for Leo?"

"Yes. I suppose. I didn't have anything better," he said. "I wanted—I don't know, family"—that was exactly what he had wanted—"and he was the closest thing."

"Gilbert's your family," she said, "and you have to have him."

I have Toby, he was about to say, I have you, and then knew what she was telling him. She wasn't sure of herself. If she left him—she knew she might—Toby would go with her. Gilbert might be all he had.

"Why did you decide you couldn't—" she used the word "—spy for Leo anymore?" she asked.

"Tasy," he said.

"You're like that for Uncle Gilbert," she said. "He was all right with Harry until you came back; I mean not all right, but—You came back. Ever since then, he does things because he thinks they're right. Because of you. He let you go because he knew you didn't want to stay. And he didn't just let you go, he let me go, both of us, though he loved me too. And now, I think, his coming here, it's a part of that. He wouldn't beg you to let him be a part of our lives, but he has. You can't imagine how he came to New York, Alexander, he didn't take anything but his dog, not even his clothes. He went on a boat; you know he's frightened of boats. You make him"—she thought of a word—"honest."

"And demanding. We would all be happier if he could be

content with Harry." He didn't want to think of Gilbert's appearance in Paris as being like his running away from Leo. "He's mistreating Harry."

"Harry knows he's second best with Gilbert—we'd all like to think it's not that way, and it's a shame it is, but it is—and Harry's got other people. It isn't comfortable but it may be right. Gilbert's got nobody but Elphinstone and us." Her voice quavered. "Scandal or no. You can't go away. You can't let him go. That's what I want."

Honest, he thought. Do I make you honest? He didn't think so. Tonight he did. Honesty, loyalty, choosing someone and not letting them go: *That was what I wanted,* he'd said to her. *Family.* It was more than Toby's hand in his. It was more than the closest thing to it, it was itself and only itself, and it was frightening, it was a risk like the edge of a precipice.

"You're right I don't trust you," he said before he could persuade himself she didn't need to know this. It had been what he thought of daily since their marriage, when he thought of her, but saying it to her felt as if he were driving her away. "You want Gilbert. You're—" he hesitated and said it "—you're blind; you can't see on the street. You're ten years younger than I am, Perdita. There's so much you don't know."

"That's all true," she said, and the tears stood in her eyes. "I know that."

"But what you say I am to Gilbert," he said, "you are to me."

There was much more to say, but that was all they could say now. He told her the rest of the story instead. "You were right about the rabbit." He told her about the Auclart uncle, the coven *A* with its aphrodisiac flying ointment, and the tunnels under the farmhouse. He told her about T. J. Blantire's past and the coven ritual.

"And she killed Mr. Blantire?" Perdita said.

"She locked him in the well cage. The carbon monoxide may have killed him."

"Did she kill—what did you call him, the Ferret?"

Reisden thought of Sabine dealing playing cards off the bottom of the deck: *Your fortune is below.* Sabine would have known about the tunnel at Montfort. Like himself, she would have wanted someone else to give Gehazy the information.

"I don't know."

"He could have blackmailed *her*," Perdita said.

"He would have if he'd known," Reisden said.

"She was a murderess. And I let her hold Toby," Perdita said.

Toby's mother and father lay together in silence. "A good journalist like Milly would have found Sabine out," she said.

"Yes. She couldn't lie very well." He thought of her the night before she died. *I didn't do anything wrong,* she'd said, indignant, sad. Perhaps her premonition of death had been the beginnings of a sense of guilt, responsibility disguising itself as punishment. Perhaps she would never have felt anything at all, except pity for herself.

Whether she had a moral sense or not, Jouvet should have protected her the way it had tried to protect André. Reisden had had two patients to protect. He had cared for only one of them.

"Who do they say killed her?" he asked.

"André."

"He didn't. I've talked with him. What happened to the guillotine?"

"Someone took some of the bunting from the platform and stuffed it into the lever that opened the lunette. The lever jammed and the lunette didn't open."

"And it was done at the last minute, because it was all right when we checked it. Anyone could have murdered her," he brooded.

"Anyone," Perdita agreed. "Two of General Pétiot's soldiers were guarding the guillotine. But they were all watching André. Anyone could have ducked under the platform behind them and not been seen because of all the bunting hanging down."

"How do they say André did it?"

"With tricks, like at his theatre," Perdita said. "Or with someone helping him. Jules. Ruthie."

"Ruthie?"

"Ruthie to jam the lever. Jules not to notice and to pull the guillotine rope. Aline won't even read me what the newspapers are saying. Milly told me Ruthie's landlady has asked her to move. I was going to tell her she was welcome here.— Who did kill Sabine, Alexander?"

"I don't know." He thought of the Necro, gimmicked in every part. "Whoever it is has to be more believable than André.—I didn't think; that's what we have to do, isn't it, find who killed her."

"That won't be easy," Perdita said, "finding someone more believable than André.—Alexander, are you hungry? Did you have dinner?"

He sat in the kitchen while she fixed him an omelette. He watched her strike the match and light the gas, and he held his breath and thought of all the layers of fear and distrust that made him think her risky. Everyone was risky but William. William said so. "I missed you," she said at the stove. "Every time I cooked anything, it wasn't for you."

"Thank you for taking care of me." He followed her with his eyes. All the implications of being taken care of, of being a child, helpless, at William's mercy. Better to keep caretaking at bay. No. But William had damaged him in ways he hadn't even considered. He thought of André, whose past had come back to haunt him when he'd married.

She had kept the newspapers. He scanned the front pages

while she cooked. The news was bad and getting worse. Lloyd George, the British prime minister, had unexpectedly directed a fiercely warmongering warning to Germany. Kinderlin-Waechter, the moderate German negotiator, wasn't being backed by his government and was threatening to resign. French and Russian government officials were returning to their capitals in the middle of what should have been summer vacation. And, last Sunday's paper reported, even Maurice Cyron had added his voice to the chorus. In Calais he had talked to a gathering of ship owners. *I, a poor actor of soldiers' roles, an old man, I will gladly put on the uniform of a simple private.*

"We have it all wrong," he told Perdita, "looking for a motive to kill Sabine. We're at war. So far it's a polite little war, off in Morocco, but war is its own motive. A soldier doesn't need an excuse for killing; he does it for his country. Leo would use anyone. Blackmail anyone. He was defending Austria. If Sabine were sleeping with a German spy—"

She put the omelette in front of him and sat down beside him. "Tell me, someday, all about that," she said. "Leo."

"Yes," he said. "Someday."

He ate and washed the plate, looking at the drinkable water splashing into the sink. If there is a war, he thought, I want Toby and Perdita in England or America.

If there is a war, and it is a short one, the Germans will win it.

They went into Toby's room. Reisden picked his sleeping boy up and held Toby's warm sweaty weight against his chest. Toby stirred, then woke abruptly and reared back to look at his father. "Yes, it's Papa," Reisden murmured. Toby smiled at him. "Da da da da da!" "Yes," said Reisden, "and I love *you*." Let there not be a war, he thought. Let there not be a war.

It was late and hot. They drew back the curtains of the

French windows and let in the trace of evening breeze. Toby and he talked for a few moments; then the cooler air made Toby yawn and he settled back to sleep on Reisden's shoulder. Reisden closed his eyes and felt the breeze on his face. Eating had exhausted him; the breeze was reminding him of something but he couldn't think what. The breeze and Cyron. He told Perdita in a whisper how, in the boves, he had tried to navigate by currents of air. "It was so cold and damp one could feel the air moving, when it moved," he said. "Most of the time it didn't. The air was dead. Damp, completely still, and smelling of stone." A small part of him wanted to howl about it, now that he was safe with her: *It was dark and cold and there were ghosts and I was scared.* He held Toby on his shoulder, with his son's small warm breath dampening his cheek, listening to the sounds of the Paris night traffic from the boulevard St.-Germain, feeling the fresh breeze.

He must call Cyron; must call Ruthie. And Gilbert. Tonight? Wait for tomorrow? Tomorrow. He had to find out who had killed Sabine. Perhaps it had been an accident. De Vere had warned them the machinery was dangerous. Reisden wasn't thinking straight; he was too tired.

"It smelled in Cyron's tunnel," he said, remembering. There had been something different about it, something familiar; it had almost reminded him of Jouvet. A chemical odor, sharp and oily. Boomer O'Connelly's black powder? No.

"What did we smell this spring?" he asked Perdita. "Before you left?"

"Paint," she said. "Wood and plaster and paint."

He was still holding Toby; he handed him to Perdita. He stood leaning on Toby's crib, half thinking, half just stunned. He understood what Cyron had been trying to do, why Pétiot had needed to pass the secret. The whole story stretched out clear

before him, as if he had shone a good light beyond the barred
door of Cyron's tunnel at Montfort and seen false perspectives, dead ends.

"I know who killed Sabine and I know why," he said.

The new plan.

"Rumors of secret fortifications. A castle being reconstructed with the help of the army. The Friends of Montfort. Great amounts of money raised. Mysterious cellars, always kept locked. Hints of something big." He wasn't making any sense to her. "Cyron's secret was a tunnel or a fortress," he said. "The entrance to it is hidden in the lowest cellar at Montfort. Jules and André and I saw it. But it doesn't exist," he said. "That's all there is to it, an entrance. A stage set. There is no secret of Montfort."

Montfort. Rising above the Flanders plains year by year, tower upon tower, inscription by inscription, stone by stone. Even Leo had been puzzled by it. "What is it *for*?" he'd asked Reisden. "Find out for me." Something to give the spies pause. Something big, something mysterious. Cyron hadn't built a fortress. He'd built a mystery.

Cyron would have been very careful to control who saw it, for how long. Françoise Auclart should have been the one to show it to Blantire, lead him down to the third cellar, give him a tantalizing glimpse of Cyron's huge project—which he could report back to Izvolsky. From the Russian Secret Service it would have got safely back to the Germans.

But it was Sabine who had taken Blantire there.

Had she been working for Cyron? He hoped so, he so much hoped so. But he didn't think so. Sabine had been risky and Cyron hadn't known it until she'd married André. Sabine had been a witch, who knew other witches, and witches meet underground, witches want water from the Holy Well. Sabine had slept with a spy. Sabine would have learned Cyron's secret and wouldn't have been able to keep it to herself.

Cyron had been in the Grand'Place, with Sabine, by the guillotine, just before they both had climbed the stairs. He would have known how to move when everyone's attention had been distracted by André. It would have taken only a moment to jam cloth into the machine.

Motive, means, and opportunity.

Reisden thought about Cyron dancing with Sabine at André's birthday party; Cyron coaching Sabine in the mad scene; Cyron reassuring Sabine she wasn't going to die. Sabine turning to Cyron just before she put her head under the blade, holding his hand, smiling up at him, saying something to him.

Cyron, the good soldier.

I can't suspect Cyron, he thought. No. Let him not have done it; let me not have to say so— Because what would it mean? It would mean, he thought with sudden icy clarity like a cold shower, that Cyron couldn't possibly risk André being innocent. If André and Jules were innocent, someone else had to have killed Sabine.

And who would be the next suspect? Who had the money from Sabine and the castle from André, if André was dead?

The telephone rang. "Will you?" he said. "Give me Toby." She went down the hall to pick up the phone in his office.

"Ruthie?" she said, and looked back in his direction helplessly. He took the phone and listened.

"Have you heard anything?" he heard Ruthie saying. "Is André *alive*, is your husband *alive*? My brother?"

Reisden listened silently to Ruthie's flood of words. Roselle, the old housekeeper at the château, had been to see Cyron. Ghosts, floating candles— Reisden put his palm over the transmitter. "Tell her you'll telephone her back," he said.

Perdita talked to Ruthie and hung up the phone. "Why couldn't we tell her?"

"Because Cyron killed Sabine," he said.

"He cried for Sabine," Perdita said. "You should have heard him cry for her."

"I cried for William." Cyron couldn't have planned the mob, or known André would be so distracting that he could gimmick the guillotine unnoticed. "I'll put Toby down." She followed him into Toby's room. He laid his baby gently in the crib. Toby stirred and muttered; they stood without speaking until he settled down.

"I don't think Cyron planned anything," Reisden whispered. He took Perdita's arm and they both moved away from Toby, to the door of the room. "It was just very convenient that André and Jules disappeared. But now they're alive and Cyron knows it, and Cyron's got used to getting away with murder.—I have to go to Montfort."

"I'll come with you."

"No, stay here with Toby. We can't take him. I don't have proof," he thought aloud. "None. And I won't get any."

"What will happen?" she asked.

This was one of the things she didn't know. He did. Leo would have had André and Jules shot trying to escape arrest.

He stood in the door of his son's nursery with Perdita next to him. "Can you imagine, love," he said, "can you imagine having to accuse Maurice Cyron of murder?"

"But you're going to have to do it," she said, "aren't you?"

"The first thing I have to do is get them to safety." Somehow. Somewhere. Impossible. Ruthie had said Roselle had seen Cyron only this evening. He had been away in Calais talking to the ship owners. How long did André and Jules have? Until tomorrow morning. Perhaps. No more.

He stood in the door of his son's nursery with Perdita next to him. Men fight wars for their sons, for the yellow-painted nursery crib and the teddy bear and the familiar sounds from the street. For the chance to do one's work. For one's friends; for one's country. "I don't blame Cyron," he said softly. "He doesn't want France invaded. He's a soldier.—What will happen to us if I say Cyron murdered Sabine? Everything we thought might happen, and more. Pétiot will provide Cyron an ironclad alibi for every moment of that afternoon, and I will be lucky if I'm not deported.—I could have him blackmailed," he said. "Pull Cyron down with someone like the Ferret. Make everyone laugh about his plaster tunnel; make it possible to say he's guilty."

What I know, he thought. What I learned from Leo. The weapons I have to protect my family. Spies' weapons. Knives in the back.

"But if I make the real secret of Montfort public," he said, "the Germans will know there's nothing to stop them on the Arras road."

Late on a Saturday night in August vacation: There would be no one in the building. "Come downstairs with me," he said.

They went together into the laboratory. He turned on the lights and looked at the double row of lab benches and enameled-steel cabinets. The techs had already claimed their territories with knickknacks on cabinets and shelves. Méraud's plants on the window ledge, Félicienne Calivart's cartoons on the supplies cabinet, Beauchêne's soccer schedules on the bulletin board. He pushed open the door of a testing cubicle. On the table were scattered pieces of a Goddard form board. That would be Ségur testing a baby's intelligence and never picking up after himself.

This is my country, he thought, mine and theirs. I am Reisden of Jouvet and I made this with them. He saw the baby's chart, left in Ségur's out-basket. No one else would have picked up Cannon's syndrome this early. We find answers. We are good.

And I'm willing to give it up, he thought, for André's sake; for one patient.

No. I'm not giving it up. Only losing it. But in the meantime I'm d——d well going to fight for it.

And that was the key to his marriage too, he thought. Not giving up, trying at least; losing it maybe; losing it probably if the war came. But not willingly or easily.

In the venerable, unchanged office that had been Dr. Jouvet's, he cranked the telephone. Toby reached for the phone cord and he took his baby's hand and kissed it while he eased the phone cord out of reach. This may be all I can give you, Toby, he thought, how to fight for who you are. "Does Gilbert have a phone yet? I want him." He jotted down phone numbers from his memory and his address book. Ruthie. Katzmann at home. Dotty. Milly Xico.

"What are you going to do?" Perdita asked.

"Fight Cyron for André. Lose, unless we get to him first. I'll try to get him away. But if I can't, I want him arrested in front of witnesses; I want someone watching him all the time, so nothing happens to him."

"Give me the list," she said. "I'll call. You don't want to spend time telling people you're alive. But I'm coming, Alexander, and we're bringing Toby if we have to."

Chapter 84

There were eight of them in the truck. The grey-haired, plump lady from the theatre. The psychiatrist snoring on a pile of quilted pads. Mr. Krauss, the cameraman, with his cap over his eyes. Mr. Krauss' camera, wrapped in a blanket, slid as the truck turned yet again. Toby was asleep on his blanket between Alexander and Perdita, his rump in the air. Gilbert had been given the job of looking after him; he hovered over Toby and clutched at Elphinstone's collar.

The sun was barely up. It shone through a crack in the panels and sliced over Perdita and Alexander, leaning against each other, arms around each other, half asleep, half thinking.

"It's like Dreyfus," Gilbert overheard her saying to Alexander. "How did Dreyfus win out?"

"Luck and fifteen years, love."

Dreyfus—? Gilbert had no idea. They were talking the private language of married couples, shared allusions and shortcuts. Gilbert would have liked to speak this family language and knew he never would; he would not be in Paris long enough.

They stopped at Amiens for coffee, at the railroad café. There was no tea; Gilbert had coffee too. In the strengthening sunlight he looked at his nephew's face. He had thought never to see it again.

Alexander shook the paper out and swore. "Kinderlen-Waechter's resigned." A group of young soldiers were reading the papers eagerly, joking, boasting, slapping their chests. A train huffed into the station and they gathered their equipment, going somewhere to the east.

"The French want Cambon to come home," Alexander translated, his eyes dark. "The negotiations are failing. That lot are going off to the frontier.—You really told Perdita you'd stay if there is a war? I hope not for that reason, Gilbert."

They watched the young men boarding. They are so young, Gilbert thought, and so bright, so cheerful, so happy on this hot morning, as if they are going to see their girlfriends. He wondered for a moment at Alexander's words. Did Alexander mean Gilbert was to stay anyway? No. Surely not.

"You must take the money," Gilbert said to Alexander.

"Tom's money. If there is going to be trouble of any kind," he didn't want to say words like *war*, "then it's better to have resources. One wants to do well," Gilbert hesitated, "to do well for oneself; one feels rather—ignored—when one is well off; it is only the money that they see and respect. But when I have gone," he was very careful to spell that out, "I would feel so relieved if I knew you had resources to spare."

The low morning sun made Alexander's face suddenly bleak. "Gilbert, I am glad of your presence. Don't think I want you to go. None of what's coming will be fun. I want friends," he said, with a little pause before *friends*.

Alexander had never talked about needing friends before, and it did not seem a comfortable admission for him now. One middle-aged lady, who had fallen asleep; the doctor, drooling a little against the quilted pads. Mr. Krauss. Me, Gilbert thought. Alexander smiled, a tightening of the corners of the mouth, as if he were a little disappointed in them. Gilbert realized, in one of those sharp-edged revelations he had with Alexander and no one else, that Tom's money might not be good for Alexander. Wealth is isolating.

"I shall be with you," Gilbert said. "I shall not go, not while you need me." Alexander looked at him questioningly.

The last soldiers were boarding. "If the war comes," Alexander said, "some of them will come back with nightmares they can't talk about. And here I am, making a stink in Pétiot's nostrils and losing the army contract so I can't help them.—Let's get on with it. Let's get to Montfort."

Chapter 85

When Cyron reached Montfort, he found Lucien Pétiot already there, standing in the courtyard, directing the soldiers.

It was the first time Cyron had been back to the castle since Sabine's funeral. She was still so here, as if she were around the corner. He had almost seen her, a flash of blonde, her soft little nasal voice. It had been a window closing, shrieking dry in the heat, or a bird crying. In a moment she would come truly into the center of his vision. But when he turned his head, she wasn't there.

Weeds were poking up between the paving-stones of the terrace. Where the grass had been plowed up by cars or carts waved blood-red poppies, the weeds of Flanders, taking root in the churned-up earth.

Methodically, from one tower to another, groups of Pétiot's soldiers were searching the buildings. It was so quiet. The sun hammered the courtyard. The men made barely a sound.

"Go home, Maurice," his friend said quietly. "I'll let you know."

Cyron squinted; the soldiers were armed with revolvers. "Surely—" he protested.

"A dangerous madman, Maurice. I'm sorry. I know he's
~ son."

r of the courtyard lay two enormous boxes, fresh
like the coffin of a beheaded giant. The guillotine

410

had been brought here from Arras. In the sun the pine smelled sharp and resinous. Cyron was suddenly back in 1870, the day he had been wounded, going up toward the line. He had passed a wagonload of coffins, smelling like that in the heat. "What do we want that here for?" Cyron said sharply. Around the guillotine the ground was red with flowers. Under a tarpaulin, the electrical ventilation fan was waiting to go back to the mines. It brought her all back, all the hopes he had had for her. He could see her blonde hair shining with Krauss' lights behind it. He had imagined once that she would bring André into line—ah, she could have done it if anyone could, sweet and stubborn Sabine. He had been half in love with her himself. When he'd thought of André's marriage to her, he had pictured himself and Sabine at the breakfast table, with André somewhere else.

More than half in love, perhaps. And André had killed her.

Cyron knew André had killed her. Somehow, some way, André had perverted the theatre. *His* theatre, Cyron's magic, Cyron's greatest weapon against the enemy. André had used it to kill his wife, to destroy his unborn child, to destroy everything Cyron had wanted. Theatre is an art. André had made it a guillotine.

Cyron went inside. Upstairs, he looked into his own room, then, hardening his heart, he opened Sabine's door. For a moment he thought he smelled flowers, her perfume, and then the dusty heat of an unused room overpowered it. Powder dusted her dresser and her box of jewelry had been rifled, spilled open. An amber necklace, an enamel bracelet for a little wrist.

"D—n you, boy," Cyron choked.

He closed her door and went back to his own room. But from his window he could see the army boys searching the stables. He went into André's room instead, looking for some clue to how everything could have gone so wrong.

It didn't seem like the room of a madman; it looked like Cyron's office at the theatre. André had a camp bedstead in one corner of the room, but the rest was all about the film. Notes on costumes. Budgets and schedules. Rehearsal times, costume preparation, scene paintings, props. The scenario, annotated with the shots André wanted.

In one corner of the study, on a table, André had set up the old puppet theatre Cyron had given him. Cyron grasped the frame of one of the puppets, an Alsatian soldier. He stood up with it. He made it salute and march, and then for a moment he rocked its frame and began to make it dance. Those first days Cyron had known him, the only thing that had amused the boy had been listening to stories and seeing the puppet dance. A grimace gripped Cyron's face, the beginnings of too much sorrow in his muscles and his skin, and he dropped the frame and kicked the puppet underneath the table. I showed him the theatre, Cyron thought.

Beside the puppet theatre was a pile of scrapbooks. Cyron opened one, expecting to see André's record of his theatre.

But everything in the scrapbooks was about him, Cyron.

There were no reviews, only interviews with him in theatrical journals, introductions he had written for plays. Interspersed with them were notes in André's hand, memos of a discussion they had had about *Le Cid*, something he had said about pacing. Cyron flipped through the pages, dismayed, horrified. Cyron had been a soldier first, then a sensation, above all a message. None of it had been an end in itself. But here it was: André had thought of him as an actor.

He wanted these scrapbooks full of André's military career. He wanted them kept by André's wife. He sat down helpless in the chair by the puppet theatre, the wrong life spread ⸮ ⸮nees in dusty brittle pieces of paper.

⸮actor, boy. I stood for something. I belonged to

Outside André's windows, a truck was coming through the Jerusalem Gate. Cyron could just see the side panel of the truck. A life-size André capered on the painted boards, pointing out the gilded, blood-dripping name of the theatre: the Grand Necropolitan.

"What now?" he said, heartsick. "What?"

He stumped downstairs.

By the time he got outside, the courtyard was full of people. A couple of men in caps, a short man smoking a cigar, two women. He recognized Reisden's baby, and then he saw Reisden at the corner of the truck.

Reisden. He might have known Reisden would be alive too. He looked thin, half-starved, and he turned and stared at Cyron almost feverishly, with the intensity of a man at the front. Cyron wouldn't go to meet him; Reisden squared his shoulders and came forward.

"You sicken me, boy," Cyron said. "If you've come to apologize I won't hear it. You ruined him. You couldn't help him. 'He's not mad, he won't hurt her,' " Cyron mimicked Reisden, giving him the Austrian drawl he'd had once. "See what you did. He killed her."

"He didn't kill her," Reisden said.

"You lie and you're a coward," Cyron said.

Lucien Pétiot was at their elbows. "What is this, why are you here?"

"We've come to help you search," Reisden said.

"Nobody needs your help," Cyron said.

"We don't need help. This is no place for civilians. Your wife, Reisden, your baby—!"

Cyron looked toward the crowd that had come with Reisden. They had moved onto the terrace to get out of the heat. By the front door stood an old man holding Reisden's baby in his arms. It was the same white-haired man who had come when Reisden was sick, and the two of them together, the old man and the child, looked like Reisden in old age, Reisden as a baby. Binny is dead and the baby she would have had, and André is dead to me, Cyron thought; and yet Reisden parades his son who looks like him and this man who looks like him, to me, as if I had no heart.

"Leave us alone."

"You've more chance of capturing André with our help than hunting him out." Reisden looked toward the hillside. Thirty soldiers at least, a long irregular blue line like a shadow on the grass. "Guns, Cyron; what are the guns for?"

"Go away."

"After I ask you one question." Reisden looked at Pétiot. "Alone."

"Wait in Arras if you like," Pétiot said.

"Alone," Reisden said.

"You should have treated André like the child he was," Cyron said bitterly. "You should have supported me when I tried to make him a man. Now he's killed her."

"Supported you in what, Cyron?" Reisden said quietly. "Making him a murderer, when he's not? Neither André nor Jules had anything to do with killing Sabine, which you should know as well as I. Pétiot is hunting them *with guns*."

"What should I know, why should I know?" The guns bothered him too. He wasn't going to say so to Reisden. "What do you think I know?" He guessed, looking at the hot dark eyes. "You think I know someone else killed my Binny, and I'm letting them go?"

He saw a flicker of uncertainty cross Reisden's face.

"Where is he, if you're going to help us find him? *You owe me that.* I married Binny off to him, and he killed her." He wanted to wail, to scream into the sky, white as a blind man's eyes, until Fate took pity on him and brought her back. "Do you know what you've done, boy?"

"Cyron," Reisden said. He was white-faced. "You have the

castle now. You'll have all of Sabine's money. *But you can't have André.* I won't let you do it. You cannot have André shot and give your big curtain speech about justice prevailing, the way you do in your plays. You bloody well aren't the hero here."

"Don't you care about *her*?" Cyron asked. "Don't you care who killed her? *Your* friend, your *patient*—"

"No," Reisden said.

"Then who? Who do you think?" Cyron said.

Reisden looked into his eyes, trying to stare him down or something. Cyron stared back. "Who?" said Cyron. "Who?"—and he understood how full of self-delusion the boy was. "You failed, you didn't even know he was as sick as he was. And now?" Cyron gestured to Pétiot. "Lucien. This boy, this *excuse* for *nothing*, he wants to blame Sabine's— Sabine's—" He could not say *murder*, not even *death*. "On me. Isn't it funny?"

He left them and stumped up the stairs to the terrace. He brushed past the people Reisden had brought. The last one was the old man with Reisden's baby; him Cyron shoved aside. Isn't it funny? The fools flourish.

He made his way blindly up the stairs to the privacy of the second floor.

Chapter 86

"Are you insane?" Pétiot asked Reisden.

Cyron didn't do it, Reisden thought. Cyron was just disappearing through the French doors, shoving aside Gilbert and Toby.

Cyron said he didn't. Reisden wanted to believe him. That didn't mean it was true.

Pétiot was glaring at him with concentrated anger. "Look at me. Where is André?"

Who could have killed her, if he didn't? "I don't know."

"You knew André was alive—how long ago? I thought you and I were on the same side. You should have told me he was alive. Immediately."

"I went to see my wife, immediately."

Pétiot gestured. "All these people. What do you mean by bringing all these people?"

"Fauchard's sister, people from the Necro; they want to see André."

"They'll only distress themselves."

"This is your manhunt?"

"This is my attempt to control things," Pétiot said. "To clean up the mess you made. I have to protect Maurice."

"Do you think Cyron needs protecting?"

"From the newspapers! We're in the middle of a national crisis." Pétiot lowered his voice. "And Maurice is a national symbol. In the middle of his personal sorrow, he's speaking in front of manufacturers, talking about the necessity of cutting ties with German companies, producing supplies for the army. But all it takes is one heckler. 'Have the police caught your son, the murderer?' " Pétiot mimicked grimly. " 'What happens if we don't want to support war production—the *guillotine*?' I want André caught."

Six weeks to conquer France. Reisden took a breath and burned his bridges. "André didn't do it."

"I honestly don't care."

"So you're hunting him down, is that it? No. No, Pétiot. Four people have died already. I will not let you hunt André and Jules."

Pétiot simply looked at him. "Do you know how many people have died in Morocco this week?—I thought I could work with you. I'm sorry."

They followed the searchers. Ruthie and Katzmann, Eli Krauss, and the technicians walked behind the line of soldiers, calling out *André! Jules!* Ruthie pinned her hat on her head and clambered up on the ramparts, cupping her hands into a megaphone. "Juley! Count André!" Reisden walked down the hill to the New Buildings, which were locked, then back up the slope to the Lion Gate. He wanted to make sure André saw he was here. If André was here.

The young soldiers kept on, methodically quartering the landscape of Montfort. They were sweating through their tunics. Reisden recognized some of them from the battle scene. They did not seem to be searching the house. Reisden got in, on the excuse of washing his hands, and looked round the first floor, which was shadowy and dusty and deserted, but had been thoroughly searched.

He went outside and sat in the shadow of the stables with Perdita and Toby. Gilbert came and sat down beside them.

"Cyron told me, 'You should have been a parent to André,' " Reisden said. " 'You should have made him grow up.' I was too much on André's side. Cyron was William to me; he was controlling, he was a moral bully, and I could think only 'André's in danger.' "

Gilbert nodded soberly.

"I hope André and Jules have left Montfort." Elphinstone came up, panting, and dropped down by Gilbert's feet. "They're not in the cellars. It would be the first place Pétiot's men would look."

Ruthie came over and sat with them, fanning her face with her hat. She was pink, distressed. Reisden took a look at her, remembering her lying in the field. "Go into the house and drink some water," he said.

"I am all right. I don't understand why anyone should think Count André could have done anything to the guillotine! Jules and you and I checked it. Nothing was wrong with it!"

"Ruthie," he said, "France needs someone to blame."

She looked at him open-mouthed, betrayed by his tone of voice. She gathered her skirts, got up, and left without another word.

Reisden walked with the soldiers, walking for the last time over the bumpy, chalky fields. The heat gathered toward midafternoon. Above them the white sky became a searchlight, a coppery glare. They all stopped for water, sitting down in the shadow of a blockhouse. "Neither Jules nor André is dangerous," Reisden said.

When he came back to the courtyard, he saw the technicians putting together the guillotine. Ruthie was directing them, wiping sweat off her face.

"What are you doing?" he asked her.

"Look, see, Count André could not have done anything to this," Ruthie said. "He was much too far away."

Pétiot came out of the house to look at it. "Take that down."

"No! Look, General." Pétiot turned on his heel. "Put it all together, every bit of it," Ruthie said. The sweating technicians hammered together the platform, then set the uprights in their places and secured them. The platform had been roughly washed, but the planks were brown with dried blood-stains. Ruthie shuddered and dumped pail after pail of water from the kitchen over the planks, into the machine.

"The blade too, miss?"

The men lifted the blade out of its box. Blood flaked from its edge. Eli Krauss, watching from the ground, took a step back and put his hands behind him.

Finally it was all complete, tall, narrow, garish, standing in the courtyard at Montfort. Behind the French windows in the dining room, two shadows moved.

"See!" Ruthie said. She made her way up the narrow stairs. "Here was my brother, sitting just here," she shouted toward the shadows of Cyron and Pétiot. She put her hand on the top step. "And here was Count André: Look, ten, eleven, twelve steps away from the platform. Twelve long steps. How could either of them have done anything?"

From inside the house, curtains slid closed over the French windows.

They looked over the mechanism. It was simple enough: levers, a latch. Threads of blood-stiff material still clogged the main lever. Ruthie picked them out with the point of her sewing scissors. Under the brown stains Reisden could see blue, white, and red. They hooked the bunting onto the plat-form. It hung down almost to the ground in gaudy swags and strips, concealing everything behind it. At the back of the platform they found a strip torn from the bottom of the bunting.

"You see?" Ruthie said. "Anyone must see! The person who stuffed the material into the mechanism must have done it from back here. Count André was out in front. My brother was on the platform. It wasn't possible for them to do it!"

Chapter 87

"I will not leave my Toby out here in the sun." Perdita marched in and took possession of the kitchen. There were no servants at Montfort; no one stopped her. She had brought food: cheese, bread, sausage, wine, food for Toby. While Toby crawled around the cool kitchen flagstones after Elphinstone, she and Ruthie and Uncle Gilbert made up plates for people. Being polite—being awfully, very polite—she took a plate in to Monsieur Cyron, negotiating the minefield of things scattered on the floor of his office, wondering if she was feeding a murderer.

"Let my husband find your André," she said to him as she left the food.

"Go away, all of you."

"I would think," she said, "I'd think that *you* would want to know where André is. *You* would want to help André."

She heard her plate of food smashing on the floor.

"He laughed when she died," André's father said. "I will never forget that. Never."

Could he have killed Sabine and say that?

While Perdita fed Toby, Ruthie tiptoed upstairs to search. She came back from Sabine's room with a tin box that had held chocolates. "Smell inside." Under the chocolate Perdita smelled old fires, traces of strange herbs, leather, grease. "That was the books," Ruthie said, "but they're gone."

Ruthie scraped out the firebox of the enormous two-ovened kitchen stove. Deep in the grate among the clinkers she found a scrap of burned leather.

"What about Mademoiselle Françoise's order book?" Perdita asked. It would show Sabine ordering mourning before her father was dead.

They sent one of the technicians in the truck to Arras. He came back with the order book.

But the page with Sabine's order had been torn out. It was gone too.

At the end of the afternoon, the soldiers found the men.

The soldiers had been working their way through the abbey, poking sticks into every hole. They had climbed the towers. They had almost finished, some of them had started on the stables, when one of the soldiers took a second look at the half-ruined, re-roofed side chapel, and saw the iron door.

Reisden was in the chapel. He had time only to see that the key was gone from above the door before one of the soldiers pulled the door open.

Jules was crouched by a pile of coffins. André exploded through the door, running, knocking aside chairs. The soldier drew his gun. "No!" Reisden ran after André, tackled him, brought him down hard on the marble pavement. "Don't say a word, André," Reisden muttered, lips by André's ear, "not a bloody word."

"He lied," André whispered. "It's not a real tunnel."

"I know. Don't say anything."

He manhandled André to his feet, standing close by him. They were surrounded by a ring of guns.

The soldiers handcuffed André and frog-marched him across the courtyard. Jules they half-dragged behind, the center of another knot of guards. Pétiot came bustling out of the house to meet them. Behind him was Cyron.

"I'm sorry to see this," Pétiot said. "I really am, Monsieur le Comte." André stared over Pétiot's head at Cyron, too, seeing perhaps what Reisden saw. André was grey with dust, his long hair was tangled, he was smiling a wide-eyed, twitching smile, no more than a stretching of the lips. His mouth had been cut when he fell. Blood ran down his chin onto his shirt.

"Hello, *Papa* Cyron. What will happen to me now?"

"Bring him into the house," Pétiot said, moving between André and Cyron as if André were something infectious. "In—" He hesitated for a moment, obviously at a loss for someplace to put André.

"The old dispensary, in the stables," André said. "Papa used to put his medicines there. There are bars on the windows and a door that locks." He smiled, weird, wild, helpful.

Jules, mute, struggled with his captors and got his hands free. He pointed to the guillotine, then to himself. I pulled the rope—I, not André! "Yes, you too," Pétiot said, shaking his head. "Put him someplace else," he said to the soldiers.

André thinks about Jules, but mostly André thinks about Papa Cyron, Papa Cyron's eyes not meeting his, Papa Cyron's mouth turning down like a sick man's.

"Dispensary," Reisden says, understanding what André has only half spelled out to himself. "Are there still medicines in it?" There are. Reisden takes a box into the little room and fills the box with bottles. André, guarded, sees the box pass him, sees faded skulls and crossbones on the labels. Mother, he thinks, and knows how people commit suicide out of despair. He knows what is going to happen, he read it in Papa Cyron's eyes and in Reisden's. He doesn't know when, how long, whether it will be painful.

It is like when Sabine gave him the poison. Eventually there is nothing else to do.

The soldiers shove him inside the dispensary, a little pantrylike stone room with wooden shelves. The bars on the window are ancient, square, rusted; the door is barred, so that André can see out into the stables. The room is filthy, covered in dust; dust motes make the light yellow. André goes over to the window. Outside he can see, on the left, the wall of es-paliered grapes and the kitchen garden. On the right is the guillotine.

Beyond the guillotine, parked on the grass, he can see the Necro's truck, and on the side is Necrosar, dancing and point-ing. Only a painted thing. Necrosar would be good to keep him company through this; Necrosar would say it's only a play.

But all he has is Reisden. Reisden brings in two chairs. The soldiers lock the door. Reisden sits on one of the chairs, back-to-front, with his arms on the back, looking up at him. André stands by the window, then goes to the barred door. The sol-diers are just outside. He stares at them, and Reisden gets up and does, too, until they move halfway down the long stables.

André comes back to the window and motions Reisden to stand by him.

"They came here last night," he says in a low voice. "Began hunting us at dawn. I shouldn't have frightened Roselle—I thought *he'd* come. He sent Pétiot. I'm frightened."

"You'll be taken to Arras, probably tonight," Reisden says, reasonable, reasonable. "Tomorrow morning you'll be ques-tioned. You'll be sent to jail or to a guarded asylum. That's all that will happen for now."

Reisden is being kind to him or thinks he's an idiot. André touches his mouth. It stings and his hand comes away bloody. "I want a bath. If I were cleaner Papa Cyron might think he could trust me."

"I'll stay with you," Reisden says. "We're all here. Every-thing will be all right."

You do think I'm an idiot, André thinks. "I picked the lock on the tunnel," he whispers. "Scratches, scratches, all around the lock. So Papa Cyron knows."

At the corner of Reisden's jaw a muscle jumps, and then his face goes completely wooden, blank, almost stolid. André knows how Reisden uses his face, André's put it on stage. Reisden isn't showing what he's thinking but he's not able to show anything else.

"He *could* trust me," André says; it's Papa Cyron he's saying it to, Reisden is only a convenient ear. "It's true I'm—a little odd—but I wouldn't tell the Germans." It's his house, after all, his countryside the secret is protecting. "If I ever wanted to say *the tunnel doesn't exist*"—he puts his face in the corner, against the cold stone—"I'd say it like this." He whispers to the wall, but what he whispers is something else.

Papa Cyron is going to murder me.

Papa Cyron needs his tunnel. Which doesn't exist. And poor odd André knows it.

Murderers are ordinary, André realizes. He has got it wrong in his theatre; the Necro vampires, the eviscerators, the ax murderers are comedy. This is real life, and there is no difference between the heroes and the villains and the victims. He and Papa Cyron used to eat breakfast together, and Reisden's a murderer, Reisden who does paperwork in the train and acts and has a little boy he loves.

That's the only way André wants to think of murder now, that it's an accident that happens to ordinary people. So it might be something that happens to him and Papa Cyron. It's nobody's fault. If it hadn't been for the tunnel, it might not have happened to them.

"Tell him to trust me. I won't tell." André sits down on the chair. He is so frightened that he needs to rock back and forth; he puts his hands between his knees and squeezes them, but his mind is perfectly clear.

"I won't leave you."

André turns around and looks at Reisden. Reisden is trying to make both of them believe that everything will come out all right. Reisden is frightened of the dark with the guns in it, of the boy who pulled the trigger; he doesn't want anyone to pull the trigger again. But he won't say that Papa Cyron will trust André.

"Papa Cyron will put me in the asylum," André says to let Reisden know that he knows what will happen. "But he'll think, it isn't safe, the boy's insane, he'll say anything to anyone.—So—"

"I will make sure one of my people is with you."

"You can't watch all the time," André says impatiently. A month, a year, two years!

"I can." Reisden's mouth twists, André doesn't know why. "I will have resources for that."

How long? And all that time Papa Cyron will have to wait, and André will have to wait. And then . . . André thinks that Papa Cyron will bring him some bottle of wine, some delicacy. Something he particularly likes. He will take it, the way he took the candy from Sabine.

Papa Cyron won't want to do it. André has seen that in Papa Cyron's grimace. And André doesn't want to die. But they are tied together, Papa Cyron and he.

"We have a journalist friend. She's going to take up your case. We'll try you in the newspapers, André, and we'll prove you innocent."

"I said I would kill her," André says.

He looks out the window. It is a beautiful late afternoon. On the wall, the grapes are shaped by the shadows and the sun. On film they would look round enough to take in the hand. "I like making films," André says, "and I won't be able to make any more in the asylum. And I don't want to spend a long time frightened. So you don't have to prove me innocent."

"I'll prove her guilty," Reisden says.

That won't work. André has been watching her through the

camera lens for weeks. He sees her in the Ball of the Dead scene, blonde, terrified, attacked by monsters: innocent as a picture. "No one would believe it."

André looks out at the good strong light. He has wanted to photograph that last scene with Cyron; when he thought the tunnel was real, he thought he would make Cyron a hero. Now the scene could play better. "Ask him to finish my film," André says. "I want him to say *I did this for France*. Tell him when he plays that to think of the tunnel. He should think of all the things he never did." André, for a moment, thinks of all the things he never did. "And I want you to say *I forgive you, Papa*."

"I don't forgive him."

"And whatever you want to do for me, I want you to do it for Jules instead."

"No," says Reisden.

"Yes. If I say I killed her, Jules will be all right," André persists.

Reisden stands up and grabs him by the shoulders. "You're not alone in this!" he says. "If you roll over and let yourself get killed, I will blame you. If you think Jules will thank you for it, or Cyron's life will be better—And if he didn't kill her, then what did he do? Nothing? And you're going to confess to murder? And then what does he do, André? And how does he feel about it afterward? He hasn't done anything to you yet. Don't let him do it. Don't do it to him. Just don't."

It is almost funny. Reisden won't let Papa Cyron kill him. Reisden wants to save both of them.

"Don't give up. I'll talk with Cyron."

"What can you tell him?" André asks, curious.

"They want to avoid scandal; they simply want the whole thing over. If you're accused it won't be over. We have a journalist friend looking into Sabine's background. Milly Xico— you know her? And I'll put Jouvet's resources behind you."

"Jouvet won't have any resources," André says. "Papa Cyron will have bigger newspapers. Bigger friends."

"We'll be able to fight him," says Reisden. He looks grim. "I have resources if I need them."

"Tell him he can trust me," André says.

Chapter 88

The coppery sky greyed; the long twilight drew in. The soldiers set up their tents around the stables. From the east, lightning made the clouds glow and thunder muttered across the fields, but not even a breeze moved the air at Montfort. Reisden sat in the kitchen with Perdita and Gilbert, feeding Toby. Eli Krauss and Ruthie were on watch by André. Katzmann was upstairs with Jules.

Perdita told him about Ruthie's search upstairs. "The books are gone. Sabine's order for mourning is gone."

Reisden took a chance and used the telephone cabinet in the Great Hall to call Milly.

"Almost none of Sabine's school friends are in Paris," Milly said over the telephone line. The connection was bad; she sounded as if she were shouting through a windy sewer pipe. He could hear Nicky barking in the background. "They've all gone to the country. But I reached one."

"What?" he enunciated back.

"She's been got to! She said Sabine was the sweetest, kindest, most considerate girl she ever knew. She was shocked,

shocked that the poor girl's died. I saw two of her school-teachers. The same. Sweet. Kind. Considerate. Bah!"

"Will you keep trying?" he asked.

Milly would. Milly gave up for nobody.

"Dreyfus will win in the end," he told her.

"Dreyfus will win. But you should have been her dog," Milly said. "I'll lose my column over this.—Never mind, I'll live off my sweetie and write my book."

After he hung up, he stood in the Great Hall, thinking: not thinking, simply waiting, for inspiration, to be clever, anything. Halfway up the wall, the entrance of André's parents' room gaped like a wound.

Pétiot was standing by the kitchen door. He moved away when Reisden approached. He had been looking at Gilbert.

In the kitchen, Gilbert had rolled up his sleeves and was washing up. Perdita was sitting on the floor, playing ball with Toby. Elphinstone was following the ball with his eyes. "Gilbert?" Reisden gestured: Come outside.

The soldiers watched them from the stables. He led Gilbert past the guillotine, through the Lazarus Gate and the grave-yard in front of the great ruined abbey doors. They sat on the grass slope beyond the abbey, watching the low sun and the ribbons of water through the fields. He looked back; Pétiot was watching them from the crown of the hill.

"I thought Cyron might have killed Sabine," Reisden told Gilbert quietly. "It's simpler than that. Cyron's reputation needs to be protected. So Sabine's murder has to be solved quickly. André's the designated murderer, probably with Jules. I won't have it."

Gilbert nodded, slowly, understanding.

"I'll take up your offer of Thomas Robert's money."

"I am glad."

Reisden wasn't. He fell back on the grass, looking up into the sky. "I don't think either of us should be glad. How do we explain why you're helping me?"

"Because I think you are right?" Gilbert said. "Because Jouvet is a good company? It is, you know."

He turned his head to look at his uncle and smiled wryly. "Thank you for that."

Pétiot was coming down the hill toward them, half-sliding on the grass. He stood in front of them, looking from one to the other.

"There are two men guarding André," he said. "Two men from you."

"I hope I'm being foolish. Pétiot, have you met Gilbert Knight?"

"I can have you deported," Pétiot said, "and I will."

"I expect you can," Reisden said. He could have added, But you can't deport Gilbert. Not our American.

"Il est un bon homme," Gilbert said in his careful French to Pétiot.

"Why is he here?" Pétiot asked Reisden.

"Monsieur le comte de Montfort et Alexandre, ils sont deux bons hommes." Both good men.

Pétiot looked at Gilbert, stroked his beard, seemed about to say something, but then abruptly headed up the slope.

I will never again be entirely Alexander Reisden of Jouvet, Reisden thought. We look too much alike. He closed his eyes, too tired even to sit up.

"Alexander," Gilbert said. "From something Perdita said, I believed you might not mind if I were to stay in Paris. For longer than we originally thought. Is that—all right?"

"What do you think about it?" Reisden asked.

"What do you, Alexander?"

He thought one of them should have an opinion. "I've told you I'm glad to have you here." It was ungracious. "I'm sorry. You're being very useful. What's going to happen won't be pleasant, Gilbert. Pétiot means to sic the government on me. Do you want to stay?" This morning, when Gilbert had talked about leaving, Reisden hadn't wanted him to go. All he needed to say now was: Don't go. He opened and closed his mouth, struggling with words. "I wish this were easier," was all he could manage.

"I am here," Gilbert said.

"I want you here," Reisden said. "As long as you want to stay."

And, yes, it was the right thing to say, and it frightened him. He was tangled with the Knights again. "I can't think about this now," he said. "I have to think about André."

They went back to the château. In the kitchen, Perdita had bathed Toby and was drying him. Reisden stood at the door, feeling drained, watching Perdita tickle Toby and Toby giggling, loving it. Oh Toby. It was clear to him, perfectly clear, that he was betraying his son for his job.

Gilbert was looking at Toby too, then turned and looked at Reisden, apprehension in his eyes. Reisden smiled at him encouragingly, and to his surprise it was a real smile. "It's all right. We'll have each other; that's the good part."

He went upstairs to see Jules but stopped at the door. Katzmann was with him, sitting and listening; puffing at his cigar but being silent, receptive. Jules had got his neck brace off and was in a padded neck-collar. He could speak, barely, in a whisper. Reisden heard the murmur. He stepped back to avoid eavesdropping, but he heard some of it.

"It was late," Jules whispered. "We had to get the shot. I hit my marks. I'd measured everything. I know I stepped on the plank that released the catch. I thought I felt the click—"

Gaunt, miserable Jules held up the hands that had pulled the rope and stared at them. He had been an ordinary man. Now, for the rest of his life, he would envy the innocent world.

He has Jouvet, Reisden thought. At least he has Jouvet.

He waited a few minutes down the hall, watching the intensity of the confession, until Jules straightened up and sat back in his chair. Katzmann puffed at his cigar, stood, and was an ordinary man again, telling jokes, trying to cheer Jules up. Jules was asking if Katzmann thought he'd be deported. "And Ruthie?" Jules managed. Reisden knocked on the doorjamb.

"Do you want some sausage?"

"I do," said the soldier who was guarding Jules.

Jules made a spooning motion with his hand: something liquid? "Soup," Reisden guessed. "I'll bring some up."

He cut through the Great Hall toward the kitchen. It was almost dark by now. The light was on in Cyron's office. Reisden stopped by the door and saw Cyron sitting at his desk, among all the paraphernalia of his theatre, the Serpent Baa, the discarded wig on the bust of Napoléon, the linking rings dangling from his chair. Cyron's head was in his hands. On the desk lay a puppet, a broken Alsatian soldier, like a broken child.

Did you kill Sabine, Cyron? It didn't matter at this moment. Cyron might be a murderer; he was a father. Reisden had thought he had two patients. He had three.

The sausage would wait. Reisden brought in a chair from the Great Hall, moved the litter aside, and set the chair down. He stood in back of it, crossed his arms on the back, and talked to Cyron.

Chapter 89

"He's your son," said Reisden. "He's what you have, and he didn't kill Sabine. This is what will happen to him. He'll be taken to an asylum. He'll be tried. He'll be convicted. He'll either be guillotined or locked up for life. I may be able to save him." At a cost too high for my son to pay. "But that's not my job. It's yours."

"He killed Sabine." Cyron's face settled into stubborn, angry lines.

"Guillotined, Cyron, or locked up for life. And one day you'll hear that André's drowned in his bath, or committed suicide, and who knows and who cares, because in spite of who he is, André's not important and you are. He is being framed to keep you a national hero of France."

Cyron turned away impatiently.

"What are you a hero for if not for your son? All you have to do, Cyron, is to say you think he may be innocent. Tell Pétiot that it is important to you to protect him."

"No."

Reisden hadn't sat down. He stood behind the chair—keeping it between him and Cyron, as if Cyron were the lion he had to tame. Even now, Reisden thought, I think he's William. "I am a father and so are you. Even if I thought Toby were guilty, I wouldn't put him through what André is going through. He doesn't know whether someone will kill him tonight or whether it'll take months."

"I'm not his father," Cyron said.

"What's the puppet for?" Reisden said.

Cyron looked down at the desk. "It was my father's. I broke it today. You've got what you want. I have no children." Cyron picked up the puppet. It hung between his hands, a dead thing.

"You need to save him."

"Go away, boy."

"We can all ruin each other, Cyron," Reisden said, and felt it was the wrong thing to say. "If your reputation is so precious that I have to ruin it, I will."

Cyron laid the puppet aside and opened the drawer of his desk. He pulled a gun out of it and held it in his hand, his finger against the trigger. It was an old army revolver, standard issue, from the army of 1870.

"Don't talk to me about loyalty, boy, because this is what I mean by loyalty. I shot men with this. I didn't want to. But I'm a soldier of France." Cyron held the gun loosely, pointing toward Reisden. "Don't you play around with me, don't you tell me he didn't do it. I don't care about my reputation except that it does some good, but *he killed her and I didn't*, so don't you threaten me."

Reisden brought his hands up slowly and tented them in front of him on the back of the chair, where Cyron could see them. Other than that he didn't move. The gun was unlikely to be loaded, he told himself. No one keeps a loaded gun in a drawer.

He watched Cyron's finger curl and half-tighten around the trigger. Cyron turned the gun away for a moment and kneaded his right hand with his left. The knuckles of both hands were white and gnarled with tension. "Walk out of here, boy," Cyron said. "Now."

And if Reisden did, that would be the end of André, of Jules, of Cyron too, though he didn't know it. Reisden thought of his family, of Jouvet, of the half-finished conversation with Gilbert. He was beginning to know how one needs families. And here he was, taking it into his work and risking everything, talking to a man with a gun.

Why he had thought Perdita was risky, he didn't know. "Threatening me wouldn't help," he said levelly. "I wrote a letter." There was no letter; it was a bluff. "I wouldn't come to accuse you, Cyron, without leaving a letter. I sent it to several friends, to be opened in the event of my death or André's. What's in it is not necessarily true, but if I'm dead it will be believed. Even if you produce the proof it isn't, Cyron. Gehazy knew. It didn't have to be true. Only scandalous."

Cyron braced his gun hand with the other and pointed it at him. Talk, Reisden told himself, and make it good.

"What's in this letter?" Cyron said. "That I killed her? Why?"

"If you didn't kill her, who did?" Reisden asked, which was what he wanted to know.

"What did you say about me?"

Reisden looked around the office. Leo had taught him how to think on his feet. Testimonials, photographs, medals. An Alsatian puppet. Wigs and props and a magic serpent. And then he realized one thing that wasn't there. He had known André and Cyron fourteen years; he had seen Cyron's office, his house, Montfort. He had never seen it. He had read about Cyron, all the hagiography. He had never read about the one moment that should be there. He thought of Katzmann, of Jules and Ruthie, of how he and Perdita would remember becoming French citizens, if he lived to do it. He took a chance.

"You were being blackmailed," Reisden said. "By Ferenc Gehazy."

Cyron puffed out his lips: Bah, for what?

"Remember it's not necessarily true, only scandalous— Because of your citizenship. You come from Alsace," Reisden said. "When the Germans captured Alsace, the French conceded the country but not the people. Any Alsatian could move to France and declare himself still a French citizen." He had read of it among the piles of naturalization information he and Perdita had got. "They called it opting for France."

Cyron frowned.

"The last date to opt for France was 1 October 1872. But from 1870 to 1874, you and your men were in hiding. During that time you were digging a tunnel into the German munitions store of the Citadel—the tunnel's still there, I think I've seen it. On 1 October 1872, you were just about to dig inside the Citadel wall. You were under the maneuvers field, scraping out dirt by teaspoons.

"What day did you opt for France? Katzmann remembers his family going to make their declaration. His mother dressed them all in mourning."

"I don't remember the day," Cyron said.

"Katzmann has his certificate framed in his kitchen. Jules and Ruthie are political refugees too; they have their certificates of citizenship framed in the front hall. Where's yours?"

"I was always French," Cyron said. "Not like them."

"But you did opt for France," Reisden said.

"Of course."

"At Arras, was it?"

"Of course at Arras."

"There'll be a record in the town hall, then."

"You're examining me as if I were a criminal."

"It must have been very dramatic. Sergeant Cyron, the guerrilla leader, making his declaration of loyalty to France at the risk of his life. I'm surprised it wasn't in your first play." He was being sarcastic. "I'm sorry. I mean that. It would have taken courage."

Cyron shook his head angrily.

"It would have been humiliating as well," Reisden said.

"Katzmann said he felt robbed of his identity. One shouldn't have to say one was French."

Cyron half-nodded. His face had fallen into bleak folds.

"Which is why you didn't do it then," Reisden said. "Katzmann's family didn't declare for France until the Dreyfus affair. They were always thinking, 'Wait a year, wait a year, Alsace will be free.' They waited more than twenty years."

By now the house was quiet. Upstairs, in another world, someone was running water. From outside, in the fields and the pond, the frogs were making a sound like scraped nerves. Cyron looked straight at him. An old man's wrinkled potato face, a big nose, no chin, the typical French workingman's face that can be so ordinary or so extraordinarily spiritual.

"You never did it," Reisden said, "did you?"

Cyron's eyes darkened. He had guessed right.

The current German ambassador to Paris was even more of a propaganda master than Izvolsky. He wouldn't quarrel with Cyron's assertion that he was French. He would simply take a box at the Théâtre Cyron and fill it with enthusiastic blond Aryans. Ah, yes, Cyron. One of ours.

"Why should I apply for what was mine, boy?" Cyron said.

"But it isn't yours," Reisden said. "You're German. The way my wife is Austrian, who's American, and I'm Austrian, who am Parisian. —I don't want to harm you." That was true, more true than Cyron knew. "But I want you to use your influence to save your son. He didn't kill Sabine. Someone else did it, or it was an accident. You do not have to solve it this way."

Cyron was still looking up at him, but his hands moved; his right hand reached into the drawer of his desk and brought out a box of bullets. He began loading them into the gun.

"I'll take my chances on the letters."

There were no letters. Cyron reached out without looking and found the wig on Napoléon's bust. He held it over the muzzle of the revolver. It would muffle the sound.

"Don't kill me," Reisden said. He thought he was telling Cyron everything he had learned from twenty-five years of being a murderer: Don't do it. I know what I am supposed to be doing now, he said silently. I am beginning to know. Don't kill me now— He realized he was pleading.

"At least tell me what really happened." He was playing for time, time to think, perhaps just time. "Did you kill Sabine?" he asked.

"André killed her."

"No. Who killed Gehazy?"

"I don't know. Do you think I know?"

"Did he blackmail you? Did you kill him?"

Cyron looked down at the gun and back up at Reisden. When you are about to shoot a man, you don't look at the gun, you look at the man; but you look at the gun beforehand to make certain it's ready. "No," Cyron said. "I didn't kill him."

"You said Gehazy was working for the Austrians," Reisden said. "He wasn't. If he had been, he wouldn't have blackmailed me. For five years the Austrians have been trying to get Jouvet patients' records from me; they wouldn't compromise that by doing this. Gehazy was working for someone else. Who was blackmailing you through him?"

Cyron's eyes flickered with a momentary uncertainty.

"I think it was the Germans. They used him too, and the Germans want the secret of Montfort, this famous whatever-it-is, which you would know. He came to you. He said he knew you were German. You agreed to give him the secret, which Pétiot wanted passed to the Germans. But the secret couldn't come from you," Reisden said, "because a hero can't be a traitor."

"This is all in your letter?"

Reisden was saying anything, like Scheherazade, telling stories to hold death at bay, looking for a way out. "You asked him to appear to blackmail another person," Reisden said.

"Jules. But Jules did two unexpected things: He went to me and his sister first, and then he came to you. Jules is an honest man. He can't lie without friends to help him. He was careful that whatever he said about Montfort wouldn't be the truth. So he was no good to you.

"So Jules was removed in favor of me. A more believable spy, who couldn't afford to be blackmailed. I was supposed to find something in the cellars." He thought of the Ball of the Dead party. "I didn't cooperate either. I wasn't going to pass the information; Pétiot knew that before I did. Gehazy may have known it too. He was around when I became— uncooperative—with Leo."

Cyron was listening. Cyron was listening, Reisden realized, as if some of this was making him think. What?

"Pétiot had to pass the secret to the Germans. The Germans wanted it. But there was no one to pass it. I think Gehazy asked still another person, or asked someone again. Who? You? And then Gehazy disappeared."

Cyron shook his head. "I didn't kill him."

"I don't say you did. I say he was a problem for you and he disappeared. You didn't have to do anything. Pétiot protects your reputation; the army protects your reputation; they want you making speeches and appearing on cigaret cards, not shooting blackmailers."

The two words hung in the air. Shooting blackmailers. You don't have to do anything to me, Reisden thought at him. Something will happen to me without your shooting me.

"André is a problem for you now," Reisden went on, keeping his voice quiet and level. "Just as Gehazy might have been. This afternoon there were thirty nervous conscripts with guns out in your fields, hunting him like a rabbit. You think nothing will happen to André in prison. It will."

"He killed Sabine," Cyron said.

"If he is suspected of it and dies, it's convenient for you. But he didn't."

"Who are you accusing? Lucien Pétiot? You think Pétiot wants to kill André so I can appear on cigaret cards?"

War is the worst kind of melodrama. There are no motives. This one knows too much, that one makes me nervous, he has too many strong friends. I don't like his sort. I need room to breathe. Murder without motives. I think André is going to die, Reisden thought, because you built a plaster tunnel, a stage set for spies, instead of a fortress; because you were a hero and not hero enough.

"I think Gehazy died because he threatened your reputation," Reisden said. "I think Jules was attacked because he was in the way."

"What about Françoise Auclart?" Cyron asked unexpectedly. "What did she do?"

"I don't know." She got in Sabine's way.

"She died by accident," Cyron said. "They all—It had nothing to do with me."

So you did wonder about her, Reisden thought. "She was the niece of one of your men," he said. Cyron nodded. You wondered about her, Reisden thought, the way you wondered about Gehazy. You think André killed Sabine. But what did Françoise Auclart do, the niece of one of your men?

"You couldn't ask about her, could you?" Reisden said. "Not when everything else was happening so conveniently. How many things have happened conveniently for you, Cyron?"

Cyron looked up at him sharply.

"You have a good reputation, and you use it for France, and it's protected. Can you control that protection? Can you give it to André? Cyron, what's going to happen to André? Blantire died. Gehazy died. Jules and Ruthie almost died. Françoise Auclart died.—Cyron," he said, "what about Sabine?"

Cyron opened his mouth as if he were about to say

something, and then stood up, pushing himself up with his hands on his desk, the gun hand and the other. Standing, he raised the gun and pointed it at Reisden.

"Sabine was a danger to you," Reisden said very quietly.

Cyron's lips moved. What do you mean, he might have said. Tell me. But if he had asked anything, he would no longer have been protected.

"Everything Ruthie said, everything André said about her, was true. She had got involved with a group that met in the boves. Your man Auclart was part of it; so was Françoise. Sabine's child may have been Blantire's. She would have been a scandal for you."

Cyron shook his head as if he couldn't speak. The gun wavered, then pointed dead straight at Reisden. Did she tell you she was leaving André, Reisden wondered; did you tell anyone else? But that wasn't what he said.

"There are two ways to treat any human being," he said, "as something and as someone. Things can be bought and sold. Things can be sacrificed. Someone decided Sabine could be sacrificed for her money and your reputation, and made her a thing. That never ends; I knew Leo; I know.—And now André will die for your reputation unless you tell whoever is doing this that he is not a thing to you, he is your son, and he cannot be sacrificed. Put your reputation on the table; put who you are; put everything. Be his father. Be his family. Save him, or André will be nothing but cards on the table, money spent to protect you, and he'll die. The way Sabine died. For you."

Cyron's mouth opened. He looked as if he were about to howl. It was theatrical, stagy, the prelude to a big speech, a vast indignation, an accusation, something that would put the attention back on him in the right way. One gunshot would stop the enemy propaganda that was pouring into his head, would turn him back into a hero. Reisden could see the broken veins in Cyron's eyes, the blank circle of the gun barrel; thought of William; thought of Toby and André; thought of Gilbert and Perdita, and what he had missed.

"Monsieur!" It was a voice from the doorway. *"Ne tuez le pas. Ne tuez le pas! Il est mon fils."*

It was Gilbert. Gilbert and Elphinstone. Gilbert came into Cyron's office and took Reisden's arm, watching Cyron and the gun all the time with horrified eyes, and pulled Reisden out of the room, into the dark hall, into safety.

Chapter 90

H e and Gilbert went out onto the terrace. Reisden stood in the darkness, leaning against the still-warm stones of the house. He was shaking with nerves. If he'd had a cigaret he would have taken up smoking again. Elphinstone came up and licked his hand.

"That was interesting."

"Alexander—"

"I pushed him further than I should have."

"Yes, you did," said Gilbert with surprising vehemence.

We sound alike, Reisden thought. We say things in the same way. Or perhaps we have just learned it from each other. Against the sky the guillotine was a vague bulk, blackness against blackness, with the shimmer of starlight along the triangular blade.

"Why did you call me your son?" Reisden asked.

"I— You had been speaking of his son. I was in the hall, taking Elphinstone out. You sounded distraught.—I saw him pointing the gun at you."

"Cyron wouldn't help André." For a moment he simply felt desolated by it. "I couldn't persuade him. I couldn't blackmail him. Nothing."

He felt exposed outside, like a target, and Gilbert by being with him was exposed too. They went back into the house. Gilbert stood between him and the Great Hall like a shield. They both went into the kitchen. Perdita was standing by sleeping Toby, frightened, her face white as milk.

"I heard you both shouting in the hall," she said, "and then nothing."

He took her in his arms. "Cyron has invited us to stay the night, though he doesn't know it. Take Toby, we're going upstairs."

He found a bedroom overlooking the courtyard. It was the room with the angel bed. He locked the door. From the deep window seat he could see the stables and the guillotine.

"What are we looking for?" Perdita fit herself next to him on the window seat. He appreciated the *we*.

"We're looking after André." We're hiding, he thought. The door was thick old oak. Not easy to shoot through. The lock was sturdy. He tried to tell himself he was not frightened.

Perdita wasn't wearing her blind watch, which would have told them the time. Toby woke up, found himself in a strange room yet again, poor child, and began to weep. Perdita held him and Reisden held them both, thinking protective thoughts.

"Alexander?" Gilbert said quietly.

Cyron was in the courtyard.

He came all alone out into the courtyard, holding a dark lantern so closed down that they could not see it was he until he stood in front of the guillotine and held the lantern up. Reisden handed Toby off to Perdita and leaned forward on the window seat. Cyron didn't look at the mechanism. He looked at the posts of the scaffold, gaily decorated with tricolor bunting. He stood in front of the posts and held up the lantern so that, if the posts had been soldiers, he could have seen their faces.

On the day Sabine had been killed, two men had stood there, two soldiers from Pétiot's staff, guarding the guillotine. No one had looked at them, of course. They were not actors, they were not important; Reisden could not even remember their faces. One had had a reddish moustache that had looked incongruous with his wig.

Light spilled over the courtyard. Someone had turned on the light in the small dining room. Pétiot bustled out onto the terrace, little Papa Pétiot in his blue uniform, his white hair and beard ruffled. He laid his hand on Cyron's arm solicitously.

And Cyron drew back, though not much, and in his face there was an unutterable shocked weariness, like a soldier who has seen too much of the war.

They negotiated on the terrace, out of sight. From above, Reisden could hear André's name but very little else. The voices died away.

I have done what I could, Reisden thought.

Perdita put Toby down to sleep on the bed, between two pillows, but the three of them stayed on watch. In case anything else should happen, perhaps; because they did not want to leave each other.

He began to tell them what had happened, softening it somewhat— And then, realizing what he was doing, he took a deep breath and told it in all its sad complexity.

"A soldier killed Sabine?" Perdita whispered.

"Why could he not apply for citizenship?" Gilbert asked.

"Will he save André?" Perdita asked.

Perdita leaned against him, tired, sighing, her arms around him. "What are you thinking?" he asked. "About Sabine," she said. "And her baby."

He thought of the German soldiers singing along the Arras road, of Cyron bullying André to be a soldier, of the German army officers driving Kinderlen-Waechter out of the negotiations in Berlin. Of Mademoiselle Françoise with her blonde curls, giggling as she was introduced, and Sabine, looking up at André in the Grand'Place with a scowl of baffled love. Like pieces of different puzzles mixed together, different stories, each trying to make itself the only puzzle, the only story. In the darkness a single bird began to sing his son's name, *Toby? Toby, Toby?* We all pay, he thought, for what one of us needs.

He leaned against the window casement and—how long later?—found himself slumped against the window thinking thick thoughts. The birds were singing in chorus. The sky had changed, was less profoundly dark. Perdita was breathing softly against his shoulder. "Gilbert?" he said into the dark. "Are you awake?"

"I'm watching," Gilbert said. "Lie down, Alexander, you'll sleep better."

Are you sure you'll stay awake, he thought; which was as much as saying, Are you sure I can trust you. "Yes," he said, "thank you." He got up stiffly and led the half-asleep Perdita over to the bed, tucked her in with Toby, and lay down beside them but on the outside of the cover, still half on watch, trying not to be. He was depending on Gilbert, not only for the money; it would help if he could trust him. He could see Gilbert's alert patient profile—Gilbert and Elphinstone—against the window tracery. It was a new thing for him to have someone else on watch even momentarily, someone taking care of his family. For a moment, disoriented, falling asleep, he felt protected, in a way that had never happened to him, or if it had he could not remember; that his father was in the room, keeping the monsters of the night away.

"Reisden!" It was Pétiot.

They all started awake but Gilbert, who was awake already. Elphinstone, who had found himself a place at the bottom of the bed, barked madly. Toby cried.

"What is it?" Reisden said.

"We have found a solution. Come outside."

Elphinstone scratched at the door. "He is accustomed to going out at this hour," Gilbert said delicately.

"Come with me."

Elphinstone made his way down the stairs clumsily, favoring his lame rear leg. Gilbert hovered, ready to grab his collar. "His dignity requires him to go downstairs himself, Alexander, but I find it a trial." Elphinstone slid but recovered. Outside, they waited for Elphinstone to splash the Lion Gate.

"A solution," Gilbert said. "Do you know what he means?"

Reisden shook his head.

"Would it mean you'd be all right?"

Something unknotted in him. "I hope so."

"You wouldn't need me, then," said Gilbert.

"No. I suppose not." He had given Gilbert the choice of whether to stay or go. He had asked him to go. No reason to be surprised if Gilbert went.

"I should go back to Boston.—I see how everyone looks at us, Alexander. You have your own life here. And you are quite right. Toby will be old enough to ask questions soon."

"And too young to hear the answers," Reisden agreed. "That's true."

"I know that," Gilbert said. "I want you to know that I have enjoyed myself very much. That doesn't affect what we should do, does it?"

"Enjoyed yourself?" Reisden said.

"I like Jouvet. A company," Gilbert said, "I think is like owning a dog. They are a great bother, but . . . he expands my life. On a cold day, you know, throwing sticks for him on Commonwealth Avenue, in the snow; one could never do that by oneself."

"Ah," said Reisden, amused.

Hearing *dog* and *stick*, Elphinstone raised his head and shook his tags. Gilbert reached down to pet him and groped on the grass for a branch to throw. Reisden found one.

"I have even thought of traveling," Gilbert said, imbuing *traveling* with the emotion of a man who spreads his handkerchief on a park bench before sitting down. "Even—Italy."

"Don't go back to Boston yet," Reisden said, wondering a bit why he was saying it. "Gilbert, there's the whole world."

"Drains," Gilbert said, shaking his head. "Hotels."

"You faced Cyron," Reisden reminded him. "That took courage. Italy can't be worse."

"Alexander, do you ever think of Father?"

"Oh yes."

"He was a great drag on the spirit. But he—" Gilbert hesitated. "Do you suppose, in a way, he might make one courageous? Simply from having to resist him?"

An expansion of life, Reisden thought. William. Like Toby. "That would be a good way to think of him," he agreed.

"Why did you name your boy Toby?" Gilbert asked, half-echoing Reisden's thoughts. "I found that—very touching. That you should take such care to name him after Tom."

"What?" Reisden turned and stared at him.

"Toby," Gilbert faltered. "Thomas Robert. I thought—"

"No, it was—" Toby had been meant to be Jean, Johannes, after Perdita's beloved Brahms. Perdita's family chose names out of Shakespeare, so they had wanted one for him. Finally they'd taken Sebastian from *Twelfth Night*. Jean-Sebastien

Louis Victor von Reisden, an awkward mouthful. But, as babies will, he had found his own name—

Yes. Toby. Thomas Robert Reisden, he thought. I named him after my father. And I thought I was running from the Knights.

Gilbert threw the stick overhead for his dog. Elphinstone rushed off at his peglegged gallop down the hill, sliding, scrambling tail-over-ears. I ran from it, Reisden thought, ran to it, like a dog with a stick, who wants it thrown far away, who wants to lose it and chase it, find it and have it thrown far again, but always to have it somewhere in his thoughts; the stick is the thing. We shall never be able to get away from each other, Gilbert and I.

"I don't know what we'll do about the resemblance," Reisden said. "Or the scandal. But, Gilbert, we shall always need an American. A large wild American, waving dollar bills, when we need to get out of the sort of problems I assume we'll get into." When there's war.

Gilbert smiled at the idea of being large and wild. "You shall have the money. That is yours anyway."

"No," Reisden said. "It's not mine. I don't want that. You would give it to Richard, and I don't want Richard. But I have a proposition, Gilbert. If you like Jouvet, I want to use that money to buy into Jouvet, as a partner with me."

Chapter 91

Everyone gathered on the terrace: Ruthie and the technicians and Eli Krauss, soldiers who had spent the night, Cyron all by himself; Gilbert and Perdita, Reisden and Toby, in a group by themselves; and, not under guard, Jules and a stunned André.

"I have an announcement to make." Plump Papa Pétiot smiled at them. "We have all been deeply saddened by the Countess of Montfort's tragic death. But it is my sad pleasure to report that we have found the explanation, and the culprit."

Exclamations and murmurs. Pétiot gestured in the direction of the guillotine. "A regrettable—accident!" said Pétiot.

"You mean nobody murdered her?" said someone, and was shushed.

"The design of the guillotine isn't to blame." Pétiot pulled up the bunting that draped the platform until the fabric was an austere scallop, barely hiding the mechanism. "This was De Vere's original design."

"I asked for more bunting," Cyron interrupted hoarsely, with the air of a man delivering bad lines. "I didn't want the crowds to see the trick. We hung the bunting from the platform, long swags, streamers. And the script called for a breeze to move the flags"—his voice trembled—"so we'd show it was one shot without any tricks."

André nodded.

Pétiot pulled the tarpaulin off the wind machine.

"The filmmakers brought this ventilator fan from the Wagny mines," he said. "To create the breeze. But it was hot in the square. For the last forty-five minutes before the accident, it was running."

He pointed at one of the soldiers. The fan had a hand crank as well as a motor. The soldier cranked the handle; the big vanes began to turn. The streamers stirred and fluttered.

"Of course this is not as powerful as it was in the Grand'-Place. And then the breeze came up too. Maurice?"

Cyron, like a man mesmerized, reached out and took one of the streamers, pulled it gently underneath the platform as if the wind had blown it.

"And you, Reisden, you tested the machine. Test it now."

He was being brought into this explanation. He climbed the stairs and stepped on the release plank. The lunette dropped open. "Again," Pétiot said. This time the lunette dropped only halfway.

"Look," Pétiot said. "Come here and look. The material's working its way into the mechanism, into the hinge."

They all looked. One of the streamers had caught in the lever.

"A tragic accident," said Pétiot.

The crowd gathered around André and Jules, cheering. Ruthie stood between them, hugging them both. The technicians grinned. Pétiot took Reisden aside. "What do you think of our story?"

"Graphic, simple, and believable." It gave everyone the truth they wanted.

"So you've won," Pétiot said.

"Have I?"

"You've made an American alliance." Pétiot nodded at Gilbert, talking to Perdita. "And now I hear you're partners with him. You're to be congratulated."

"News travels quickly," Reisden said.

"You did tell me," Pétiot said. " 'His lawyers thought I was an unofficial relative.' Are you his son?"

"Am I?" Reisden said.

"I should say so," said Pétiot. "You have the contract, if you still want it."

Reisden thought of soldiers laughing as they boarded the train east; soldiers marching down a road. "Yes."

Pétiot brought something out of his pocket. It was the lock from Cyron's false tunnel. The edge of the keyhole was bright with scratches. "I don't suppose you recognize this?"

"I can't say," Reisden said.

"You accused Maurice of so many things last night," Pétiot said, "all of them wrong, of course. You never accused him of failing at anything. I found that impressive."

"Failing at what?" said Reisden.

Pétiot looked over at André, standing on the terrace with Eli Krauss and Ruthie, pointing up at the guillotine. "Will that one really keep his mouth shut?"

"Oddly enough, he will."

"Make sure of it.—Encourage him to stay in Paris. Not that I wished the boves on him, but I really did think we'd seen the last of that boy." Pétiot made a wry face.

André was talking with Jules and Ruthie now. What will happen to those three, Reisden thought; what will happen to André? Ruthie was looking up at André with a shy longing that, sometime in these last days, had crossed the line between service and adoration. Jules was looking from his sister to André, and André, as usual, was oblivious. Not quite oblivious. Through the crowds, Cyron had blustered his way forward to greet his son, and André simply looked at him, like a specimen, like raw material for the Necro. This was the middle of a story, not the end.

"Maurice was bothered when you said it was for the money,"

Pétiot said. "Not that we don't need it. We're still trying. We don't give up.—But no, it wasn't for the money." Pétiot was putting on his gloves. "There was an incident in the Countess's life. A school friend, a necklace Sabine wanted. 'You'll die soon. Leave it to me.' The girl did die. Maurice should have consulted me." Pétiot adjusted the gloves, pulling fastidiously at each finger to straighten the seams. "That was what Gehazy knew. He came to Maurice and Maurice came to me. I am not sorry about Gehazy, no, not at all. But the girl . . . It was a shame. It was really deplorable."

"No one gave you the job of being her judge and jury."

"You are wrong about that," said Pétiot.

"Did Cyron know she was going to be killed?"

Pétiot looked toward Cyron, standing alone on the terrace by the guillotine.

"Maurice is—protected. The odd thing is," Pétiot said, "I don't really *believe* in what Maurice does. I know the world admires him, the theatre, the pictures in the newspapers, but *Citizen Mabet*—" He shrugged. "Madame Mabet in particular. 'I've done wrong. I'm going mad.' Doing wrong? The world is full of people doing wrong. I admired her. She wouldn't have gone mad. She would have done very well, Sabine. But she married the wrong man's stepson. It was one of those things."

André was sending people off in all directions: Krauss and the technicians toward the truck, Ruthie toward Cyron. Reisden watched them curiously. Krauss came back with his camera. "Do you know," Pétiot said, "I believe your André is going to film something?"

Trust André. "He never did get Cyron's last speech."

Pétiot gave a last tug to his gloves and smoothed his beard. They were almost done with each other for now. Reisden and he would have to work with each other. Pétiot looked up at Reisden as if something had been left unsaid, something that would have made a difference to him. Then he shrugged, accepting some advantage.

And Reisden knew what it was. He had failed completely to see what Pétiot was doing with Gehazy. "One question," he said. "When you told me to meet Gehazy at Saint-Vaast, he was already dead, wasn't he? But you wanted me to pass the message. To incriminate myself?" He answered his own question. "For the fourth floor of Jouvet?"

Pétiot looked up at him for a long, long moment. "For all of it. Ask your wife. I would have been the chief of the trustees."

"I must set up a good board," Reisden said, "in case anything happens to me."

"Always wise to take precautions," Pétiot said. "Until September, then. Unless there's a war."

"Will there be a war?"

Pétiot looked up at him. Here we are, his look said. Two men in a world where men are things, counters to be sacrificed. And you ask me—?

"Not this year, I think," Pétiot said, and beamed with all his teeth, almost like Father Christmas.

Chapter 92

There is an advantage in being just a little odd. André looks at Papa Cyron and sees an expression he has never seen before: a loneliness, a terror. It is the Necro, beyond Necro. The sun has risen. André calculates foot candles and sends a technician for lights.

"Come," he says to Papa Cyron. He leads him up the stairs to the guillotine. The lights go on.

André is seeing a ghost. On the terrace, Sabine in her rainbow robe embroidered with insects, brushing out her yellow hair. On the sun side of the hill, Sabine in a pink eighteenth-century dress and a wig, reading the movies pages of one of Papa Cyron's theatre magazines. Sabine is at Papa Cyron's side, smiling up at him, asking him *Did I do well?* And here she is, too, here at the guillotine, turning to look at him and laying her head on the block.

"Do your speech now," says André. He has set Krauss up on the platform itself. Even the shortest lens is almost in Papa Cyron's face. " 'What I have done, I did for France. . . .' "

Behind the camera, André looks at him. "What I have done, I did for France," Papa Cyron says. He gives his beautiful speech. He pleads for understanding. He says how much he has lost. "For France I have lost everything." Now Méduc should kneel at his feet, saying, *Father, you have not lost your son*. But Reisden isn't here. And Papa Cyron runs out of words to say, waiting for André to say "Cut," looking finally into the camera itself, wondering why it is all continuing, and André waits, getting the expression he wants. When he edits this scene, André will cut in a shot of Méduc. But the last shot of all will be this, a puzzled old soldier just beginning to get angry, wondering why he is still onstage.

When André finally shuts off the camera, Cyron gives a little speech to the young soldiers who have made up the crowd. "Keep up your courage! Sharpen your swords, clean your guns! The enemy is always at hand," he says, "the enemy attacks our hearts, unless we give ourselves wholly to our beloved country!"

Ever since Sabine died, something has been wrong with Cyron's eyes. In the audiences at his speeches, in the young soldiers shining up at him now, there are patches of greyness, shifting veils. It feels to Cyron like an absence; their faces are somehow unfinished, too bright, too eager, young faces in which there is no shadow of an old age to come.

He is getting old, he thinks.

In his memory Sabine is already taking on the same glamour, the beauty of youth that will never age. Cyron is already seeing the need to forget her. There were problems there. One has to forget. One has to move on. Mistakes have been made. It was an accident.

There are some things that shouldn't happen, some facts that shouldn't be. It's every man's job to change what shouldn't be into what is.

On the terrace, for a moment, Cyron sees not one ghost but three. There is a man with a puppet theatre on the sidewalk. A maiden and an Alsatian soldier are hanging from the puppet-rack and the puppeteer is dancing with the puppet of a bird. On the other side of the street a man with a low flat hat and side curls mutters *"Narishkeit!"* and tries to drag his son away. The son, little Morrie, cranes his neck back desperately, seeing only the name. THÉÂTRE CYRON.

But Cyron ignores all these ghosts. He has always been Maurice Cyron.

"Think of nothing but this," Cyron says to his audience, "that the right is on your side, that victory is within your grasp. Forward! Forward! Always forward! Morocco is ours—Alsace will be ours—Berlin will be ours!"

And they cheer him, his children.

Perdita is changing Toby, pinning a diaper on her wriggly little boy, and Uncle Gilbert has taken the old diaper off to the bucket when Alexander tells her Gilbert is staying in Paris.

"Is anything wrong?" he says, looking at her face. She ought to be happy. She is happy, she tells herself. But what she feels most clearly, most keenly, is something ending.

"I won't have anyone to visit in Boston," she says. Ridiculous. She has lost a country, the landscape of her childhood, the house in Boston with Uncle Gilbert there, unchangeable, waiting forever for Richard to come home.

"Gilbert is leasing an apartment," Alexander says. "Actually I think he's buying a building. In New York. For when you're there, between tours."

"New York?" she says, and wants to kick herself for sounding so happy.

"Happy birthday from him. I've lost track of the days; I didn't remember."

Her birthday, she realizes—she has forgot it too—was the night he came back from the boves. Idiot, idiot Alexander. "You won't make me stay in New York all the time," she says, "when my family is in Paris?" That is not quite what she means. She means, will you understand I want to be there and here? All of us together, will we be family enough for you?

"You must come back to save me from Gilbert's money. There's too much of it."

"Gilbert's money will be all right." She is still holding Toby on the table with one hand; the other arm she puts around her husband. "I hope everything will." I have gathered everyone I love in France, she thinks, but I miss America still. Will it be all right? What have I done?

"You can come to New York," she says. "When I'm there? Come with me, sometime?"

"I suppose I can," he says. "If we are to have the scandal of kidnapping Gilbert, I suppose I can visit America.—New York's an interesting city."

"You have no idea— Just let me put Toby down." She sets Toby on the floor, turns back to Alexander, and puts both her arms around him. What have I done? "Love," he says. Inside her head they feel like question and answer. What have I done? Love. Not live happily ever after, not know all the answers, just love him. It is no solution but a dilemma, a house half-finished, something always needing fixing; too big, half-explored; something to live up to, to grow into; home. The place where one lives.

"Love," she says.

One of the technicians goes into the cellar and brings out champagne, for a toast. André takes a glass. *Citizen Mabet is over.* The filming will recede into the mists of theatrical horror stories, and months from now they will go to the premiere and see half-recognizable grey fragments of what they remember doing, being.

Reisden is saying something to his wife. The old man, Gilbert Knight, has swung the baby up on his shoulders and the baby is pulling at the old man's hair.

André has never liked families. He thinks about Mama, Papa. He thinks about Mama's gloves and Papa working on the greenhouse. There's more to life than death; there's all the rest, and André doesn't know much about it. He knows it hurts. He knows it makes men cowards sometimes; it makes them bullies, and afraid, and mad. But he wonders if he will envy Reisden.

He thinks about Ruthie and Jules. If he has a family, it will be them.

"Who's the old guy?" one of the techs says.

"Aah, look at them. That's Reisden's dad. That's baby's grandpa, Reisden?"

Reisden looks up sharply, the old American too, the same movement, the same set of the shoulders. They have their own ghost, André thinks, someone they will see whenever they see each other. It is like a moment out of the Necro; André wants to wrap a play around it.

But a new kind, a kind he doesn't even know yet. A horror story with a different ending. Where no one disappears and no one escapes, where the survivors have to live with the ghosts and the villains are only heroes with different lighting.

"No," says Reisden. "That's not baby's grandpa."

"Yes," says André.

He cannot write this play yet, but he knows what to do. "Ladies, gentlemen, and madmen! Gather round!" He spreads his arms; he fixes the tech with Necrosar's fateful blue eye. "A night dark as the pit," he intones. "Thunder rumbles in the distance," he is making all this up as he goes along, "a door creaks open—" André looks into Reisden's eyes. I am giving you the theatre, André tells him silently. I am giving you what I have, Necrosar's freedom, to tell the truth and have no one believe it. "And who enters?" He turns and points at the old American. "It's Reisden's secret father!"

Reisden understands what he is trying to do, and something in his face changes. He looks once at Gilbert Knight, as if conferring with him on something that he already knows he is going to do anyway. "You have it wrong. Not nearly Necro enough, André. I am Richard Knight, the Vanished Child." He is almost laughing, but look at his eyes; it is as if years of being hunted fall away from him; it is a moment André will remember forever, a moment to get on film too, though he never will.

"No," says the old American earnestly. "Richard is dead. You must not believe *anything* else."

"Everyone always believes the worst," Reisden says. "So we shall make it worse. I murdered William Knight."

The techs look at each other; they don't know who William Knight is. They look at André for the next piece of the entertainment.

"Horribly," André agrees. "Hacked him to pieces. Fed him to hogs. Big hogs. When the hogs were butchered, the butcher found—"

Reisden holds up his hand. "Too far, André."

"Make it vile," André counsels.

"As bad as possible, that's what everyone believes," Reisden says, "and they may believe it if they please. But if I have to choose which I prefer, let me be Gilbert's son. Don't you think so, Toby?" Reisden looks at the old man and the child. He picks up his son and holds him out, and the old man reaches to take him. "Toby," he says, "this is your grandfather."

Gilbert Knight's dog barks once. "And this is your dog," Reisden says.

So there is that story at an end, the story of Richard Knight. Not even a horrible death lasts, André thinks; then how can anything last, and especially this happy family Reisden wants for his boy? It can't. André leaves them and looks one last time at the guillotine, which is already half taken apart. Without its blade it looks like two posts, unfamiliar, with an unknown purpose. By the front door of Montfort the straw man still stands, its arms outstretched, its wheat-sheaf head nodding. André raises his arms high, mimicking it, like a sorcerer. He goes out through the Jerusalem Gate and looks across the fields. The sun is warm on André's shoulders. In the green fields, the sugar-beet leaves are steaming. A row of workers is moving through the field, picking beets and piling them in baskets. André watches the rhythmical wave of the movement.

"Count André?" It is Ruthie, with Jules behind her.

"Look." He points the movement out to them.

Behind them, on the terrace, he can still hear Papa Cyron haranguing the soldiers.

People make the most sense together, André thinks. It is people who hurt each other worst, but it is also people who look after each other. People are like pieces of film, nothing in themselves, nothing but bits of light and darkness, ghosts of meaning without each other.

Far away, across the valley, a line of light flickers, moving up the side of Vimy Ridge. It looks like the guns of the soldiers in the battle scene. Jules points; André squints.

But today it is only the farmers at Vimy with their tools, making the harvest, and André takes Jules' arm and Ruthie's and stands between them.

They will not be safe forever. No one ever is. They are happy today.

Afterword and Acknowledgments

> *At Arras . . . the British hold the town, the Germans hold a northern suburb; at one point near the river the trenches are just four metres apart. . . . The Hôtel de Ville, the Grand'Place and the cathedral are mostly heaps of litter. . . . The streets are strangely quiet and grass grows between the stones.*
> —H. G. WELLS, describing Arras, September 1916 from *Italy, France, and Britain at War*

The Agadir crisis of 1911 was resolved, a month past the date of this book, by an unlikely coalition of international bankers, organized by the French diplomat Joseph Cambon, and the German Socialist Party. A form of peace would last for three more years.

In August 1914 Europe went to war.

In early September 1914, only four weeks into the war, the Germans almost captured Paris. The French army beat them back to the countryside just east of Arras. There both armies dug in. They would fight on Vimy Ridge until the Canadians finally captured it in 1917.

Of the places in this book, only the boves and the château I have called Montfort still exist in anything like their former state. In Arras, the Grand'Place and the town hall are reproductions from the 1920s. Cemeteries now dominate the Vimy road. The fields around Vimy Ridge cannot be plowed because of unexploded bombs. Villages, woods, houses and trees and gardens, chalk pits, sheep and shepherds disappeared in bombs and shrapnel, victims of the war; with them went most of the culture of prewar French Flanders, including its witchcraft.

For bringing it back to life, particular thanks to Jacques Borgé and Nicolas Viasnoff's *Archives du nord*; Marguerite Yourcenar's two memoirs; Alcius Leduin's important compilation of folk beliefs, *Traditions populaires de Demuin* (1892); and Maxence van der Meersch's *Invasion 1914* and Nigel Cave's *Arras/Vimy Ridge* for chalk pits and tunneling. For help in finding these and other sources, thanks to the staff of Widener Library, Harvard University, and the Brookline Public Library, Brookline, Massachusetts. For aid on site, I am grateful to the Bibliothèque municipale de la ville d'Arras, the staff of the Arras Office of Tourism, and the people of the commune of Mont-St.-Eloi, Pas-de-Calais, France. Though they share some architectural features, my Montfort and the extraordinary Mont-St.-Eloi are not the same.

Nor is Count André de Montfort the same as Count André de Lorde, cofounder of the Grand Guignol—though they, too, share some architectural features. For sending me to André de Lorde, I am grateful to Laurence Senelick, who also read this book in manuscript and taught me, among many other useful facts, that quintessence of French culture, the difference between a *baguette* and a *ficelle*.

Sabine's ideas of witchcraft should not be taken as typical of anything we know; Flanders witchcraft was different in many ways from Wicca and modern paganism. Nevertheless I have used bits of them and other pagan traditions as "frog DNA" where the details of the culture aren't known; thanks to Alan Seeking Wolf Bosell, Kirsten Houseknecht, and others for sharing their religious experiences. Katherine Neville shared her experiences of magic, and Michele Slung, as good a friend as she is an anthologist, found and passed on to me A. E. Waite's *Ceremonial Magic*. Thanks also to U.S. Games Systems.

Many friends of historical stage magic shared their expertise. Yvette Grimes, magician and generous friend, unstintingly loaned books and videos from her enormous collection; thank you, Yvette. Thanks also to John Stanley at the John Carter Brown Library at Brown University; the Harvard Theater Collection; Ricky Jay; Valentino (the magician of *Magic's Greatest Secrets Revealed*); and Cesareo Pelaez (Marco the Magi) and Le Grand David, national treasures of magic.

My knowledge of early films developed in part through the generous support of a Fulbright fellowship and a fellowship at the American Film Institute. Of the many people with whom I've had the privilege to talk about film, I am especially grateful to Thorold Dickinson, W. K. Everson, and Vlada Petric. Robert B. Wyatt, film fan and collector, loaned me his copy of *Les Vampires*; thanks also to the generous Joe Blades and to Lew Gamerman, video lover extraordinaire.

The members of the Cambridge Speculative Fiction Workshop (David A. Smith, Steve Popkes, Kelly Link, Brian Yamauchi, and Mary Tafuri Ross) and the members of the Ladies' Main Thang (Delia Sherman, Phyllis Birnbaum, and Kelly Link again) read this book in manuscript. They and Laurence Senelick saved me from many mistakes. I've kept a few, though. Thank you all. Thank you, Delia, for those sanity-saving lunches, Kelly for the inspiration your own magical stories provide me, and David and Steve for good tough criticism. Thanks to Ellen Kushner, a light to all who know her and an instant purveyor of emergency Yiddish, and to Andreas Teuber, who shared with me his experiences of acting with Richard Burton.

I am grateful to H. R. F. Keating for a conversation about political mysteries at St. Hilda's Mystery Conference in

1996. Thanks to Philip Kerr for the inspiration of his great trilogy, *Berlin Noir*.

Toby thanks Simon Jablokow, Peter Cramer Hartwell, and Benjamin Zimmerman Popkes, and his literary mother thanks their parents, especially Kathryn Cramer.

Thank you, dearest Fred, Mariah, Justus, and Helen (and Gracie and Pombo), for letting me spend so long at this. Thanks to my agent, Jane Otte, and to my editor, Joe Blades, associate publisher of Ballantine Books, for your support and enthusiasm.

And a special thanks to some other people who made this book possible.

While this book was being written, three remarkable people died prematurely. Kate Ross was a mystery writer, honored and loved by her peers. Gerald Hoeffel was a student of the French left. Michael McDowell, partner in life of Laurence Senelick, was a novelist and screenwriter, known among other works for the cult favorite *Beetlejuice*. Jerry I knew only through his many friends. Michael and Kate were dear to me: Michael, unfailingly generous with his time and expertise over many years, and Kate, a friend I wish I had met earlier and known much longer. Kate and Michael, I miss you both greatly.

Through the kindness of Edward Ross, Kate's father, and Jane Otte, Jerry's sister, I have had the privilege of enriching my library with books from theirs. Some of the details in this book come from their libraries. Thank you, Ed and Jane.

Michael, Kate, and Jerry all collected the sort of obscure information that finds its way into writers' libraries, and after writing a book like this, I am particularly grateful to them for being collectors. Obscure information is the only way we now know prewar Flanders. The world disappeared, down to the soil itself. The words and photographs remain.

In publishing, we hear a great deal about books being measured by bestsellerdom and publishers and booksellers by their size. But in writing about Flanders I have seen how precious and important, how necessary, all books are. We know much of what we know about the past because bookshops sell old books, librarians and collectors keep them safe, and, most of all, publishers and writers have created them.

Thank you all who do that work.

—Sarah Smith
September 1997–September 1999

**If you enjoyed *A Citizen of the Country*,
venture back to the beginning of the trilogy**

THE VANISHED CHILD

A *New York Times* Notable Book

New England, 1887. A millionaire is brutally murdered. The only witness, his young grandchild, mysteriously disappears. . . . Eighteen years later, in Switzerland, a man with no memory is "recognized" as Richard Knight, the missing child. Thus begins a masterpiece of historical suspense, as one man's obsession leads him toward a shattering truth—and to a killer, still at large. . . .

"Stunning . . .
[A] tale of murder and duplicity . . .
Stately prose that subtly enhances the
psychological horrors."
—*The New York Times Book Review*

"[A] deliciously intriguing tale. . .
An artful literary puzzler featuring the kind of
thick period detail and narrative intricacy
mastered by Charles Dickens . . .
This one belongs on the permanent shelf."
—*The Philadelphia Inquirer*

*And don't miss the second novel
in Sarah Smith's mesmerizing trilogy:*

THE KNOWLEDGE
OF WATER
A *New York Times* Notable Book

An enigmatic man haunted by guilt and a dark secret
from the past . . . A beautiful young woman con-
sumed by a desire that could destroy her lifelong
dream . . . A madman who stalks them both in retri-
bution for a murder they know nothing about.
They all play a part in Sarah Smith's captivating,
critically acclaimed novel of suspense.

"Compelling . . . Engrossing . . .
Envelop[s] the reader with history,
mystery, and passion."
—*The Boston Herald*

"A haunting tale . . .
An accessible mix of historical speculation,
literary allusion, and suspense,
[this novel] could become this year's
Name of the Rose."
—*Entertainment Weekly*

In paperback from Fawcett Books.
Available wherever books are sold.